Marc Alexander ha[...] when he was fifteen, and became a full-time writer in 1972 of both fiction and non-fiction. He is an established writer of horror novels under a pseudonym. He is at present working on the second title in the fantasy quartet *The Wells of Ythan*.

Ancient Dreams

Part the First of
The Wells of Ythan

Marc Alexander

HEADLINE

ISBN 0 7472 3025 0

Printed and bound in Great Britain by
Collins, Glasgow

HEADLINE BOOK PUBLISHING PLC
Headline House
79 Great Titchfield Street
London W1P 7FN

For Maisie

White Virgins

High Wald

River
Garde

Toyheim

The Wald

THE OUTLANDS

THE LAND OF
BLIGHT

The
Shallows

Ruined
Towers

The River of Night

YTHAN
The Pilgrims' Way

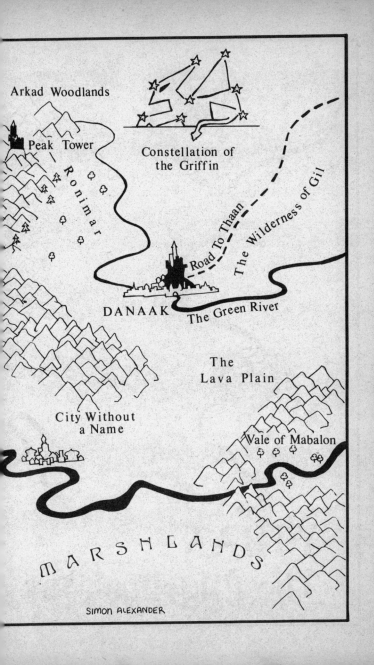

Arkad Woodlands

Peak Tower

Ronimar

Constellation of
the Griffin

Road To Thaan

The Wilderness of Gil

DANAAK

The Green River

The
Lava Plain

City Without
a Name

Vale of Mabalon

MARSHLANDS

SIMON ALEXANDER

Ancient Dreams

Book One

In a land of lost Illusions
Where the power of Splendour fails,
Where men's Joy remains unbidden
And Love hides in nursery tales . . .
At a time when spreading shadow
Veils forever Hope's last gleams . . .
Then pilgrim, prophet, star-eyed sailor
Seek the path of Ancient Dreams.

– lines from the commonplace book of
Lady Eloira, Reeve of the High Wald

ONE
River Garde

Black pennants streamed against the saffron and rose of the sunset sky and beneath their silhouettes sentinels on the ramparts of River Garde were touched by the magic of the moment. Each man sensed a portent in the westering splendour and even the most hardened veteran felt an ache as though something of great worth and beauty was about to pass forever. Below the castle's revetment the expanse of water, usually so sombre that the old minstrels of Ythan named it the 'River of Night' in their epics, reflected a brief golden sheen as though it, too, could not escape the apocalyptic glory.

The river's surface was oil smooth, yet beneath it, like the sinews and muscles which writhe beneath the fairest skin, were currents hungry for any man hapless enough to fall into its clutch, hungry to suck him down to the deeps which the riverfolk believed were the homes of pikemaids. This made it an ideal frontier, dividing the rolling hills of the Wald from the flat Outlands as neatly as a black boundary line drawn on a map. On its far shore began the grass plain which rare travellers who braved it likened to a sea. Waist high and stirred by the steppe wind, it was in perpetual motion; rippling, threshing and undulating like an ocean of drab green.

Now herons stirred uneasily on legs in the sedge at the rapping of hammers from the timber bridge spanning the river, the only link between the vast kingdom of Ythan and the barbarian world. And as these unaccustomed sounds re-echoed from the ivied stones of the castle, Grimwald VII, Hereditary Lord of the River March, leaned on the parapet of its slender watchtower and eyed the scores of leather-canopied wagons lining the opposite bank. Each vehicle had a pole erected mast-like behind the teamster's seat, and each pole was capped with a white emblem.

Beside the burly Grimwald the Lady Demara, his beloved young bride, followed his gaze while the Outlands' wind teased her hair into the likeness of corn-coloured flames.

'So there is truth in the old tales,' she murmured. 'They came like ships over the plain.'

Drawing his forest-green cloak closer about him, the River Lord nodded his leonine head.

'A wanderer once told me that the nomads hoisted sails above their carts to give them speed and lighten the work of their horses so they could cover great distances,' he said. 'But until I saw them approach like a fleet of windboats I had not believed it.'

The Lady Demara laid her fingertips on his shoulder as though to gain reassurance by touching him.

'Have no fear, dearheart, they cannot cross the water or pass River Garde,' he continued, glancing with pride at his men-at-arms statue-like in the crenels of the walls below, their weapons gilded by the setting sun.

'But why have they come?' the girl asked. 'Among the things that I have learned in the short time that I have been in your domain . . .' She coloured as though her words held some subtle innuendo '. . . is that occasionally a small band of nomad reivers may attempt to cross over to loot a village, but that is an army camped there.'

'When the Wolf King's herald stood before our portcullis and tried to get his tongue round our speech, I put that question to him but he made no answer,' Grimwald replied. 'I agree that it is strange that they have come in such numbers because since history began they have been bred to the plain and abhor forests. Perhaps they have fled from a plague, perhaps the auroch herds have failed them this season. Tomorrow I shall learn the truth when I meet the Wolf King face to face.'

'Wolf King!' she exclaimed and he sensed her shudder. 'That title has a ring of terror about it. The peasants believe that the nomads have the power of shape-changing, that they are werewolves.'

He laughed at her wide-eyed expression.

'They are barbarians and the wolf is merely their totem, but that is enough to make gossips mumble about were-wolves on winter nights. They love to scare themselves with such things as pikemaids and pottons. I am sure the only wolf-like thing about the nomads' leader is his fur jacket. Let me show you something.'

He led her to the centre of the tower's flat roof where a great bowl-shaped mirror of burnished silver was pivoted amid brass rods and cunningly geared cogs. Beside it stood a graceful young man in doeskin breeches and tunic who, as Demara approached him with a smile, tried to conceal the flush which suffused his features by fingering his fair moustache. His hair was parted in the centre and fell on each side of his handsome face whose straight nose, determined chin and blue eyes were said to mirror the appearance of his father at that age.

He was only three years younger than his stepmother – and he had never seen a more beautiful young woman in his life.

At the wedding feast he had been overjoyed that his father's long years as a widower were at an end because he knew that, while the River Lord could have made a convenient marriage many times over, he had preferred to wait until he met someone to wed for shared love

7

rather than political convenience. Grimwald adored the girl who, though half his age, brought such companionship to his days and such joy to his nights. As yet he had no inkling that his only son adored her as well.

'Alfrith is skilled in the use of this mechanism,' Grimwald explained when they stood beneath the mirror. 'It is said that such devices were in common use before The Enchantment, but now it is the only one left in the Wald. It still serves us well in keeping watch, and many a marauding rogue has had cause to curse it. Son, aim the Eye so that my lady may view the decoration the nomads put atop their masts.'

The youth bowed slightly to Demara. His pulse quickened as he caught a breath of her perfume and he tried to curb his guilty thoughts by concentrating on the focussing wheels.

'I have it, father,' he announced a minute later. 'Lady, if you will look into the crystal . . .'

He indicated a small luminous globe mounted on fine spokes angled below the reflector. Demara started back with a gasp of fear as, putting her eye close to the crystal, she beheld a wolf skull leering at her.

'Be not alarmed, it is merely an image – a reflection of something that lies far across the water,' said Alfrith gently. 'Watch, I shall give the picture greater breadth.'

As he adjusted a wheel it seemed to Demara that the skull receded while other details swam into view, firstly the mast to which it was attached and then the wagon beneath with wheels higher than the squat, leather-faced men lounging beside it. Shaggy hair fell over their foreheads almost obscuring their yellowish eyes. They wore fur jackets and baggy trousers and were armed with axes whose hafts were so long they slung them across their backs in the same way that Grimwald's archers carried their bows.

Demara turned away.

8

'So ugly!' she exclaimed. 'Well can I believe the terrible stories about them with which my nurse punished me. My lord, the thought that you should meet with one of these creatures makes me ill.'

'All necessary precautions for the parley are being taken,' said Grimwald, secretly basking in her concern. 'Alfrith, let us see how the work progresses before the light fails.'

Squinting along a sight, his son made adjustments and stood back, treacherous memory recalling a vision of the Lady Demara as he had glimpsed her early one morning through the window of his father's chamber . . .

The crystal now showed a hut-like structure which had been hastily erected in the middle of the bridge. Carpenters from River Garde were putting finishing touches to it while on the far side several nomads watched impassively.

'There can be no treachery there,' Grimwald said with satisfaction. 'Tomorrow I shall enter it alone, as will the Wolf King from his side, and there we will talk through the double oaken grille which divides the chamber without fear of each other . . . or of spying ears.'

'A plan of great prudence, father,' Alfrith remarked with an air of importance, 'but I shall stand guard on our side of the bridge and should there be treachery I shall see to it that our foresters axe the supports before the barbarians can cross. Without the bridge they would be impotent because it is a well-known fact that they are born with a dread of water and none can swim.'

The River Lord chuckled.

'At least let me get to safety before you topple it. I have no wish for you to change your name to Alwald just yet.' He was referring to the custom of Wald nobility to alter their names to incorporate the name of their domain on their succession.

'Still I fear for you, my lord,' said Demara, refusing to

be comforted by her husband's light tone. She returned to the parapet and gazed over the darkening water. By now the sun had sunk behind the horizon and purple shadow engulfed the plain; along the opposite bank tiny points of light flickered through the dusk as the nomads' dung campfires were lit.

'At least this parley is giving us a little time to be prepared for any eventuality,' said Grimwald, joining her. 'News of this was immediately sent to Danaak by carrier bird . . .'

Demara gave an ironical laugh.

'And what use will that be?' she demanded, for once dropping her role of subservient bride. 'All that the Regent will do will be to remind you that your family retains the marcher lands of the Wald in return for safeguarding it against the barbarians, and to get on with the task. No succour was sent to Lord Radnord when the sea kings pillaged his coast or to the Lady Isa when reivers overran her husband's fief . . .'

'You are right,' said Alfrith vehemently. 'Danaak is so far from the boundaries of the kingdom and it matters not there what happens to provinces of which the city folk have hardly heard tell. It is all part of the malaise which has hung over Ythan since The Enchantment.'

'It is not quite that simple,' said Grimwald quietly. 'Some might say that the invaders did the Regent's work for him. It is no secret that Radnord and Lady Isa had incurred his displeasure. But enough, such talk is unwise even in this place.'

'Grimwald, my cherished lord, your lineage is ten times older and more honourable than any upstart regent, the scions of your family were all champions of Ythan's kings – so what do you have to fear in your own stronghold?'

'Spies!' he answered, in his vehemence forgetting his caution of a moment ago. 'They infest every corner of the realm and since The Enchantment times have so changed that ancient lineage counts for nothing. To belong to a noble house, to have old loyalties in the blood, is to be born under suspicion. Ythan has been corrupted and is held together by corruption and practices which were once blasphemy to mention. Good traditions have withered like trees in the Land of Blight; it is as though an endless night has fallen and, alas, there are so few of us to light the way.'

At these last intense words Demara lowered her tone to his.

'Grimwald, so little time has passed since our wedding and I find that each day there is something more to be learned about you, and everything I learn makes my love for you greater. Now from your words it would seem that you are telling me that you follow the Pilgrim Path.'

The River Lord inclined his head, thinking once more how fortunate he was to have found such a bride in his middle years.

'Yet I have heard it said that the pilgrims and their quest are no more than a myth born in the troubled times which followed The Enchantment. Surely if the search be real she would have been found by now – if she was somewhere to be found . . .'

'No myth, my sweet Demara. In telling you this – by admitting that I am one – I give you my final confidence. I place my life, and that of my son, in your hands, for should our secret be revealed the greatest mercy we can expect is the garroter's thread. Yes, the quest must go on because it holds the only hope for the kingdom, and if it has failed so far it is because there have been so many false leads and the lands to be searched are so vast.'

'Do you mean there are those who are still seeking the Princess Livia?'

He smiled slightly and said, 'Each of us plays our part on the path as best we can. Not all are required to make

11

perilous journeys, there are other tasks perhaps equally perilous to be performed. And we are not the only seekers; the Regent has his secret searchers and there is little need to explain why. If he should find that secret place he will ensure that the princess will never awaken from her glamour so the empty throne will remain that way forever.'

'Somewhere in the world . . .' began Alfrith, anxious that Demara should be aware of his involvement in the treason.

'But The Enchantment came when our grandsires were children,' she interrupted. 'It is not possible that she could still be alive. Indeed, I believed that if there was a quest it was a symbol for those who wish to see the end of rule by regents.'

Grimwald shrugged.

'The search is real enough. Long ago the seers told us she is in an endless sleep and though it is difficult to comprehend ancient sorcery today, when the quest succeeds it will signal the end of the regency. When the first regent authorized the Guild of Witchfinders it was not only to curb heresy but more importantly from his point of view to seek out pilgrims and condemn them as heretics.'

The wind seemed suddenly cold and the River Lord felt his bride shiver against him.

'We will talk of this matter at a later time,' he said. 'At the moment our main concern lies across the water. Come. Let us go down to the hall, wine is needed both for our bodies and our spirits.'

But the Lady Demara made no move. She gazed anxiously at the far shore where scores of fires now flickered, each reflected as a lurid streak on the black river surface. Above, the constellation known as The Griffin was, as ever, the first to glitter in the darkling sky.

'When I was a child I used to wish upon The Griffin,'

she mused. 'Now I wish that we shall sleep through the night in safety and that you will not meet treachery on the morrow.'

'There is no need to invoke the stars,' said Grimwald, leading her by the hand to the staircase with Alfrith following. 'Even if the Wolf King concealed a dagger he could not reach me through the bars, and as for tonight I tell you that beneath the decking of the bridge are tubs of pitch and until dawn our sentinels will stay in boats beside them with flints ready. Should the nomads attempt to cross secretly the bridge will be ablaze before they reach the parley chamber. So you may rest easy in my arms.'

'So far I have had little rest in such circumstances,' Demara laughed with a sudden shift of mood. Grimwald laughed too as he led her down the spiral stairs, followed by his son who struggled to resist the imp of jealousy which threatened to sour his heart.

Above the tower, caught by the dark wind which at this time of evening flowed more strongly across the Outlands, the pennants cracked like whips, each report causing Affleck the watchman to wince. During his training in far Danaak to become a spy his ears had been plugged with wax for a year to make his hearing more acute.

TWO
The Crystal Bird

Half asleep and yet unable to sleep Krispin made his way
from the pink-washed cottage, with its fretwork shutters
and hanging flower baskets, to the pump at the end of the
cobbled yard. Grasping its carved handle he worked it
until its screech put to shame Father Tammas's cockerel
and water spurted from its ornamental dragon's mouth.
The youth thrust his head beneath the icy stream and
combed his fingers through his auburn hair which, like the
other apprentices in the toymakers' village, he wore
shoulder length.

When the noise of the plunger ceased he straightened
up and viewed his world through bedewed lashes. The
lower half of the valley was a lake of mist; above it the
forest of dripping evergreens, which marched menacingly
down the slopes towards the cluster of cottages, was still
in shadow, but the peaks beyond – the White Virgins who
never lost their snow mantles – sparkled in the fresh
sunlight.

And although it was early, pencil lines of smoke were
already rising above the steep red roofs of the village, for
today was the most important in Toyheim's calendar – the
day of The Choosing.

Krispin guessed that most of the lads of his age had
worked through the night like him in locked workshops,

14

adjusting and polishing their exhibits until the eastern sky grew wan.

As he bent and towelled his hair – too pretty for a boy, the village dames said behind his back – his sleeping robe slipped to his ankles and he grinned as he noticed the curls below his belly where a few weeks ago there had only been down. He ran his palm down his chest and was disappointed to find it as smooth as ever while his face, despite frequent assaults with Father Tammas's razor, still refused to turn its soft growth into manly stubble. What good was the first emblem of his new manhood if it was hidden away!

Straightening up, he saw a face at a diamond-paned window beneath the eaves and he grabbed for his robe. Another sign of approaching maturity. Not so long ago it would not have mattered if Jennet had seen him naked, but now the fact that she had glimpsed him had the most surprising effect. Loosening his robe to accommodate it and trying to muster his dignity, he strode back to the cottage.

Here he found that Jennet was the only one astir, and already dressed in her favourite long-skirted gown of pale blue ninon whose colour complimented her spun-gold hair which, when not braided for formal occasions, fell to her waist.

'Kris, you look dreadful,' she accused as she leant over the newel post of the crooked staircase. 'I vow it was only an hour ago that I heard you go to your room.'

He loosened his robe some more, half proud and half ashamed at the way part of him seemed to have developed an independent will.

He was afraid the girl might mock him but her eyes remained anxiously on his face.

'You should go back to bed and sleep.'

'How can I on this day of all days?'

He was almost angry with her for not fully appreciating

15

its importance, but then girls did not have to go through the ordeal of The Choosing.

'At cockcrow all tools must be laid aside,' she continued, 'so what more can you do now?'

He raised his shoulders and then let them drop.

'I feel so nervous, Jen, I don't know what to do with myself.'

She thought for a minute.

'I shall help you take your exhibit to the hall, and then you must put it out of your mind until tonight. Come into the woods and perhaps I'll be able to show you something secret.'

He nodded his agreement and she rushed on, 'I know it is the rule that it has to be veiled until the ceremony but I would love to see your work . . .'

'Nobody is supposed to see the exhibits before tonight.'

'But I am not nobody, I am Jennet, remember?'

He grinned.

'All right, Jen. The pottons take tradition!'

'Good boy. I shall meet you in the workshop after you have dressed.'

A few minutes later, in white shirt and brown breeches and wearing an apron of red canvas which another tradition decreed must be worn by Toyheim apprentices, Krispin came into the kitchen and smiled as he heard Father Tammas snoring in the room above. At least his slumber was not disturbed; his choosing had been thirty years ago and since then he had become revered as the leading craftsman in the valley.

Pausing only to drink from a pitcher of yellow milk, the youth hurried to the workshop where Jennet sat on a bench, swinging her legs so that her toes furrowed the fragrant shavings which carpeted the floor. Her eyes were fixed on a shrouded object at the far end.

'Large,' she commented.

He bit his lip nervously as he took hold of the cloth

16

cover. Although such a short time had elapsed since he had made the final adjustments, he wondered if his work was as good as he had believed or whether he had been deluded by fatigue and lantern light.

'You may be surprised,' he said quietly and tugged the sheet away to reveal a large, doll-like figure with tow hair falling to the waist of her blue dress.

'It is me!' cried Jennet. 'You meant her to look like me.'

'I must have had you on my mind when I carved the face,' he said, anxious not to admit to her, or himself, how much he had thought about her during the long and lonely nights when he had been working on his automaton.

'And that dress. I used to wear it when I was eight. You must have found it in the attic.'

'Yes.'

'But surely for The Choosing she must be more than a carving . . .'

'Watch.'

Krispin stood behind the figure, and putting his hand through a slit in the back of her dress, worked a hidden control. A heavy ticking was heard as springs and gears moved into clockwork life. The head, which had been drooping, rose defiantly and the eyelids opened to disclose glass eyes of a blue close to those of the girl's.

'A marionette without strings,' he announced.

Stiffly at first the doll advanced several steps and then began a slow dance, her cherry lips set in a smile that never altered even when the mechanisms hidden in her body ran down and her movements slowed into graceless jerks.

Jennet clapped her hands as she had done when she was a small girl.

'Oh Kris, she is magnificent,' she declared, her heart

17

warmed by the fact that she had been the unwitting model for the toy. 'There will be nothing to match her.'

As she said these words a sense of sadness filled her as she realized the loneliness which would be her lot if her words proved true.

'We must take her to the hall,' she continued, anxious that he should not immediately respond to her mood as he usually did, just as she so often mirrored his feelings.

'Just let me wind her up again,' he answered, all his attention upon his creation. He fitted a crank into a hidden socket, and when the sound of the ratchet ceased he gently closed her eyes with finger and thumb, an oddly gentle gesture which made Jennet shiver.

The cover was replaced and secured with many more cords than were necessary. Then on a hand barrow the shrouded figure was rolled out of the workshop through a flutter of hens, and along the street of high-gabled dwellings so neat and colourful that they might have been dolls' houses that had been enlarged magically to real-life size.

'I never thought you would try to construct anything so difficult,' Jennet said as they passed the Jack-in-the-Box Inn, its great sign, which depicted the Jack, creaking beneath a gallows-like arm high above the cobbles. Already, little maids in lace caps and full-skirted dresses were busy preparing for the inn's busiest night of the year.

'I have hardly seen you for these last three months,' the girl continued. 'And when I did you were so bad tempered.'

'I did not think it would be possible to finish her in time,' Krispin said apologetically. 'Her main spring snapped three times and I could not get the counter-weights which give her balance to work properly.'

Curious eyes watched the couple from through bottle-glass panes, and behind them another youth appeared with a well-wrapped burden on his shoulder.

'What gave you the idea of making a dancer?' Jennet

asked as they passed Dame Norbet's school, silent for once as no one could expect her little pupils to concentrate on their pothooks on such a day.

'In Danaak the Regent collects automata,' Krispin replied. 'It is said to be his passion and I have heard that he has a brass warrior who wields a mace to protect his bed while he sleeps and a maid life-sized and so beautiful that . . .'

He stopped, not wishing to repeat the obscene rumour he had heard in the Jack from a wandering packman.

'Danaak is far from here – thanks be! – and there is little chance of the Regent ever seeing your toy,' Jennet said.

Krispin raised his shoulders in a characteristic gesture and said with a laugh, 'True, but one has to have hope while one works.'

'Good fortune, Krispin,' an old man called from his doorway whose pilasters and lintel, like the others of the village, were intricately carved in the style of the toymaking owner.

'My thanks, sir,' Krispin responded, touching his forehead with his fingertips which was the customary apprentice's salute to a toymaker.

He felt a pang of disquiet when it occurred to him that his days of such deference might be over. Suppose it should be his fate tonight to leave the village with its cheerful well-being, its people whose kindness was only equalled by their passion for their craft. How could he part from the man they called father who had, in fact, been *more* than a father to Jennet and himself after the horror of the forest, and not only given them a home during their growing-up years but had taught him his trade – and Jennet, too. Most of the village women envied her skill when it came to dressing dolls which was the traditional work of womenfolk.

Krispin paused to gaze up the green slopes of the valley

to the crystalline mountains which filled him with awe even though he saw them every day of his life. Ranged like distant ramparts, they were the eternal guardians of Toyheim, protecting it from the stain of the outside world which, according to the few travellers who in spring came through the passes to purchase the villagers' winter work, was filled by people made restless and brutal by injustice and secret fear. How could he ever venture beyond the friendly mountains into such a world, how could he ever leave Jennet and his fellow apprentices with whom he got merry on apple ale on restday eve? For a sick moment he wanted to turn back and hide his dancer away, but pride in his craftsmanship overcame the base thought.

'. . . a secret for a secret,' Jennet was saying light-heartedly. 'Do come with me into the forest and I may be able to show you a marvel.'

'It could be no worse than moping here,' he replied. 'Everyone is strange on Choosing Day.'

'How graciously put! If you had not shown me your dancer I would certainly not allow you to come with me after such a gallant acceptance.'

Krispin lowered the barrow handles and, with a sudden even-toothed smile lighting his face, said, 'Forgive me, my lady. My words do but prove how The Choosing can rob a man of his manners. Permit me to accompany you into the greenwood as your protector against bears and pottons.'

'That is better, sir,' laughed Jennet. 'We shall go as soon as you have put your exhibit in place.'

Of the buildings which made up the village, the hall was the most ornate. Since the toymakers had arrived with their families following persecution by the witchfin-ders, it had become the custom for each craftsman to leave his decorative mark upon it. Every handspan of woodwork was carved with folktale characters; gargoyles sneered from its gables and weather-vanes mounted on its shingled roof performed curiously when even the lightest breeze blew across the common meadow.

Inside the building, used mainly for name day dances and full moon feasts, the walls were now hung with ceremonial drapes of indigo emblazoned with silver stars. On the elders' dais at the far end the beadle stood guard with his halberd of office, a necessary presence because there had been shameful occasions in the past when the tension of The Choosing had driven desperate apprentices to destroy rival exhibits.

Without saying a word – as convention demanded – Krispin and Jennet hoisted their shrouded burden on to the platform and hurried back into the early sunshine where the youth felt the lifting of an invisible weight which had oppressed him for many weeks. Everything was out of his hands now and the thought of getting away from the village for a few hours with Jennet seemed the best idea in the world.

He sat her in the barrow as he had done when she was small, and, while she screamed with mock terror and laughter, raced her back to the cottage. Here she packed bread, cheese and cold meat in a basket, along with a bottle of black wine from the vineyards of Ronimar, while in the workshop Krispin thrust a small hand axe into his belt just in case his joke about bears should prove more than funny.

Then they were away, racing hand-in-hand with Jennet using her free hand to hold the hem of her gown above her knees, just as they had done as children when released from workbench and sewing table. They followed the path across the common meadow where the goose girl's charges hissed them and goats followed their laughing progress with satanic eyes.

Only at the edge of the forest did they falter to a walk, regaining their breath before wading through the ferns which grew in tender profusion between the tree trunks.

21

A warm stillness brooded beneath their boughs and sunlight filtering through their leaves took on a greenish cast.

'Am I to be told what this surprise is, or do I have to wait?' Krispin asked, lowering his voice as though afraid to disturb the hush surrounding them.

'I shall tell you. It is the crystal bird – at least, that is what I have privately called it since I first saw it.'

'You mean you found a glass bird in the forest?'

'No, it is real but it looks as though it is made of crystal, especially when it takes to the air and the light shines through it.'

'You are making this up. It sounds too much like a story in a chapbook. If it were true, why have you not told me about it before?'

'Because, when I first saw it, I felt that the moment was something which was my very own. It was the only thing that was really mine apart from my dresses, and even those had been passed on to Tammas for me by the village dames. Besides, if I had told you about it, you would have teased me until I no longer believed it myself.'

'I am sorry about the teasing,' said Krispin, embarrassed by guilty memories. 'I do not know why I did it, especially as when I made you cry I felt like crying myself. But tell me more about your bird.'

'I first saw it two years ago. Like today, I wanted to get away from the village, so I went up to the mere and sat on the bank. And then I saw it, my crystal bird . . .'

She paused as if struck by poignant memory.

'It was resting on the water and I watched it for a long time. Often, when it moved and the sunlight caught it, it seemed as though it was created from a rainbow. At midday it spread its wings and flew until it vanished over the White Virgins.'

'And you saw it again?'

'Oh yes. Exactly a twelvemonth ago. I remembered it

on the last Choosing Day, and I went to the mere and though I did not really expect to see anything, there it was. And at midday – just as it had before – it flew away. I think it makes the same journey at the same time every year so perhaps we shall be lucky and see it today.'

'And you say it was formed of crystal?'

'A living bird could not be glass, so I supposed it just looked as though it was. On the water it seemed to have light in it, like the conjure woman's pendant, but when it was in the air it was a mixture of the blue of the sky and the green of the forest and the sparkles of the sun . . .'

Her voice trailed off as she realized the inadequacy of her description.

Krispin laughed softly.

'A fey bird perhaps?'

Jennet glanced anxiously about her.

Everyone in the village knew that there were still some fey folk left in the High Wald, survivors from a magical race who had resented the arrival of outsiders after The Enchantment. Because of this a superstition had evolved that it was very unwise to refer to them aloud in the forest.

As the pair continued through the trees their fingers remained locked as they had done when they were small. Then it had signified companionship, and earlier, during the terrible time before Father Tammas found them, a spark of comfort in the night of fear. But now there was something different, some osmotic current of excitement passing from skin to skin.

Half an hour later they entered a huge natural clearing where the slope had levelled. Its grass was rank for no village kine grazed here; there were large patches of magenta willowherb and, in the shadow of fallen trees, yellow flowers of wolfsbane which they avoided. In the centre gleamed the mere, half-screened by rushes above which dragonflies performed iridescent ballets.

'It is ages since we used to come here together,' Krispin murmured. 'I had almost forgotten it.'

'I kept coming alone,' said Jennet. 'It became my secret place when I was unhappy.'

'Why should you be unhappy?' He sounded genuinely surprised.

'How could you understand? Because you were a boy you were able to become an apprentice and Father Tammas taught you his skills so that you are likely to become a toymaker yourself.'

'So?'

'It could not happen if you had been a girl . . . no chance of being chosen if you are a girl, no travel for a year and a day or a banquet on your return as a master craftsman, no bright silver for your work! If you had been a girl in Toyheim you would do nothing but stitch, stitch, stitch. I am troll-sick of making dolls' clothes! Why should I not make proper toys if I want to, travel if I want to, get drunk and sing rude songs in the Jack if I want to?'

'Because that is how it has always been. Do not blame me, blame the All Father who first decreed everything. Only princesses can do as they like.'

'Little good did that do for the last one, poor thing. How much life did she enjoy before the curse fell upon her?'

Kris laughed softly.

'That is just a legend, invented long ago to give people something to hope for in bad times. Why, if she was still alive she would be over a century old . . .'

'Sssh, there is something on the water.'

Krispin became silent. He had an understanding of Jennet's desire for the freedom to do as she wished and knowing such a desire was impossible made him uncomfortable. Any other village lad would have guffawed at her words, but there had always been a special understanding between them.

24

'There!'

He looked and saw a mirror-flash from the mere. 'Come,' whispered Jennet, and she led him beneath a bank from which writhed the serpentine roots of a grandfather tree whose branches spread over them protectingly as they knelt in flower-starred grass at the water's edge. In this sheltered spot there were no rushes to obscure their view of the calm water in the centre of which Krispin beheld Jennet's wondrous bird.

It threw rays of light into his eyes and, dazzled, he turned to the girl who gazed ecstatically across the sky-tinted surface.

'It came,' she murmured. 'My crystal bird came.'

'It did,' he agreed in an awed voice.

As they remained kneeling they were oblivious to everything but the glory of the bird floating in a halo of its own light. Wavelets whispered unheard as they lost themselves in the duckweed along the margin and the call of a bellbird from the forest fell upon deaf ears.

Suddenly the bird stretched its long neck upwards, its pinions beat the water briefly and then it launched itself into the air to circle the mere. At a certain angle the sun caught its wings and it became a creature fashioned from a spectrum of colour, a living prism, and as it rose it seemed to Krispin that it was accompanied by ethereal flute music which seemed to be inside his head rather than in the air about him.

A tear rolled down Jennet's cheek and he knew that she could hear it too.

With a heavy wing beat the bird passed over their heads and seconds later it was lost behind the tree which reared above them. Krispin leaned sideways and kissed away Jennet's tear as he had done once before when they were bewildered children lost among colonnades of tree trunks.

And, as had happened then, she clung to him – only this time it was not terror which tightened her arms about

25

his neck. Now her lips brushed his face until they found his mouth, and she kissed him with an eagerness that was a revelation. His whole body felt as though a rare sparkling wine was bubbling through it, his heart fluttered like a trapped bird and newly awakened instincts made him press his fingers cruelly into her back. Through the softness of her mouth he could feel the hardness of her teeth as she responded with all her strength.

At length she pushed her hands against his chest and, breathless, he released her.

For one moment he feared he had given her offence, embracing her so closely that she could not have been unaware of his growing need; then he saw that she was reaching behind her neck, fumbling with the buttons of her gown. As the soft material slid to her waist he felt that it was he who was coming under an enchantment. Music still filled his head and all that he could comprehend was the pale beauty of her body in the dappled sunlight – only that.

Jennet was still girlishly thin but her breasts were well formed, and the sight of their points taut with excitement sent a thrill through Krispin's being and a rush of blood to his loins. As though aware of his urge Jennet rose to her feet so that the gown rustled to her ankles and he realized that, like him, she now had the silken symbol of maturity.

Repeating her name in a low murmur, he knelt upright and, throwing his arms about her slender legs, pressed his face against the curve of her belly.

For a long moment they remained thus, her eyes downcast upon him, almost thoughtful while her fingers twined his hair. Then, as his embrace became unbearable, she tumbled back and lay upon the springy grass so that its tiny flowers printed themselves upon her skin. He lay beside her, his hand caressing her body from breast to thigh and thigh to breast while his other hand fought to unfasten his belt buckle.

A moment later she bit back a cry as he rolled upon her and she suffered his thrusting until she guided him with her hand, and this time she did cry out with the spasm of pain this brought. As his desperation was replaced by pleasure she closed her eyes to the hurt and her heart sang with the joy of encompassing this beloved brother whom she had secretly worshipped for as long as she could remember.

For a fleeting moment she found that she was able to share the bodily delight before she felt a sudden flood of warmth within her. Krispin shuddered and raised himself up on his arms, his bottom lip clamped between his teeth and his face sheened with tears or sweat or both, and then with a smile of gratitude he collapsed beside her, an arm across her body and his lips against her cheek.

'My love,' she whispered, 'now you are properly mine. It is the gift of the bird.'

THREE
The Wolf King

At midmorning Lord Grimwald, attired in his finest ceremonial robe, strode out beneath the portcullis of River Garde and surveyed the expanse of grey-green river and the frail bridge spanning it. From the roof of the parley chamber, which had been hastily constructed half way across it the day before, rose two tall poles. One supported the wolf skull emblem of the nomads; from the other flapped the black pennant of the Wald.

'My lord . . .' began the Lady Demara at his side.

'Fret not, dearheart,' he interrupted. 'To please you I am wearing mail beneath my doublet.'

At his sign trumpeters on top of the donjon sent a silvery fanfare rolling over the water to announce that the River Lord was ready to parley. It was answered by thudding drums from the wagon camp lining the opposite bank.

Grimwald kissed his bride and approached the bridge with his son while his herald Jonal followed a respectful four paces behind.

'Father, I shall be on guard outside the chamber while you face the Wolf King,' Alfrith said. 'Should there be treachery I can rush to your aid.'

'No,' said Grimwald, lowering his voice so that Demara would not hear. 'If there should be treachery it would be ill for the Wald if we were both to perish. Jonal will keep watch on the bridge and aid me should it be necessary. You take Demara to the watchtower and follow the proceedings through the Eye.'

At these words the young man halted his protestations.

'Keep watch on the barbarians and upon the first sign of anything untoward have the alarm sounded for the bridge to be brought down – *even if I am still upon it*. It must be destroyed before they can cross for without it they will never gain our shore.'

'I understand, father.'

'And, Alfrith, although I do not believe there is anything to fear, should it be that the Dark Maid awaits me upon the bridge I entrust Demara to your care.'

Alfrith said nothing but lowered his head in obedience, and in the hope that the guilt spawned by the insane and wicked thoughts that invaded his mind like a hellish whirlwind would remain hidden. True it was that the Master of Lies sought to corrupt the most upright minds with unhallowed visions!

'Protect thy child,' he murmured as he made the sign of the Mother.

'And there is one other thing,' said Grimwald lowering his voice still further. 'As you know it has been the duty of our family down the generations to protect the march, and I am proud to say that thanks to our forebears the Wald has remained comparatively secure and peaceful even when death and fear and famine rode through the kingdom after The Enchantment. Even now the waldmen and the riverfolk and the others who live in our domain enjoy lives of peace which are unique in Ythan.'

Alfrith nodded.

'But I want you to know there is a deeper loyalty . . .'

'The Pilgrim Path.'

'Yes. Only by following that can we guarantee the future safety of the Wald. An evil stain spreads from Danaak like pus from a canker; sooner or later it will

29

infect the Wald and other outlying provinces, and therefore it is our duty to halt the source of the corruption. All this you know, but should River Garde fall . . .'

He waved away the protestations Alfrith was about to utter.

'. . . I am speaking only of a very unlikely occurrence but we must be prepared for every eventuality – and in this I see the Regent a far greater threat to me than those simple barbarians over there. I repeat – should River Garde fall and I with it, you must forget about being a hero and hurry to the High Wald and put yourself in the hands of the Lady Eloira, the Reeve of the High Wald. She shares our aspirations and will tell you how best you can serve it.'

'The Lady Eloira!' Alfrith exclaimed. 'She's as old as the mountains and they say she holds on to life by witchcraft.'

'That is the talk witchfinders love to hear,' said Grimwald disgustedly. 'The truth is she is as wise as she is old, and she has knowledge which was gleaned and hoarded by her ancestors who were scholars long before The Enchantment. Give me your vow that should calamity ever befall River Garde you will seek her and heed her.'

'This is gloomy talk,' Alfrith said, 'but if you wish it you have my word.'

'Excellent!' exclaimed Grimwald, his usual good humour returning. With a joke to the men-at-arms stationed at the end of the bridge he mounted it and began a dignified walk over the creaking planks towards the centre.

His father was close to the parley chamber when Alfrith, breathless from running up the spiral staircase with Demara close behind him, focused the mirror of the Eye and in its crystal beheld the Wolf King approaching from his side. The youth drew in his breath at the contrast between the elegant River Lord and the barbarian in his grotesque garb of furs and cap fashioned from a wolf's head which gave him the appearance of a shape-changer who had figured frighteningly in Alfrith's nursery tales.

Before entering the rough structure, Grimwald turned his head and felt a combination of pride and reassurance at the sight of the honey-hued walls and towers of River Garde, and the ranks of armoured men shining behind its crenellations. No matter what the nomads might be up to, they could never be a real threat to the Wald as long as its frontier was dominated by this graceful stronghold. And he smiled at the added thought that without a fleet of boats they could not even cross the River of Night to test the castle's defences.

He waved, turned and entered the parley chamber.

On the watchtower the Lady Demara put her hand to her mouth as she watched the distant doll-like figure of her lord and lover vanish into the structure, regretting that she had not told him of her growing certainty that their child was quick within her. She decided that she would wait no longer for the chirurgeon to pronounce upon the matter; *she knew* and she would tell Grimwald the moment he returned.

It is a pity that he already has an heir, she mused, and then tried to banish her ignoble thought.

Alfrith looked up from the mechanism of the Eye and gave her a smile which she returned warmly. Everything was suddenly beautiful to her. She gazed across the river to the plain and even that seemed beautiful with the vast sky above it.

'I am going to get my cape from Margan,' she said.

After the bright morning light the interior of the parley chamber was dark and it took Grimwald's eyes several moments to adjust before he was able to see the double row of stout oaken bars dividing it. Although he had spoken confidently to his young bride about his meeting with the barbarian, he had no illusions about his devious

31

nature. For generations the Wald folk had mistrusted the nomads – a mistrust based on their attempts to reive villages along the river – and it was this mistrust which had prompted Grimwald to speak with unusual gravity to his son.

He looked about him to make sure there was no flaw in the precautions his carpenters had taken against the possibility of a treacherous attack and his hand was gripping one of the bars to satisfy himself of its strength when the nomads' leader entered through the opposite doorway. At the sight of him the River Lord involuntarily stepped back and made the sign of the Mother; the nomad was dressed in wolfskins like a shaman and the mask of a great wolf which he wore as headgear was drawn so far forward that his face was hardly visible.

'Greetings, Wolf King,' declared Grimwald, resuming his dignity. 'Let us talk fair and open and learn what is in each other's minds.'

The barbarian responded with a guttural affirmative – more like a growl than normal speech, Grimwald decided with distaste.

'Tell me, what brings you and your people to the River of Night when you have all the Outlands to wander over?' he continued.

The Wolf King came right up to the bars and grinned, and Grimwald was conscious of his noisome breath – it must be true that on their long migrations over the vast grasslands the nomads lived on raw horseflesh.

'The Wald,' said the nomad. 'The Wolf-in-the-Sky . . . he tell us . . . you go into Wald . . . bad time coming to Outlands . . . we do what he say . . . you let us cross.'

Grimwald had a desire to laugh at the broken sentences. Wolf-in-the-Sky indeed! A fine excuse for pillage and plunder. But he kept a solemn face and said, 'You must know, O Wolf King, that all men have their places – we have the Wald for our home, you have the Outlands.

Such was ordained by the All Father and it is not for us to alter the destiny laid down for the world.'

'All Father! The Mother!' The Wolf King spat between his feet. 'Old gods gone . . . only god now Wolf-in-the-Sky . . . we must do what he say . . . we come into Wald . . . bad time come to Outlands.'

'Bad time come to the Wald if you enter it,' Grimwald said. 'Go back to the plain which is your homeland and both our peoples can live peacefully . . .'

'Wolf-in-the-Sky say let us cross or die,' interrupted the barbarian.

Grimwald abandoned diplomacy and laughed.

'You cannot cross the river or pass River Garde. In the past your ancestors tried but they never succeeded . . .'

'Wolf-in-the-Sky tell us how.'

The River Lord's habitual curiosity now surfaced.

'Tell me, Wolf King, how does your god speak to you?'

'Like this.'

The barbarian stretched his arms wide and seized a bar in each taloned hand, bringing his face close to the barrier. In the dim light it seemed to Grimwald that his amber eyes glowed and then the wind-tanned skin of his face began to *ripple* . . .

For a long moment he clung to the bars to support himself like someone in the grip of a seizure. He shook his head painfully from side to side moaning, and a long thread of saliva drooled from the corner of his mouth.

What happened next was so extraordinary that disbelief rooted Grimwald to the spot. The Wolf King straightened up, and now his eyes were full of yellow light, and with the cry of a beast rather than a man he wrenched the bars he was holding from their fastenings. Reports of snapping stakes filled the chamber as he smashed aside those in front of him.

Only as the second barrier was splintering under his demoniac strength did the River Lord shake off his paralysis. Turning to flee, he screamed 'Betrayed!' to the herald stationed outside on the bridge.

Jonal sprinted to his master's aid but at the doorway he collapsed to his knees at the sight of Lord Grimwald spread-eagled on the floor with his throat torn. And even as bile filled the herald's mouth he looked up and saw the bloodied jaws of a wolf descending upon him.

FOUR
The Bone Piper

It was music – like bubbles rising from the darkest, most secret depths to burst in the light – which brought consciousness to Krispin. For a moment he lay supine while his eyes opened on the flushed face of Jennet who had followed him into slumber. Then he looked beyond her high up the bank; seated on a huge root which curled from the base of an ancient tree, was a bent figure in a cloak of shadowy grey. His face was as brown and sere as an autumn leaf and he played a white pipe which had been carved from a bone.

The music this pipe made was high-pitched and strange, as though floating from a dream world, and completely unlike the music of the village band of tarbuts and drums. No one in Toyheim played the flute, and this ethereal sound was to haunt the youth for years to come. He realized that this was the same music which had accompanied the flight of the crystal bird.

Jennet stirred.

'What is it?'

'Hush. Someone is playing on a bone.'

'Is he looking at us?' she asked, more alert as she drew her discarded gown over her naked body.

'He seems to be looking over the mere. Lie still, he may not notice . . .'

The music ceased, its final note seeming to linger like a

poignant memory, a scrap of fantasy so slow in dissolving into silence. And then the silence was absolute; no bellbird chimed, no bee dared to drone its worksong. Krispin looked up the bank and found that the piper was gone, almost as though he had melted into the warm air which hung over the forest. Despite this warmth Jennet shivered and pulled her gown closer about her.

'Do you think he was of the fey?' she whispered. 'It is said that they like to spy on the love-making of mortals because they are so old they have grown weary of their own kind . . . What is it, Kris? If it was fey music, it has stopped now so fear not.'

The youth was running his fingers over his face in a distracted way. The languor which followed the wonderful merging of their bodies – and more than their bodies, it had seemed! – was ebbing. Remorse and vague fears were replacing it.

'It was wrong what I did,' he said in a low voice. 'I would ask forgiveness of you but that would not be enough – it could not alter what has happened.'

'Forgiveness!' Jennet exclaimed in amazement. 'Forgive you for making me into a woman!'

The idea was so absurd that all thoughts of the fey folk left her.

'You cannot know how much I have wanted to lie with you these last months,' she continued, 'but I dared not distract you from your work.'

His look of disbelief irritated her further.

'You are a loon. My forgiveness, indeed! Did it seem like a rape to you?'

He shook his head and said slowly, 'It is a terrible wrong for a man to lie with his sister, an abomination against the Mother. We both knew that, and yet . . .'

'Who is to say we are brother and sister?'

'Of course you are my sister.'

'There is no proof of it. We do not look alike, not even our eyes. Yours are greeny and mine are blue . . .'

Krispin shook his head again, refusing to abandon the guilt which replaced the joy he had known such a short while ago.

'We have been together ever since I can remember.'

'But how much do you remember of the time before Father Tammas found us? Do you ever think about it now?'

'Hardly ever. It is something best forgotten. But,' he added reluctantly, 'I sometimes have nightmares about the forest . . . you know, after what happened with the old woman.'

'Let's think about it now,' said the girl in a practical voice. 'My first memory is of a street in a town. There were people – I suppose they were dead people – lying in doorways and piled in a cart. And there were fires burning.'

'Yes, I remember bonfires at the street corners. The smoke smelled of sulphur and made my eyes stream. There must have been a plague.'

'The Red Death.'

He nodded, becoming absorbed in recollection as it became clearer.

'I held your hand and a grown-up held mine. I do not know who it was, perhaps our mother . . .'

'I remember a long walk away from the town. My shoes pinched and I was so tired I could not stop crying, and I was so afraid of the trees. They looked like green giants. What happened then?'

'The woodcutter. His little house in the glade. It is all vague now, though I remember that his wife always seemed to be cross with us. And there was a cat! A black cat with the palest green eyes. I loved that cat. What was his name?'

'How do I know? But I do remember the snow, walking

through the white winter forest with the woodcutter. We had all been so hungry, and I was pleased when he sat us down under a tree and gave us a piece of bread each. It was lovely . . . until we found that he had gone.'

'He had been kindly enough in his way but there was hardly any food in his larder that winter. It must have been his wife who made him abandon us. I wonder how long it was before we came upon the old woman's cottage.'

'Let us not think about it. I still dream about her pebble glasses.'

'She must have been a witch.'

'Or worse.'

They fell silent.

'It is running through the forest afterwards that I dream about,' Krispin said finally. 'It seemed to go on for ever and ever after . . . you know. I suppose I thought her ghost might be after us.'

'I cannot remember Father Tammas finding us. In one way it seems as though we have always been in his home, being looked after as though we were his own children. What happened before he took pity on us seems like a dream.'

'Just like a dream,' Krispin agreed thoughtfully. 'Tammas has made up for everything.'

'But that does not make us brother and sister!'

'Somehow I must find out the truth. Should I be chosen tonight and permitted my year and a day away from Toyheim I shall search for it. Perhaps I could find the town – though no one here has any idea where it could be – and there might be someone there who remembers, perhaps even the woodcutter . . .'

'Is it so important?'

He seized her wrists.

'Yes! Yes! Yes! If I could prove that we are not related I would beg you to be my wife.'

She looked at him in amazement, eyes shining.

'If you feel like that it matters not whether we are related,' she said. 'We could leave the village in secret and travel to some place where we are not known, and there we could be wed.'

He shook his head.

'Impossible. You know the penalty for what we have done. In this gentle place we would be driven into the forest like outlaws; in Danaak we would be put in the cage high on The Citadel wall for the citizens to gawp at until we rotted. We could not live under such a threat. Besides . . .'

He paused unhappily.

'. . . besides, should we have a child it could be monstrous.'

His eyes were moist and he gazed away over the mere.

'I love you, Kris,' Jennet said quietly. 'And I know there can be nothing evil in what we have done. It was the blessing of the crystal bird.'

She rose to her feet, standing above him pale and slender as a willow wand.

'I *shall* find the truth about us,' he muttered. 'Pray that I am chosen tonight.'

Then, with alarm in his voice, he cried, 'You bleed. Already you are being punished for my folly.'

The girl laughed.

'Punishment! That is my maid's blood, ignorant one.'

'Does it happen every time?' he asked while she shrugged her gown over her shoulders.

'Of course not – only the first time, but that is why a beldame can still remember her first lover when those who came after are forgotten. And that is why I am grateful it was you. Next time I shall enjoy it as much as you.'

Krispin gazed at the bruised flowers where they had lain and at the stain on the grass which seemed like a pagan libation. For a moment the wonder of all that had happened, the flashing bird, the joy of their lovemaking and the haunting music of the mysterious piper filled him with such emotion that tears rolled down his cheeks.

'I shall find out the truth,' he repeated, his hand caressing the bloodied grass.

FIVE
The Revel Master

Gambal, a ludicrous masked figure in the pied garb of the Regent's Revel Master, stood hidden by the crimson draperies which divided the luxury of the flambeaux-lit hall from the squalor of the kitchens. Before long the election ceremony – always a foregone conclusion – would take place and after that he would come face to face with his destiny. He would discover whether his desperate efforts to escape the ghastly slaughterhouses of Danaak, the dreaming capital of Ythan whose spires were said to touch heaven while its foundations were rooted in hell, would bring the success he ached for or whether he would be doomed to return to his lowly beginnings.

This was not the time to doubt! he told himself sternly. Having paid so much attention to the Regent's bizarre interests, he could not fail with Silvermane.

His deceptively innocent eyes roved along the hundreds of guests seated at long tables ranged round the largest hall in The Citadel – important men in rare brocades, fleshy with affluence, and beside them their ladies in shimmering gowns whose most sincere smiles were those of disdain.

The order of precedence was carefully observed; the tables furthest from the High Table with its halo of golden candle light held the hereditary lords, governors and military commanders from Ythan's remote provinces;

next were seated the dignitaries from other cities and towns of the sprawling kingdom – their opulence in high contrast to the wretches they ruled. Beneath the High Table sat the burghers of Danaak in their traditional cloth-of-gold caps, and above them at a raised table were the six members of the Regent's Council who whispered flinty-eyed among themselves, and only smiled when the Regent made one of his sardonic jokes.

Unlike many of the guests whose boorish manners and appetites had increased with privilege, the Council was formed of five men and one woman who in public possessed the dignity of their exalted office.

In Gambal's ears the clatter of the kitchen behind his back seemed to fade as his gaze came to rest on the tall, over-fleshed form of the Regent himself. He sat alone on a dais above the councillors to the right of the traditionally empty Throne of Kingship. Although his once-muscular body had been softened by years of easy living and hard indulgence, it still generated an aura of harsh strength and his inflamed face beneath glossy black hair, cut straight above the eyebrows, expressed almost royal authority. At a distance his appearance suggested a strong but benign ruler, but close up his usual smile was belied by adamantine eyes whose coldness became even bleaker with anger – a quality which had sent not a few officials from his audience chamber with soaking hose or worse.

With such a presence the Regent never needed to waste words, and such was his whispered reputation for ingenious cruelty that the words he did utter in his unexpectedly high-pitched voice were obeyed with fervour. That reputation coupled with the efficiency of the Regent's Guard – curiously named the Companions of the Rose – had enabled him to survive a dozen conspiracies and attempted revolts since his first election as many years ago. The one thing he had in common with lesser men was that he liked to be amused.

42

Serene Mother! How he likes to be amused! thought Gambal. *And what amusements!*

A surge of panic made the youth close his eyes behind the grinning gold-lipped mask. As yet the Lord Regent was not aware that an unknown upstart was replacing old Wilk who had devoted his life to studying his master's humours.

Now old Wilk lay stupefied and incapable in his remote chamber because Gambal had made a study of *his* tastes.

It had begun a year ago in one of the subterranean slaughter houses of the city when the old revel master had descended into the blood-reeking hell to select a new hog's bladder which, when cleansed and inflated and attached to an ivory wand, was the emblem of his calling. As he stood surrounded by the steam from the fat cauldrons, the corpulent master butcher called to Gambal who, for twelve hours every day, disembowelled still twitching animals, hauled out their guts hand-over-hand and coiled them in tubs of salted water.

'Get the Mesire Wilk a bladder in a trice or it will be your bladder he will have on the end of his rod,' he roared. 'The poor gentleman is not used to the perfumes of our delicate trade.'

Gambal scurried away through the steam in which spectral figures of butchers and skinners and trimmers fought to keep pace with the endless line of animals driven down the ramp from the upper world.

When he returned with a bladder Wilk saw that his thin face, rosy with blood smears and the glow of the furnaces, was remarkably unspoiled and almost attractive compared with the ghouls who moved about him.

'You are a comely lad,' he said as Gambal wrapped the bladder in a piece of sacking. 'How is it that one such as you is content to work in this pit?'

Gambal's thin lips curled back at the irony of the old man's remark but before he could reply the master

43

butcher shouted, 'Back to your chain, turd. You are falling behind and there is a new drove of beeves arriving.'

Wilk watched as the youth obediently stepped across the grease-rimed cobbles to where several newly slaughtered sheep hung like criminals from chains attached to rails beneath the shadowed roof. He sucked in his breath through worn teeth as Gambal flicked the thin blade of his knife along the steel which hung from his broad leather belt with a reflex gesture before deftly slitting the carcass so that its offal burst forth.

'Will that be all, mesire?' asked the master butcher, and when Wilk nodded he vanished through the vapours in the direction of the killing pens where the crack of the herdsmen's whips was briefly blotted out by a bellow of animal agony. Lifting the skirts of his gown, the old man picked his way over blood-flowing gutters to where Gambal sent the de-gutted carcass spinning away from him and prepared to run his knife down the belly of the next.

'Young man,' he hissed through the clamour of the slaughter, 'bring this to the gate of The Citadel when you are free. I want to express my thanks . . .'

Without a word Gambal took the piece of folded parchment and hastily thrust it into the pocket of his canvas apron, hoping that none of the other labourers had seen it and would hold him over the rendering vat until he gave up what they would believe to be a tip.

When the moon hung low over the spires of Danaak, Gambal hurried through streets in which timber-framed houses leaned towards each other as though confiding ancient secrets, to the bronze gates of The Citadel standing on the enormous rock hill around which Danaak had grown over the centuries.

A sentry squinted at the piece of parchment by torchlight, showed it to a superior who recognized the marks upon it with a sour expression, after which the youth was led through a maze of cold stone corridors by a silent usher and up hollowed steps to a remote tower.

'In there,' said his guide and Gambal was left to knock on a worm-pitted door.

After the hovel near the caravanserai which Gambal shared with his mad mother, the dingy chamber seemed luxurious. Wilk, attired in a lounging robe of raw wool, offered him wine the like of which he had never tasted and whose scent was enough to put his tired senses in a whirl. But though he thanked the old man and drank his heady wine he retained his gutter cunning. When Wilk sat beside him and, in remarking that a young man like him should not have to work in such ghastly conditions, let his hand rest on his thigh, Gambal casually drew out his wicked butcher knife and toyed with it like one deep in thought.

And when Wilk asked how it had come to pass that he should have to do such shameful work, he told him a tale, invented on the spur of the moment, of how his father had been a prosperous merchant who had borrowed heavily to finance a trading expedition to Ronimar for casks of the famous black wine. On the return journey the caravan had been pillaged in the wilderness by outcasts and his father, unable to meet his obligations, had been sold into slavery by his creditors. In order to support his broken-hearted mother Gambal had been forced to give up studying the physic arts.

The truth was somewhat different. True, his drunken father had been sold into slavery – as punishment for purse-cutting – and true, he did support his mother, an ex-tavern-dancer who, after her man had gone to the mines, addled her mind with fumes of Moon Bloom petals, but there any hint of similarity ended.

The nearest Gambal had got to medical studies was dissecting the beasts which hung from the chains; all he

45

could remember was the hated abattoir into which his mother had sold him when he was little more than a child.

As he spun his tragic fabrication, he remembered the horror of his first days in the slaughterhouse when the cries of the animals made him cringe, when he was constantly tensed for casual blows from the butchers and when the amalgam of blood, dung, warm fat and human sweat made him gag. His particular horror was when worn-out drongs were brought for slaughter. These tall animals had to be bled to death – some said because of a half-forgotten religious edict, others that the practice was to improve the meat – and after their veins had been opened, while they slipped and rolled in their own rich smoking gore, their cries were like those of panicked children.

Brutality brutalizes or fires revolt, and as Gambal grew in strength through the punishing work there evolved within him a desperate urge to find a better life. On the surface he made things as easy for himself as possible by subservience to his masters – while in his fantasies he tugged out their entrails as they dangled heads-down from the chains. And at each false dawn when he left his mother's hovel he vowed that somehow, someday, he would escape to the upper world no matter the cost to himself or anyone else, and in this he had two unrecognized qualities – innocent, if pallid, good looks and a rare and ruthless mind.

Despite the moment of the butcher's knife, old Wilk felt genuine pity for the enslaved merchant's son. After another visit he arranged for Gambal – so full of respect, so eager to become his unpaid servant – to be released from the Slaughterers' Guild and after burning his blood-stiffened garments, dressed him in a cast-off page's uniform and allowed him to run his errands.

Gambal learned everything he could of the revel master's work by watching Wilk night and day, drinking in his boastful reminiscences and his monologues on the nature of the Lord Regent and his court.

The youth also learned that the old man was experiencing a renewal of lust in the way that a candle flares before guttering out. Seeing his chance, Gambal fathomed his pathetic vices and then, disguising him under the veil of a survivor of the Red Death, he led him to the vilest of the city's stews. Here Wilk slaked his desire with weeping boys or the most violated little virgins on the market – he cared not their sex provided they were *young*.

Depravity became the old man's drug, and night after night the ill-assorted pair roamed the darkest alleys of Danaak in search of more perverse pleasures, more degraded drabs and pathics, until Wilk's health faltered under his excesses and only by the use of stimulants provided by his ever-attentive servant – still unpaid but steadily robbing him – was he able to continue with his duties.

Meanwhile Gambal laid his plans which included night visits to the caravansarai where he met with a deformed drong-rider descriptively known as The Hump, and through him he had conversations with his master who had traded along perilous routes to the outermost corners of the kingdom. Finally an agreement was reached and the silver he had filched from Wilk's pallet was transferred to the merchant's money pouch. Now, at the approach of the traditional re-election of the Regent, it seemed that the potions which had supported the old man through his excesses became inexplicably unobtainable.

'It will be sure to come on the next caravan,' Gambal answered soothingly when Wilk demanded and then whined for his sustaining substance. Curiously there was no shortage of another drug which had the effect of raising desire in the mind without helping the body to gratify it, and even after the revel master had taken to his bed he still ordered Gambal to procure for him. Each morning, after some young whore had been conducted out through little-used passages by his servant, Wilk would declare in a quavering voice, 'Tomorrow I shall be better and rehearse my lord's feast.'

'Surely, master,' Gambal would agree, having bribed a seamstress to alter Wilk's traditional motley to fit him.

On the eve of the banquet Wilk had sunk into a stupor on his befouled pallet and Gambal went ahead with his plan to replace him.

And now as he watched from the curtains he put thoughts of the past out of his head. All that mattered in his life was *now*, this thin strip of consciousness between the past and the future. Everything depended upon the next few minutes – they could mean a return to gut-pulling or rising to a position of which he had hardly dared to dream. He looked over his shoulder to his drummers ready to announce him with thunderous rata-plan, and at the four liveried footmen – hired with the last of Wilk's silver crowns – at the corners of the tall cage which had remained shrouded in black samite since its arrival at The Citadel.

An inquisitive serving girl, chosen for a figure that seemed about to burst her bodice ribbons, tried to part the draperies as she flounced past. Immediately Gambal was beside her, his hand shooting clawlike to the bosom which a moment ago had been the toast of her table, and she gave a cry, lost in the kitchen noise, as his fingers dug into her powdered flesh.

'Be not curious, sister,' he hissed. 'My playful pinch is nothing to what you might find behind that curtain.'

Slowly and deliberately he turned his wrist and then released her so that, ashen-faced, she reeled away in tears.

'Silvermane,' Gambal murmured close to the samite, 'soon it will be your great moment. Let me know that all is well.'

From within the swathed cage came a knock so heavy that the footmen glanced at each other with apprehension.

Gambal allowed himself a smile of satisfaction and turned his eyes back to the banquet.

SIX

The Choosing

The lament of a moon-haunted wolf echoed across the valley as the oaken gate of the Peak Tower swung back and the black, heavily curtained coach of Lady Eloira, Reeve of the High Wald, rolled out on to the narrow road which plunged zig-zag down the forested mountain-side, crossed timber bridges above cararacts from the high snow fields and skirted the rims of precipices. With its wooden brake screeching and its team of six horses shying and skidding, the vehicle began its descent from the awesome rock formation on which the tower-like castle shredded fast-moving cloud with its pinnacles.

Once the sombre carriage reached the lower slope of the valley the coachman wiped away the sweat that bedewed his face despite the night air, and released the smoking brake. After half an hour's travelling on a more gentle road the lathered horses approached a cluster of yellow lights and knew from past experience that soon they would be able to rest their strained muscles and thrust their noses into generous buckets of oats.

As the equipage neared the first of the village cottages the two outriders raised auroch horns to their lips so that the toymakers would be prepared to greet their patroness.

The driver drew up skilfully opposite the series of evergreen arches which had been erected for the Reeve to pass through into the hall – like most things on this special night, the arches were the product of tradition. A servant, his livery almost as aged as he, climbed down with creaking joints from the rear of the vehicle and opened its door. Silent villagers doffed caps or curtsied as from its dark interior stepped Lady Eloira, a tall old woman with silver hair parted in the centre so that it fell in a wave on each side of her face which had gained a fragile fine-boned beauty with the long passage of the years.

No one knew her age, but the older men of the village swore that she had hardly altered in appearance since their apprentice days.

Drawing her cloak of blue-grey spider silk about her, she walked determinedly erect beneath the evergreens into the hall where, on this most important night of the year, the stage area was brilliant with the light of a hundred candles and stifling with their heat.

Still without a word, as custom demanded, Lady Eloira seated herself in the chair of honour, a throne-like example of the finest carving that could be found in this village of obsessive craftsmen. The villagers trooped in after her, taking their places according to status with rehearsed ease. Then rotund Tammas, as leading toy-maker, bowed before her, squinted through his square spectacles at a creased parchment and began the traditional preamble while the Reeve gazed at the grotesquely figured rafters without expression.

Few would have guessed that she was counting the minutes to when she would be back in her library, surrounded by the odour of antique bindings and time-faded scrolls, a crystal goblet of sweet wine close to hand and a grimoire of forbidden knowledge open upon her slender knees. Thus she passed most of her nights for with her many years the need for sleep had lessened and she only took to her bed when the dawn eagles soared above the conical roofs of her castle. Tonight she found her

51

ceremonial duty more than usually oppressive, for a few hours earlier she had experienced a dim premonition of approaching malfeasance.

Over her long life she had learned to respect such warnings but as yet she had no inkling of what form the threat might take. The High Wald was so remote from Danaak and the machinations of the Regent that she felt no greater apprehension than usual in that quarter, and as far as she knew the lives of the scattered folk who lived in her forested domain continued their even tenor. And yet . . .

Such were the distances between the villages of the Wald, between her Castle of the Peak and River Garde, that news was slow to travel. The Lady Eloira knew that until several days had elapsed without some ill word reaching her she would be unable to free herself from this sense of foreboding.

Her mind wandered while Tammas's ritualistic monologue – suitably sprinkled with archaic phrases – told how, in the chaos which followed The Enchantment, toymakers were among those persecuted by mobs whose puritanical leaders blamed their heretical frivolities for the judgement brought upon Ythan. They inveighed against music which, under old King Johan, had become an obsession with his subjects; the painters who were no longer content to limn the faces of men and women but the dreams behind them; and the Guild of Toymakers whose members had become less and less interested in making kites and rocking horses but turned their skills to automata whose jerky imitations of the living were a blasphemy.

Carrying what tools they could salvage, the toymakers quit the smouldering towns and took to the forest tracks in search of a haven away from the hysteria of the darkening world. Finally, after a winter-long march, the survivors entered this sheltered valley in the High Wald and the then Reeve, Lady Eloira's grandsire, generously granted them permission to build their village in return for the right to select the finest piece of work produced by the apprentices each year. This light-hearted pepper-corn condition evolved into the solemn choosing ceremony.

'. . . and now My Lady Eloira, Reeve of the High Wald, Guardian of the Forest Ways, Friend of the Fey Folk . . .' (here several villagers made the sign of the Mother) '. . . and Protector of Toyheim, shall exercise her right,' Tammas intoned from his parchment. 'And whosoever's work she chooses shall quit the village for a year and a day to travel the great world beyond, living by his craft, and learning from his wayfaring until his return whereupon he shall be deemed a guild member and shall be allowed to work accordingly, receiving his fair allot-ment of profit earned by the Guild. Is this fully accepted by all?'

'Aye!' came the answering chorus while Lady Eloira inclined her head slightly and wished that they would get on with it.

'Let the unveiling proceed.'

Tammas wiped his ruddy face in a gesture of relief and like everyone else turned his gaze to the ten swathed objects in a line on the dais. A silver bell, said to have been brought to the village by its founding fathers, was rung and the beadle in a uniform reminiscent of a toy soldier marched forward stiff-legged, as custom yet again demanded, and cut the cords round the first bundle with ceremonial shears. Immediately his assistant snatched away the covering.

There was an intake of breath as a magnificent rocking horse was revealed, so cunningly carved that he appeared about to spring from his rockers at any moment. His flaring nostrils showed carmine, his wicked eye regarded the villagers as though he was only half-tamed, and silver stars decorated his chest and flanks. Silver, too, were the threads which made up his mane and tail, while his saddlery was of the softest leather dyed the deep blue of the sky just after sunset.

The Reeve sighed. Already her attics contained a score of rocking horses.

She nodded and the next exhibit was unwrapped and a model castle, based on fabled River Garde, shone in the candlelight. Accompanied by the ticking of clockwork, a line of tiny sentries patrolled its diminutive ramparts. There was stifled applause and the ceremony continued.

Krispin's palms were greasy with sweat when the cloth fell away from his dancer and he stepped forward to touch the concealed lever which activated her repertoire of movement. Father Tammas, whose eyes flicked constantly between the toy and the Reeve, was gratified to see a quick look of surprise cross the old lady's impassive face. Jennet felt a glow of pride in her brother – she believed him to be that despite her words by the mere – as she noticed how Lady Eloira's gaze remained upon the face of the automaton even when she was performing her most intricate steps.

It is the quality of the carving she appreciates, she thought.

The next exhibit – a comical cow – was the last.

The Reeve rose from her seat of honour and walked along the exhibits until she reached Krispin's where she stopped and intoned the customary words, 'The Reeve has chosen. Forward, toymaker.'

Filled with fierce pride, Krispin advanced to receive the purse filled with silver to enable him to commence his year as a wandering journeyman. He told his name – Krispin Tammasson, a gesture which all the village appreciated – and then he could hardly believe his ears when the Reeve announced that she wanted him to return with her to the Peak Tower where he would be given instruction on his journey. It was an honour which had never been bestowed before and Father Tammas trumpeted into his handkerchief to hide his tears of joy.

The tarbuts and drums struck up and the women of the village began their traditional doll dance.

At midnight Lady Eloira gratefully rose from her seat of honour to return to the Peak Tower and while the villagers lined up one by one to make their ceremonial farewells, Krispin sought Jennet in a corner of the hall where guttering candles cast intimate shadow.

'Why do you cry?' he asked in a falsely cheerful voice. 'Tonight you should be happy for me.'

'Oh my dear, but I am,' she replied between sobs, trying to brush away the tears which furrowed her thick doll make-up. 'I am so proud of you, but it means you leaving Toyheim . . .'

'But I'll soon be back from the Tower.'

'Only to set out on a year of wandering.'

'At least let us be happy until that parting. And the year will soon pass . . .'

'For you perhaps because everything will be new and wonderful, but for me here in the village it will be a lifetime.'

'I shall use that year to find out who we really are, I promise you. Somehow I shall learn the truth and – the Mother willing – we may be able to spend the rest of our lives together properly as man and wife.'

Apple ale had given him confidence and he held her closely while she pressed her cheek against his.

'Where is that boy?' boomed Father Tammas. 'Her ladyship's coach is waiting.'

'Never forget the crystal bird,' whispered Jennet.

'Never.'

Krispin released her and hurried into the cold night air where from far away came the cry of a lone wolf.

SEVEN

Mandraga

In the Great Hall of the Citadel servants removed platters with the remains of dyed meats on them, more wine flacons were circulated and a tide of rising voices drowned the music of the harpers. Seated beside the empty throne, the Regent gazed over the animated scene with hooded eyes and smiling mouth. Behind him his personal body-guard, six specially selected Companions of the Rose, stood as immobile as a line of statues with gauntleted hands on the hafts of their halberds, their visors down.

These men gave him a comforting sense of protection, as did his taster and his avenger who stood with his crossbow cocked and eyes restless behind his silver mask. It was his duty, should his master be attacked or murdered, to fire a triple-barbed bolt not at the assassin but into the heart of the person present most likely to profit by the Regent's death.

The Regent had found this innovation remarkably effective. The last time there had been an attempted assassination at a court ceremony he had noted that a certain noble was unexpectedly absent from the function and who had later confessed to the conspiracy in the clutch of the Iron Virgin.

Despite his spies and precautions the Regent was well aware there were still those who would hazard everything in the hope of ending his reign – not to overthrow regency rule as the Pilgrims wished but to usurp his power for themselves. With such thoughts in mind he scanned the faces of the councillors – which of them would be the next to try and become the master of Ythan? His gaze lingered on the aristocratic features of Lord Odo, the spokesman of the Council who, the Regent knew, would lead the clamour for his ritual re-election.

He smiled encouragingly over his goblet of black wine at Lord Odo who inclined his silvered head in recognition of the favour.

'And what has your revel master planned for us tonight, my lord?' he asked in his cultured voice.

'I believe there is some surprise afoot,' the Regent replied, 'though to me the surprise will be if the old goat can perform at all. When I last saw him he appeared like something summoned by a necromancer. A lusting pestle is a greater danger to the old than the Red Death.'

The councillors chuckled appreciatively and Lord Odo wondered if there was any possibility that the remark had been directed at him. Surely he could not know about Urwen whose young body had brought such joy to his bed. He comforted himself with the thought that before the next full moon that false smile would be wiped from the Regent's face and all his guards and his avenger would avail him nothing.

While Lord Odo savoured his wine and his thoughts, the Regent unfastened a small vellum scroll which had been handed to him by a page whose fair locks and innocent features appeared girlish to guests who had been invited to The Citadel for the first time and who did not know of the Regent's penchant for female pages.

So, thought the Regent as he crumpled the missive, the nomads mass opposite the Wald and the River Lord looks for help. Excellent! That extraordinary Wolf King is on time, it seems, and while his little demons will rid me of a

Pilgrim there is nothing like a threat from without to make discontent less vocal within.

'Blood-letting is still the chirurgeon's best cure,' he remarked to the councillors.

'My lord?'

'I was thinking of a distemper which has become too prevalent in some parts of the realm,' he answered, his eyes so like dark ice that those below the high table were relieved when an ascending fanfare of ivory trumpets filled the hall and a herald proclaimed, 'Now hear the words of Mandraga, Lore Mistress of Ythan!'

Through the far doorway a beautiful boy appeared scattering drops of red wine from a ewer of finely decorated electrum in a ritual whose origins had been long forgotten. His youth emphasised the great age of the woman who followed him, supporting herself by a T-shaped crutch. Sparse white hair floated round her wizen face, her back bent like a bow and her shuffling progress was painfully slow.

In the body of the hall men froze in the midst of laughter, nodded ponderously to each other, sealed lips with be-ringed fingers and controlled their belches and farts with a parody of dignity. They gazed at the creeping beldame with a mixture of repugnance and fascination, and not a little fear.

When Mandraga reached the centre of the crimson-carpeted floor her curved spine straightened, and those seated nearest to her noticed uneasily that her slate blue eyes held a curious luminosity suggesting youth . . . more, there was a worrying illusion that for brief moments her features and figure seemed to blur and change so that spectators could have sworn that for an instant there was a full-fleshed young woman standing in the sable robe of the Lore Mistress.

Gambal, waiting in the shadows, was not the only one present who recalled whispered hints about her studies

58

relating to the Philosopher's Stone. There were those in the innermost circles of The Citadel who were more wary of the Lore Mistress than their master the Regent who, despite his enormous power, was still flesh and blood, whereas at times she was frightening with her power of weird-sight. Having regained her breath the old woman raised her hand and intoned the traditional runer's opening, 'Listen!'

'We listen,' the assemblage responded.

'One hundred seasons have come and gone since the year of The Enchantment,' she proclaimed in a voice which, though it quavered, reached the furthest recesses of the Great Hall. 'In that year of the Serene Mother the realm of Ythan was prosperous and at peace under the reign of King Johan, the thirty-third monarch of Ythan's royal line. As is known to all, the Princess Livia, the sole issue of the king, was abducted by magical means to some unknown place where, if there be truth in ancient prophecy, she would remain entranced.'

While Mandraga paused for breath, the Regent surveyed the faces of the guests – rapt or bored or drunken in the torchlight – and wondered how many believed her words. It was something each had learned at his or her mother's knee, yet how many considered it a historical fact as they grew older and how many regarded it as a convenient myth such as the fall of the All Father? Certainly the Pilgrims believed the story of the princess as literal truth – which was the one thing they had in common with the Regent.

'Worn out by grief and fruitless questing, the old king reached the end of his span and left an empty throne,' the Lore Mistress continued. 'To overcome the troubles which followed and preserve the kingdom until the return of its rightful inheritor, the first Regent was elected and in turn he created the High Council to aid him in his task of governing. And it was decreed that on each and every anniversary of The Enchantment, the reigning Regent must be reaffirmed in his role by persons of consequence listed in the Rolls of Entitlement, or if it be deemed that he has not fulfilled his office with honour and nobility a new Regent must be named before midnight . . .'

As Mandraga continued her recital the Regent continued to look about the hall.

. . . *with honour and nobility!* he mused. And with bribes and preferments for which this rabble would auction their souls. And with fear – oh yes, very much with fear – and, for those who would usurp me, the reality of fear.

He decided that when this tiresome rigmarole was over he would descend the secret stairway to the special dungeons cut in the rock beneath The Citadel's foundations and pay an overdue visit to his 'pets' as he termed the special prisoners incarcerated there – it would be more amusing than this buffoonery.

Finally the Lore Mistress demanded that those assembled decide if it was their wish that the Regent should rule for another term.

The expected roar of affirmation curtailed the Regent's pleasurable thoughts and he rose to his feet, hands raised as though in benediction while the old woman hobbled from the hall. She appeared even more hag-like from her exertions yet for odd seconds she seemed to dissolve into a different form which, it was agreed afterwards, must have been a trick of the flambeaux.

When the acclaim had died and the Regent seated himself after his ritualistic response, Gambal snapped his fingers at his retinue and then, with extravagant gestures and old Wilk's scarlet-dyed hog's bladder bobbing at the end of his ivory wand, he marched forth into the torchlight to the rolling beat of his drummers while behind him the footmen wheeled the shrouded cage. When he halted before the High Table the drumbeats died and he threw away his mask.

60

'Mesire Regent and honoured gentlefolk,' he declaimed, 'on this auspicious night our revered Wilk, forced to take to his bed at the zenith of his prowess . . .'

Laughter.

'. . . has entrusted me, your humble servant Gambal Gut-Stretcher . . .'

More laughter.

'. . . to take his place. So overwhelmed was I at this honour that I determined to make my debut one that will remain fresh in your memories. And so, I give you . . . Silvermane!'

At the last word drums rolled afresh and the footmen snatched away the covering. Men shouted in astonishment, some women screamed but the Regent rose to his feet and for once his eyes lost their bleakness.

EIGHT

Smoke In The Forest

Krispin was still intoxicated by a combination of apple ale and success when the Reeve's swaying coach approached the final stretch of road leading up to the Peak Tower, so steep that a team of oxen waited ready-yoked to lend their massive strength, their drivers laughing and waving their goads while the coachman split the night with his whipcracks.

For most of the journey Lady Eloira sat in a reverie against the corner cushions, only once looking up at the youth seated opposite and asking, 'That face. How did you put such a face on your dancer?'

'After I had carved it, my lady, I used special waxes to make the surface as much like skin as possible . . .'

'You misunderstand. Where did you find the picture you copied it from?'

'It was no copy, my lady. I based it on my . . . my sister.'

'No village chit could have such features.'

'Jennet has. She was there in the hall, but she had her hair under a scarf and two red patches were painted on her cheeks for the doll dance.'

'No wonder I did not recognise her.'

In the warm darkness Krispin shrugged and nothing more was said until the coach halted in the castle court-yard where servants waited with flambeaux.

With a nod Lady Eloira left her guest to be escorted to his room. He found it so high in a turret that as he gazed from its tiny window it seemed that he was looking down on the whole world – hills, forests and valley lit by the gibbous moon – while the peaks of the White Virgins gave the illusion of being level with him.

What dreams awaited Krispin that night as he sank – yes, sank into a mattress of eiderdown such as was given to princesses in the old tales because of the softness of their skins. Exhausted after the long day with its conflicting emotions, he was assailed by images; Jennet's slender body as she stood above him; the glitter of the crystal bird; the joy on Father Tammas's face when the Reeve touched his dancer; and then the old dreaded dream of fleeing through the forest.

He rose late the next morning, his head thick and the taste of fermented apples still in his mouth. After he had toyed with breakfast in the vaulted kitchen, an old man-servant announced that Lady Eloira would see him in her solar. As Krispin followed the shambling figure up a circular staircase in the central tower it occurred to him that everyone he had seen in the castle, even the maids, were very, very old.

He was finally led into a chamber at the top of the tower which appeared to be lined with cabinets and shelves packed with leather-bound tomes of all sizes and condition. A herb-scented fire glowed in the hearth by which the Reeve sat, a grey, malignant-eyed cat named Smoke on her lap, for all the world like a village grandmother.

'Sit,' said the old woman, indicating a chair on the opposite side of the fireplace. She turned to a table beside her on which stood a brass-bound box, and after unlocking it she produced a miniature portrait which she held so that Krispin could see the face behind the crystal.

'Jennet!' he exclaimed.

The old woman turned her head from side to side.

'This is the likeness of Princess Livia – painted when the kingdom of Ythan was at its noonday – who vanished as the result of malefic sorcery. Now you may understand why I was drawn to you and your dancer.'

'I know little about the Princess Livia, only what is told in children's tales,' said Krispin. 'They say that in some secret place she lies in an enchanted sleep waiting for a hero to awaken her so that she can claim the Empty Throne, but I vow I had no inkling of her looks.'

Lady Eloira sighed and replaced the miniature.

'You may be an excellent toymaker but you and your remarkable sister are not of the village – are you, Krispin Tammasson?'

'No, my lady. Tammas found us wandering in the forest and brought us up as his own.'

'I recall hearing about that years ago. Do you have any idea who you really are?'

'Would that I did!'

She looked at him quickly, then from a decanter poured a goblet of her favourite sparkling wine.

'This will revive you after last night's celebration.'

He took the glass and noticed that when the light shone through it the wine had a faint hint of green. As he drank it seemed as chill as a mountain torrent, he felt as though icy bubbles were bursting within him, and then cold fire danced along his veins to clear his head. Everything became more vivid: the perfume from the burning fire, the colours of the tapestries glowed, and he was suddenly aware of a beauty that shone through Eloira's finely wrinkled skin.

'Wonderful,' he exclaimed.

'It is,' she agreed with a smile. 'It comes from a vineyard on the far side of Ythan, a year's caravan journey away, and these days it is my greatest indulgence – that, and ancient dreams –'

For a moment she stared into the fire, her thin fingers furrowing the fur of her cat; then, as though recollecting herself, she turned her gaze back to Krispin and began questioning him.

Perhaps it was the wine which he continued to sip, perhaps it was because he felt flattered by her interest, but he found himself talking in a way that had only happened on certain occasions with Jennet.

Lady Eloira suddenly held up her hand.

'You are leaving something out – after you and your sister were abandoned something happened before the toymaker found you. There is a shadow in your voice.'

'It was a long time ago, I forget . . .'

'But not that. Do not think that you can gull me, young man.'

Krispin heard himself tell how hand-in-hand with Jennet he had wandered into a glade in the centre of which stood a delightful little house. A red rose and a white twined above the door, herbs grew in pots beneath the leaded windows and the walls were decorated with floral pargetting – and to the exhausted children it was like a dream come true.

'It is all hazy, but I seem to remember a lady coming to the door,' Krispin continued. 'She wore blue spectacles which made us scared but we were hungry and when she offered us food we went inside. She said we were to stay with her, and once we got used to her spectacles we were happy for a while . . .'

'And what happened?'

He shivered.

'She . . . she was unkind. Not at first but . . .'

'And what happened?'

'We ran away. Through the forest. It was frightening. Sometimes I have nightmares of running through the trees with Jennet.'

65

'So you left the dream house. You do not remember the name of the owner?'

Krispin shook his head.

'Of course, to you, it is so long ago,' said Lady Eloira soothingly. 'Tell me, young sir, what do you plan to do when you leave your sheltered valley?'

'To search . . .' he began and then paused in confusion.

The old woman poured him more wine.

'For more seasons than I care to recall I have watched over your village,' she said. 'Your people are dear to me, and you, as one of them, are therefore special. I sense that despite the fact that you have had the honour of being chosen your heart is troubled. Why not ease the burden, tell me . . .'

And he did.

The words seemed to tumble from him as he explained about his love for the girl who might or might not be his sister, and how he was ready to search the world to find the truth in the hope they could marry.

'And supposing you find the truth and the truth is that Jennet is your sister and forbidden to you.'

'That is a risk I must take.'

'You seem a very determined young man. Perhaps I could help you . . . if you would be prepared to undertake a task for me.'

Krispin looked enquiringly.

'You are thinking that it is not possible for a woman as old as I, living high on a mountain away from the outside world, to help you in your search, but I still have those who would serve me in different parts of the realm – and my knowledge is not just the kind that one finds in those – ' She raised her hand from Smoke and waved it at the rows of books.

'For example, I can tell you the name of the woman you and Jennet met in the forest. Does Mistress Good-heart have any meaning for you?'

Krispin put his hand to his mouth.

'What else do you know about her?'

'Nothing that need concern us.'

For a while they sat in silence, and Krispin was conscious of the moan of the wind round the tower.

'That wind sweeps across the world,' said the old woman softly. 'It carries its secrets from the Outlands, over the Wald and the mountains, over wilderness and woodland, over farms and fens, over desert and the Land of Blight to Danaak itself, and there are those who can read its secrets. Have you not heard of Wind Runes?'

'No, but it sounds like sorcery.'

Lady Eloira laughed softly.

'What would you hazard for your Jennet?'

'My life.'

'Brave words, but I believe you mean them – at least while you are comfortable before a fire.'

'I mean them, my lady.'

'Good. I need a – what shall we say? – a messenger to carry out a commission for me, a secret commission which could have its dangers. You see, Krispin, there are those of us who believe that Princess Livia still lives . . .'

'I have heard tell something of it in the Jack. Packmen come and . . .'

'Did your packmen tell you that to attempt to find her can bring a charge of treason and its inevitable penalty. Would you risk that for Jennet?'

'If I must, but . . .'

'I shall make a bargain with you – be my messenger when you leave on your wandering and when the year-and-a-day is over I shall have the truth about Jennet for you.'

Krispin looked at the old woman who he had been taught as a child was the generous protector of his village and he had no doubt of her words as he agreed.

'Tell me what I must do.'

'If I do that there is the possibility that, should you be questioned by those who serve the Regent, you would be forced to reveal that which would put you, and others, in jeopardy. Your safety will be the fact that you will know nothing.'

'But how can I . . .?'

'I shall store what you need to know in the recesses of your mind, and as each stage of your task is undertaken that part of the knowledge you need to carry out your errand will come into your head – it will seem as though you have just remembered it.'

He looked doubtful.

'Be assured it will work, as it has worked with others.'

'And you will be able to find out about my sis . . . Jennet?'

'Oh yes, I am vastly interested in that young woman. Tonight I shall put you in a trance and tomorrow you may return to Toyheim to prepare for your journey.'

Lady Eloira rang a brass bell and the aged servant appeared to lead Krispin back to his chamber where he stretched out on his bed and found the sunset was staining the mountain snows pink when he next opened his eyes. He decided that her ladyship's sparkling wine must be far stronger than he had imagined, and he began to wonder just to what it was he had agreed.

He had little time for his doubts to grow. After a quick supper in the kitchen he found himself once more in the Reeve's high chamber. He sat opposite Lady Eloira as before. She began to swing a pearl pendant before his eyes, talking gently as she did so.

And then it seemed that everything became strange and distorted and at the soft insistence of Lady Eloira's voice his eyelids drooped and he remembered nothing more until it seemed he heard her voice from a long distance urging him back to consciousness. He woke to find himself gazing into the old woman's grey eyes.

'When you have returned to your village you will set off on your journey through the pass and as it progresses it will become clear what you must do,' she said. 'And tell your Jennet that I wish her to come to the tower.'

Next morning Krispin set off whistling from the castle to begin his year of wandering with a small vellum map folded in his new purse of silver coins. The events of the previous day and evening now seemed dreamlike, indeed he almost wondered if he had dreamed his agreement with the old woman, but his spirits were high and he looked forward to a brief return to make his farewells and enjoy his departure celebration, and above all to spending a few precious hours with Jennet.

It took him most of the morning to follow the road down the valley, and as he recognized landmarks which told him he was nearing the village, his mood abruptly changed as he realized that life would never be the same again.

As he drew closer an acrid smell assailed his nostrils.

Surely it was too early for the husbandmen to be burning stubble on the lower meadows. Could one of the cottages have caught fire? He began to run until he reached a bend in the forest road and saw the village – or what was left of it. Smoke drifted lazily and whole houses were missing.

He ran forward, stumbling desperately and ignoring the stitch which was like a slender knife in his side. Nothing mattered except the scene of horror ahead.

The roof of the Jack-in-the-Box was still burning, and it was not the Jack's sign which hung from the gallows-like arm but Mine Host Lubin with purpled face and protruding tongue blackened by flies, his codpiece burst by the pressure of the hanged man's final stiffening.

Krispin ran on, to find that his home had been razed and saw a mound – a man-shaped mound of ash – which he knew if he kicked it away would reveal the body of Father Tammas. Other villagers lay where they had been butchered, mostly with their heads axe-cloven, but some with arrows which had been shot into their backs as they had attempted to flee.

'Jennet! Jennet!' he cried.

Apart from a steady insect hum there was no answer.

'Jennet! Jennet!'

He must be the only living being in the village. Even cattle and swine lay on their bloated sides, victims of axe blows.

In his search he passed the little school which was still intact. He looked inside and saw Dame Nobert sprawled on the floor, her skirt hoisted above her thighs which were grotesquely apart with the hilt of a dagger showing how one of her attackers had avenged his impotence.

Up and down the village street the youth roamed with a madman's energy, turning over half-burnt corpses, kicking up clouds of ash, closing the eyes of friends who had been gazing at the fluffy clouds with sightless intensity, and vomiting at what he found in a wine cellar.

Back at the ruin of Father Tammas's cottage he picked up a singed doll which Jennet had recently finished dressing, and as she gazed up at him with china eyes and eternal smile his tears fell upon her rosy face. Then he thrust her into his shirt.

'Are you the only one left?'

Krispin spun round.

A young man with a bloodied cloth round his neck swayed in the saddle of his spent horse. Blood was also seeping through his woollen jerkin.

'I have just come back,' Krispin answered tonelessly. 'I cannot find Jennet.'

'I am Alfrith . . . Alwald,' the stranger said with difficulty. 'My father was murdered on the bridge.'

His words meant nothing to Krispin, but seeing him

slump forward he lifted him down and laid him in the shade of a tree.

'Who did this?' he asked as he brought water from the pump for the wounded rider.

'The Wolf King. His barbarians came over the plain in wagons with sails, but we never believed they could cross the river once the bridge was down.'

'What happened?' asked Krispin as he began to remove the sodden bandage.

'The moment the Wolf King killed my father they rolled their wagons into the water . . . they were boats on wheels.'

His next words were lost in a crackling roar as a nearby house burst into flames.

NINE
Silvermane

The ancient city of Danaak was bathed in the radiance of a moon swelling to fullness. The plain on which it lay appeared as a shadow stretching to the horizon, but the Green River which meandered across it and entered the city at the eastern watergate, and left it by the western, appeared like a serpent of pure silver. The massive walls of the city, the steep gabled roofs of the houses within them, the graceful buildings surrounding the outcrop of black rock around which the city grew, the spired shrines dedicated to the Mother and a plethora of saints crowding its lower slopes, and the magnificent Citadel towering above them appeared as though lit by stage lighting.

As the midnight gong reverberated, torch-bearing sentries on the ramparts were relieved, singing revellers rolled out of taverns along the river bank, watchmen assured honest householders that all was well, and in the darker thoroughfares, potholed and uriniferous, cloaked figures hurried on ill-boding missions. The guests from the Regent's election feast sought their carriages and litters. In the banqueting hall flambeaux were doused and candles snuffed, and in a crimson-draped apartment the Regent rested his bulk on a damask divan and surveyed the two figures standing uneasily at the far end of the chamber.

72

One was Gambal, still in his old master's costume, and the other was the lovely yet curious creature whom he had referred to as Silvermane. It was an obvious name; the girl had silver hair which appeared to flow down her back but on close inspection it would be seen that the hair actually grew down the back of her neck and continued below the level of her shoulders. Her features were even and in terms of physical beauty there were few young women in Ythan who could match her. Her eyes were large and liquid brown, their extreme gentleness in contrast to the haughty curve of her nostril and the finely chiselled mouth.

Although she wore a smock of rich gauzy material provided by Gambal, it did not hide the litheness of her body or the shapeliness of her small breasts. But it was from her waist down that held the gaze of the Regent. The pale skin of her thighs was covered with short silver hair, and her slender legs were those of a young horse complete with delicate hoofs. From the base of her spine hair hung in the form of a pony's tail and as she stood with her head bowed under the searching gaze of the Regent it occasionally swished as though under its own volition.

'And what is the name given to such freaks?' the Regent asked. 'Was she the monstrous issue of some cursed woman who gave herself to a stallion or is she one of an unknown breed?'

'I do not know what her kind are called,' replied Gambal, speaking carefully as the Regent's cold eyes swivelled to him. 'But I understand that there is a race of such creatures in the forests far beyond the Waste of Baal where few men dare venture.'

'What tongue does she speak?'

'Those who brought her here have not heard her speak her tongue, but she has some understanding of what we say.'

Silvermane inclined her head.

'She does not seemed affrighted.'

'I believe she was looked after kindly by the merchant who brought her to Danaak.'

'I have no doubt,' said the Regent, climbing to his feet and approaching the horse-girl. He raised her smock.

'At least she is a woman in her vital part,' he said. 'Now tell me, how many crowns did you pay this clever young actress to make up for this evening's entertainment?'

'I assure you, my lord, she is genuine . . . why I paid . . .' He stopped himself speaking further.

The Regent circled Silvermane, then entwined his powerful fingers in the coarse hair of her mane, teasing and tugging until she gave a long-drawn cry.

'Serene Mother! She *is* real!'

The girl's flanks quivered horse-like as he ran his hands over her.

'There is no sorcery about this?' he demanded as he returned to his divan and signed to his silent page to hand him a goblet of Ronimar wine.

'Oh no, my lord. There are some men who adventure into distant parts of the kingdom to seek unusual creatures which they bring to sell in the city. Wishing to provide an unusual spectacle for your feast, I spent time at the caravanserai until I was introduced to the merchant who had brought her to Danaak.'

'And did you learn if she had been used as slaves usually are on such journeys?'

'She was well respected . . .'

'So you were told. Perhaps it will be put to the test.'

He turned to the page.

'Get servants to take her to a chamber in the Tower of the Moon where she will be comfortable. Does she eat hay? Does she sleep on the floor or a bed?'

'She eats the same food as us, my lord, though she has

74

little liking for meat. And she has learned to lie on a pallet.'

'Good. I want a tutor to try and teach her to use our speech for there is much I would question her on.'

When the silent horse-girl had been led away the Regent gestured to a chair. Everything about him suggested geniality except his eyes.

'Having worked so hard to come to my notice you deserve a few minutes of conversation. Page, pour my guest some wine.'

As he sat face-to-face with the Regent in the glow of amber lamps burning perfumed oil, Gambal felt intoxicated even though he had hardly sipped the cup of black wine he held in his hand. So far his audacious plan had worked beyond his dreams, but through the euphoria of the moment he warned himself that he must keep his wits about him more than ever.

'So you are the butcher lad who has murdered my faithful Wilk,' said the Regent.

'Murdered, my lord? I – I merely took his place . . . poor Wilk is ill . . .'

The euphoria was replaced with a feeling of cold sickness.

'Come now, let us not be squeamish over the choice of words. At this moment Wilk lies dead – I had word of his passing during the banquet – and you killed him as surely by your pandering as if you had put viperherb in his drink or slipped a bodkin up his nostril. Tell me, when you led him through the stews what did he favour . . . boys, girls, cripples, whipping whores, or old strumpets whose experience made up for their lack of flesh?'

'Youth,' said Gambal. 'He yearned for youth.'

'Ah yes,' said the Regent reflectively. 'I am told that as a young man it was his ambition to be a poet. He could get words to rhyme but not to sing, and so he became a

75

revel master. I wonder what the young poet would have thought of the old lecher hungering for brothel children.'

The Regent raised his goblet but his eyes never left Gambal's face which had become greasy with perspiration.

'You know the penalty for murder in Danaak?'

'The Cage?' the youth muttered.

'Yes. The Cage. A fate worse than death that finally ends in death. I am told that when the bones of the condemned finally drop through the bars there are craftsmen who collect them and carve them into mementos . . . a thigh-bone flute, a skull vase, necklets of fingerbones. Curious the preoccupation some have with the Dark Maid . . . do you think your thigh bones would have good pitch?'

The Regent's high voice was chuckling, teasing.

'I never meant the old man to die,' stammered Gambal.

'Wilk's death matters not – except to Wilk,' said the Regent with a change of tone. 'We are realists, you and I. If I was to give a minute's concern to each life that has been ended at my decree I would have precious little time for anything else. I know there are those who hate me for this but desperate ills need desperate remedies. After The Enchantment the kingdom lost all unity. Every second man believed he knew the answer to government, and so there was no government. Holy men led crusades against each other on such liturgical questions as to whether the eyes of the Mother were blue or brown. The peasants hanged their landlords and then starved because they had no masters to make them work the land. False messiahs led folk into deserts to die of thirst and illusions and every man's hand was against his neighbour because he was richer or poorer or his skin marked him as a stranger.

'Warlords set up their own little kingdoms, civil war followed and pestilence and madness stalked hand-in-hand. Soon the reign of old King Johan was looked back upon as a mythical golden age. So the Regency was formed and only by pitiless methods was some form of order restored.'

Gambal had a sudden picture of the orderly way sheep trooped down the ramps to the slaughterboards in the bloody cavern where he had spent most of his life; the animals were goaded and smelled death and were filled with fear but they were orderly.

'The chirurgeon's blade feels no remorse when it slices flesh to remove a canker,' the Regent continued reflectively.

'But before . . . before The Enchantment,' said Gambal. 'You say it was a golden age, and all men believe it was different then.'

'Of course it was,' the Regent said. 'The only wars were to protect the frontiers of the realm against barbarians, spies were few and there were more minstrels than beggars in the land. It truly was a golden age because the minds of the people were attuned to living under benign kings – when the monarchy ended they were lost. Such rule held the seeds of its own destruction. It was like a lush garden where everything was allowed to flourish – including sorcery, and in the end it was sorcery which brought the blight.'

'It is whispered that sorcery is returning,' Gambal said.

'I know it is whispered – and it is true.'

A water clock gave forth a musical note to indicate that another hour had passed. At the sound the Regent's tone changed.

'Enough of old history. The present is what matters and I must decide your reward for that fine gift you gave me, not with your own silver I will be bound but I admire your enterprise. Tell me, what do you wish?'

'To serve you, my lord,' said Gambal in a voice he had rehearsed many times in his daydreams.

'Very wise. Better than the gut bucket, eh?'

'You know . . . about the slaughterhouse?'

'Of course. I make a point of knowing what goes on in The Citadel – and Ythan. With such a background you could become an apprentice torturer. You might even perfect a new mode. The most stubborn prisoner might be inclined to confess when he saw his umbles appearing handspan by handspan through his navel. But perhaps you are weary of blood. How do you think you could serve me best?'

'During the past months I did learn something of a revel master's duties from my master Wilk.'

'Then you can try the motley, and if you continue as you have done I may have more important work for you than waving a bladder about on the end of a stick. You had better prepare for the Feast of Fools when the moon makes his next crescent though by then perhaps I shall have more useful work for you to do. I recognize you for what you are . . .'

The lamps suddenly flickered as the door of the apartment swung open and Lord Odo, sword in hand, strode in, followed by the captain of the Regent's Guard and two Companions of the Rose, one of whom hastily closed the door and shot its heavy bolt.

'What . . .' began the Regent, half rising from his divan. 'Even you have no right to make such an entry.'

'It is not a question of entry, my lord, but treason,' the noble said coldly. 'You are my prisoner.'

The Regent laughed.

'Captain, take the councillor to his chambers to sleep off his wine, and if he is not drunk take him to the Hall of the Mad.'

The soldiers did not move.

'The Companions of the Rose have given me their favour,' said Odo, unable to restrain a note of triumph. 'The days of your arrant rule are over. Within the hour couriers shall ride forth to the furtherest corners of Ythan with the news that freedom is at last restored . . .'

'With my Lord Odo as the new protector of the realm,' sneered the Regent.

Lord Odo affirmed with an ironical smile. The Regent turned to the three impassive guards, and wide-eyed Gambal was shocked to see that there was a pleading look on his fleshy face.

'Captain Bors, I remember the day you took the blood oath in the Shrine of the Mother to protect your Regent. And you two, you bring shame on the Companions of the Rose.'

'Times change, my lord,' said Bors.

There was a short silence broken only by the sniffling of the little page.

'Tell me,' said the Regent with an effort to regain his composure. 'Is this plot all your own work, Odo, because if it is the Council will not support you.'

'You have always underestimated me, but I am not the fool you thought. The Lady Thesa is with me, as is Lord Wode, which means the rest of the Council will follow.'

The Regent nodded.

'It is true, I did not give you credit. Nor did my spies, it seems.'

'Silver bought your spies . . .'

'And my guards,' the Regent said ruefully.

Captain Bors stepped forward and raised his arm to bring his gauntlet across the face of his erstwhile master.

'No!' Lord Odo exclaimed.

The metalled fist dropped.

'There must be no mark on the body,' Odo continued as he withdrew a parchment from his doublet.

'So it is to be like that,' said the Regent.

Odo nodded.

'It will be perfectly simple. You will sign this will naming me as your successor. When your body is displayed in

79

state in the Shrine of the Mother the folk of Danaak will conclude that your death has been natural.' He smiled with self satisfaction. 'For some time my agents have been spreading rumours in the taverns that your health has been failing.'

'And why should I sign?'

'Because I have two powders, one of which will be added to your Ronimar wine. If you sign it will be the white powder which will give you a death no more unpleasant than going to sleep. If you do not sign it will be the purple powder ground from firewort which, as I am sure you know from your own experience, will burn you within until your fundament smokes. Either way the final result will be the same, so why not sign and pass peacefully from this world.'

The Regent nodded.

'Let us get it over,' he said heavily. 'Inkstick.'

Sobbing, the page handed him the writing implement and Odo passed him the parchment which he signed without troubling to read.

'Now the wine.' He turned to Gambal. 'How ill your fortune has turned out, my lad. These gentlemen cannot allow witnesses to this night's work, and soon you will join Wilk in the charnal pit.'

Lord Odo took up the goblet of black wine and sprinkled a spill of white powder on the surface so that for a moment the dark liquid seethed. At that moment Gambal launched himself forward and knocked it from his hand.

TEN
Mist Magic

Hot smoke rolled towards Krispin as the house of Old Master Wykin collapsed in a shower of sparks. He straightened up from beside the wounded youth who had whispered that his name was Alwald, and sought to gentle the horse which had borne him from River Garde. As he did so a fragment of glass in a broken cottage casement flashed in the bright morning sunlight; flashed like a message mirror . . . or a crystal bird!

A desperate hope surged through Krispin.

'Rest here in the shade, sir,' he said to Alwald who was now muttering incoherently. 'I shall be back to help you shortly.'

Then he was running through the common meadow as he had never run before, running over the path that he and Jennet had followed on the morning of The Choosing; but now there were no snow white geese to hiss them and no goose girl to grin at their playfulness. That had only been the morning before last, but a barrier of time divided him from that happy moment with the same inevitability as if it had been a century.

He was relieved to enter the cool air of the forest and though shafts of sunlight which pierced its foliage looked solid in the smoke haze which drifted fog-like between the tree trunks, there was something reassuring about its stillness. His footfalls were silenced by the loam of a thousand leaf falls.

After a few minutes he had to slow to regain his breath, and as he did so he was conscious of something moving against the skin beneath his shirt. He slipped his fingers inside expecting the squirm of an insect, instead they touched a cool metal disk suspended from a fine chain. Puzzled, he unfastened his buttons and drew it into the light. It was the size of a silver crown but had been fashioned from a yellow metal which gleamed richly even in the subdued woodland light.

Looking at it closely he saw that on each side there were engraved curious rune-like marks in the form of a spiral.

It was very strange. He had no recollection of how he had come by it. Probably it was a Choosing gift, like the purse of silver, and he had taken too much ale to remember it being given to him. He buttoned his shirt and ran on despite the pain in his side. He would find out about the medallion at some future time.

At last he broke from the trees into the great natural clearing with the mere shimmering through its margin of black reeds . . . and there on the bank, beneath the roots of the grandfather tree, Jennet sat with her legs curled beneath her, making a daisy chain.

For a long moment Krispin lost the power of speech. His eyes closed as he mentally formed an inarticulate prayer of gratitude to the Mother for this mercy, and when he opened them again he saw Jennet peeping at him through her circle of little flowers.

'Please, sir,' she said in the voice of a child which sent a chill through Krispin, 'have you seen my brother? He was with me a little while ago watching the pretty bird, but he left me . . .'

For a moment her eyes filled with tears, as indeed did Krispin's, and then she smiled and held the chain out to him.

'Please take me to Kris,' she said.

'Of course,' he managed to murmur. He stretched out his hand and, taking it, she stood up and slipped the linked flowers over his head.

'That is for being kind,' she said solemnly.

'Come,' he said and led her into the trees.

When they reached the edge of the forest he did not take her across the common meadow, but made a wide circle round the smouldering village to the road which led up the valley to the Peak Tower.

'I am going to take you to a nice lady,' he said.

'Will my brother be there?'

'Oh yes, he will be there.'

He wanted to get away from here as fast as he could in case the marauders should return, and he hurried along the road holding Jennet firmly by the hand. Then his step slowed as he remembered the young man he had left in the village. He stopped. He had been shown a mercy, how then could he deny mercy to another?

There was a stile in the hedge at the roadside and he led Jennet to it.

'Climb over that and wait behind the hedge,' he said gently. 'I want you to stay hidden until I come back with a friend.'

'Like hide-and-seek?'

'Just like hide-and-seek.'

He ran back down the road to where smoke wraiths from the village drifted across it. Again tears welled in his eyes at the sight of the devastation and the sprawled forms of slaughtered neighbours and friends. He found Alwald just as he left him, mouthing deliriously.

For a moment Krispin looked down on him and heard himself say in a panic, 'What can I do? What can I do?'

He heard an uneasy whicker from the tethered horse, and summoning his strength he lifted Alwald upright and then managed to hoist him so that he lay across the high-pommelled saddle, head and arms dangling on one side, his legs on the other. He loosened the young man's belt and refastened it round the pommel to prevent him slipping off. Then leading the well-trained horse by the reins he thankfully left the smoke and the reek of burnt flesh.

Once more on the road, he saw that Jennet was sitting on the stile.

'I got tired of hide-and-seek,' she told him. 'Are we going to see Krispin now? Is your friend dead?'

'He is sick,' he answered. 'We must hurry.'

As the road grew steeper Jennet complained that she was tired.

'I feel I have been running hard but I cannot remember. Is it far to go?'

'Soon be there, then you can rest as much as you like.'

As he spoke he anxiously scanned the valley, looking for some movement that would indicate the presence of the enemy. But the only unusual aspect of the familiar scene was the lazy column of dirty smoke above the trees.

He tried to keep Jennet's attention from her weariness by singing childish rhymes with her – rhymes that they had chanted together when they were small. Sometimes they would be startled by a shout from Alwald. It seemed he was calling a woman's name in his delirium, but it was too indistinct to have meaning.

'Soon be there,' Krispin said grimly, and realized that he was now saying it for his own benefit.

It was late in the afternoon when the incongruous party arrived at the gates of the Peak Tower. Krispin struck the gong beside the entrance with all his remaining strength and as its droning note died among the mountains the old gateman allowed them to enter.

At the sight of Alwald slumped over his saddle the castle servants exclaimed, wrung their hands and cried for their mistress. When the Lady Eloira arrived in the courtyard she immediately restored order. Alwald was carried away to be put to bed under the care of her chirurgeon, the exhausted horse was led to the stables to be cared for and Krispin and Jennet found themselves in her solar while she ordered refreshing draughts for them.

'I did not expect to see you back so soon,' she said, turning to Krispin while Jennet gazed in childish wonder at the pictures on the wall tapestries.

'And I am back with terrible news,' he replied. 'Toyheim is no more. That young man comes from River Garde. He told me that the Wald has been invaded . . .' And in broken sentences he began to tell of what he had found on his return to the village.

'Wait,' said Eloira, holding up her slender hand. 'This is not suitable for childish ears.' And she glanced significantly at Jennet who had seated herself on the carpet and was waving her finger in play with the Reeve's grey cat.

She rang a bell and when an elderly maid appeared she told her to give food to the young lady and then install her in the most comfortable guest chamber.

'Her mind suffers from what she has witnessed and has escaped into the past,' Eloira told the woman. She went to a cabinet from which she took an exquisitely costumed doll.

'Here, my dear,' she said, handing it to Jennet. 'Dolly gave me comfort more years ago than I can recall – I hope she still has the power to do the same for you.'

Jennet jumped up, holding the doll to her chest.

'Lovely,' she exclaimed. 'And will I see Krispin soon?'

'I hope so,' said Eloira.

When Jennet had been led away the old woman turned to Krispin whose eyes gleamed with unshed tears at the scene which had just taken place.

'I can see that she was the model for your automaton,' she said. 'Her likeness to the portrait of Princess Livia is remarkable . . . remarkable. Now that she is being cared for, tell me everything that happened, young man.'

'She does not recognize me,' Krispin muttered. 'Tell me, lady, will her mind return to the present?'

'I cannot give you an easy answer,' she replied. 'She may remain a child in a woman's body for years, perhaps slowly growing up in her mind as a child does, or perhaps she will wake up one day her proper self as though nothing has happened. But rest assured that here she will have the best of care . . . oh yes, your Jennet will be cherished. Now your story.'

When Krispin finished his simple recital Eloira said, 'It is obviously the Wolf Horde from the Outlands that has crossed into the Wald, barbarians whose god is a great wolf who they say prowls across the Bridge of Stars. But there is more to this than a foraging raid, much more. My old friend Grimwald is dead, his son sore hurt and River Garde overrun. Soon I must expect a visit from the pack.'

'If River Garde could not withstand them, what chance is there if you remain here with – forgive my bluntness – old retainers who could hardly lift a broadsword?' said Krispin with inward concern for Jennet's safety.

'River Garde was taken by surprise,' said Eloira. 'And there is more to defence than broadswords and slingbows. It is something that I must attend to immediately. You will eat and rest and we will talk again later.'

When the young toymaker had been taken to the tower's kitchen Eloira rose wearily and, taking a jar of peacock blue porcelain from the cabinet which had housed her doll, she made her way to the flat roof of the main tower.

The sun was now low, bringing a faint blush of pink to the peaks of the White Virgins while a tumbled bank of clouds above the River of Night far, far beyond the valley took on a menacing purple as though reflecting the doom which lay below them.

The old woman sighed as she stood with her arms resting on the parapet surrounding the roof, recalling how as a young woman she used to come up here with her father and he would read to her from vellum scrolls and give her instruction in arts that had been handed on from his father. How happy she had been then, her body filled with the well-being of youth and her mind stimulated by the words that he made come alive from the sepia hieroglyphs that so few in Ythan could read today.

Where had that happy time gone?

Her father had long lain with his fathers in the catacomb cut deep into the mountain, the hopes that he had engendered within her as his heir had come to nought despite the fact she had devoted herself to fulfilling them – *Serene Mother, how she had tried!* – but the power of the Regency or the wilfulness of fate had always proved too strong. Now she was to have her last throw with destiny's dice, and she had little optimism.

She sighed again and turned her back on the tree-carpeted valley and the distant peaks, and surveyed the roof area with fond nostalgia. Hardy plants in antique urns, weather-stained statues of past members of her family and marble benches were placed on it to give the impression of a garden in the sky. On a plinth in the centre was mounted a large astrolabe – or a bronze instrument resembling an astrolabe – the use of which, she remembered, had taken her so long to master that even her father's phenomenal patience had begun to run out.

Beside the plinth was a tripod supporting a bowl whose corrosion was another reminder of time's passage.

Eloira blew a spider from the bowl, laid a piece of glowing tinder within it and sprinkled brown powder over it. Immediately the ground spices and resins glowed and white smoke poured from the censer. The burning of incense would have no effect on what was about to happen

87

next but the Reeve, like many magi, had a sense of theatre; besides, she relished the perfumed fumes which swirled about her.

Next she carefully removed the stopper from the jar and took from it an arm's length of black cord. There were a couple of intricate knots tied at one end, and several kinks in the silky fibre indicated that in the past there had been other knots.

Nervously she ran the cord through her fingers and inhaled the aromatic smoke as though to draw an illusion of strength from it. Years had passed since she had undertaken such a ritual, and, simple though it was, she desperately tried to summon up her old confidence.

From far across the forest rolling below the tower came an ululating cry – the call of a wolf. But was it one of the solitary timber wolves who roamed the lower slopes – or a barbarian signal?

Whatever the origin of the sound, it lent urgency to the old woman. She began to unpick one of the knots, murmuring a monotonous litany which she interspersed with gasps of exasperation as her old fingers trembled. Her task was not helped by the curious fact that as she attempted to loosen the tightly drawn loops the cord caused her skin to burn as though she had plucked a mandrake from the ground.

Tears welled in her eyes as it seemed the cord was actively resisting her efforts and her nails broke as she continued to struggle with the knot which had been tied by powerful hands long before her birth.

Then she felt a slight loosening and the cord came to life snake-like in her fingers, untwined itself and, snake-like, it flowed to the floor.

There was a mutter of far thunder and Eloira returned to the parapet and gazed down the valley. At first it seemed that the air below was thickening with the approach of dusk, then she saw that instead of the blueness of evening it was becoming opaque. Pale patches of mist formed in hollows, more flowed like a silent white river down the zig-zag road. It welled up in the forest until only the tops of the tallest trees rose above it and then they too were swiftly submerged.

Soon the vapour could no longer be likened to a river or lake, it was a sea covering everything below, a spectral tide which rose until it was level with the castle gate. The aroma of the incense was drowned by the clammy smell of the fog which continued to rise until its tendrils spilled over the roof wall; and then it stilled and lay like a vast snow plain above which only the peaks of the White Virgins were visible, now golden in the final rays of the sun.

ELEVEN
The Nether World

Gambal launched himself forward and knocked the goblet from Lord Odo's hand. Crystal shattered into diamond fragments on the marble tiling and spilled wine bubbled as it spread.

The gauntlet of one of the companions fell on the youth's shoulder, metal fingers propelled him back to his seat.

'Now lad, do not ask for more trouble than is already coming,' the man said gruffly from behind his lowered visor.

Grey-faced and trembling, Gambal sank back into the chair in which, a short time ago, he had believed his schemes had succeeded better than he had ever dared hope. Now, within minutes the Regent would be a dead man, and so would he – and as he swallowed a sob which threatened to burst from his throat he was conscious of the Regent's cold eyes resting upon him curiously. His calmness in the face of approaching oblivion steadied the young man and he made an effort to retain his dignity. For a moment he had a mental picture of the slaughter-house and beasts being driven down the ramp to the butchers . . .

'That was unfortunate for you,' said Lord Odo, beckoning the weeping page to bring more wine. 'I only had one spill of each powder. Needs must that you will now have to take the essence of viperherb. Your bowels will burn to ash before the Dark Maid arrives, but that is only just for one who has burnt so many . . .'

'There is no call for moralizing, Odo,' sighed the Regent. 'Let us conclude this business . . . I am surprised that Grimwald is not supporting you.'

'He is too self-righteous for such intrigue,' Odo said as he poured purple powder into the wine which immediately frothed. 'He is a dreamer like all Pilgrims, and his treason is to believe that all will be well in Ythan if an entranced girl can be found . . .'

'But there must have been someone of great importance to help you plan such a coup,' the Regent persisted. 'I have always recognized your ability but as for poor old Wode and the Lady Thesa . . . well, they are hardly of the stuff that changes the destiny of the kingdom. No, even with me out of the way you will have need of someone with great influence to endorse you. Without that . . .'

His words hung in the air as Odo approached him with the bubbling wine while one of the Companions of the Rose laid his gauntlet on Gambal's arm.

'Never fear, I shall have all the endorsement I need,' Odo said with self satisfaction. 'Archpriest Gregon . . .'

'Gregon, of course. I congratulate you, Odo. He is exactly the man you need to hold the people for you, especially as the shrines have always resented the power of the Citadel. But watch him, Odo, he too may have dreams of an earthly kingdom.'

'I can take care of myself,' Odo retorted.

'I am sure you can. But before you give me that vile toxin, cannot you find it in your heart to show mercy. I have never harmed you personally so why take on the guilt of my murder? Secret exile would serve equally well. I could be no threat to you on an island in the Cold Sea . . .'

'Drink,' said Odo, holding out the goblet. 'Captain Bors, hold his wrist so he cannot spill it.'

'There is no need for that,' said the Regent, and, as Gambal watched in frozen terror, he raised the glass almost to his lips.

'On second thoughts,' he continued, gazing into the wine's dark depths, 'I find I am not thirsty.'

'Seize him, men,' Odo ordered angrily. 'Bors, put the funnel down his throat.'

The companions did not move while the captain took a slender leather funnel from under his cloak and laid it on a table.

'Quick, men . . .' Odo began, sensing a subtle change in the atmosphere.

The Regent leaned to one side and carefully set the goblet beside the funnel.

'Captain Bors,' he said. 'Do your duty.'

The captain turned about and drawing his falchion declared, 'My lord, I arrest you for treason.'

'Betrayed!' It was a moan rather than a word.

'From the first whisper of your plans,' said the Regent, standing up and stretching. 'I knew even before Captain Bors reported your attempt to buy his allegiance. You as a councillor should have known, Odo, that the Companions of the Rose have a code of loyalty to the regency that has never wavered.'

Lord Odo stood biting his bottom lip, his face as bloodless as the parchment the Regent had signed.

'I demand my hereditary right as Lord of the West Marshes to be tried by my peers,' he said in a voice that he tried desperately to control.

'That might be difficult,' the Regent chuckled. 'After our conversation just now some of your peers will not be at liberty much longer. I must tell you that I am against a trial. The result would be a foregone conclusion but it would make the populace restless – and think of the distress it would cause your family.'

'Then perhaps I could trade my life for information. Many were involved in the plot. Scores of names I could provide in return for exile . . .'

'On an island in the Cold Sea? My agent has already given me a copy of the list you kept in a black casket hidden in your sleeping chamber. I believe it also contained a charm for reviving your manhood . . .'

'Who . . .?' Odo asked, aghast.

The Regent clapped his hands. A curtain at the far end of the room moved and a beautiful red-haired girl walked into the light, her greenish eyes fixed on Odo with cold curiosity.

'Urwen!'

'That is the name you knew her by,' said the Regent. 'To me she is known by a more important one. You have done well, my dear.'

'Urwen, why? Did I not give you all . . .' Odo's voice quavered. The inbred confidence that his aristocracy had given him broke. A tear crawled down his cheek.

'Urwen, I – I loved you.'

'Yes. Such loves invites betrayal.' There was a discreet knock at the door.

The Regent nodded and one of the companions opened it a handspan. A small roll of parchment was passed through.

'*The time has come*,' the Regent read after he had broken the wax seal. A smile of intense satisfaction briefly lit his broad features.

'I have pressing business,' he said with a new briskness. 'To save a scandal, Odo, I shall use your methods. Here's your wine to drink my health.'

Shaking his head from side to side like a petulant child, the noble backed away. The two companions seized him and Captain Bors forced the end of the funnel between his teeth.

'You, butcher boy, give the gentleman his drink.'

Gambal slowly rose to his feet.

'Hurry! After helping Wilk into the hereafter you can have no qualms over this little task.'

The young man tried to say something but if he did get the words out they were lost in the companions' laughter at the sounds being emitted from the funnel. That interruption gave Gambal enough time to save his career. He bit back his refusal, realizing in that instant that, if he was not to throw away everything he had schemed for, he must show obedience to his new master.

Taking a deep breath he picked up the goblet of black wine and while the guards held the sagging prisoner he carefully poured some of the dark liquid into the funnel mouth.

As Lord Odo felt it trickle into his throat a convulsion jerked his body so wildly that he almost freed himself, a wailing cry gurgled from him and he sank to his knees.

'Step back,' the captain said to the guards. 'If what I hear about viperherb is true he will fart flame.'

Odo clutched at his heart and rolled sideways on to the marble where he lay still.

'Justice has been done,' said Captain Bors heavily.

'Not yet, oh no, not yet,' chuckled the Regent and taking the goblet from Gambal drained the remainder of the Ronimar wine. 'It is only Odo's fear that has laid him there and he will soon wake up to wish that the poison had been real. Urwen had made sure that his toxic powders were no more dangerous than sherbet. To the lowest level with him after which you will receive reward for the parts you have played in this comedy. Bors, you should have been an actor.'

The captain grinned and asked for orders regarding the other conspirators.

94

'Do nothing yet. Leave them to wonder what has gone wrong, to fear the footfall in the night, and when my Whisperers start a rumour that it was Gregon who betrayed Odo the wolf will be among the sheep.'

The Regent turned to Gambal.

'You have served me well this night and in the future you shall serve me better. Go with the companions and learn some of the Citadel's secrets.'

One of the companions shrugged off his long maroon cloak and, wrapping it round the unconscious form of the rebel lord, hoisted him over his shoulder. Captain Bors led the way out of the apartment and, as he passed through the door, he darted a glance backwards to see the girl Urwen kneeling before the Regent.

In silence the three elite guards marched along a corridor until they came to a wide stairwell in which steps spiralled down into gloom relieved at intervals by lurid flambeaux light. Twice they passed servants coming up the stairs, but where they saw the visored helmets of the companions they averted their eyes. Gambal had been in the Citadel long enough to know that the Regent's guard inspired a sense of dread in the menials.

Determined not to be classed with the lower orders, Gambal said conversationally, 'Where are we going, captain?'

'The nether world – the dungeons. They upset strangers at first, but from what I saw of you tonight your stomach should stand it.'

A moan came from the bundle slung over the companion's shoulder. The other said something and gave a chuckle muffled by his visor.

As they proceeded further down the stairwell Gambal was aware of the air becoming clammy. An indistinct sound floated up from the depths, a sound that could have been made by wind soughing through a forest, or by human voices chorusing a dirge. It grew louder until, finally reaching the floor of the circular pit, Gambal gazed through an archway into a cavernous hall. Also lit by flambeaux, it reminded Gambal vividly of the slaughterhouse where he had spent most of his life.

There were differences. The vapours in the slaughterhouse came from boiling vats, here the vapours were chill and moist; in the slaughterhouse it was beasts which were driven through the leaping shadows, here it was men and women – or creatures that had once been men and women.

Several score of them were pushing against the beam-like levers of a huge capstan set in the centre of the hall. Clothed in the remains of what they were wearing when they had been brought from the world above, they staggered in an endless circle round the creaking pivot, often slipping in ordure. From their throats came the wordless dirge that Gambal had first heard on the stairs.

He gazed in fearful fascination at the grotesque scene. As his eyes grew more accustomed to the gloom he saw that some of the prisoners were naked, and some of the men had filthy beards hanging down to their bellies. The one thing that all had in common were the gyves on their wrists which were linked to heavy staples in the beams. One emaciated captive had fainted or died, and he was dragged round the eternal circle by his arms while the lower half of his body trailed over the filthy paving.

The guard in charge refused to stop the capstan to release him; whatever happened, the great wheel had to keep turning except for the few minutes when the exhausted wretches were unshackled and a new shift began the creaking round.

'What does it do?' Gambal asked.

'Drives machinery somewhere, what I do not know,' replied Captain Bors carelessly.

'And those prisoners . . .'

'You could call them minor offenders. This is only the first level.'

Nodding to the respectful guard, the captain led the way round the capstan, through another archway and along a short passage. Gambal saw nitre hanging in white webs from the mortar which held the ancient stones in the curved roof, and the dank smell grew stronger. Then ahead of him he saw the gleam of black oil-smooth water, and found himself on a quay along one wall of a wide brick-lined tunnel.

'The river,' said the captain. 'It goes under the Citadel rock and comes out at the watergate. Prisoners arrive here. Very discreet and convenient.'

The small party passed through another arch at the end of the quay and followed a passage descending at a steep angle into living rock down which water continuously trickled. Another level was reached, another hall with black silhouettes of guards sitting close round a brazier whose ruddy glow was lost in the mouths of tunnels cut in the walls. The captain told him that each was lined with tomb-like cells.

As the journey downwards continued Gambal began to shudder, but it was not entirely due to the ever-increasing cold or the endless dripping of river water from the ceiling or even the psychic sense of despair which haunted the passages. He realized that he had been sent with the companions as an object lesson of the dismal fate awaiting those on whom the displeasure of the Regent fell.

'Springtime brings us games of love,' sang one of the companions merrily.

> 'So play the pipe and hark the dove.
> Winter has a hand of ice
> To freeze our dreams of paradise,
> Yet life is joy in winter snow
> Compared to pining here below.'

Gambal lost all sense of direction. Down ramps and staircases, through torch-lit halls and along passages the three guards marched with an air of purpose, but all he knew was that they were going deeper and deeper into the rock on which the Citadel was built and, as the wetness of the walls testified, they were now far below the subterranean river.

Sometimes he caught glimpses of the denizens of the cold, nether world; grey cowled figures wheeling a rumbling iron-wheeled cart piled high with shrouded shapes that could only be corpses; a line of pallid prisoners whose wrists were shackled to a heavy slithering chain crossing a cavern – and everywhere *rats*. Myriads of red eyes peered at the intruders like embers glowing in the deep shadow, and when one ran across his feet Gambal saw with a start of alarm that its fur was thick and long, increasing its size to that of a cat.

'They grow like that because of the cold,' Captain Bors explained when he saw the young man's expression of disgust. 'And they have teeth to match as many a poor wretch has found out.'

It was not only the miasma floating through the passages which raised Gambal's bile.

'This is the lowest level,' Bors announced when they reached the foot of a broad stone staircase. 'In the world above the higher you go the more aristocratic life becomes.' He gave his rare dry chuckle. 'Here it is the exact opposite. Lord Odo will be accommodated with the aristocrats of the dungeons.'

A warder, steel-booted and wearing a hide jerkin, came out of the shadows, rubbing his hands so hard that his hoop of keys clashed like a barbarian dancer's anklets.

After Bors spoke in his ear he nodded ponderously, having been without speech from birth like all warders on the lower levels. He led the way along a passage whose only illumination was his swinging lantern and stopped before an iron-bound door which he heaved open after much fumbling at its keyholes.

Gambal saw that the ceiling was so low that the tall guards had to bend double as they dragged the prisoner to the pillar in the centre. The floor was covered with straw still reeking from the last inmate, and there was a brief squeal as the warder exultantly brought his metal-shod foot down on a rodent lurking in it.

By now Lord Odo had recovered sufficiently from his seizure to look about him with increasing terror as his wrists were chained to staples in the central column. There were not enough links to allow him to sit and the rough-hewn ceiling was too low to permit him to stand.

'Mercy, for the love of the Mother,' he moaned as the Companions of the Rose left him crouching.

'For the love of the Mother!' they responded piously.

TWELVE
Alwald's Tale

Alwald painfully opened his eyes to see the Lady Eloira sitting in the dimmed light by his bed.

'Demara,' he gasped through a mouth dust dry.

'Do not talk yet,' said the old woman and, taking a spouted vessel, allowed soothing liquid to trickle between his burning lips.

'You are ill with poison from your wounds,' she told him, 'but do not fear, the Dark Maid is not claiming you yet.'

He swallowed greedily, and as his eyes rolled he saw there was someone else in the small chamber.

'That is Krispin,' said Eloira, seeing the direction of his glance. 'You owe your life to him. He brought you here and he has watched over you, waiting for your fever to break. He was a toymaker, but it will be a while before he carves a dancing doll again.'

'Where . . . is this . . . place?' Alwald gasped.

'This is the Peak Tower.'

'The horde . . . they will come . . .'

'Hush, we are safe here thanks to my forefathers' sorcery. A bewitching mist lies around us. No one can find his way through it for it has the quality of beguiling men so that if they enter they will wander until they find themselves back where they started. Not even foresters

100

who have known the High Wald since childhood could trace their way to our gate.'

'River Garde . . . I should have stayed . . .'

'We will talk about that later. You will go back to sleep now.' And as Eloira spoke, the drug in the drink she had given him drew down his eyelids.

'Your vigil is over now,' said Eloira to Krispin. 'He will sleep and heal.'

'He kept muttering the name Demara.'

'She is his step-mother, though she would have been no more than two or three years older than he.' Eloira sighed. 'She was the wife of Grimwald VII.'

'Then she must be dead . . . like everyone else.'

'Dead, or worse. Now, go and see Jennet, your company may be of help in bringing her back to the present.'

'Lady, it breaks my heart when I see her sitting with a doll.'

'Better that than Demara's fate. Who can say what happened or what she saw before she fled into the forest. It was a miracle that you found her.'

'Oh no, my lady, I knew where to look. I knew that if she had escaped from the village she would have gone to where she saw her crystal bird . . .'

'Her crystal bird?'

'Yes. It was real enough. I saw it too, on the morning of The Choosing.'

'Tell me about it. Everything.' Her voice took on a new timbre.

Krispin recounted how they had escaped the oppressive atmosphere that always affected Toyheim on The Choosing, and as pictures of Jennet in the forest and at the margin of the mere returned to his inward eye a tear rolled unnoticed down each cheek.

'I had hoped when we made our bargain – that you would find out who we really are if I would journey as you told me – but now . . .'

101

'The bargain still stands,' said Eloira, rising. 'More than ever it stands. Now go and play with Jennet, and perhaps your love will restore her. Love is the most powerful sorcery in the Three Worlds.'

During the next two days the potions that Lady Eloira administered to the drowsing Alwald were so effective that the livid marks spreading from his wounds faded and the wounds themselves ceased suppurating and began to heal.

Early on the third morning after the fever had left him Eloira went to his chamber and found that he had risen from his bed and was standing at the mullion window, watching the sun rising over the lake of opaline vapour stretching from the tower to the distant peaks of the White Virgins.

'The mist does not move,' he said as he crossed unsteadily to the bed.

'Nor will it until the horde returns to the Outlands,' the old woman replied. 'My sorcery is still strong enough to hold a cloud.'

'Sorcery,' Alwald exclaimed. 'It was sorcery that killed my father.'

'Was it? Do you feel strong enough to tell me what happened at River Garde?'

He rubbed his hand over his stubbled face, nodded and then with closed eyes recounted how the Wolf Horde had arrived with their wagons and camped on the far bank of the River of Night, how it had been agreed that his father would parley with the Wolf King in a chamber which was believed to be proof against treachery, and how at the meeting the Wolf King had burst through the double grille.

'He is a shape-changer,' he whispered. 'When I heard my father's herald scream I forgot my orders and ran down to the bridge and I saw him. He had the head of a

102

wolf, I swear, and his muzzle was gleaming with blood . . . the blood of my . . .'

'Be calm,' said Eloira. 'Even by then your father's agony was over, it is those who remain who continue the pain.'

'Easy words,' murmured Alwald. 'But you did not see what I saw in that shambles. It was a beast – a fanged beast – that had rent them.'

'What happened next?'

'It was confused. I seem to remember that wolf-headed creature looming up in front of me. He swung his arm and I felt his talons tear my chest.'

Eloira nodded.

'And then?'

'I remembered my duty, I ran back along the bridge, shouting to the axemen to bring it down. By the time I reached the bank the axes were thudding into its supports and it was already buckling. A minute later it collapsed into the river and I believed that River Garde was safe. My thought was that I must be the one to break the news to Demara, although she probably knew by then that her lord was dead. But before I could enter the castle I saw the nomads rolling their wagons into the water to become boats. They were full of men and the steppe wind drove them across.'

Alwald went on to describe how archers on the walls of River Garde sent volleys of arrows sleeting on to the wagon-boats but while a number of nomads were transfixed it did not halt the progress of the makeshift fleet across the broad river.

'As soon as the leading boats touched the reed-fringed shore the enemy sprang ashore, moving more like animals than men. Their long-handled axes made arcs of silver as they hurled themselves against the line of men-at-arms drawn up to meet them.

'The line reeled under the impact, it broke and the

nomads surged about the castle walls with pockets of soldiers still fighting desperately. Then came the ultimate treachery. Even as the archers fired from the battlements and boiling oil gushed from the mouths of the gargoyles, the portcullis was raised and the howling men rushed into the castle.'

Alwald stopped.

Eloira waited patiently, waited while he regained control of his voice and went on to describe the slaughter, how the gargoyles no longer spewed oil but blood.

'I tried to fight my way into the castle to find Demara – I truly tried – but it was impossible. By then I was wounded and suddenly it seemed as though I could hear my father's last instructions ringing in my head.'

'And those were?'

'If River Garde should ever fall he wanted me to come to you.'

Eloira nodded.

'You knew that your father and I shared a dream.'

'You are a Pilgrim.'

'Yes. The only hope for the kingdom is for Princess Livia to be found and for her to take her place on her rightful throne. The Pilgrim tradition was as strong in my House as it was in yours. But tell me what happened next.'

'I hardly remember. One minute I was fighting, the next I found myself at the back of the castle. I saw my groom leading two horses.

'"Hurry, mesire," I heard him call. Although I was now weak I managed to haul myself into the saddle and we galloped off along the forest road.'

'"Good work, Brin," I shouted to the groom.

'"Your father told me . . ." he began to reply, then he vomited blood and fell to the ground. When I got down beside him I saw that he had a terrible axe wound in his side. Then through the trees came the howling of the Wolf Horde – I say "howling" because that was just what

104

it sounded like – and I rode off along a trail that I hoped would bring me to you.

'I rode all day, climbing through the trees until I reached the High Wald. In the evening I tethered my horse, drank the last of the water in the canteen and rolled myself in the horse blanket.

'I slept badly. By now I had periods of delirium, and when my mind cleared I was racked with shame that I had left Demara in the castle.'

'Perhaps it was not storybook heroic but it was the only thing you could do other than get yourself killed. And it was correct that you should follow your father's last wishes.'

Alwald gave the old woman a look of gratitude.

He said he remembered little of the next day. After wandering among the trees he found a narrow road which led to the toymakers' village, a place that he had only visited once before as a child when his father took him there to choose a set of wooden soldiers.

'When I reached the village I found that the nomads had arrived ahead of me and had razed it. Then it seems I met a young man. He was well mannered but strange. He helped me into the shade of a tree, and the next thing I can recall was opening my eyes in this room.'

'That is enough for now,' Eloira said, alarmed by the effect his own words were having upon him. 'Rest now and I shall return at noon and then it will be me who does the talking.'

The old woman walked through the castle corridors to a doorway leading into a courtyard where she paused to watch Krispin and Jennet. The girl was sitting with her doll on her lap while Smoke the cat rubbed its fur against her ankles. The youth appeared to be telling her a story while she gazed at him with rapt eyes.

'You may hear the tale later on,' said Eloira coming forward. 'I must have speech with the story-teller.'

'Oh!' Jennet pouted like a six-year-old. 'We are just at the part where the Minstrel King comes seeking Princess One-wish.'

'The story can wait but there is a tart going cold in the kitchen, so if you want Cook to give you a warm slice you should hurry.'

Jennet laughed merrily at the bribe and hurried off to claim it.

'You agreed to act as a secret messenger for me,' said Eloira.

Krispin inclined his head.

'My reason for asking you was that as a toymaker on your year of wandering you had excuse for travelling the realm, and as your instructions were buried deep in your mind so that you would not be aware of them until it was necessary, you would not have been at great risk.'

'I am still ready to serve you.'

'And I thank you. But the world is changing and now I am asking if you will undertake a much more perilous mission.'

'Could I leave Jennet in your care?'

'That is understood.'

'Then what is the mission, lady?'

'It is in my mind to send young Alfrith – Alwald, now! – on a quest of great importance not only to the Wald but the whole of Ythan. He has the nature for such adventure. Allegiance to the princess is in his blood, he has the chivalry of a noble house and he is well trained in the use of arms. Added to that he has lost his domain and his bitterness will hone his determination.'

She paused and regarded Krispin reflectively.

'I want you to journey with him.'

'But, lady, I have no knowledge of weaponry . . . I am just a toymaker . . .'

'I am the judge of your qualities, and you have one that is of utmost value.'

Krispin's face expressed his doubt.

'I realized when I entranced you with my pendant that there are few who could have accepted my directions as readily. Thus, as before, I want to plant knowledge in your memory so that you will be able to act as the way-finder. And so that no Regent's spy could learn the secret of your route you will make the journey in stages, each of which will only become known to you by the recognition of some landmark.

'And if you undertake this our agreement will remain. I shall find the truth about who you and Jennet really are, and she will be cared for as my daughter while you are gone.'

'When would this quest begin?'

'As soon as Alwald is healed which should be soon for he is a healthy youth and my potions are strong.'

'Then so be it.'

THIRTEEN

A Tear In The Moonlight

From where the Hump sat on the balcony of the caravanserai inn the gibbous moon appeared to balance on the highest pinnacle of the Citadel. The rock out of which the great edifice rose, the throng of city houses crowding its lower slopes and Danaak's fortifications threw the caravanserai into a gulf of shadow. Only a few oil lamps glimmered in its sprawling collection of doss houses, inns, compounds and marts. The last drunken drong driver had been thrown out of the rowdiest tavern, the girls in the Traveller's Dream had finally collapsed on their pallets to sleep thankfully alone, and the star dials told the watcher that the false dawn was only an hour away.

This was the Hump's favourite time, a time when he felt safely alone in the darkling world, when no one would stare at the bow-like curve in his spine which inspired his nickname – the only name he knew. At this hour he chewed rare and expensive sooma seeds to ease the nagging ache between his shoulders and induce a state of dreamy wellbeing when his thoughts drifted into the realm of the fantastical.

This night he had neglected to take the sooma seeds, and the beautiful silvered city rearing against the luminous sky failed to fill him with its usual awe. A tear slowly rolled down his bronzed cheek, something that those who knew him during the day on long treks would have found unbelievable. This solitary pearl of reflected moonlight did not spring from self-pity or bereavement or for lost innocence – self-pity was an unknown luxury to the Hump, he had no one to mourn and beneath his strange self-sufficient exterior his innocence remained intact. The tear sprang from thoughts of what-might-have-been, of a love that was hopeless, of the memory of a bright being who had seen beyond his ungainly form.

Twenty years ago the captain of a caravan making its painful way through the Wilderness of Gil spied a movement beneath a thorn bush and swung down from his horse to investigate. In the stippled shadow he found a naked infant, a wizen male baby too exhausted to cry. There was no clue as to how the child had got there, caravans risking the journey across the wilderness were few and certainly no human kind had lived in its arid solitude for centuries. The mystery of the Hump's origins led to the story that he had been hatched from an egg, references to which were shouted after him by street urchins.

The caravan girls – the temporary mistresses of merchants and drong-drivers who travelled endlessly along the far-flung trade routes of Ythan – revived the silent babe and swamped it with affection until the cavalcade finally reached Danaak with its profitable cargo of sweet-scented timber. Before setting off on a new trading expedition the kindly captain took the child to a motherly widow in the caravanserai and paid enough crowns to board the waif for several years.

Although the sweet-faced, ample-bosomed dame may have been motherly to her own offspring long ago, her only interest in the infant was the silver coins which accompanied him. And while she did not set out to be unkind any more than she tried to be kind, she had a revulsion for deformity. When the child reached the stage of walking and his back curved unnaturally she found the sight of him so distasteful that he was removed to a shed behind her lodging house. Here he was left to his own devices apart from a daily bowl of kitchen scraps.

Sometimes, when she had drunk more barley beer than usual with her cronies, she would return home determined to do something about her charge and his disgusting hump which, at times like this, she decided was due to an evil perversity on his part not to hold himself erect. So, for his own good, she would beat him across the offending malformation.

When word reached her that the good captain had perished from the black sickness on the shores of the Cold Sea and therefore would not be paying another instalment, she calculated the exact day when she could morally relinquish her fostering. She was a very correct dame as her regular attendance at the shrine testified. While on occasion she might beat the little cripple until his hump glowed, she would not throw him out while he was in credit.

As it turned out his expulsion was unnecessary – he ran away. Perhaps the last beating had been too painful, perhaps he had reached the stage when the jeers of other children made him want to get away, but away he went inside an empty drong pannier with a caravan headed for the Crystal Ranges.

The motley collection of men who chose the vagabond life of the caravans tended to share a rough good humour and when the Hump – he had his name now – was finally forced by thirst to show himself they responded with food rather than blows and allowed him to continue with them. In return he made himself as useful as he knew how. He would be up before the dawn with the cooks and at sunset he would help to feed and water the drongs, fetch firewood and – the task which he pridefully made his very own – replenish the watch lanterns with oil.

His great joy in his newfound situation was when the caravan was on the march, when there were no chores to be performed and he perched high on a swaying bale of merchandise. Then his eyes roved hungrily the vast sky-scapes, or feasted themselves upon distant mountains, or peered through the gloom of forests, and he knew that he could only be happy following the caravan trails.

For several boyhood years he did menial work with pack trains, content to receive his rations and cast-offs as payment, his real reward the far horizons and the pleasure of new and strange lands. Then, when fourteen years had gone by since he was found by the thicket, he was with a caravan of a merchant who, eager to trade more profitably away from the usual routes, set out across an unmapped waste and after several days of wandering found himself as lost as if he had been drifting at sea in a derelict ship. Water ran low as the caravan crawled over terrain which was so monotonous, so devoid of landmarks that for all the travellers knew they may have been going in vast circles. Sun and stars were no help as the sky was obscured by low stratus cloud which, despite the curses of the thirsty caravaneers, refused to yield rain.

Despair finally overtook the straggling column when it reached the ashes of one of its previous campfires and it was realized that they had been moving in a circle. There was screaming as several men and women vented their frustration and fear on the caravan scryer for her lack of foresight.

Suddenly the Hump knew what he must do. Climbing on to the back of one of the drongs still capable of walking he shouted hoarsely, 'Follow me. I know the way to water.'

Some of the guards and drivers mocked him, but a few ready to clutch at any straw remounted their animals and, huskily promising fearful retribution if he should make fools of them, formed up behind him. Half a day later they reached the bank of a slow river where man and beast floundered blissfully in the shallows.

Full water bags were taken back to the main party, and then the Hump guided the column across the plain to a remote trail which eventually led them back to a recognized track. How he accomplished this he could never explain, he just *knew* the direction to take.

News of how the hump-backed youth had saved the caravan spread along the trade routes and suddenly the Hump found himself in demand as a guide. In this role, his crooked figure perched high on the leading drong, he piloted caravans to far corners of the kingdom with almost supernatural success. Apart from his mysterious ability to find the way when a normal guide would have been lost, the Hump was quick to grasp the pattern of caravan routes. Details of terrain and hazards likely to be encountered remained imprinted vividly in his mind, not only from his own experience but from trailside conversation with grizzled pilots who lost their professional secrecy when talking to this strange youth.

For the last couple of years the Hump had worked for an adventurous merchant named Azrul, an olive-complexioned man from a distant coast whose ancestors had been sea traders. Rather than finance conventional caravan journeys, he made expeditions with a small number of attendants and pack beasts into the remote parts in search of curiosities which would be light to transport and at the same time fetch high prices in the auctions of Danaak.

The last journey had taken them to a warm forest land to trade with swarthy-skinned natives. In return for metal arrow-heads, daggers and sword blades, they bought colourful birds, the like of which had never been seen before in Danaak, and tamed cats with unusual white and brown fur who could become the rage as pets in aristo-cratic households.

When the animals were all in makeshift cages and the caravaneers were preparing for the hazardous march back to Danaak, a band of natives approached the encampment with what appeared to be a human captive. It was only as they drew nearer that Azrul cried out that here was one of the creatures which, according to legend, lived far outside the realms of men before The Enchantment. The prisoner was a beautiful girl with a silver mane of hair and whose graceful lower limbs were those of a horse.

Although the natives surrounded her in order to pre-vent her escaping, they appeared to treat her with respect.

During the sign-language haggling which followed she remained dignified and aloof, and when the natives departed, laden with the metal weapons they so dearly loved, she regarded her new owner with an almost mock-ing smile while he endeavoured to convey to her that she had nothing to fear, that she would be as well-cared for as if she were a normal human being and escape would be unwise as she would be better off with civilized people than those who had traded her.

She accepted this with a brief nod and went to rest in a tent which was erected for her while the last-minute preparations for the journey were made. Like the others the Hump was awed by the sight of what seemed to be a mythological creature, and there was much speculation as to where she had come from. On the journey Azrul attempted to learn her story by teaching her to speak the common language but though she learned some words and phrases, she remained uncommunicative about her past.

At night the merchant was amused to see that she preferred to sit by his guide in the firelight.

'Doubtless she feels more at home in the company of a fellow freak,' he remarked to his captain.

'What would be the result if they mated?' the captain laughed. 'A hump-backed horse!'

Sometimes when she wanted exercise she would run beside the drongs, her hair flowing behind her which inspired the name of Silvermane. From his high seat on the leading animal the Hump would draw in his breath at the gracefulness which was in such contrast to his bent body. It was true that his limbs were straight, and he was very strong and perhaps his face with its unusually high cheekbones and dark restless eyes was not exactly repulsive, but nothing could hide the ugly curvature which seemed to become more pronounced and painful as he got older.

By the time the caravan reached one of the regular stone-paved highways which ran to Danaak through smiling farmland and pleasant woods, the Hump was inwardly struggling to come to terms with an emotion which he had not experienced before – he was in love with the horsemaid.

It was madness of course.

A creature as beautiful as she could never feel more than a passing friendship for someone as ungainly as he. On top of this she was the property of his master and in Danaak she would be sold into a life of luxury.

What added to the confusion of his new-found emotion was the fact that when they made the evening halt at one of the many inns scattered along the high road she appeared to like his company.

After the drongs had been watered and tethered for the night and the watchmen posted, the caravaneers would take their supper on scrubbed tables and then sit round the fire to drink and tell tales of journeys into remote territories, of outcast attacks and battles with basilisks. The merchant sat at the board of honour with his captain and sergeant of guards and, though he would invite the Hump to join him, the guide preferred to sit alone at a table in the shadows where his deformity, which he partly concealed during the day by wearing a voluminous cloak, was out of sight, and therefore out of mind.

It was then that Silvermane would sit beside him. She hardly said a word but sipped her cup of cheap wine and gazed dreamily into the firelight. Of course the Hump realized why she chose to do so; he was ever-conscious of a remark he had overheard about 'fellow freaks', and doubtless she preferred his companionable silence to the crudity of the caravaneers. While such men, bitten by wanderlust and the call of adventure, were in the main a rough good-hearted crowd, their language was coarse and, apart from gambling, their pleasures were simple and bawdy. Hardly a night passed when some inn wench was not flattered into unlacing her bodice and dropping her skirt to display her charms to their salacious comments.

Not infrequently such displays developed into much lewder performances, and then the Hump would lead Silvermane into the night. They would stroll past the snoring and spluttering drongs, past the watchmen bent over their gaming board, and along the highway stretching like a stone artery to the heart of the kingdom, the golden city of Danaak, where all journeys end and with them such fleeting companionship.

Sometimes she would lay her hand on his arm when crossing rough cobbles – her delicate hooves were used to a softer floor – and his heart would beat faster until he told himself that the gesture had no more significance than the need to steady herself.

Occasionally they would exchange a few words. She had learned enough to express simple ideas, but all that he ever learned about her past was that there were others of her kind; she had not been a freak born to human parents. But as to where these horse people dwelled, or how she came to be taken by the natives, she said nothing.

It was as though she had a need to protect herself with silence.

When the journey finally ended at the great caravanserai of Danaak where the hired drongs were returned to the paddocks of their enriched owners and the merchandise stored, Azrul arranged for Silvermane to have a room to herself in one of the quieter inns. He posted a guard outside her door every night and day to discourage the curious as, despite oaths of secrecy sworn by the caravan drivers and guards and the concealing of Silverman's equine limbs beneath a floor-length gown, the caravanserai was rife with rumour about her.

The Hump only saw her briefly when she came out on to the balcony of her chamber, only fleeting glimpses but they made his face pale beneath its trail tan. At night he could no longer be alone with his thoughts and sooma seeds, instead he frequented the darker taverns.

It was in one of these that a young man sat at his table. His face was so haggard that he felt a necessity to mention it when he saw the Hump give him a sympathetic look.

'It is not the sickness,' he said. 'I have to accompany my master who seeks the well of youth in the city stews. Tonight he is so exhausted by his debaucheries that he lies on his bed like one who awaits the Dark Maid, and for once I can have some hours of quiet. Let me order a flagon to celebrate my evening of tranquil freedom.'

It was one of the rare occasions when the Hump yearned for company, and as the young man did not seem the sort who would suddenly ask whether he was born or hatched, he agreed to share the wine. As the evening wore on he found the young man to be a most sympathetic listener. Though unaccustomed to heavy drinking, the Hump found that there was always more wine on table.

When the Hump woke the next morning the pain in his head was only equalled by a nagging sense of remorse for having opened his heart to the stranger. His guilt was made worse by the fact that he could not recall what he had actually said or if he had cheapened his love by maudlin revelations. All that he could remember was that he had given a promise to introduce the young man to Azrul on account of 'some business' he could put his way.

The morning bustle of the caravanserai had reached its height when the young man arrived at the Hump's lodging. He gave a taciturn greeting and led him along the lanes to the merchant's inn. The harsh cries of the stall women, the shrill pleas of the holy mendicants, hot gusts of music from whorehouse and tavern, the booming patter of auctioneers, the cursing of impatient drong drivers and the guttural protest of their beasts combined to batter the Hump's frayed senses. A convoy of prisoners sentenced to slavery was leaving for the mines of Endor and the wailing of their families, the crack of whips and the drumbeat of their guards added to the din, and to his discomfort.

It was a relief to enter the comparative quiet of the room where the merchant sat with his abacus and a ledger scroll before him. As usual he greeted the Hump with a smile, having a special regard for the crooked guide with whom he had travelled thousands of leagues.

Before the Hump could introduce the young man, the merchant said, 'I was about to send for you. I want you to take a chest of spices to a country estate. They are of a special kind' – he winked – 'and too valuable to trust to a hired messenger. Also, Lord Odo wants it urgently for a banquet and if you get it to him in time he will pay handsomely, and – as the Mother knows! – I need money.'

The Hump said he would leave immediately – he would be glad to be away from the noise and dust of the caravanserai – and after introducing the young man whose name he remembered just in time as Gambal, he left.

Half an hour later, as he passed Silvermane's inn, he

saw her come on to her balcony. Perched high on the tall drong, he was almost level with the balustrade.

'You go?' she asked.

'A short journey. I shall return in three days with luck.'

She held out a small bunch of blue flowers, weeds which grew beneath the walls of the caravanserai.

'You take. All I have to give.'

His rein-calloused hand brushed hers as he took them, and looking up he saw that her large eyes of darkest brown were moist.

'Forget me not,' she said.

A surge of hope filled him.

Could it be that he had mistaken her attitude on the journey? Had she sought his company for something more than the reassurance of a fellow outsider?

'Forget me not.'

He shook his head, afraid to release a babble of words and angry with himself for being unable to say what was in his heart. Instead he smiled, held the flower to his lips and urged the drong forward.

When he returned from Lord Odo's estate, where the household was in turmoil preparing for a gala to be held after the re-election of the Regent, the Hump found that Silvermane had been sold.

'I could not refuse the offer,' the merchant said. 'The way those rainbow birds died on the journey back nearly ruined me but now we will be able to go to the High Wald and buy toys in time for the Festival of Fools. The horsemaid will be well-cared for in the Citadel . . .'

The Citadel!

Like everyone else the Hump had heard stories of the Regent's private menagerie, his collection of strange automata and his obsession with freaks and legendary creatures.

'Gambal swore that she would be treated with honour . . .'

The Hump's frozen expression did not alter.

The merchant shrugged, muttered about the stupidity of becoming sentimental over a something that was as much horse as human, and turned irritably to his scrolls.

Now the Hump stared sorrowfully at the silvered spires of the Citadel. His hand stole inside his shirt and he fingered the ivory locket which contained the petals of the little flowers she had given to him.

Forget me not!

Her last words to him, and he felt that he had betrayed her. If he had not drunkenly confided in Gambal his attention would never have been drawn to her, and he would have bought some other alien being for the Regent's pleasure.

If only he had had the courage to find out her feelings exactly so that, if love had touched her too, they could have fled on a fast drong to a land far from gross humanity. He had made the error of seeing himself as others saw him – a feckless cripple whose only value was a curious sense of direction.

The back of his hand smeared the tear on his cheek.

Perhaps it was not too late to seek her, to free her from her dark master – and if he failed and had to suffer the inevitable consequence he would go to the square of executions knowing that at least he had tried to help his beloved. Even that would be better than the blank existence stretching ahead of him.

His first step would be to seek Gambal. His hand slid down to check the needle-pointed drong-rider's spike sheathed on his thigh, then his misshapen shadow was lost in deeper shadow as he hurried away.

FOURTEEN

Woundflame

As the unexpected note of the gong echoed through the Peak tower the elderly retainers stared at each other with alarm. What sort of traveller could have penetrated the magical mist which enshrouded them? Certainly no ordinary stranger could have found his way here from Lower Wald, not even the woodcutters and charcoal burners who spent their lives under the evergreen boughs of the vast forest.

The Lady Eloira hurried to the courtyard and ordered the gatemen to raise the iron portcullis and draw back the great oaken doors. When they did so they beheld a slender figure standing motionless against a backdrop of the white vapour. His cloak could only be described as the colour of rain and his high-crowned hat, whose broad brim covered most of his face, was the same indefinite hue. The only definite thing about him seemed to be an ivory-white pipe which he held half concealed.

'I bring greetings from the forest folk,' he said in a voice which was sweet and soft like the sound of trees stirred by a breeze, and like such a sound it managed to reach the furthest scullion gaping from the kitchen door.

'You are welcome by dayshine or starshine,' Eloira responded, 'no iron will harm you, no spell will charm you.'

'Very good,' said the stranger, walking through the stone archway.

'Close the gate but leave the portcullis high,' Eloira ordered the gatemen.

In the shadow of his strange hat he smiled his appreciation of her realization that his kind could not be at ease if iron barred their way.

'Your father taught you well. The last time I was here you were at his knee, looking at the pictures in his grimoire. Strange fare for a child, I thought.'

'I remember you, and your pipe-playing. I was a child then and now I am old but you have not gained a wrinkle.'

'Our days are numbered differently to yours,' he said with a sigh. 'Men envy us because their lives are short, we envy men because death gives them a sense of purpose.'

'Come to my solar, these are sad times for the Wald and I doubt not that you have much to tell me.'

'The world is changing, mistress. For men and forest folk the world is changing.'

'I hear the crystal bird has been seen,' Eloira said as she led him across the courtyard and through the banqueting hall. The servants drew back awed and respectful as they passed, and the last words they heard him say to their mistress before they vanished up the stairs were, 'The time of prophecy is at hand.'

At midnight only the watchman was awake to see the stranger dissolve into the moon-pearled mist after Eloira herself had opened the postern, and he surreptitiously made the Circle of the Mother.

The next noon Alwald entered the Lady Eloira's apartment to find her sitting close to the fire, a heavy tome upon her thin knees and her grey cat purring sonorously beside her.

'Sit down at once,' she said, indicating a high-winged chair opposite. 'Are you healing well?'

'Your chirurgeon must be a magician,' he replied, and then pursed his lips at what he had said.

'He has no need of magic when he has an excellent herbal to consult – a herbal that the first Reeve of the High Wald brought when he came to this tower,' Eloira said. 'And now I shall give you some of my special elixir, a spirit distilled from such rare flowers that it takes my women a summer season to gather enough to make a pitcherful.'

From a crystal flask she poured a small amount of ruby liquor into a silver wine cup. She looked at the flask for a moment and then decided to pour some for herself.

'We may need this to give us strength for what lies ahead,' she said.

Alwald raised his cup in a toast to her and when he sipped the spirit it seemed as though his mouth had been filled with sunshine; his throat warmed and then a glow suffused his whole body. For the first time the gloom which had made his waking hours wretched lifted and he wondered whether he was drinking a potation from the ancient herbal.

'I understand that your father told you that if River Garde should ever fall you were to place yourself in my hands,' the old woman said as the drink brought a slight colour to her pale cheeks.

'Yes, my lady, those were his last words to me. I did not take them gravely as at the time it seemed impossible that such a calamity could befall us.'

'And now?'

'I shall do my best to obey my father's wishes, especially as I understand you and he followed the same path.'

'Yes, I am a Pilgrim. Like him, I have worked in my way for the restoration of the Princess Livia and the overthrow of the rule that has corrupted this once fair kingdom.'

She raised her cup.

'Do you know why we are called Pilgrims?'

He shook his head. 'The word was so familiar to me that I never queried i

'When chaos reigned after The Enchantment and warfare and pestilence filled the land there was such fear of strangers that walls were built across the highroads and warlords refused all entry to their petty kingdoms. It was only those making a holy pilgrimage from one miraculous shrine to another who could journey unhindered, for even the warlords would not dare harm those holy ones who gave their lives up to the Mother.

'Bloody-footed, wearing rags and living on acorns and scant charity these fanatics struggled behind their white banners from one end of Ythan to the other in an attempt to pray at each of the three hundred and sixty-five sites dedicated to the Mother. For those seeking the enchanted princess the only way to move about the country was in the disguise of a pilgrim, and it worked well until the regency gained power and the witchfinders put an end to pilgrimage. So many were spiked that the great plain round Danaak had a new forest – of gibbets.

'Since those days Pilgrims – I mean those who believed in Livia – have continued to go in secret quest of her. They have followed the great caravan routes and travelled the seaways, even to the Cold Sea, in the hope of finding some scrap of information that would lead to her resting place. Others ventured into the Outlands, explored dead cities in the wastes, braved Upas forests, scaled the highest peaks and plumbed the deepest caverns. Many died from the natural dangers, more from the attentions of the witchfinders and the Regent's spies.'

'And all in vain,' said Alwald with a sigh. 'An army of heroes lost for nothing.'

'Certainly they will have died vainly if their cause is not finally won,' Eloira said. 'And now the time is at hand when it will be decided whether the shadow which has been growing over Ythan will become eternal night, or whether the bright days of the olden times will return; whether Princess Livia will be found or whether she must stay in her glamour for ever.'

Her fingertips fluttered over the vellum page of her book.

'Long before The Enchantment, it was prophesied by the Sage Omgarth, and now come omens that his prognostication of vast change is at hand.'

'Does his prediction tell what the outcome of this change will be?'

The old woman shook her head.

'His soothe is locked in riddles that are solved only as certain portents come to pass. This is one of the few books of his wisdom to have survived the Great Burnings of the witchfinders.'

For a moment the eyes of Eloira glazed as though her mind strayed into a different world. In a voice as soft as a sigh she murmured:

'Then Pilgrim, prophet, starry-eyed sailor,
Seek the path of Ancient Dreams.'

She blinked as though awakening from a dream herself.

'Livia must be found,' she murmured. 'Do you not agree to that, young Lord of the River March?'

Alwald shifted uncomfortably.

'Being the son of my father I have always believed in the Pilgrim's Path as a way to rid Ythan of tyranny, but I saw the story of Princess Livia as . . . as a symbol of the golden age. In my inner heart I found it hard to believe that, even if her tomb were found, it would be possible to awaken her. So much time has passed . . .'

'Yes, it was easier for us old ones,' said Eloira. 'We were born closer to the high days of magic. Here in the Wald there is little to remind us of the hidden forces. In

River Garde you believed your enemies were flesh and blood men from the Outlands, and the greatest force you knew was the west wind that swept the skies and rent the forest, yet in the last days you have seen a little of the nightside of the world. Was not your father slain by a werewolf, and is it not a spell which keeps this tower hidden from the invaders?

'I find it hard to adjust my thoughts since that black day.'

He raised his silver cup to his lips as though to gain courage from the fragrant spirit after the cruel mention of Grimwald's death.

'Listen, Alwald, though many have failed to find Princess Livia there is hope at last that we will learn the secret of her resting place.'

'But, from what you have said, generations of Pilgrims have searched the kingdom from end to end . . .'

'True, but at last the way may be found from the only person who truly knows it.'

'My lady, how could anyone know?'

'One who was involved in The Enchantment. He was known as The Mage in the olden days, and it was thought that he died long ago. Now it has become known to certain Pilgrims that he lives almost beyond the ken of men, in a tower on a desolate shore.'

'But how could he survive so long?'

'You forget magic. I know not whether it be true, but in his time it was rumoured that he had found the Philosopher's Stone. Because the Regent's spies are everywhere no Pilgrim knows a jot more than is necessary for him or her to play their part, and all I know is that The Mage lives and a journey must be made to question him.'

Trying to mask his doubtful expression, Alwald asked why, if a Pilgrim managed to reach The Mage, he should part with his secret.

'He will trade it for something he covets above all else. He will also know the ritual for breaking Livia's entrancement.'

Despite his doubts Alwald felt his interest stirring. What the old woman said reminded him of tales he had been told in the nursery, and he remembered Erlwald's devotion to the Pilgrim's Path and the Lord of River Garde was certainly not a man to be deluded by wishful thinking. He wondered at her purpose for telling him this.

'What I am going to say to you is what your father would say if he still lived,' Eloira continued. 'You are the one who must journey to The Mage.'

Alwald said nothing. So often since his arrival ghastly pictures had tormented his mind. Again he saw the body of his father and the red-muzzled Wolf King; the flotilla of boats speeding across the river while the bridge collapsed; the howling nomads surging round the out-numbered men-at-arms and then their rush through the gate which was inexplicably opened. After that all he could remember was his delirious flight through the forest, his face lashed by branches and the blood from his wounds hot on his skin.

Guilt sickened his soul after such memories haunted him – guilt that he should have survived when his companions had been slain, guilt that he had fled when the castle fell, and above all guilt over the fate of Demara. Now the old woman's words offered a slight hope of redemption.

When he did not answer immediately, Eloira said, 'I take it that you are still willing to honour your father's hopes and give your loyalty to me.'

'It is my duty to follow his command, only . . .'

'Only?'

'Only I believe it is my duty to discover the fate of Demara, my father's wife . . . widow. Perhaps she still lives as a hostage. I will never rest until I know her fate.

Therefore I want to return to River Garde and – by the Mother! – if she lives I shall rescue her.'

'Brave words but foolish . . .'

'No more foolish than searching for an entranced princess . . . no more foolish than believing folktales . . .'

Eloira regarded him with a slight smile.

'Your father's new wife, she was young and beautiful I hear. You were in love with her?'

'I – I adored her,' he admitted, with a burning face.

'Then, by following my wishes you will have a chance to avenge her fate, the death of your father and the fall of River Garde.'

'My lady, I do not see how seeking out some faraway mage could bring retribution to the Wolf King.'

'The Wolf King was merely the weapon of your real enemy. Do you think those barbarians alone would have had the wit to make boats on wheels? Do you think they would have ever entered River Garde without treachery? Why after hundreds of years of wandering the grass plain howling to their Wolf-in-the-Sky should they suddenly decide to invade the Wald with its hated forests? No, my poor Alwald, they did it at the behest of someone who had much to gain by their arrival, someone who mistrusted your father and the independence of River Garde, someone who would profit by the fear that the Wolf Horde inspires. Simple folk forget tyranny when threatened by an enemy from without; like children their cruel parent becomes their protector . . .'

'The Regent?'

'The Regent!'

'But, lady, how do you know this?'

'To me it is manifest, but for proof I have the word of one of the forest folk named Piper. When he travels the greenwood he is no more than a shadow among shadows, and he has watched the Wolf Horde marching towards the pass in the White Virgins with two Companions of the

Rose to guide them, and he has seen your watchman honoured as a lord by the new masters of River Garde. Would those barbarians treat him so if he had not opened the gate for them on the command of his master in Danaak?'

'Affleck!' the young man murmured. 'He came as a stranger, one of the few of our men who was not Waldborn. He must have been the spy my father feared . . . My lady, if the quest you ask of me should help to end the rule of the Regent then I am yours.'

'Spoken like a knight errant of old,' murmured Eloira with approval. 'And as such you shall have your squire. Look.'

She crossed to a diamond-paned casement and nodded to a courtyard below. Vines covered its walls and small flowering trees grew in antique urns. With her doll on her lap Jennet sat on a rustic seat while Krispin amused her by making cats'-cradles.

'The toymaker,' exclaimed Alwald. 'I owe him much, but when it comes to undertaking a perilous journey at least I have noble lineage and have been trained in the use of arms, whereas he . . .'

'Do not underrate Krispin,' said Eloira. 'There is more to him than he probably realizes himself. It is he who will lead you on the quest.'

'Surely it should be I who am told the way.'

'As is the Pilgrims' practice the less one knows the better, so that should one fall into the hands of the witchfinders one cannot bring misfortune to others.'

'But why should you trust a village apprentice more than I?'

'He is not aware of instructions that he carries in his mind. Before his village was razed and he was to leave it for a year and a day as was the custom of the toymakers, I struck a bargain with him. He needed my help and then I needed a messenger to carry a token to Danaak. Only when he recognizes certain signs and landmarks will an intimation of the next step swim into his mind like a returning memory. Even if he was tormented by the Regent's creatures in the dungeons of the Citadel he could not say a word that would betray those on the path ahead.'

'More magic, my lady?'

'Not necromancy but a skill used by conjure men to put thoughts into the minds of those they would have obey them. Come, finish your drink, we will need its comfort for the ordeal that must now be faced. Light that lanthorn from the fire and bring it with you.'

When they had drained their wine cups Eloira wrapped herself in a heavy hooded cloak of grey wool and led the way down a narrow staircase to a deserted bailey whose far wall was a scarp of living rock.

Alwald shivered as he looked over the deserted scene illuminated by light from the nacreous mist which hung overhead and coiled in pallid tendrils down the damp walls.

The young man and the old woman halted before a bronze door set between pilasters carved from the rock-face. Funerary runes were incised upon its greening surface.

'This is the sepulchre of the Reeves of the High Wald,' Eloira said. 'I must warn you that it was the practice for them to be laid to rest uncoffined.'

She inserted a key in a massive lock and after she had turned it Alwald helped to push the groaning door inward. A breath of ice-cold air caressed his face and when he held up the lamp he saw by its dancing light a long hall down the middle of which were two lines of marble slabs, each carved with intricate garlands surrounding heraldic devices. On each stone a human form lay like an effigy, each in full armour. As they proceeded into the vault

Alwald saw bone fingers resting on the hilts of swords while skulls smiled grim white smiles within their helms.

They halted at the sight of a fully-fleshed figure. On his pale finger a ring caught the yellow light and returned it as a spark of green fire; beneath his raised visor his bearded face was in repose with his full lips set in a faintly ironic smile.

'Father!' cried Eloira with a sob in her voice. 'Oh, father!'

At that moment the air of the vault, which had been still for half a century, was stirred by a faint gust of wind through the entrance. There was a sigh no louder than the fall of leaves, and as Alwald and Eloira watched in horror, the face before them moved slightly as though briefly reanimated, then the dust of which it was composed flowed from the bone beneath. Within seconds the slight smile was lost forever and long teeth and empty sockets took on the grisly expression of the other inmates of the vault.

Alwald felt thin fingers clutch his arm.

'Come,' Eloira whispered in a taut voice.

She piloted him between the twin rows of her ancestral dead to an altar at the far end of the vault. On it lay utensils and ritualistic instruments, and in the centre, its point fitted in a deep groove, stood a sword like a pagan cross.

'Woundflame!' Eloira exclaimed.

Alwald held his lamp high to look at the weapon. It had a plain old-fashioned hilt bound by silver wire which had gone black with age; its broad double-edged blade did not gleam like the weapons in the armoury of River Garde. It was dull and discoloured, its only decoration was a pebble-like moonstone set in the pommel, and Alwald wondered why such a nondescript object should be displayed in the place of honour.

'Look at that sword,' whispered the old woman beside

him. 'Ages ago it was cast by Wayland the Swordsmith on the shore of the Cold Sea where he collected nuggets of iron from a mountain which spewed flame from the gut of the earth. In his forge he melted those pebbles until he had molten iron which he cast into strips which he cooled in troughs of slave blood, for there is that in the blood of men which hardens iron. He twined the strips into a pattern, weaving into it his immemorial spells, and when it was white hot from his driftwood charcoal he beat it into the shape you see, sharpened it on a lodestone and polished it with lime from a hero's bones.

'It was carried by my ancestor Rusthal when he came south from the snow forests at the head of his warriors and took the High Wald by right of conquest long before the reign of good King Johan. With Woundflame, as Wayland named it, he drove out the creatures who held court here and became the first Reeve. Only with such a weapon could he have conquered and he set it here as you see, to remain until there was true need of it.'

She reached out her hand and her blue-veined fingers caressed the blade.

'Several times it has been taken from here by my forefathers to become the bane of the Peak's enemies.'

'Who did your ancestor conquer to take possession of the High Wald?' Alwald asked.

'Dark creatures. The few who escaped the wrath of Rusthal hid themselves beneath the earth so that later the peasants feared them as pottons. Now Woundflame will once more come into the light. For your quest I give you this fell blade. Take it.'

Looking up at the dulled metal Alwald decided how much he preferred his own weapon of bright steel with its begemmed hilt and niello decoration. Nevertheless he had no wish to offend the old woman who put such store by the ancient relic, and leaning forward he grasped the blade – which he noted was in need of a weaponsmith's

131

grindstone – and raised it from its notch. As he did so another soft sigh seemed to hang in the cold air of the vault, and when he lowered it and clasped his hand round the tarnished grip a curious tingle ran up his arm.

'May you wield it for the cause of Livia,' said Eloira. 'May it defend you from dark powers, may it lay your foes for the horn-beaked raven. Now let us leave my fathers in their timeless sleep.'

It was with relief that he followed her to the entrance and helped her to close the heavy bronze door which she carefully locked. In the sickly light he examined the antique sword and though he could appreciate its value to the Reeve as a family heirloom, it did not impress him as a weapon.

'There is more to Woundflame than meets the eye as you may learn,' said Eloira as they recrossed the bailey. 'Let me tell you of one attribute. When conflict is nigh it warns its master with a death sweat.'

'I have heard something of that in legend, but I thought it an invention of romancers.'

'Like a man a sword has a life, Alwald, which is what makes it the king of weapons. Like men, swords have names of their own and, according to the spells that were woven into their iron, certain powers. The death sweat of Woundflame appears like drops of blood upon the blade, and should you ever see that be warned that your enemies are at hand.'

The young man examined the metal carefully but all he could see were spots of rust.

FIFTEEN
Mirror, Mirror

In the Regent's austere bedchamber the page removed her master's ceremonial garments – spider silk, brocade and deep purple damask which he had worn at the re-election banquet – until he stood brooding in his undershirt of the softest silver chain mail ever woven by Ythan's finest armourers. A hooded robe of the kind worn by priests and witchfinders at tribunals was placed over it. Calling his dwarf lamp-bearer to light his way, the Regent set out into a corridor lit at intervals by flambeaux. At each turning a Companion of the Rose, visor down and halberd in hand, stiffened to attention as the tall figure stalked past.

After the long day and the drama of Lord Odo's abortive attempt to overthrow him, the Regent was weary and the flesh of his broad face sagged. Only his black eyes glittered with an almost feverish intensity.

Tonight of all nights he had no wish to rest, for, if the message he had been handed were true, it would be a night of triumph. Reaching a small door guarded by another metal-masked sentinel the Regent unlocked it and entered a long hall. It was his private domain, a domain within a domain where few dared enter. The dwarf's light threw feeble rays on the rows of grotesque figures lining the walls, for it was here that the Regent's collection of automata was housed.

Most of the figures lining the walls were covered with dustsheets which only allowed vague and disturbing hints of what lay beneath. Here and there an unshrouded automaton appeared out of the shadows as the dwarf's lamp passed by, life-sized dolls ranging from the beautiful to the grotesque. An armoured knight stood with raised war axe, a glass-eyed beauty was frozen in an erotic pose, a winged lion crouched with a perpetual snarl – all waiting for the click of a key or the tug of a hidden lever which would give them brief clockwork life.

'Ah, master, you have come to play?'

The voice was sibilant, fawning.

'The executioner has been repaired and waits to swing his great axe for you, oh yes, his very great axe. All are dusted, all are ready, all are *eager*, oh yes, very eager. They want to come to life for you. Timbal wants to play his lute, oh yes, he does. Give the word and I'll set him playing, and look, Merlinda has her pretty new petticoats. Let me light the chandeliers and you will see.'

From the shadows danced the crouching figure of a man, little taller than the Regent's lamp-bearer, waving a duster in one hand. His pebble glasses caught the light like the eyes of a cat at night as he bobbed before the Regent.

'No games tonight, Prince,' said the Regent in an indulgent tone. 'I have graver matters to claim me.'

The little man flicked his duster with exasperation and then in his fawning way said, 'It is not like the old days. Every night you came to your family. And they loved you, oh yes, the toys loved you. Now we wait in the shadows and silence. They hate the silence. Look, the drummer has his sticks poised to beat you a rataplan . . .'

'I shall come again, Prince, but of late there has been much on my mind, much to be done and never enough time.'

He nodded to the dwarf who started towards the end of the hall.

'We will wait for you,' the voice hissed from the darkness. 'You will tire of other pleasures, you will want your family again, and we will wait, oh yes, we will wait.'

The burly Regent followed the dwarf through an archway and up a flight of steps to a landing where a sentry sheathed in plate armour stood statue still with a mace held in his gauntleted hand.

'Advance,' the Regent said.

The dwarf threw him a look of supplication, then shrugged and stepped forward. There was a faint creak from the floorboards and the arm of the mechanical sentinel swept in a blurred arc, the mace hissing a finger breadth above the ceremonial headgear of the midget who gave a squeal of terror.

'What an excellent guard,' said the Regent in good humour. 'He cares not for rations or bribes. Would that I had an army of such. You, Fozo, do not grow or the next time he will have your head off.'

The dwarf bowed and presented the lamp to his master.

'I shall wait as usual, my lord?'

'As usual.'

The Regent walked past the automaton who, jerk by jerk, was raising his arm back into its defensive posture; and after unlocking a heavy door he passed through with the lamp and locked it behind him.

The dwarf sighed, spat in the direction of the metal figure and curled up on a musty palliasse in the corner. He wondered briefly what it was that could occupy the Regent for so many night hours in the tower above, but he shrugged the thought away – he had long learned that in the Citadel there were many questions and few answers. He ritually cursed the Mother for not allowing him to grow as other men and began to snore.

Behind the locked door the Regent ascended a spiral staircase with an eager step. Sometimes he would pause for breath by a lancet window whose slender aperture was filled with the lights of Danaak below. At length he reached the top of the stairwell and found himself in a large octagonal room which was situated beneath one of the characteristic Citadel spires.

At first sight the scene was one of wild disorder. Against several of its walls were benches littered with crucibles, scales, retorts, spirit lamps and curious instruments of use only to alchemists; on shelves stood rows of flasks blown from ruby, emerald and clear glass; beside them were storage urns filled with age-stained scrolls. Above the great fireplace, in which a fire leapt and kept the chamber unnaturally hot, a water clock gurgled the minutes away. On the floor lay priceless rugs sacrilegiously holed by acid spills, just as pieces of haphazardly placed furniture were stained and chipped.

The Regent sank on to a divan from which horsehair burst in profusion and looked at the old man who climbed from a high-backed chair by the fire. He was dressed in a robe that was so grimy that its original colour was hard to determine, and it contrasted with his skin which had the pallor of one who has lived long without sunlight.

'You have come quickly, my lord,' he said, blinking and running crooked fingers through his dirty white hair. It was obvious that he had been dozing in the warmth and was trying to gather his startled wits.

'And I hope my effort will not be wasted,' the Regent replied. 'If you have succeeded this time, Leodore, you shall have what you ask.'

'This time . . . this time,' Leodore said, his head nodding in confirmation of his words. 'How many years have you kept me locked in this tower, Lord Regent?'

'I forget, Leodore,' the Regent replied carelessly. 'And be thankful that I have. Had I not spirited you here you would have known the tug of the garroter's wire after the witchfinders discovered what you were up to. To attempt to imitate life is the greatest blasphemy against the Serene

Mother in the eyes of her priests – next to denial of the fall of the All-Father. After The Enchantment the punishment meted out for blasphemy was often the fiery cauldron, but here in the Citadel you have been safe from priest and witchfinder. You have had peace and all you needed for your work – and your little pleasures. Soon it will be dawn, so let me see if your creation lives.'

Leodore shuffled to a table in the centre of the room and cleared it by the simple method of sweeping his arm across it, then from one of the benches he carefully carried two large objects wrapped round with cloth.

'Each time I have started to grow them I have failed in the final process,' he said with an unexpected briskness. 'It has been a question of getting the ingredients of the elixir into harmony. I have tried a hundred variations, but at last I have the perfect blend.'

'That we will know in a few minutes,' said the Regent.

'I have tested it on that,' Leodore said, pointing to a jar in which a tiny human foetus swam in spirits of wine. 'It showed signs of animation when I added a drop to the solution. Lord Regent, it *moved*.'

'But from the time its father's seed flowed into its mother it knew life in her womb,' said the Regent, standing up to his full height. 'We are not necromancers trying to animate the dead. Our little friends have never known life.'

'But it does indicate the power of the elixir,' the old man said stubbornly. He held up a glass flask filled with white liquid.

'With this I believe I am close to the secret of the Philosopher's Stone – already I believe it will restore youth, at least for a while. It is possible, Lord Regent. It is said that there was a mage who was close to finding it before The Enchantment.'

As the alchemist spoke he carefully unfastened the cloth which bound two large vessels of clear glass, their wide necks sealed with wax plugs. Each was filled with a colourless fluid and, floating in each, rather as the foetus floated in its spirit of wine, was a homunculus.

The Regent leaned forward and stared in fascination at the two tiny travesties of the human figure. Both were in adult form, one obviously female and the other male with a penis out of proportion to his corpse-white body.

The little creatures were broad and without grace: their faces resembled wide masks with gash-like mouths and flaring nostrils set in flat rudimentary noses; ears were mere flaps of puckered skin and the closed eyes bulbous. The breasts of the female were pendulous and without nipples; neither had a suggestion of hair and their hands and feet were grotesquely large for their body size.

For a long time the Regent stared into the bottles.

'They look much more close to humankind than your last pair,' he said at length.

'This time you have been generous with the supply of blood and I have been able to distil it closer to its spiritual element than before,' said Leodore. 'But would that I had water from the Wells of Ythan, for it is believed that life formed spontaneously in it.'

'You might as well ask for dust from the moon; the wells are long dry and lost,' the Regent said. 'Are you ready to try if the elixir can animate these stocks?'

Leodore nodded and carefully unsealed the vessels. As he did so a dank smell of still water rose from them.

'Which first, Lord Regent?'

'The female.'

The alchemist's stained fingers carefully removed the stopper from the flask on the table beside the homunculi's vessels and using an apothecary's measure he poured a modicum of the white fluid it contained into the jar in which the female floated lazily upright. The contents of the vessel clouded until all that the two intent watchers could discern of the homunculus was a shadow.

138

'A movement,' the Regent whispered.

'Wait till the solution clears,' Leodore said in an equally low voice.

'If they survive, you believe they can be grown to human size?'

'Or bigger. The laws which govern our natures will not apply to these. There is no reason why they should not become giants as long as they are fed substances which give them growth.'

'Imagine an army of such creatures, without souls and unafraid of death, blindly loyal to those who created them, patient in labour and terrible in battle.'

'The jar is clearing.'

'Could they breed? Could we raise them like beeves . . .'

'They are open!' Leodore shouted. 'Her eyes are open.'

The Regent bent so that his face was close to the glass. Two tiny black eyes glared back at him, then the lipless mouth opened revealing teeth like ivory needles and he realized she was smiling at him.

'She lives,' murmured the alchemist, awed by his own work. 'I have created life.'

'A parody of life at least,' said the Regent. 'But she no more has anima than my automata.'

'That you cannot say.'

'*In the beginning the All Father blew his breath upon the world and his breath became the life, and from his breath was formed the Mother and out of her womb were born those with souls and they only had souls and their children,*' quoted the Regent.

The homunculus stretched her arms in a pathetically human-like gesture and then propelled herself through the liquid to press the palms of her ugly hands against the glass.

'She can see her mate,' Leodore said.

'Then let him see her.'

139

Drops of white fluid splashed into the male's vessel, and again the liquid clouded.

'He, too, is moving,' said the Regent. 'I congratulate you on your persistence, Master Leodore, after all the failures you have braved.'

In the jar the male homunculus gazed about him with coal black eyes, bewildered by the light and his surroundings. For a while he revolved like a swimmer allowing himself to drift with the tide, then he touched the glass and glared through it.

'Look! At least he shares man's deepest urge,' breathed the alchemist.

As the manikin had caught sight of his female counterpart his monstrous penis immediately distended giving him the appearance of possessing a fifth limb.

'The little demon wants her,' chuckled the Regent. 'Are they able to live outside their jars yet?'

'They must soon or they will not learn to breathe.'

'Then free him and see what happens.'

Leodore cast a suspicious glance at the Regent who watched the two creatures with a curious smile.

'You cannot let him . . . he would kill her like that . . . they are not like the creatures you mate in your menagerie.'

'Do as I say. Let us see how he fares outside the glass.'

With a sigh the alchemist picked up a pair of tongs he had shaped especially for the purpose and, gently lifting the struggling homunculus out of the fluid in which he had been formed, placed him on the table top. For a minute he lay on his side, his chest rising and falling and his slash of a mouth opening and closing like a stranded fish. As he became accustomed to breathing air he pushed himself on to his knees and once more caught sight of the female.

'Get her out.'

Leodore did nothing, horrified that this culmination of

140

his life's work might be destroyed to gratify his master's voyeurism.

'Lord Regent, I beg you . . . there will be time enough when they are grown. They are only minutes old, the exertion could kill them both.'

'Fear not, Leodore, I shall not allow him to mount her.'

The Regent watched as the male managed to climb into a crouching position, then stagger forward and, with arms outspread, press himself against the transparent wall of the female's container. Taking the tongs, the Regent carefully lifted her out and held her high to inspect her closely.

'She is no beauty, Leodore, but she is complete. I congratulate you.'

He placed the female on the far end of the table and without thinking tossed the curved tongs to one side. Like the male she struggled for breath for a minute before she was able to sit up. From his place by the jar the male turned his head, peering with black eyes until the image of the female swam into his hazy vision. With guttural cries he went towards her supporting his swollen member in his hand.

'No, my little fellow, your time to mate is not yet,' murmured the Regent as the doll-sized figure fell several times in his eagerness. Suddenly finding his balance, he ran forward and pushed the female down on the surface of the table, falling upon her and thrusting madly while she shrilled her agony.

Unable to lay his hand upon the tongs, the Regent encircled the waist of the homunculus with thumb and forefinger and plucked him into the air. Turning his head on his short neck the homunculus snarled his frustration and then sank his teeth into the hand of his tormentor.

The Regent gave a cry of disgust as the needle teeth pierced deep into the flesh and pain streaked up his arm. With an oath he sent the creature spinning into the heart of the fire. Even though the homunculus was so small his shriek filled the chamber and for several seconds he danced wildly on the glowing coals until a spurt of flame consumed him.

The old alchemist collapsed into a chair, tears streaming down his cheeks and ugly sobs rasping from his throat.

The Regent held his right wrist while blood trickled from the wound.

'Another! Make another!' he told Leodore and quitted the chamber.

Later, when the morning sun caught the tallest spires of Danaak in her beams, the Regent awoke sweat-soaked from a nightmare. His swollen hand throbbed painfully and holding up his arm he saw that the veins running from his wrist were raised and evil-coloured as though an artist had painted them in vermilion. The thought of infection following the bite of the homunculus made him shudder.

As he hauled himself into a sitting position with his left hand he saw the figure of an old woman leaning on a crutch beyond the black drapes of his four-poster bed.

Mandraga, Lore Mistress of Ythan and the only person in the Citadel who could freely pass the Companions of the Rose into the Regent's apartments, gazed at the figure on the rumpled bed with a hint of mockery on her withered features.

'You are in pain, my son?'

'The bite of a wild creature, nothing more. It will heal.'

'The bite of a homunculus can be as venomous as a serpent,' she said. 'I shall send you a salve for you will need all the strength of your cunning in the season to come.'

Once again the Regent wondered uneasily at the old witch's uncanny awareness of the Citadel's most guarded secrets, but thankfully her loyalty to him was without question.

'Last night my mirror clouded and then I saw a crystal

142

bird flying over snow-capped mountains, an omen long foretold,' she continued. 'It has much meaning for you – and Ythan.'

'Yes?'

'A time of change and danger lies ahead . . .'

'Times of change and danger always lie ahead.'

'Of course, but this period is the one predicted in the Book of Omgarth.'

'No doubt mountains will shake and the seas turn bloody. It seems to me that prophets believe they will be honoured only if they predict cataclysms . . .'

'What living prophet is honoured? Who dares prophesy since the witchfinders cry treason across the land? Only the words of the long dead give us an inkling of what is to come.'

The Regent stirred uncomfortably. His fingers tightened on his wrist to block the pain flowing from his hand.

'A new quest for the Princess Livia is to begin. The prophecies of Omgarth have inspired the Pilgrims as well as brought warning to us. From the mirror I learned that this time it is possible they have new knowledge to guide them. You must find Livia before your enemies, otherwise the days of the regency – of the new order you have worked for so long – will be numbered.'

'You know my spies have sought her with the same resolve as the Pilgrims. Sometimes I wonder . . .'

'She is no myth, my son,' said Mandraga, anticipating his thought. 'While she is a symbol of the Golden Age she is no myth. Once men believe, so it is . . .'

'This quest?' the Regent interrupted. 'Do you know where? Can you give me names?'

'The Spirit of the Mirror did not tell. All I can say is that the future divides; if *our* future is to come to pass you must counter opposition in every form, find the princess and end her slumbering power for all time.'

'How?' The Regent's voice was exasperated. 'I am commanded to do things but never told how.'

'My son, your strength is that you always find a way. I suggest you let the Pilgrims lead you to her.'

'I shall consider your words.'

'Act upon them, my son. The wheel of destiny is about to turn and there is little time.'

The Regent nodded.

'I act,' he said sombrely. 'Soon I will send an army to level the apostate stronghold of Thaan, an offering to the priesthood which they will find most acceptable.'

'Save the books. Those green-robed heretics have a treasury of ancient lore which I could well use.'

'As you wish. Arrange to have them spirited away before the witchfinders move in.'

The old woman straightened up on her crutch. For a moment the lines of her visage softened, for a moment it appeared youthful.

'I will send you the salve, my son.'

Book Two

Like an evil serpent of darkness
That winds through the country of blight,
Through the land where no man wanders,
Flows the dreadful River of Night.
Only fools and the dead dare to follow
Its course past the shallows of shame,
In the region of long-ago madness,
To the city without a name.

*– lines from an
old minstrel lay*

ONE

The Shining Path

Krispin leaned against the parapet and gazed sombrely across the sea of cloud to where the peaks of the distant White Virgins blushed in the dying glow of the sun. Behind him Jennet trailed a yellow ribbon round the base of the great astrolabe for the Lady Eliora's cat to chase. The Reeve had granted permission for the two to spend time on the terrace where she had performed her magical ceremony. She understood that the mist she had conjured up had a depressive effect on the mind of the girl who had been shocked from reality back into childhood.

High up on the tower Jennet was able to escape the opaque shroud and the dreary light it cast to play with her doll beneath a bright sky and watch the ever-changing hues of the distant mountains.

Krispin turned to her and once more felt a pang of sorrow as he watched the full-grown girl – the girl with whom he had shared a forbidden act of love – holding her doll by the arm and tantalizing the cat with the laughter of a dozen years gone.

'Jen,' he called. 'Come here, my dear, there is something I want to tell you.'

She immediately surrendered the ribbon to Smoke and came to Krispin's side.

'Is it a secret?' she asked. 'I love secrets.'

'It can be if you wish,' he answered.

'Then tell me.'

'Tonight I have to go away.'

'Oh.'

She looked at him with disappointment.

'I do not want you to go. You have been very kind to me. Do you really have to?'

'Yes, my love . . .'

The last sad word slipped out but it meant nothing to Jennet.

'Will my brother come while you are away?'

Krispin could not think of an answer. Ever since he had brought her to the safety of the Peak she had asked about her brother – the brother he had been long ago.

'The kind lady will look after you.'

'But who shall I play with?'

There are none but the old in this place, he thought, but aloud he said, 'Smoke will be your playmate.'

'I am going to be sad,' she announced and he could see a tear trembling on the edge of her eye.

'Someday I shall return, and all will be well.' He repeated 'all will be well' like a verbal talisman and ran his fingers through her hair. 'You will be safe here.'

'Yes, I never want to go into the forest again. There was such a lovely house, but we ran away. Krispin held my hand and we ran through the dark trees, but his hand was all sticky . . .'

'Look at the lovely colours on the mountains,' he interrupted. 'See how pink they are as the sun makes her goodbye to the world. When you see them at this time I want you to remember me.'

'I shall,' she said. 'Can I go back to Smoke now?'

'Of course.'

A black eagle rose from the vapour and soared into the dusk-filled air before swooping and skimming over the white carpet. To the youth it seemed that the bird's lonely flight held a mysterious significance if only he had the wit to comprehend it.

'Suppertime, my pet,' came the voice of Lady Eloira. 'Take Smoke down to the hall.'

Jennet picked up the heavy cat and turned to Krispin. For a moment a forlorn look crossed her features, her eyes looked at him imploringly and her lips soundlessly parted. He wondered with wild hope if there was some mature idea in her mind struggling to come through the barrier of her resumed childhood. Then the expression passed.

'Goodbye,' she said, and with her doll and Smoke clasped in her arms she left the terrace.

'I will look after her well while you are gone,' said Eloira. 'And when you return I hope I shall know who you and she really are.'

Krispin shook his head.

'Even if you find we are not brother and sister, the barrier between a man and a child would remain.'

'The physician is hopeful that her mind will return to the present. He says it could happen in an instant . . .'

'Lady, you know the working of magic, you conjured this great cloud to protect us – could you not work a spell to give her back the years that are missing?'

'You do not understand the nature of sorcery,' said Eloira. 'It is not a universal cure-all, otherwise in the days of the great and good sorcerers there would not have been a cripple in Ythan. Some things follow natural law and some magical, and to use one law over the other produces an abomination. You might say that strong gramarye can raise the dead and it is true, but the result is the vampire. Courage, Krispin, there may be much joy for you both when you return.'

'Never joy,' he said dolefully. 'For both of us the village is no more; our friends are dead, our home razed and Tammas . . . You promise me this journey may help bring

151

down those who allowed such a massacre. There is much that I do not understand but you I trust, and on such assurance I shall go just as I promised after The Choosing . . .'

'I feel your pain,' said Eloira, 'but do not let it destroy you. Keep the village and its folk forever in your mind so that something of the past remains to console you.'

The far peaks were now black triangles against indigo sky. From afar came the howl of a wolf.

'It is time to prepare,' Eloira said. 'The path will be marked by the forest folk so you will find your way through the mist. Beyond that it will lead you safely away from the barbarians, who hold the High Wald pass, to begin the first stage of the quest.'

'I feel like a man about to swim in a dark lake at midnight. I have no idea of where I am going.'

'You will know clearly enough when the time comes,' said Eloira with confidence.

An hour later night lay heavy on the High Wald and Krispin and Alwald, wearing the dark travelling cloaks of wandering pedlars, stood at the postern gate.

'You go as youths; you will be men when you return,' said Eloira. 'You will have seen marvels that no longer exist in such settled places as the Wald or the countryside round Danaak; you will have walked in lands nameless to men, and you will have survived hunger and despair and the dread which stalks men in the wilderness – and for the rest of your lives you will know no masters but yourselves.'

Neither young man spoke, each was thinking that the possibility of return became more remote with each of Eloira's words.

From somewhere in the night came the note of a distant pipe, and Krispin was reminded of the ethereal sound he had heard by the mere above Toyheim.

'Do not leave the path and do not tarry,' Eloira told

them as the postern was opened. 'It can only be seen at night for in olden times the Fey used it for their trade.'

Krispin shivered. Tonight there was more than a hint of strange in the clammy air as he followed Alwald through the portal.

'Remember the Esav . . .' The Reeve's soft voice floated after them, then the door closed, its locks clicked and crossbars creaked into position.

Before them a shining path descended into the mist. It was made up of a myriad specks of green light as though all the fireworms of the Wald were in procession.

The two looked at each other with some embarrassment. They had hardly met while Alwald's wounds were healing and the thought that they must be companions when they hardly knew each other made them awkward.

'We may as well start,' said Alwald.

'Yes, the lady wants us clear by dawn,' Krispin said, adding 'After you', in tacit recognition that as a noble Alwald was the leader.

'Before we go, have you a sword?' Alwald asked.

'Only a hunting knife.'

'Then take this,' he said, and unstrapping the belt beneath his cloak he handed Woundflame in its scabbard to Krispin. 'It is a blade more suited to such as you – by which I mean, of course, that being light it is easier for one who has not learned swordplay.'

From his long pack Alwald brought out his own weapon, an aristocrat's sword with an ornate hilt, bejewelled pommel and fine chasing on its rare steel blade. He sighed with satisfaction as he slipped on its baldric, thankful to be rid of the dull iron relic that the old woman had forced him to take. He admitted that the Lady Eloira had a store of arcane knowledge but when it came to weapons she knew no more than any housedame.

'I am honoured with your gift,' said Krispin politely. 'On our journey I hope I shall prove myself worthy of it.'

153

'I am sure you will, lad,' responded Alwald in the tone he would have used to a recruit at River Garde.

With the unaccustomed scabbard knocking his leg, the toymaker followed as Alwald marched resolutely along the green-starred path.

Casting a final glance over his shoulder, Krispin saw that the rough-hewed masonry of the castle was already sheeted by the formless vapour whose moisture dripped steadily from the forest boughs. Occasionally a sound other than the patter of drops on leaves would cause him to look to one side or the other, and he dimly perceived slender shapes moving through the mist as though a band of shadows were escorting them. Although he knew that it was they who had created the shining path for their protection, he still had the old mortal suspicion of the Fey. It would be a relief when the Wald and its dangers were behind them and they were on the proper road – wherever that might be.

As he walked he felt something smooth against his chest, and his fingers slipped inside his shirt to feel the medallion with its curious rune spiral. He had meant to ask the Lady Eloira if it were a gift from her – it was the only possible explanation – and why she had given it to him, but every time he met her he forgot and most of the time he was not even aware that he was wearing it.

The path plunged steeply and often curved so that for many a moment it seemed the glowing pinpoints had come to an end. Then as the travellers rounded a bend it stretched ahead once more, its faint luminosity silhouetting the tree trunks through which it passed. Krispin had no idea of what part of the forest they were in, though the fact that the path led downward for much of the time told him that they were not heading for the peaks which would have been the usual way of leaving the valley. He remembered the Lady Eloira saying that the Wolf Horde held the passes.

'For how long I cannot guess,' she had said, 'but sooner or later a yearning for their nomad life on the steppe will free us from them.'

Although Alwald's wounds were healed he still suffered from their effects and several times he had to sit on a bank and rest, and when this happened the specks of light went out to leave them in darkness. Having been bidden to be silent both felt it a relief not to have to make conversation. Frequently they heard wolf calls echo and re-echo but whether they were from the animals who dwelt deep in the forest or whether it was the invaders signalling to each other they could not tell.

The feeling of apprehension caused by these mournful cries was forgotten when the travellers rounded the bole of a spreading tree and saw by the glow of the path a body hanging from a branch.

It must have been dangling there for several days and the forest ravens had mutilated its face.

'A forester?' asked Krispin, unable to take his gaze from the grisly sight which brought back memories of what he had seen on his return to Toyheim.

'A charcoal burner by his apron,' Alwald answered. 'There must be many such berries hanging in the Wald by now.'

'I'll cut him down,' said Krispin, unsheathing his hunting knife.

'Leave him be,' Alwald said. 'It matters not to him now, his spirit is with the Mother, and time is pressing.' He pointed above his head where an aureole of pale light glimmered through the mist. 'The moon is high and we still have far to go.'

Reluctantly Krispin sheathed his knife and circled the corpse to follow Alwald.

'Do you know where we have to go?' he whispered but Alwald made no reply.

Sometime later a distant murmur came through the forest, a sweet sound they both recognized.

'The Falls of Cramel Linn,' Alwald cried excitedly.

'Now I know where we are,' said Krispin. 'Toyheim is three leagues to the north.'

'Yes, and the stream goes down through the forest to River Garde. We used its water because it was purer than that of the river. Come, the track leads towards them.'

As they followed the stardust path the murmur grew louder until they reached a rock bluff over which several phosphorescent tongues of water tumbled to a pool below. The path skirted this and disappeared into the trees but the travellers knelt on a spongy bank and drank cold water from their cupped hands.

'I can easily reach the castle by following the stream,' Alwald whispered.

'But the path goes in a different direction,' Krispin objected.

'The time has come to tell you what is in my mind,' Alwald continued. 'You, who found me near to death in the ruins of your village, know my story well enough, how my father was treacherously slain and also by treachery River Garde was captured. In war each must bear his grief alone and you, too, know sorrow thanks to the barbarians.'

He paused and Krispin was conscious of the dim Fey shadows waiting in the mist.

'What adds to my despair is the fate of Demara – of my father's wife . . .'

His voice wavered. To cover his loss of control he took another mouthful of water.

'My wound . . . cursed spells of weakness . . . I was saying, the fate of the Lady Demara. As consort of the Hereditary Lord of the River March the barbarians must have realized her value as a hostage . . . they could not have . . .'

156

'I understand,' said Krispin. 'She may be captive.'

'It is a possibility I cannot ignore. I intend to find out and if she remains in the castle I shall win her freedom.'

'By ransom?'

Alwald laughed bitterly and then lowered his voice again.

'What a simple fellow you are! How could I pay a ransom when I have nothing left of value but my sword. No ransom! If Demara is a prisoner in River Garde we will rescue her.'

'What you say is true, I am a simple fellow,' said Krispin, endeavouring to keep the irritation out of his voice, 'but I am not too simple to understand that what you say is impossible.'

'You think so?'

'Of course. Firstly River Garde is in the hands of the Wolf Horde. It would take an imperial army to enter it, and the Mother alone knows what would happen to the prisoners during a siege. Secondly, you talk of making a rescue but you are still so weak that perforce you must rest every half hour merely from walking. And thirdly you do not know the fate of the lady. As a hostage she may have been taken to some other place across the River of Night. And there is something else . . .'

'Do you think I do not recognize the difficulties? But tell me, master toymaker, what else?'

'We both swore to the Reeve of the High Wald to go on a mission for her. If we were to leave the path we would be breaking our oaths. It is a question of honour.'

The breath hissed from Alwald's nostrils in exasperation.

'What does a promise to an old dame matter when the fate of . . . of the River Lord's widow is at stake. And, if it will help your village conscience, I promise to undertake the quest when Demara is safe . . .'

'If the path is left tonight the way will be lost,' Krispin

157

retorted. 'The route is in my head, and only by recognizing certain landmarks will it come from my memory. If I leave the path now I shall never find the landmarks.'

'And does it matter? Is it not better to save a living noblewoman than wander across the kingdom in search of a clue to a princess who was spirited away a century ago!'

As Alwald's voice rose in anger the glow of the path dimmed and then all was darkness. For a long moment the only sound was the song of the waterfall. Then Alwald, his voice shamed back to a whisper, said, 'You may think you impress me with your easy talk of honour, but is it not true that you have undertaken this mission because you made a bargain with the dame? Your words are not inspired by honour but self-interest. I cannot expect a village apprentice to understand true honour, but if you did you would know that true honour would not allow me to leave the Wald without attempting to save Demara.'

'Should she be alive,' Krispin said cruelly.

'Enough, enough. I have wasted enough words. I am going to follow the stream to River Garde, and if you have not the courage to join me you can follow the Fey path to the world's end for all I care.'

'Then go – and the pottons take you.'

Alwald hauled himself to his feet by means of his staff. By the faint moonglow filtering through the mist, which had thinned as they had travelled further from the Peak, he caught the faint gleam of the stream flowing from the pool and he made his way along its bank.

For a long time Krispin sat with anger seething in his heart. To think that the quest should end like this within hours of them setting out! And Alwald's talk of true honour when he was the one who had fled from River Garde! Now, if he wanted to assuage his guilt by some suicidal exploit he was welcome!

As Krispin grew calmer the Fey lights began to glimmer

158

again and the shining path stretched away through the night as though inviting him to follow.

'If I must continue alone then alone I must,' he muttered aloud. 'I have sworn to the quest and only by keeping to the vow have I any chance of happiness.'

It did not occur to him then, as he set out along the enchanted trail, that Alwald had the same reason for breaking his vow. Krispin's thoughts were concentrated on Jennet, not in her present childish state but as he had known her up until The Choosing, and he felt a guilty twinge of erotic pleasure as once more his mind returned to the scene by the mere when they had lain in the flowered grass. And then it occurred to him that her present condition was like a divine punishment on them both for defying one of the most important of the Mother's Commandments. Yet he was the one who should have been punished, for it was taught that evil was male, hence the fall of the All Father.

He hurried on in the forlorn hope that by following the quest he would in some way make retribution to his sister.

TWO
Death Dew

Mentally cursing Krispin for a fool, and himself for his bodily weakness, Alwald made his difficult way along the bank of the stream. The going was made hard by trunks of trees which overhung the water or thick bushes that blocked his way and clutched at his pack and staff as he worked his way round them. The one thing in his favour was that as he made his painful progress the vapour which pressed upon the High Wald thinned, became ragged and ceased, allowing the light of the declining moon to turn the fast-flowing stream into a torrent of quicksilver and enabling the young man to pick his way with more certainty.

Although he occasionally heard the faraway lament of a wolf, there was nothing in the surrounding forest to unduly alarm him and he hoped that despite his weariness he would be close to River Garde by dawn. His plan of action after that was vague. He would find a hiding place and rest during the day – he knew the very spot – and then he would see what fate handed him. He held one secret which would make his venture less forlorn than the village oaf believed.

Sanctimonious clod!

Of course his real motive for wishing to continue along the path was one of fear, Alwald told himself. All the lad wanted was to quit the territory occupied by the Wolf

160

Horde as quickly as possible! But what more could one expect from someone who had spent all his days among workshop shavings learning to make rocking horses. Now he wondered at the sanity of old Eloira in suggesting that Krispin would be his esquire on the quest. Old age must have taken its toll of her wits since his father had last met her, otherwise the River Lord would have never placed his son in her care.

At the thought of his father Alwald felt a pang of guilt.

By disobeying the instructions of the old woman he was in a sense disregarding his father's wishes; on the other hand, had his father known the terrible outcome of his meeting with the Wolf King would he not have expected him to act as he was now doing.

And then the demon deep in the being of every man whispered: *And should you keep faith with Grimwald by rescuing his wife you will be able to have her for yourself!*

His pulses quickened with remembered pictures of the girl, especially one of an accidental glimpse he had had of her through her chamber window early one morning. Had he hated his father at that moment for the shameless intimacy which brought a smile to her face? Had he not dreamed of her lewdly after that, imagined that it was he who knelt before her . . .'

'Serene Mother!' he muttered aloud. 'Rid me of my demon! Let me do what I must with a pure heart!'

As though in answer to his plea erotic fancy faded.

Once more his mind was clear, and as he trudged through ferns lining the stream his hand brushed against his sword hilt. He grinned with relief that he'd had the sense to bring it in his pack and let the toymaker have the blunt relic which had gathered rust in Eloira's family tomb. At the time he had been impressed – who could fail to be in such a drear place! – but thankfully he was now free of the old dame's witchery.

The intervals at which he had to rest and regain his

161

breath became more frequent. Thanks to the skill of the Reeve's chirurgeon there was no danger of his wound opening but its effect on his constitution had left him weaker than he had at first thought. When the false dawn diluted the dark of the eastern sky he had to admit that he would not be able to reach his planned destination before daylight. His body cried out for rest and he decided to find a hiding place where he could sleep and bide his time until it would be safe to resume his trek to River Garde.

Leaving the stream he cautiously ventured between tree trunks until he came to a bracken-floored clearing not much larger than his old sleeping chamber. Its advantage was that the trees surrounding it were so thick, their branches so entwined, that anyone resting there would be screened from any enemy following the course of the stream.

Thankfully Alwald removed his heavy pack which he used as a pillow, rolled himself in his thick cloak and, with his hand clasping the grip of his fine sword, went to sleep on a natural mattress of vegetation.

Meanwhile Krispin plodded along the Fey path, tormented by conflicting ideas. At first he had been buoyed by his anger against the arrogant young noble who had so soon betrayed Lady Eloira's trust, but as his anger abated he began to question his own situation. Was it right for him to go on alone or should he return to the Peak and report what had happened? The latter course savoured unpleasantly of tale-bearing – the most despicable offence among the apprentices of Toyheim – yet he would betray his trust if by stubbornly tackling the mission alone he brought about its failure.

He tried to imagine how the Lady Eloira would respond to the news if he decided to return. The danger was that she might turn her wrath on *him;* should he have not been capable of talking Alwald out of his folly or even prevented him going to certain death by force if necessary? And, if she so lost patience with him that she chose others for her quest, how would Jennet be affected?

The day before, Eloira had come to him on the terrace where as usual he was doing his best to amuse his sister, and in the course of her talk about the mysterious quest she said, 'I entrust the safe-keeping of Alwald to you. He is linked closer to me than he realizes and while he has had the benefit of a noble upbringing, in that he can slay innocent animals perfectly in accord with the chivalry of the chase, give his fencing master as good as he gets and recite his ancestral tree backwards, he could not boil a pan of water. You are no stranger to honest work and you have the simple good sense of one who has to live by it, and so I want you to excuse his affectations – which will soon wear off on the quest – and be his guardian.'

Echoes of *excuse his affectations and be his guardian* returned uneasily to Krispin's mind. They stopped him in his tracks. He raged at how wrong everything had become. It was such a short while ago that he had felt so confident with a happy home, the love of Jennet, the guidance of Father Tammas and his own skill as a craftsman borne out by his success at The Choosing. Who at the ceremony that night could have dreamed of the calamity advancing upon the village!

'Serene Mother,' he muttered, 'what must I do? What must I do?'

But he did not need divine revelation to tell him. He knew that he must go back after the cursed young noble.

As he turned on the path the shadows which had kept pace with him seemed to take on more substance as they came closer, their arms beckoning him forward again. The greenish stardust stretching through the forest rippled as though to attract his attention while faintly to his ears came soft voices chorusing a wordless entreaty which

163

changed to lamentation as he continued to retrace his steps.

The fireworm lights went out with the suddenness of a candle flame being snuffed.

Krispin had never felt more alone in his life, yet it did not occur to him to wonder why such signs of Fey disapproval had not been manifested when Alwald quit the path. He shrugged the straps of his pack into a more comfortable position and began to walk back to the falls. Within the first few minutes he tripped several times over roots and fallen branches and switches of twigs drew blood on his face. What was worse, he realized that he had completely lost his sense of direction.

Having grown up in a forest village Krispin knew the futility and danger of continuing under such circumstances – woodman's lore told him to remain where he was until daylight and the position of the sun would orient him. He consoled himself that being in better physical condition than Alwald he would still be able to overtake him before he was close to River Garde.

He removed a strap from his pack, then hid the pack among some bushes and climbed the nearest tree until he was among the highest branches. He sat on one of these with his legs dangling, passed the strap round his body and the tree trunk and buckled it so that, should he fall asleep, it would prevent him sliding off. He then put his arm affectionately round the trunk and laid his cheek against its bark.

In order to keep himself awake he tried to remember everything that the Lady Eloira had said to him, but it was curious how much now seemed hazy, especially during his first stay at the tower. It was as though there was much that was on the edge of his memory; if only he could make the right effort much would become clear. He was attempting to make the effort when his eyes closed with weariness and he slept, his arm still embracing the tree.

When Krispin awoke he was first conscious of a bright brown eye gazing inquisitively into his, then the squirrel spun round and fled along a branch with his tail floating behind him. The forest rang with early birdsong and when the young man glanced at the leafy canopy above him he saw scraps of blue sky. Looking to the east through a large gap in the leaves he saw what looked like a white precipice and realized that this was the edge of the enchanted mist which protected the Peak.

Once he had moved his cramped limbs and the agony of the returning blood was fading, he unbuckled the strap and cautiously descended. Ghosts of natural mist floated low over the ground but nothing else moved. Reassured he took up his pack and walked over the sound-deadening mould which had resulted from centuries of leaf fall.

From afar came a steady murmur of tumbling water and Krispin thankfully headed towards it. An hour later he found the falls and the pool – now sparkling in the sunlight – and set off along the bank of the stream which flowed from it. Here and there a broken branch, a thread dangling from a thorn bush and crushed ferns affirmed that he was on Alwald's track.

Conscious that having abandoned the shining path he was on his own in enemy territory, Krispin frequently paused and listened until the blood roared in his eardrums for any hint of others moving through the forest, but all he heard was the ringing note of the bellbird and the hiss and gurgle of the stream.

As he worked his way along its bank the unfamiliar rubbing of the scabbard against his leg irritated him and he decided to remove it and carry it in his pack. Gentle-folk could wear swords with ease. Alwald wore his as though it was part of his dress, but Krispin had to admit to himself that his upbringing in a workshop left such social graces to be desired.

Curious to see the weapon in daylight, he withdrew it from the scabbard – even this was done with an unseemly struggle – and was surprised at its dull appearance. No wonder Alwald had presented it to him!

Yet, although it could not compare in brightness or design with Alwald's noble blade, there was something about it which drew Krispin's attention. The silver wire which bound the grip was blackened with age but the moonstone mounted on the pommel above it appeared to shine with an inner light, and when Krispin laid his fingertips on it a tingling sensation ran up his arm, reminding him of times when lightning was in the air and he had picked up iron tools.

Another curious thing was the reddish spots which beaded the blade. In the mirror he had seen similar droplets when he had scraped his skin too close with Father Tammas's razor. He dabbed his finger on the metal with the result that a reddish stain appeared on the skin. He supposed that it was some form of rust, probably the result of the interior of the scabbard being damp. He sheathed the sword and slid it under the pack straps, after which he proceeded more easily.

The downward slope of the forest terrain became more gentle the further it was from the peak; for a stretch it would be flat allowing the stream to meander, then there would be a steep decline so that the terrain descended in a series of vast steps towards the lower Wald. At each declivity the stream became a cataract, throwing up spray fountains as it flung itself against boulders, boiling in miniature whirlpools and trapping rainbows in its spray as it leapt over rock ledges.

It was the noise of one of these torrents which saved Krispin as he descended it rock by rock. So intent was he on watching that he did not slip on their slimy surfaces that he was half way down when he raised his head and froze.

Over the aeons the water had worn itself a shallow pool in the rock at the bottom of its race and in a clearing beside it were four nomads with wolf skull helmets. Under the threat of their long-hafted axes were two prisoners, one of whom was Alwald.

Both captives had their hands tied with leather thongs. Alwald's companion in misfortune was a tall man in ragged garments, his forehead stained with blood while the lower part of his face was masked by a growth of grey stubble. Alwald appeared to be unhurt though the expression on his face told of his anger and humiliation at having been caught. Their captors appeared to be arguing among themselves, frequently gesticulating with their axes, and Krispin had an idea that it was the fate of their prisoners they were debating. One held up Alwald's sword, pointed to the gems glittering on its hilt, pointed to Alwald and then pointed down the stream in the direction of River Garde.

After a minute the others nodded and the nomad turned to the bloodied man with a gesture of contempt.

Krispin remained frozen.

He knew that he ought to attempt the rescue of Alwald and the unknown prisoner from these savages whose ghastly handiwork he had seen at first hand – but how? He was not a warrior, the nearest thing to a weapon he had ever handled was a chisel, and he was out-numbered four to one by these wiry barbarians who had toy axes pressed into their infant hands before they could walk.

To attack the nomads could only end in death.

In his mind Krispin cursed Alwald. If he had not broken his vow to the Lady Eloira and left the path this horrendous situation would never have arisen.

Below him two of the nomads threw the tall man on to his back. He kicked wildly until one of his captors sat on his knees. Another knelt behind him and seizing his long hair brutally pulled his head back so that his throat was stretched taut.

Guessing what was about to happen Alwald, ignoring his pinioned wrist, sprang forward and was halted by the honed edge of an axe blade held against his face. Meanwhile the remaining nomad took up a stance above the pinioned man whose gaze followed the gleaming axe as it was slowly raised.

'Serene Mother, into your hands . . .' Krispin murmured as he unslung his pack.

With a cry that rose above the noise of the torrent, the nomad swung his weapon down in a glittering arc but such was his skill that he deflected the axe away when it was a handspan above the victim's throat. His companions laughed their approval. Again he raised the axe, and at the same time Krispin raised a river boulder with both hands and hurled it at him.

The stone was too heavy to travel far but it did not need to. The height from which it had been launched gave it all the impetus it required. It felled the axeman so that he collapsed across the man holding the victim's hair.

Before the nomads could recover from the surprise of this bolt from the sky, Krispin was leaping down upon them with a flashing blade in his hand.

Something wondrous had happened when he had taken it from its scabbard. It was no longer rust dull but shone as though it had been newly burnished, the moonstone glowing with some essence of light stored within it.

The most remarkable thing about Woundflame's transformation was the effect it had upon the youth who was wielding it. For Krispin time slowed. As he bounded from rock to rock he felt he was floating with all the time he needed to choose secure footholds and direct his feet to them. With his final leap he found himself waist deep in the pool and glittering drops of spray, which had soared about him, remained suspended as he watched two of the nomads rise leisurely to their feet. The one who had been holding Alwald entered the pool with slow strides.

Krispin moved through the frozen splash to meet him, and as the nomad's axe swung towards him he was able to duck beneath its slow arc. He straightened up and some instinct told him to grasp Woundflame with both hands as he brought it down upon his enemy. The blade caught the man's upper arm and to Krispin's astonishment it sliced through flesh, grated on bone and continued its terrible journey.

The severed arm, its fingers still gripping the haft of the axe, fell away; a black fount spurted from the barbarian's stump as he toppled, his scream endless in Krispin's ears.

On the bank the remaining two nomads faced Krispin with raised weapons, unaware that behind them Alwald bent to seize the executioner's axe in his bound hands.

The weight of the water slowed Krispin's advance. He was not prepared for the axe which its skilful master aimed in a cruel upward stroke and he sought to counter it with Woundflame. The result was that the sword was snatched from his hands and went spinning high into the air.

Immediately he lost it, time became normal for Krispin. Instinctively he threw himself back and floundered in the bloodied water as the second axe stroke hissed dangerously close. Uttering an ululating cry like that of the animal who was his totem, the nomad waded into the water with his weapon raised high. But, before he could bring it down, Krispin surprised him by launching himself forward and locking his arms round his broad torso.

Under the impact the wolf man's feet slipped on the weeds lining the pool floor and he fell backwards. Krispin kept his grip, locking his fingers behind his adversary's back just as he would have done in the village wrestling contests in which he had once won a keg of apple ale.

The nomad let go his axe in order to free himself from the young man trying to force him beneath the surface, but Krispin only increased his hold and buried his chin in his chest to protect his throat. Under his weight the nomad's head submerged until he shifted his arms to raise himself up.

For a seemingly endless moment – a moment that he was to relive in many nightmares – Krispin gazed into the face that was only a hand's width from his own. He was acutely aware of every detail; the coarse black hair cut in a straight fringe beneath the wolf skull, the eyes whose yellow irises shone with hate, the coarse skin with its grease-blocked pores, the wolf pad tattoo on the cheek, the long hairs straggling from the chin.

For a seemingly endless moment the two stared at each other in the knowledge that death was at hand for one of them . . .

For a seemingly endless moment their muscles strained agonizingly as the urge to survive swept through their beings. Then the weed of the pool once more favoured Krispin – the heel of the barbarian's palm slid from a slime-coated stone and his head and shoulders fell back.

Desperately Krispin changed his hold. His hands sought the barbarian's face and he pressed with all his strength to keep it below the surface. He was aware of the nomad's eyes blazing up through the foam-flecked water, then bubbles streamed from the broad nostrils, more burst from the mouth which suddenly gaped and the body beneath him convulsed.

Krispin withdrew his hands and rolled away from the corpse. He was trembling as though in the last stages of the Red Death, and his throat burned as bile rose in it.

The surge of strength which had saved him ebbed and with great difficulty he climbed to his feet to stand knee-deep in the pool. On the bank he saw Alwald standing with the haft of a nomad's axe between his bound hands, its crescent blade still embedded in the wolf skull of the last barbarian who had been felled before he could have come to the aid of his comrade.

The two young men looked at each other unable to speak, then the bile burst from Krispin's mouth.

When the retching finished he heard a commanding voice say, 'That's enough, son. Come and cut me free.'

He nodded numbly and waded to the bank where he unsheathed his hunting knife and sawed through the thongs binding the wrists of the ragged man.

'And now his lordship,' the erstwhile victim said and obediently Krispin turned to Alwald and freed him. For a minute no one spoke as fingers massaged the blue grooves left by the rawhide and Krispin leaned against the trunk of a tree. In the pool the current teased the two bodies, turned them slowly until they were caught in the outflow of the stream and mercifully borne away between its bracken-fringed banks.

The ragged man was the first to speak.

'I felt the Dark Maid touch my shoulder then,' he said. 'I owe you, son. You arrived like a hero in an epic. Only once before have I seen a foeman's limb actually shorn off, and that was when our company had to hold the Ogre Pass against the White Strangers some years before I took service at River Garde.'

'If Alwald had not seized the axe when he did we would all be dead now – I had no strength left,' said Krispin generously.

The words – the act of talking – restored the balance of reality.

'If you had obeyed me I would never have been captured,' Alwald said bitterly. 'I could not keep watch

171

and sleep, and when I awoke those devils were standing over me.'

'If you had kept your vow and stayed on the path you would never have been captured,' said Krispin with equal bitterness. 'We would have been leagues away by now. As it is the path is lost and the quest . . .'

'Pox the quest!'

'This is no time for harsh words,' said the ragged man. 'Let us be thankful that we can still breathe the Mother's sweet air.'

'You are right,' said Alwald. He held out his hand. 'Krispin, I am sorry my anxieties have come between us.'

Krispin grasped the proffered hand.

'I too am sorry for my words.'

'Good,' said the ragged man. 'There are enough enemies in the Wald without us needing to fall out. I am Emon, lately Lord Grimwald's master-at-arms, and before that I was warrior first class in the old Black Storm Company. Frontier work mainly. I was taken prisoner yesterday after escaping from the castle.'

'How . . .' began Alwald.

'We can talk later,' said Emon. 'There may be other wolf men about. Throw those bodies into the water. If they are found downstream they will not betray our whereabouts.'

Trying to check his revulsion, Krispin took the feet of the nomad whose head was split beneath his shattered wolf skull; Alwald seized his wrists and together they swung him to and fro like children teasing a playmate, then released him so he splashed into the pool to be carried away by the current.

Krispin turned to the man he had struck with the boulder.

'He is still alive,' he exclaimed in a voice that reflected his horror of what he might be expected to do next.

172

'So he is,' said Emon carelessly. 'But he will not be for long.'

With ease he picked up the dangling figure, carried it to the bank of the stream and dropped it into the rushing water.

THREE

Return To River Garde

'Not my favourite weapon but better than none,' said
Emon, picking up one of the nomad axes which lay beside
the pool and testing its balance. 'You had better arm
yourself with one,' he added to Krispin who had just
collected his pack from where he had laid it on a rock in
the cataract.

'I shall seek my sword,' he said.

'There is no time,' said Alwald testily. 'Emon is right,
we cannot stay here. Sounds of the fight may have reached
enemy ears and it is madness to tarry.'

He retrieved his own sword which lay on the ground
along with his pack.

'It will not take me long,' said Krispin, wading into the
water.

'You would be better off with an axe anyway. That
sword was blunt and rusted . . .'

'That did not seem to matter when I held it,' Krispin
retorted as he slid his feet along the bottom of the pool
where he thought it might lie after it had been sent
spinning out of his grasp.

'True,' said Alwald thoughtfully. 'Perhaps there was
something special about it after all. You could hardly
have done what you did on your own, but come away.
You will not find it and every minute is precious.'

'As my sword is to me,' muttered Krispin, now waist

174

deep. 'Go if you must, I shall soon be accustomed to your departures.'

Alwald was about to reply with a cutting remark but checked himself.

'I am ready, let us go,' he said quietly to Emon. 'Once we have found a secure place I will give you food and a salve for your wound.'

'It was healing well until I was caught,' he said. 'Come now, son,' he called to Krispin. 'You'll not find it on the murky bottom. Take an axe and hurry.'

Krispin ignored him and continued with his search.

'Leave him,' said Alwald to the soldier. 'He'll soon scamper after us when he sees us go.'

'Perhaps not, I can see he has a stubborn streak.'

'I cannot risk what I have to do for his stubbornness. We go now, and that is an order, master-at-arms.'

Emon gave him a look of respect.

'Of course, my lord.'

The two men turned and walked into the trees.

At that moment Krispin saw what appeared to be a sparkle shining through the stippled surface of the pool. He reached in its direction but could feel nothing until he held his breath and ducked his head under. In the pale underwater light he saw Woundflame resting on a patch of flaccid weed, its moonstone glowing brightly and its blade shining. His fingers closed on the grip and when he straightened up he brandished the sword in triumph.

He splashed to the bank, wiped the blade carefully with a spare shirt from his pack, sheathed it and then followed the direction taken by Alwald and Emon. Soon he overtook them and was happy to obey the soldier's signal to remain silent.

Overhead the blue sky of the early morning was becoming overshadowed as a rising wind from the great Outland plain rolled up banks of sombre cloud. Far away the first thunder rumbled and not long afterwards heavy drops splashed through the leaves above them.

Krispin consoled himself with the thought that he could not get any more wet than he already was but still he was thankful when Emon, who was in the lead, signed them to halt. They were beside an earthen bank above which a huge and ancient oak spread its branches. Its exposed roots writhed down the incline like a family of serpents, and almost invisible among them – and partially screened by a lush growth of dark ferns – was a narrow opening.

'In there,' said Emon.

'It looks a real potton hole,' Krispin muttered as he unslung his pack in order to follow the others through it.

'Better that than another meeting with the Wolf King's subjects,' said Emon. 'I have never seen a potton but I have felt the metal of the barbarians.'

The interior of the cave, a natural cellar which had been eroded from beneath the tree roots, was dry, and just enough light filtered through the entrance for them to see that they were not sharing it with anything more harmful than pale spiders who had festooned its earth-and-root ceiling with their filaments. The floor was covered with dry fronds of ferns which had bravely tried to grow in its deep shade and withered in the attempt.

Emon grunted with satisfaction and, laying his axe in readiness beside him, leaned against the loam-smelling wall. Alwald fumbled in his pack and produced a flat loaf of hard traveller's bread and breaking off a piece he passed it to the soldier who chewed it eagerly. Krispin opened his pack and with some difficulty in the confined space managed to squirm into dry garments. After he had wrung out his wet ones, he too bit into a crust of traveller's bread.

Outside the opening, raindrops fell faster until the ferns were dancing under their impact and occasional lightning flashes bleached the trees, the following thunder drowning the forest's windsong.

'Rain as hard as you like, old weather spirit,' laughed the soldier as he applied Alwald's salve to the gash in his forehead. 'Wash away our spoor and keep the wolf men in their lairs.'

In the semi-darkness he turned to Alwald.

'My lord, I have not had a chance to say how gladdened I am that you escaped. Until this morning I had no knowledge of your fate after the barbarians rolled their wagons into the river and were blown across by their infernal wind.'

'Caught outside the walls, I fought with our men until they were cut down and the Wolf Horde entered the gate,' Alwald said.

'A miracle that you kept your life,' murmured the soldier.

'The Mother shielded me that day. I seem not to be able to remember much of the fighting – though I know my sword was bloodied to the hilt – and after I was wounded I was dragged away otherwise I would have fought on . . . the enemy must have lost interest in me once the gate was opened . . .'

He was relieved when Emon exclaimed, 'Such treachery! I was firing from a casemate when suddenly there was a pack of those dog turds behind me. I did not even know they had entered until then. I dropped my shotbow and was drawing my blade when an axe blow caught me. By the grace of the Mother it was not deep enough to sunder the bone but its force knocked me senseless. The nomad must have thought he had killed me because I was left where I fell.'

He paused as Alwald handed him a small flask of spirit. He took a mouthful with evident satisfaction and passed it to Krispin who was still shivering from the effect of his wet clothing. He raised the flask in a toast of thanks to

Alwald who, irritated with himself for having expected too much from a village apprentice, acknowledged the gesture with a friendly nod.

'What followed, Master Emon?' he asked.

'It was night when I came to in the casemate. I was soaked with blood but once I wiped it from my eyes I could see the glow of the great fire the nomads had made out of furniture in the courtyard. They had sacked the cellars and were howling their pagan songs to the moon. I crawled out and saw the bodies of our men lying where they had fallen, and several were headless. You know the Outlanders' trick of mounting heads on poles alongside their wolf skulls.'

'The women?' demanded Alwald. 'What happened to our women?'

'Some must have suffered rape after the attack because blood makes men randy as goats, but when I came round the nomad womenfolk had crossed the river and were as drunk as the men.'

Alwald steeled himself to ask the question he had been dreading to ask.

'Do you know the fate of the Lady Demara?'

'To be sure. She lives.'

Alwald closed his eyes, afraid that even in the gloom his tears of relief might show.

'Tell me.'

'When I saw the nomads were carousing round the fire and too full of wine to keep watch, I crawled from one pile of bodies to another until I was able to stagger into the armoury. From time to time nomads came with more barrels of drink, and more furniture to throw on the blaze, but I kept to the shadows and at last was able to climb up the stairs. I thought that the best place to hide would be beneath the roof where I could rest until I got my strength back.'

'And Demara?'

'I am con[...] [...]at, my lord. I hid myself in the space between the ce[ili]ng rafters and the roof beams. There is a lumber room . . .'

'I know,' said Alwald. 'I used to hide there when I was small. Once you pull up the ladder no one would think of looking there.'

'Some of your toys were still there,' said Emon. 'When I had hauled up the ladder like you I stayed there, sleeping most of the time.'

'How did you keep yourself alive?'

'I caught mice. For drink I unfastened some slates above the guttering and scooped up water which lay in it. It was through this hole I saw the Lady Demara.'

He paused and sighed wearily.

Alwald passed him the flask.

'The room at the top of the white turret is level with the armoury roof.'

Alwald nodded and Emon continued, 'From the hole I had made I could see it clear, and through the window I saw your father's lady. Sometimes she would come to the window and look down on the castle and wring her hands.'

'How did she look?'

'Pale. Her hair was not braided like she often wore it. Most of the time she sat at a spinning wheel.'

'How strange. Do think she had been . . .'

'I could not say how she has been treated, my lord, but it seems to me that the lady of River Garde would be too valuable as a hostage, even to barbarians, to become brothel meat – begging your pardon for the expression.'

'You see, Krispin, I was right.' Alwald could not hide the triumph in his voice. 'She is being kept as a hostage. By the grace of the Mother we will rescue her.'

'That is my hope, too,' said Emon. 'It was with that thought in my head that I left River Garde when my wound was healed enough.'

'How did you manage that?'

'Every castle ever built has an escape passage, and the one which leads from River Garde was more widely known among the lads than you and your father guessed. Many a willing wench has been smuggled in to entertain the guardroom along it.'

'It was my idea to use it to enter the castle,' Alwald said.

'I believed that there might be some of our men hiding in the forest and if I could find them, or recruit loyal rivermen, I could return to River Garde and rescue her,' said the soldier.

'The difficulty would be to get to her in the white turret. The Wolf King will have posted guards on its stairs and there is no other way in.'

'With the right men we could kill the guards.'

'But not before her keepers did her harm.'

'As it turned out I did not find any fugitives in the forest, instead those wolf men found me. Last night I was taken when I went to the stream to drink. They decided to have some fun with me after they had stumbled upon a better prize . . .'

'A notion has just come into my head,' said Krispin. 'You say, sir, that the Lady Demara spends her hours at a spinning wheel. Surely that is an unusual thing for a highborn lady to do when her home has fallen to the enemy.'

'I suppose it helps her to pass the time,' said Alwald.

'Did she do much spinning before the castle fell?'

Alwald laughed at the toymaker's naivety.

'What a question! Of course not. We had spinsters and weavers to do such work.'

'Then it could be that she is spinning a rope.'

'You have listened to too many folktales in your village.'

'Wait,' said Emon with excitement. 'I told you she often came to the window. I thought it was to get air, or to look out upon the fair forest, but I did notice that she always looked downwards. It could be that she was reckoning the length of rope she would need to reach the courtyard below.'

'Did she know about the secret passage?' Krispin asked.

'It would be very unlikely if my father did not tell her of it.'

'I think it could be in her mind to leave her chamber by a rope she has spun and quit the castle by the tunnel.'

'If so we must reach her first because she will be in terrible danger if she tries to reach the passage entrance,' said Emon.

'Then we must make the attempt tonight,' said Krispin. 'If this storm continues it will help us. I am sure guards are never so alert in the rain.'

'*We?*' echoed Alwald. 'Did I hear you use the word *we*?'

'Your ears did not deceive you,' Krispin replied.

'But after what you said last night . . .'

'That was last night. Now the quest is abandoned some other good may as well come out of it. Last night I did not think it possible that the Lady Demara could still be alive, now I know how I would feel if Jennet was held by the Wolf King.'

'After what I have seen of his sword work he would be a useful man to have along,' Emon said.

Alwald said, 'Of course. And Krispin, in the fullness of time, I shall see to it that you are well rewarded.'

'I seek no reward from you,' Krispin answered quietly. 'But should we succeed I want you to swear that you will return with me to the Peak so that we can set out on Lady Eloira's quest once more.'

'Of course.'

'Swear.'

'Listen to me, son,' said Emon heavily, 'no commoner asks a noble like Lord Alwald to swear oaths. If he agrees

181

that is enough and as binding as a vow taken at a holy shrine.'

'It seems to me,' said Krispin, 'that the days of noble and commoner are over in the Wald. We are three fugitives from the barbarians and nothing more than that – and tomorrow we may be no more than carrion for the ravens.'

'By the Mother, you forget your place!' cried Emon. 'If I had you in my company you would soon learn to speak civil and respect your betters.'

'You have no company, any more than Alwald has a castle or I have my village.'

'I still have a soldier's code . . .'

'Krispin is right,' said Alwald. 'We have all lost our position and what we hold dear. All that matters now is that we can meet the present perils with honour. Now let us rest a while.'

The two young men wrapped themselves in their cloaks, and Emon in a blanket from Alwald's pack, and all laid themselves on the soft floor with their weapons close to hand.

'Let me look at the sword I gave you,' Alwald said to Krispin. 'At the pool it seemed brighter than I remembered it.'

The lightning flickering over the forest was now so frequent that the cave was often illuminated with steely light. As Krispin withdrew the sword from its scabbard he saw that the blade had become dull again and without a word he handed it to Alwald who gazed at it curiously.

'I cannot believe this is the same sword you used this morning.'

'I have no other,' Krispin said, taking it back.

As he lay back with his head against his pack and his fingers on the tarnished grip of Woundflame, he looked back on the morning's events almost as though they had happened to another person. He had done an act which a few days ago he would not have dreamed possible – he had brought death to fellow creatures. With Woundflame glittering its murderous magic, he had robbed them of the years they might otherwise have enjoyed.

On the other hand if he had not done so Emon would have been beheaded, so it seemed that either way life had to be given up. The ways of the Mother are beyond our understanding, he thought, but why? He knew there was no answer, which was one of the dearest tenets of the priests who exhorted worshippers to have faith without understanding.

'Can you find the way to the tunnel?' he heard Alwald ask Emon.

'I believe so, my lord,' the soldier replied. 'It is about a two-hour march from here.'

'What troubles me is how to alert the Lady Demara once we are in the castle.'

'That we can only decide when we are there, my lord.'

Krispin drifted into sleep and dreams. Once more he was with Jennet on the day of The Choosing, running through the home meadow while the geese scattered and the goose girl laughed.

And almost immediately it seemed there was a hand on his shoulder shaking him into wakefulness.

'Time to move, son,' said Emon. 'If we leave it any later it will be too dark to see our way.'

Krispin sat up and saw that the rain was still falling past the entrance, hissing into pools of its own making.

'We will take our packs and leave them in the tunnel,' Alwald said as he prepared to venture out. Krispin nodded. Apart from clothing and food in his pack, there was the leather purse of silver crowns the Lady Eloira had given him before he left and he was concerned for its safety.

'It may seem a small fortune now,' she had said, 'but

you will need every crown on your journey. Husband it well.'

He pulled the hood of his heavy cloak over his head and splashed into the rain, Emon following in an assortment of garments which the two younger men had given him.

'I shall lead,' he said. 'Do not talk and do not follow too close. If we are ambushed we will need space to use our weapons. This reminds me of the campaign in the Weeping Woods – well named they were, it was always raining. Armour rusty, bread soaked to mush, dwarfs using poisoned arrows, forest fever . . . who would be a soldier!'

He squelched off, Alwald followed three paces behind, and Krispin, already shivering with the cold carried by the rain, brought up the rear. He had never seen the forest so gloomy. Toymakers had the good sense to stay close to their glowing fireplaces in such weather, drinking apple ale, whittling and scaring the children delightfully with tales of bears who had silver mail beneath their fur, evil pottons who lived deep in underground grottos and princesses who had to be rescued from terrible perils.

The last thought brought a wry twist to Krispin's lips. The idea of attempting to rescue the Lady Demara from the clutches of the Wolf King was the stuff of folktales, yet he could not have felt less like a hero. He wondered if she had listened to such tales in her nursery, and if so, would she see herself as a beautiful princess locked in an ogre's tower?

The raindrops splashed monotonously from leaf to trembling leaf, marl beneath their feet had become mud and the wind keened in the treetops like a despairing spirit. And even though there were a couple of hours before the sun went to her rest, the light was dim and sad dusk lurked beneath the trees.

Suddenly Emon halted and held up his hand in warning.

K....... moved forward and found they were on the edge of a clearing. A smell, a dreadful dank smell, reached them. It was the odour of a burnt home whose ashes have become rain soaked, and it came from a roofless ruin ahead of them.

'We are on the right track,' said Emon. 'That was Hab the Woodcutter's cottage.'

Nothing stirred in the dismal scene and the three crossed the clearing. As Krispin passed the ruin he looked sideways and saw a broken image of the Mother – in her Lady of the Forest form – lying beside a doll on churned-up earth that had once been a garden patch. The sight of these symbols – the comforts of childhood and adulthood – brought back the horror of Toyheim, and Krispin felt less perturbed over the fate of the nomads that morning.

At length as a deeper darkness was descending they emerged from the trees to find themselves on the brink of a deep gully. Ferns overhung the edge and creepers straggled down its rock walls; stunted bushes grew on its floor between which a leaden stream flowed sluggishly out of sight.

'You have guided us well,' said Alwald.

'The path is over here, my lord,' Emon replied, pointing to where a ledge sloped at a steep angle down the rockface.

The soldier descended with the confidence of one who had made the journey more than once. Alwald followed without difficulty, but when Krispin put his foot on the ledge he was dismayed at its narrowness, and added to this was the film of water flowing down the rock which made his feet slither alarmingly. He clutched creepers and exposed roots and inched downwards while his companions, already at the bottom, hissed at him to hurry. When he finally joined them his legs were trembling with fatigue. He was surprised how well Alwald was standing up to the

185

journey, and then realized that it was the thought of Lady Demara which had given him new strength.

There was no time for him to get his breath back, Emon was off again, pushing his way between bushes and tall rushes which lined the stream until he halted by a stunted crack willow.

'We made it, my lord,' Emon said with self-satisfaction. 'They used to call me Master Never-lost in the old company.'

Resting against the creepered bank opposite the willow was a flat boulder which put Krispin in mind of a large millstone. The soldier put his shoulder to it and rolled it to one side as easily as if it was a cartwheel, to reveal a tunnel entrance. Once inside, Alwald felt in his pack and produced a flint and steel, a tinder box and a fat candle which was soon casting its yellow light. Emon replaced the stone while his two companions stacked their packs and unsheathed their weapons. Alwald cast a curious look at Woundflame but it appeared to him just as he had seen it before. He was unaware of the tingle which shot up Krispin's arm as his fingers tightened on the grip.

'Forward, my lord,' said Emon encouragingly, and holding his candle high, Alwald set out along the passage, the roof of which he almost touched with his head. Krispin saw that the tunnel had been excavated in the same manner as the old lead mines, abandoned in the days of The Enchantment, in the slopes above Toyheim. Pick marks still showed on the rock walls and where there were faults brick arches supported the roof.

After five hundred steps – Krispin counted them as he trudged after his companions – the passage opened into a circular shaft. The candlelight was reflected from still water an arm's length below the tunnel floor. Iron rungs had been hammered into the masonry above, and Krispin realized that the escape route led from the castle well.

'Before we go up I want to say something,' he said in a hushed voice.

Alwald drew back and shielded the candle.

'Say on,' he whispered.

'Do you know the story of Princess One-wish?'

'I beg your pardon?'

'Princess One-wish . . .'

'You want to tell folktales at a time like this?'

'Everyone knows that story,' said Emon unexpectedly. 'Many a time I heard it at my mother's knee. When the princess was named the Fey came with a gift – she could ask for one wish to be granted in her lifetime.'

'And what happened?' Krispin asked.

'Why, son, when she grew up she refused to marry an ugly old king that her cruel father had chosen for her, and he locked her in the top of a tower with a loaf of bread and a pitcher of water until she would change her mind or starve to death. But she was not likely to change her mind because she was already in love with a total stranger who had come as a minstrel to her father's palace . . .'

'Madness!' Alwald hissed.

Krispin ignored him and asked the soldier to continue.

'The princess had a pet bird, an owl who could speak, and one day when she saw her minstrel in the courtyard below looking sadly up at the tower she sent the bird down to him with a message. It said that she had thought of a way of escape and he was to find the two fastest horses in the kingdom, and when he had them saddled and ready he was to bring them to the tower at midnight and at his signal she would escape and they would ride off together. Of course, as it turned out he was a king from a far land who, having heard of her beauty, had come in disguise to see for himself and had fallen in love with her.'

By now Alwald was listening because he realized that Krispin must have a serious purpose.

'Do you remember how she escaped from the tower?' Krispin asked.

'She used her one wish,' the soldier replied enthusiastically. 'She wished that her hair might grow and grow until it was long enough to reach the ground from her window. And sure enough it grew, and she cut it off and plaited it into a rope which she used to climb down to the minstrel king.'

'You see why I have asked you the story?'

'I am starting to have an idea.'

'Do you remember how the minstrel king signalled to her?'

'Now that I do forget.'

'The minstrel king was told that he must hoot like an owl four times and the hair rope would be lowered. And when this happened the guards took no notice because they thought it was the princess's owl that was hooting.

'Every child in the kingdom must have been told that story and if she remembers it the Lady Demara will understand its meaning. Do you have owls in River Garde?'

'The river hawks keep them away.'

'Good. Then the lady will not think it is a real owl when we signal.'

'I congratulate you, Krispin, but one thing troubles me – supposing Demara has not spun a rope?'

'Then we shall kill her guards,' said Emon. 'But first let us try the owl cries.'

'Normally the castle takes its water from a stream because it is fresher,' said Alwald. 'This well is a reserve that would only be used if the castle was besieged. Its head is in the armoury which, let us pray, is deserted. From there it is easy to get to the courtyard beneath the white turret. If that is clear, and it probably will be as the nomads must dislike the rain as much as anyone else, I want you two to guard the entrance while I signal.'

'That is straightforward enough,' said Emon. 'I shall go up first because I know the well.'

They returned to the shaft and Alwald allowed just enough light for the soldier to reach out and grasp the first of the rungs. A moment later he had climbed out of sight and soon his whisper echoed eerily down to them.

'All is clear.'

'You next,' said Alwald. 'I'll hold the candle so you can find the hand-holds. And Krispin . . .'

'Yes?'

'I hope I am as good at mimicking an owl as you are at remembering tales.'

Krispin leaned out over the water as Emon had done and soon he was following his shadow up the rungs. The soldier helped him over the coping and soon Alwald joined them in the old hall which had been a weapons store until the nomads had looted it.

With their weapons ready, the three stole to the doorway beyond which light rain fell into the court between the armoury and the keep. It was deserted, and apart from the sound of water gushing from the gutters' gargoyle spouts, there was no sound. River Garde could have been deserted, and Alwald wondered how many nomads now garrisoned it. He had learned from the Lady Eloira that groups of them were roving the forest to bring terror to the Wald folk, and a large detachment had travelled to the mountains to seal the High Pass.

For a moment he feared that the castle might have been abandoned and Demara taken over the river to the Outlands, then he looked up to where the white turret capped the corner of the keep and although it was merely a blurred outline, saw a square of yellow light marking its single window.

While Krispin and Emon took up position on each side of the arch leading into the court, Alwald moved beneath the turret and after filling his lungs and cupping his hands round his mouth, sent an owl-like cry ringing into the night.

He drew breath and again the long-drawn call rose from the court. With each cry Alwald straightened a finger from his fist, and when four were outstretched he stepped back to get a better view of the window. For a moment a silhouette appeared against the light and he could have shouted with joy as he recognized the figure of Demara.

The silhouette opened the casement and leaned into the rain to gaze into the court below.

Alwald waved his arms, hoping against the odds that she would see him, recognize him even, and that she would have a rope to throw.

At the archway Krispin gripped the grip of Woundflame and darted a glance at the lightened window. Demara's shadow vanished, reappeared, leaned over the sill and appeared to be lowering something. Relief surged through him that his folktale idea was not a failure. If only the lady could climb down the rope safely they could be back in the escape tunnel in two or three minutes.

Alwald saw the rope descend through the rain until its end dangled an arm's length above his head. He reached up and just managed to grasp it in order to hold it steady. When Demara came down he would have to catch her. The light shining from the turret room was briefly diminished as a female form clambered out of the window, clung to the ledge and then began to slide down the line. A shriek rent the night as she plunged faster and faster, her scorched palms unable to slow her.

With the cry still issuing from her mouth she reached the end of the rope and dropped into Alwald's waiting arms. His knees buckled under the impact, both sprawled painfully on the cobbles and then he had a greater shock – the woman was not Demara.

FOUR

The Black Boat

'Margan, where is your mistress?' hissed Alwald as he helped Demara's maid to her feet.

'My lord, I came first to make sure that the way was safe, that the owl calls were not some trick,' she gasped. 'Tug the rope and my lady will come.'

Alwald reached up, caught the end of the dancing rope and pulled. The light above was briefly obscured and Demara came down the rope at a safer speed than her maid. This time he did not stumble and for a blissful moment he held her in his arms.

'Alwald, I knew if anyone would help me it would be you,' she murmured. 'True son of your father.'

'You have no hurt?'

'Only in my heart, dear Alwald. As Princess One-wish I am well. Thanks be to the Mother there was a spinning wheel in that tower room and plenty of horsehair in our mattresses. The nomads left us alone once we were locked away and when we heard the guard coming with food we were able to hide the rope.'

At the archway Emon cursed and ran to the trio beneath the turret, Krispin close behind.

'Happy to see you, my lady,' the soldier said. 'My lord, nomads are coming, I saw their lanthorns in the ward. They must have heard the cry.'

'To the well,' Alwald cried and taking Demara by the

arm he ran towards the armoury door. The others followed as bobbing lamps appeared below the archway.

On reaching the entrance to the armoury Krispin turned and saw that the maid had fallen behind them.

'Run for your life, girl!' he called.

'My ankle is hurt,' she cried.

With Woundflame in hand he ran back and, placing his free arm round her waist, dragged her to the doorway. Inside the candle burned steadily on the well coping, spreading enough light for them to see the rungs set in the glistening wall of the shaft.

'I'll go first and help you down,' said Alwald. He swung himself over the edge, climbed down several hand-holds and waited for Demara to follow.

'You next,' Krispin told the maid. In the candle light he could see that she was a girl of his own age who, if her face had not been tense with terror and streaked with wet strands of raven hair, possessed a merry smile and uncommon prettiness. Her skin had a rosy hue and this, coupled with large dark eyes, reminded Krispin of the comely dolls which had been produced in Toyheim.

He helped her over the coping, held her arms while her uninjured foot sought a rung, and then returned to the doorway behind which Emon waited with poised axe.

'We can win them a few minutes here, son,' he muttered. 'Here come the potton turds.'

There was a sound of soft-soled boots on the cobbles and the leading nomad rushed through the doorway holding high his lanthorn. Emon's axe fell in a hissing sweep. The nomad's wolf skull shattered into white fragments and, groaning, he fell back into the arms of his comrades. They waited on one side of the entrance, Krispin and Emon waited on the other.

'Get down the well, son,' the soldier whispered.

'What about you?'

'They think we are trapped so they may take their time.

I will follow you. Spring to it and take the candle down with you.'

Krispin obeyed and when he stepped into the tunnel mouth Demara sighed with relief at the light shed by the wavering candle flame.

'Ever since I was a child I have feared the dark,' she smiled.

'Meet Krispin,' Alwald said. 'He is a toymaker but he has a good memory for old tales.'

Krispin inclined his head to the young woman. Even in the uncertain light he was conscious of her beauty, though her skin was without powder or rouge, and her corn-hued hair was no longer dressed as befitted the mistress of River Garde. It was merely pulled back and held by a ribbon of soiled samite. Her dress was more suitable for a maidservant, and Krispin rightly guessed that she had abandoned her usual flowing gown for one of Margan's dresses in order to be unencumbered if she had to descend the rope she had spun. Yet, despite her humble appearance and the fact she had been held captive by barbarians, she retained the poise which had first drawn Grimwald towards her.

The Lady Demara was about to say something to Krispin when baying cries echoed down the well shaft. There was a clash of metal weapons, then the water below the tunnel entrance fountained high as Emon plummeted into it feet first.

As the two young men hauled him out they glanced upwards and saw the circular opening above was ringed with lamps.

Once the soldier was safely in the passage Alwald took the candle and, shielding it against the draught of their flight, led the way with Demara running close behind. Emon followed to give protection to his master and mistress, while Krispin once more supported the girl Margan. Although she hobbled as fast as she could,

Krispin saw with alarm that they were being left behind. The bobbing light became smaller and smaller and for a frightening moment they found themselves in the dark when the passage curved sharply. To add to their fear, the cries of their pursuers resounded about them in the confined space like the jabbering of demons.

'I cannot keep up,' sobbed the girl. 'I cannot keep up.'

He did his best to reassure her but when he looked back he saw pinpoints of light and, pausing only to sheath Woundflame, he hoisted her over his shoulder and broke into a stumbling run after the others.

With his breath searing his throat Krispin caught up with them just as Emon was rolling back the wheel-shaped boulder covering the exit. He and Alwald hastily collected their packs and followed the women into the open air. Outside the rain had lessened to a drizzle and above the wind harried tattered cloud across a sky which, from moment to moment, was illumined by the moon shining like an enormous pearl through the rack.

Having put the boulder back into position, and propped large stones and a heavy willow branch against it to hinder their pursuers, the party set off beside the stream which gleamed like pewter whenever the moon showed his face. As the sides of the gully were too slippery and steep to climb, the only way they could go was upstream or down, and they chose the latter in the belief that the nomads would expect them to make their way back to the forest.

After a while the rocky walls on either side fell away and the stream lost itself in water meadows.

'We are close to the river margin,' said Alwald as their feet sank through the covering of grass into mud beneath.

'Then where can we flee?' asked Demara through chattering teeth.

'If we could take a boat . . .' Alwald began.

'I think there is little chance of that until daylight, my

lord,' Emon said. 'If we find a place of refuge for my lady to rest, I shall scout for a craft at first light.'

'Then let us seek a hiding place.'

They blundered on, Krispin supporting Margan and the soldier peering anxiously for the enemy's lights though none appeared in the shadowed gully.

As they continued further into the water meadows they were forced to skirt tussocks of tall rushes and shallow pools of stagnant water, and the fear of quagmire became as strong as fear of their pursuers. Then, as the moon once more sailed from behind streamers of cloud, they beheld a sag-roofed cabin raised on stilts.

'A fowler's hut,' exclaimed Alwald with relief.

Emon splashed forward, climbed inside and reported that it was safe for them to enter. It contained no more than two rooms and by the moonshine coming through the unshuttered window spaces they saw that one was a kitchen with a rust red stove, a table, and walls hung with a wildfowler's gear. The smaller room was fitted with a bunk bed and this was taken over by the two young women who were given blankets from the packs.

'I thank you for your kindness to me,' said Margan quietly as Krispin handed his blanket to her. 'Without your help I would be in the hands of the barbarians. You will find that I am not ungrateful.'

He shrugged away her thanks, wished her peaceful sleep and went to the other room where he lay on the creaking floorboards beside Alwald, unaware that a couple of handspans below him the bodies of the murdered fowler and his ravaged woman lay together in the ooze.

It was the harsh cronking of a marsh wader which roused Krispin. No one else stirred in the hut and by dawn light filling the window he saw that even Emon's watch had ended with his head drooped on his chest. He stretched his cramped limbs, painfully climbed to his feet and crossed to the window where he saw that the pale sky was completely cleared of yesterday's rain cloud.

But he saw more than that. To the west was an expanse of sombre, slow-moving river beyond which a line of grassy plain ruled off the horizon, to the north the tallest tower of River Garde was visible and to the south, and much closer to hand, he saw a cone-shaped hill on the summit of which a dead tree raised its whitened branches like the despairing hand of a buried giant.

Krispin had a strange feeling that the scene was familiar, especially the hill with its lone tree. He had never before travelled to the River of Night, yet he *remembered* it and knew for certain how the hill would appear from the other side. Then he understood and sighed with satisfaction.

'Alwald, wake up,' he said as he shook his companion's shoulder. The young man came out of sleep with a cry and his hand clutched the ornate grip of his sword.

'What? What?'

'Listen, you remember that the Lady Eloira said that on the quest I should know what to do when I recognized landmarks on the way?'

Alwald rubbed his hand over his stubble and squinted at Krispin in bewilderment.

'I recognize a hill out there. It is one of the landmarks. I do believe that if we had followed the shining path all the way it would have ended there. It feels odd – a memory of something I have never experienced – but I know exactly what must be done.'

Alwald still regarded him blankly.

'Do you not understand? We can carry on with our mission.'

'Serene Mother! Are you on about that again?'

'Your oath, Alwald, to the Lady Eloira; your word to me.'

'Later, Krispin, later. How can we go on such a journey with Demara? First we must get her to safety.'

'It would be dangerous to go back through the forest. Even if we missed the wolf men seeking us we should get lost in the magical mist surrounding the Peak. To stay here would be madness. Our only chance is to continue the quest. To do so will get us away from the Wolf Horde.'

'You are sure of what you say?'

'Did not the Lady Eloira tell you directions for our journey were buried in my mind so that it would be impossible for me to reveal them to an enemy.'

'She did. Yes, she did.'

'Then let us put it to the test, and right away. The light is getting stronger by the moment and the nomads have keen eyes.'

'So be it.'

Soon Krispin led his fellow fugitives from the fowler's hut. Hardly a word was spoken as they chewed dry traveller's bread and picked their way over rivulets and round pools. Flocks of birds rose screeching from curtains of reeds at their approach, a myriad black specks against the pale rose of the dawn.

The Lady Demara, her maid limping beside her, had no idea where they were going, Alwald having said that there was no time for explanations but she would understand soon enough.

Several times she looked sadly over her shoulder at the distant tower of River Garde and thought of her lost happiness. In particular she recalled the evening when she and her husband had stood together on top of the tower and watched the camp fires of the nomads twinkling across the River of Night. Later, in their bed, Grimwald had made love to her so beautifully that she knew it would be impossible for her ever to feel such ecstasy again.

When they left the water meadows for firme[...]
Krispin said, 'We must go round the hill to where [...]
to the river. There is a copse of trees close to the w[...]
and in it the remains of a shrine.'

'Are you sure you have never been here before?' said
Alwald suspiciously.

'Since my childhood I never left Toyheim except to
walk in the mountains,' Krispin answered. 'Am I correct
in what I say?'

'Quite correct. Sometimes when I was a boy I came
here looking for adventures. The ruin is very old, probably older than River Garde. It was supposed to have
been built by a holy man after he'd had a vision of the
Mother. As children we believed that the Fey danced
there at the moon's fullness.'

As Krispin looked up at the hill, with the dead tree
appearing to claw the sky, he was filled with a strange
confidence. He knew exactly what he would find at the
ruined shrine, and exactly what he must do after that.
The idea of returning to the quest lightened his heart; by
keeping faith with the Lady Eloira he felt he was keeping
faith with Jennet. Although it was such a short time since
he had left her, so much had happened to him that it
seemed they were separated by a chasm of time and
distance.

They reached the base of the hill and in his eagerness
Krispin ran round its slope until he was out of sight.
When the others caught him up he was gazing with
satisfaction at a circular coppice of hoary trees which grew
almost at the edge of the broad river.

'Follow me,' he said. 'If the promise be true we will
soon be on our way.'

Pushing his way through the undergrowth round the
tree trunks, he soon reached the ruin. It had been roofless
for centuries, its walls of rough-hewed stone were so
mossed that it hardly stood out against the surrounding

greenery and only the Circle of the Mother, cut deep above its arched portal, suggested its original purpose.

'Help me to drag the boat out,' Krispin said. 'It will be heavy.'

With these words he entered the ruin. Diamantine cobwebs hung in the angles of its walls, from the earthen floor weeds grew unnaturally tall in their contest for the light, livid fungi spread over the ancient altar stone – but there was no boat.

Krispin's gaze swept the rank growth covering the floor, the time-eroded walls overhung by branches of encircling trees and the altar which the forgotten hermit had raised in gratitude for mystical confirmation of his belief. Memory told him there was a boat in the shrine but the shrine was empty and he became assailed by doubt. Why had he recognized the hill he had never seen before, been able to describe the shrine before they reached it and yet be wrong in the most important aspect?

'Boat, son?' growled Emon. 'I see no boat.'

'It seems you are mistaken after all,' said Alwald quietly. 'We had better decide what to do without it.'

Margan gave him a sympathetic look, a return for the help he had given her the night before.

'What made him think there was a boat here?' the Lady Demara asked Alwald. As briefly as possible he explained about the quest.

'But perhaps there was a boat here and the nomads took it,' she said when he had finished.

'It is unlikely it would have been left so the wolf men could find it,' Krispin muttered. 'It must be hidden.'

'Then why do you not know the secret?' Emon grumbled. He turned to Alwald. 'My lord, I am a soldier plain and simple and I have no time for gramarye or the Fey who are no better than dwarfs . . .'

While he spoke Krispin felt a thought rising to the surface of his mind and heard a voice murmuring indistinct words

199

in his inner ear, but it was hard to concentrate with Emon holding forth. He turned away from his companions and, resting his elbows on the altar stone, lowered his head on his hands in an effort to concentrate. As he did so the disk with its spiral of tiny runes fell from his shirt and swung on the end of its chain. Immediately the voice in his head became stronger, and Krispin turned, held up his disk by its chain and intoned sonorous words of which he had no understanding.

The other four looked at each other in puzzlement and then in alarm as the air about them took on a strange luminosity. And not only were their eyes playing tricks but their ears, as it seemed as though notes of unearthly pipe music reached them from afar. They were filled with a glorious sense of well-being; Alwald and Emon were no longer wearied by their recent wounds, Margan's ankle ceased to throb and Demara's desperate grief became sorrow without desperation.

With his talisman still swinging, Krispin saw the bright aura about them become shot with colours as though they were within a rainbow. The mysterious music swelled and died, the brightness dimmed and when the fugitives' dazzled eyes could focus once more they beheld a craft in the centre of the weeds. It was long enough to hold at least six people and was beautifully constructed from black, highly polished wood with oars of similar wood stowed beneath the thwarts.

The soldier broke the silence.

'What was that?'

'Gramarye,' said Krispin. 'Come, we must launch her and be on our way.'

'Who taught you Old Ythan?' Alwald demanded.

'No one. The words just came into my head. It was as the Lady Eloira said.'

The men lifted the boat and half carrying and half sliding its keel over the grass managed to take it to the river bank where Krispin waded in and held the painter while it was launched through a fringe of spiky rushes. Alwald helped the Lady Demara and her maid aboard to sit on the comfortable seat in the bows and then boarded with Emon.

'A pity we have to row against the current,' he said as he fitted an oar between its thole pins.

'We are going downstream,' Krispin told him. 'That is the direction I was given.'

'No,' said Alwald. 'That cannot be right. Do you know where the river flows to?'

Krispin shook his head.

'I have no knowledge of these parts.'

'It flows,' said Alwald, 'through the Land of Blight.'

Margan gave an exclamation and Demara bit her underlip.

'No one goes there, it is a domain of the dead,' Alwald continued, 'so turn the prow in the right direction and let us be gone.'

'We have to go downstream,' Krispin said stubbornly. 'As it turned out I was right about the boat and I am right in this.'

'I admit the witchcraft, but I refuse to go to certain death and worse.'

'My lord, I can see riders,' said Emon. 'Let us cast off before they notice us.'

Krispin turned the bow, hauled on the gunwale hand-over-hand to get the craft into the current and climbed over the transom where he took the tiller. Alwald and Emon each heaved on his oar and the black boat shot towards the middle of the dark water.

'Steer upstream,' said Alwald but Krispin swung the rudder in the opposite direction.

'The quest is to the south.'

'My lord, we should go downstream,' declared Emon unexpectedly. 'To go north we would have to pass River

Garde where the nomads are camped on either side of the river. We would be an easy target for their bowmen while we rowed against the current.'

As though to lend weight to his words an arrow with a cruelly barbed head hissed into the water at arm's length from the side.

'The riders have seen us!' the soldier exclaimed. 'Row for your life, my lord.'

Turning his head Krispin saw that a line of horsemen were galloping along the bank, drawing back their short horn bows as they rode. Arrows fell about the craft, one thrummed into the planking and another buried itself into Krispin's pack while he steered to the middle of the river where the current was strongest. Alwald and Emon rowed with heaving chests and the boat skimmed over the oily surface so the distance between them and the nomad patrol gradually increased. Arrows fell astern and then ceased to fall, and looking back, Krispin saw that the enemy had given up the chase.

'Safe at last,' he said while the two men hung over their oars and wiped the sweat from their faces with their sleeves.

'But not for long,' said Alwald. 'You have no idea what lies ahead, Krispin.'

'Tell me about this place,' Krispin said. 'I only heard vague talk about it in Toyheim.'

'All I know is that long ago it was a fair country with goodly pastures, pleasant villages and a great city which thrived on the river trade,' said Alwald. 'Then came the Blight. What it was no man can say today, all that is known is that overnight pastures withered, orchard and forest became skeletons of trees and all living things sickened to death.

'It is said that there were strange lights in the sky and great columns of smoke which could be seen even from River Garde, and when the sun set she set in skies of blood. For a long time the river merchants did not dare go near for fear of plague and bands of crazed wretches who lurked in ruins or wandered the blackened countryside.

'When at last a merchant went downstream he saw the fair country had become a waste, the city – whose name is now forgotten – was falling into ruin and nothing stirred. When he returned he said that at night unearthly lights glimmered above the horizon and a doleful moaning filled the air.

'After that the river merchants abandoned their barges and went to other parts of the kingdom to trade and few went willingly downriver. Those who did went in search of valuables which must lie in the ruins, but none returned. There is an evil which broods over the land – and that is where you are taking us.'

FIVE

The Shallows

There was a dreamlike quality about the next two days. Once safely out of range of the nomads only one of the men needed to row at a time, and then only enough to give steerage to the black craft which was borne along by the broad river whose glassy surface, despite the bright sunshine which followed the rain, remained as dark as ever. A rolled-up canopy of black samite was found in the bow of the boat, and this was erected on four slender poles at the stern to give shade to the two young women.

After the fear and exertion all had suffered, a somnolence descended upon them. Alwald said no more about the Land of Blight but dozed in the bows, Krispin let his mind drift far away as he sat over the oars and Emon, hand on tiller, looked back on his campaigning days through a golden mist. Beneath the canopy the Lady Demara reclined blank-eyed with her hands clasped before her while her maid Margan trailed her hand in the water with her dreamy gaze on the face of the oarsman. An hour or more would pass without a word being spoken.

The landscape gave no hint of the blighted land lying to the south. To the west the Outland plain of waving grass stretched to the horizon, its utter flatness emphasizing the vastness of the sky above which gave to someone like Krispin, who had grown up in a valley surrounded by forested hills, such a sense of limitless space that he felt almost dizzy when he contemplated it. The Wald still stretched along the east bank, its hills gradually rising to the distant ranges, its forest rolling down to the water's edge. Here and there the trees gave way to glades where deer grazed peacefully. In small man-made clearings the travellers glimpsed cottages of river folk but no smoke plumed from their chimneys, no dogs barked and no figures lounged on the jetties with fishing lines. It was obvious they had been abandoned when word of the nomad invasion passed along the river.

Only once were any barbarians sighted, and then the scene was so peaceful that it was hard to believe the menace they held. A small group of them sat round a fire on a sand spit over which fishes were grilling. Their laughter sounded as innocent as that of children as it floated over the water, and when they saw the boat far out on the river they merely waved.

The creak of the oars and the chuckle of the water beneath the bows had a soporific effect on Krispin and often his eyelids narrowed as he rowed gently. Alwald and Emon had both offered to take their turn but as both were getting over wounds he let them rest. He knew he had much to think about but at this time he was content to let his thoughts drift without purpose, thankful for the sun on his back after the hours spent in soaking garments, thankful for the crust of traveller's bread which kept his belly comfortable and thankful that by accident he had been able to resume the quest and keep faith with the Lady Eloira. As to what lay ahead he repeated a village maxim, 'I shall worry about Moonday on Moonday.'

In the late afternoon they came to a narrow island in the middle of the river. Safe from marauding barbarians, it was an ideal spot to spend the night and the boat was beached on a reed-fringed bank. Once there was enough dusk in the air to hide the smoke, Alwald lit a fire in the

205

centre of the island where the thick bushes covering it hid the glow. It was with a feeling of well-being that the five sat round the fire while Emon, like the old campaigner he was, made a stew out of strips of dried meat, lentils and traveller's bread which Krispin and Alwald carried in their packs.

It was hardly the fare that any of them were accustomed to, yet as the smell rose from the light cooking pot – again a necessity from one of the packs – their appetites sharpened with pleasure. It was as though they were children again having a secret feast in the woods, and the holiday feeling was enhanced when Alwald passed round his flask. This night they closed their minds to the horrors they had all witnessed, to the loss of companions and loved ones, and lived only for the moment – the hot stew, the hotter spirit, the fragrant woodsmoke and the comforting sound of water plashing past the shore. Even Demara lost the faraway look in her eyes.

Above all they had a feeling of closeness with each other, of being part of a family, albeit an overnight one, and Alwald and Krispin grinned at each other as though they were the best friends in the world.

Inspired by the flask Emon entertained them with tales of his days in the army campaigning on the farthest frontiers of Ythan. He told of the treachery and ambuscades, of the women warriors in the mountain region of Ilona, of the ghost temples in the desert and how once, by a far seashore, he had glimpsed a griffin soaring on golden-feathered wings.

'I did not know you had seen so much,' said Alwald as he laid more sticks on the fire.

'I learned not to tell my tales in River Garde, my lord,' the soldier replied. 'Those who have never been out of the Wald – begging your pardon – have no idea of what lies out yonder. If I told of the creatures that live beyond the domain of men I would have been jeered at for a liar.'

'What sort of creatures?' asked Margan, her eyes bright in the glow of the fire.

'Creatures such as . . . as the stonelings – stones shaped in the form of men which come to life on the fullness of the moon.'

'Have you seen a stoneling?'

'To be honest I cannot say I have, though I knew a lancer in the old White Horse Company who said he had and he never lied. And that reminds me that I did once see a manhorse . . .'

'You mean a horseman?' Margan asked.

'No, lass, a manhorse. He had been captured by the natives in the Arkad woodlands – poisonous lot they were! – and they wanted to sell him to us but we were too busy pursuing an outcast band.'

'But what was he?'

'He was like a man from the waist up, but from the waist down his legs were like those of a horse.'

Margan made a sound of disgust.

'The odd thing was that he did not look like a freak, if you take my meaning. He was a well-built handsome fellow and even the horse part of him was . . . well . . . graceful. If only someone could have taken him to Danaak they would have made a fortune out of him. Rich old widows would have bid up to their last crown in the slave mart. When we returned, the natives told us he had died. Pity.'

When the fire was reduced to embers they bade each other warm goodnights and the men rolled themselves in their cloaks while the Lady Demara and her maid went to sleep beneath the black canopy of the boat.

Demara was in the thoughts of Alwald as he lay with his head on his arm watching the dying fire. Seeing her again only confirmed his passion for her, and once she was over the shock of the recent days he would gently, very gently, reveal his feelings. Perhaps the fact that they were heading for the Land of Blight was not such a bad thing – there she would come to rely upon his protection more than ever.

For the first time since the burning of Toyheim Krispin thought about his craft. Having listened to the wonders described by Emon he pondered on the possibility of making a griffin that could flap its wings, perhaps even fly a few handspans above the ground!

Emon tried to calculate how much he and his comrades would have earned if they had been able to take the manhorse to Danaak.

The next morning they woke early, cleansed themselves in little inlets among the reeds and rowed into another golden day.

Again they were silent for most of the time but it was a companionable silence broken only by the regular drip from the oar blades and the occasional screech of a fishing eagle. It seemed to Krispin that they were in a time out from time in which the terrors behind them and the mystery of what lay ahead had no reality.

By the middle of the day the terrain of the east bank had changed; the hills of the Wald became lower until the forest merely appeared to undulate and the ranges were lost to sight.

'We will soon be leaving my father's . . . my domain,' Alwald said. 'The tenure of the river lords ends at the Shallows. Beyond them the river runs through empty country until it reaches the Land of Blight.'

As the afternoon wore on Krispin noticed changes in the river. It broadened considerably, and at the same time it became shallow so that instead of one broad flow there was a diversity of currents. And with the land to the east becoming as flat as that on the west, the travellers had a sense of mounting insignificance on such a broad expanse of water beneath the enormous sky. Krispin thought of the black boat as a tiny water beetle in the centre of a large pond.

When the sun was hanging low over the Outlands, Alwald called from the bow, 'There they are – the Shallows.'

Krispin turned his head and saw what appeared to be a green line stretching across the river which, as they drew nearer, changed into a number of islets and sandbanks clothed with trees so stunted they were little larger than bushes.

'There is no way round them,' Alwald continued. 'We will have to work our way through the channels.'

Krispin turned back to Emon who was at the tiller and caught him making the Circle of the Mother.

'Is there something wrong?' he asked.

'No, son,' the soldier replied. 'It is just that sometimes I get a feeling a goose is crossing my grave.'

He moved the tiller so they headed for the widest gap between the islets. As he did so a boat came into view with a man rowing rapidly against the current, bundles of nets piled in the bows proclaiming that he was a fowler.

He appeared to be so astonished at seeing another craft in this remote place that he actually stood up and shouted something across the water, but the distance was too great for them to distinguish his words. He then made an extravagant gesture towards the sun, sat down again and began rowing with such powerful strokes that soon he was nothing more than a dwindling dot.

As Krispin rowed into a channel there was a sudden startling chorus of protest as a flock of wading birds took to the air with trailing legs; a sandbank seemed to come to shivering life for a moment as freshwater crabs covering it scuttled into the water, and Margan jerked her hand out of the water as she caught sight of a sinuous shape gliding through the water below them.

209

'I shall keep going until it is dusk,' Krispin said. 'There is no shortage of places to camp.'

'And no shortage of crabs!' muttered Margan.

'Good,' said Emon. 'Crab soup tonight.'

As the sun neared the horizon the Shallows became a place of unusual beauty. Its lagoons reflected the delicately tinted, feather-like clouds above so that for a breathless moment it was possible to imagine that they were actually rowing over the sky. Narrow waterways changed from pink to crimson within minutes and the pale leaves of the ugly trees were transmuted to gold. Then, abruptly and dramatically, the Shallows were transformed; with the sun gone the gloaming thickened over the lagoons, channels which had been paths of glory became sinister stretches of black water while the trees lost their gold and were nothing more than dark smudges against a darkening sky.

'Should we not make camp before it gets any darker?' said Demara anxiously.

'Yes, my lady, I am steering for that island ahead,' replied Emon. 'It seems night falls fast in these parts.'

The boat grounded on a sandspit and after tying the painter to an overhanging branch Alwald and Krispin helped the women ashore and then shouldered their packs. At its widest point the island was no more than fifty paces across but its advantage was that the trees left a sandy space in the centre, and here it was that the campfire was lit and cloaks and blankets spread out.

Emon set the cooking pot to boil while Krispin continually fed sticks to the flames. Margan nearby sat gently massaging her leg and further off Alwald spoke softly to Demara. Everything was similar to the night before; they were on an island, they were round a fire and they had food, yet the warm feeling they had shared was missing.

Was it something about the Shallows which made them feel alien, trespassers in a world to which they had no right? Was there something disturbing about the night breeze which set the trees sighing – or was it the black water lapping at the islet like some restless primal force?

Tonight there were no tall stories. Each was wrapped in his or her own thoughts and gloomy ones they seemed. Before long, in the darkest part of the night before the moonrise, the travellers spread out and wrapped themselves in their cloaks and blankets to sleep. By unspoken agreement Demara and her maid did not retire to the boat; there was a desire to remain together.

Alwald lay listening to the rustle of branches above, his head filled with thoughts of Demara. Today he had found she was more ready to talk though, strangely, she hardly mentioned his father except when he told her at length about the quest he had undertaken and temporarily abandoned in order to seek her.

'Your father spoke to me about Lady Eloira, and the Pilgrim Path,' she said. 'He believed that only by the return of the Princess Livia will the good days return to Ythan. It is something that, as I was only just beginning to learn from him, I do not yet fully understand but I am overjoyed that you followed his last request by going to Eloira, and that we are on the Path.'

'We?'

'Of course, dear Alfrith . . .'

She paused and a sad expression crossed her face.

'. . . Alwald. Sometimes I find it hard to remember that your name changed on my lord's death, but I must accept that from now on it must always be Alwald by tradition of your House. As I was saying, I rejoice that we are following the Pilgrims' way . . .'

'But the quest has already proved its dangers.'

'The dangers came about through rescuing me, not through the quest. It may not be any more hazardous than any other journey in lonely places. And Krispin does seem to have a power given to him which will help us.

211

Imagine what would have happened if he had not possessed the magic to find the boat!'

'It is not his magic,' murmured Alwald. 'He merely carries it for the old sorceress.'

'It matters not where it comes from if it works, Alfrith. What matters is that together we are carrying out Grimwald's wishes.'

'But he would have wanted you to . . .'

'Hush. I am going to accompany you and there is nothing more to be said. And if you disagree, what will become of me? How can I return to my father's court when the Wolf Horde holds the Wald?' She sighed. 'Poor father, I wonder if the envoy has reached him yet with the demand for my ransom. I only hope news of my rescue reaches him before he pays.'

Looking back on the conversation Alwald found there was much in it to please him; she had called him 'dear Alfrith' and seemed determined to stay with him on the journey, and yet he wanted more. In his moments of wildest longing he wanted what he had always wanted, he wanted to kiss her not as 'dear Alfrith' but as her lover; he wanted to feel the curve of her beautiful breasts, he wanted to gaze at her as her gown slipped from her body . . .

Erotic visions taunted him.

Demonic whispers.

All are asleep. She is lying close to you. Perhaps she dreams of you as you do of her. Did she not flirt with you every day? Go and lie beside her, run your hands over her body, explore her secrets, let her feel the warmth of your youth. That is what she needs, that is what she is waiting for.

'No!' Alwald heard himself cry out.

Was he going mad?

He had suffered from his guilty longing for Demara

before, but never had it been as urgent as this nor had such sensual images filled his mind. He must do something to clear his mind.

Alwald rolled out of his cloak and stood up. Near him, her breast rising and falling peacefully in sleep, Demara lay beneath her blanket. Moonlight, which was starting to filter through the low trees, caught her hair. Her beauty was breath-taking, her expression of almost childish innocence doubled his guilt and he fled to a strip of shore where he stood gazing at black silver-edged ripples whispering towards his feet.

Gradually he calmed. He knew it was the imp of the perverse that sent such thoughts, and as in the past he sent a prayer rising to the Mother for spiritual strength. The only reassuring thing was that Demara could have no inkling of these mad moments of lust. If she guessed that he could desire her so carnally after her bereavement – so soon after the death of her husband and *his* father – she would rightly regard him as a depraved monster.

Is it usual for men to become so obsessed by the women they love? he wondered. During the last few years as he approached manhood he had been aware of the courtships that were part of castle life, but behind the placid faces of the retainers and their wenches he had not sensed the fire that burned him when he thought about Demara. But did he show it? Of course not. Perhaps all lovers shared the same secret desires.

He sighed and lay down on the sand.

And then it seemed that his sigh was echoed but softly, as softly as a lover's breath upon one's cheek.

The night breeze, Alwald thought. The breeze that comes hundreds of leagues from the Outland to sigh over him and then flow on to other unknown lands.

But it was not the night breeze.

It was a young woman emerging from the shadows.

'Demara!' he breathed.

213

Her face was white, its normal complexion blanched by the moonlight. Even the lips, to which she raised her forefinger, were white.

She moved forward and stood looking down at him with an enigmatic smile. Her head was slightly on one side in the pose of someone weighing up another, then her hands reached down and cool fingertips slid through his hair.

'Demara,' he repeated in a whisper.

Again the ethereal sigh, again the fingertip to the lips.

Of course she would not want the others to know that she had followed him from the campfire.

He nodded his understanding.

She smiled, a different smile this time – a smile of complicity, a smile of enjoyment at her inward thoughts.

Her hands – those white moon-marbled hands – disappeared behind her back, her shoulders moved and her gown slid to her feet. Then with her feet planted firmly apart she put her hands on her hips in an attitude of challenge.

It was as though one of Alwald's dreams had come true, yet to see it here in this wanton stance repelled him. His desires were based in fantasy and the reality momentarily frightened him. What sort of a man was he to be gazing at the naked body of his father's widow – and what sort of woman was she to encourage it?

He dropped his eyes, but she bent forward and her hands followed the outline of her legs and body in a gesture of invitation to admire her. Alwald could not resist – curiosity drove him on. He had wondered so often what Demara would be like stripped of her garments.

Now his eyes followed the elegant hands, observing her neat feet and well-shaped ankles, the perfect curve of her calves, the slightly heavy thighs leading his intent gaze to the swansdown covering her lower belly. With a conspiratorial smile she moved her position so that he could see the full-lipped cleft which was more arousing to him than it had been in his wildest imaginings.

Thoughts of propriety, of his dead father, vanished as he feasted upon the sight of her. With a further motion of her hands she drew his eyes further, inviting him to look up to her breasts with their dark aureoles. She placed her hand beneath one, her fingers digging deep into her own firm flesh, and kneeling astride him she offered it to him as a mother might offer suck to a baby.

Alwald rose to meet the gift, his arm encircling her slim flanks while his face rejoiced in the smooth coolness of her skin – a coolness that was in contrast to the heat that surged through him – and his lips greedily seized upon her. Their touch released an excitement in her. Up to this point she had been artful, intent on arousing him, but now she threw back her head with her eyes closed in elation.

It seemed to Alwald that time stood still while they remained thus, a moon-drenched tableau reflected in black water; then the lady changed her position, placed her hands on his shoulders and with a gleaming smile pressed him back on to the soft sand.

'Demara,' he breathed but again she crossed her lips.

Then her fingers were moving over his garments, unbuttoning his jerkin and the shirt beneath, untying the points of his breeches, until he was able to shrug off his clothing to be as naked as her. There could be no hiding the effect she had upon him, and she looked upon him greedily. He moved to stand up, desperate to take the play further but she pushed him back, roughly this time, and with a practised movement set herself astride him.

Alwald bit back a shout of exultation as he felt her warmth close about him, as her rippling clasp teased him into a plunging response – he had achieved what he had secretly desired ever since Demara's arrival in River Garde.

On and on went the wild contest of the rider and the rode, their bodies lathered, their hearts hammering and their loins locked in a compulsion which only orgasm or death would release. And then it seemed to Alwald that the bubble of his being burst; as his body pumped in climax he felt drained of the force which had swept him along, but this was replaced by a growing contentment and he looked up at the lady's bedewed face with gratitude and love.

Still astride him, she returned his smile with one of mockery. It was a smile that went on and on, pulling her mouth into an expression of cruelty that he had never thought Demara could wear.

It was the disturbing nature of the smile which shocked Alwald back to reality, and gazing up at the body above him in the pitiless moonlight his eyes widened as the lady began to change. Bluish shadows appeared beneath her alabaster skin, her breasts sagged to mere folds and the nails of the fingers resting on his chest lengthened and twisted. The smiling lips shrivelled.

More change followed. Flesh resting upon Alwald lost its fullness and he became aware of the hardness of bone, the skin of her chest shrunk until the ribs protruded and then burst through their parchment covering. The only aspect not altering was the glossy hair flowing over the bony shoulders.

Unable to tear his eyes from the visage above him, Alwald saw that it had lost all resemblance to the Lady Demara. It was the face of a stranger, a face whose bitter lines melted as the skin divided into curling strips and revealed the putrefaction beneath . . .

A scream tore from Alwald's throat as he found his gaze returned by eyeless sockets.

SIX

The River Of Night

The Lady Demara woke from a chaotic dream and looked about her. Much of the clearing was in shadow, only a few carmine embers marked the remains of the fire. She could just make out the blanketed shapes of her companions apart from Alwald. His heavy packman's cloak lay in a tangle near her and for a moment she felt a pang of anxiety, then told herself that he must have gone into the trees to relieve himself.

A movement on the deepest shadow gave weight to this idea – until a figure moved forward and the upper part of his body emerged from shadow.

For a moment Demara thought she was going to faint.

'Grimwald!' she breathed.

He stepped forward again and she saw that he wore his dark green hunting cloak and beneath that a shirt of white wool which showed no sign of his bloody fate.

'Wife.'

The word seemed to come from a distance, yet as she looked at his leonine head, the powerful hands extended to her, that dear affectionate smile with which he used to regard her, she found it hard to believe that he was an apparition.

'Fear not, beloved,' he said. 'I have learned that death is not the gulf we believed.'

217

Filled with wonder that the bond between them had enabled him to return, she could only repeat his name.

'It was a cruel parting,' the faint voice continued. 'But the memory of your love, of your warm body, remained with me. Those nights we spent can never die. Now we can once more know the delight of each other.'

He took another step forward and with a characteristic gesture shrugged off his cloak.

'My lord, we must talk,' she murmured. 'I must tell you . . .'

'Please wife, you know what I want – what I have made the dark journey for.'

Without thought her hand moved to the lace which bordered her chemise, just as it would have when he was her living husband.

'Good.' The word was long drawn and soft. 'Good.'

There was so much to tell him, yet a curious amorous lethargy was sapping her will to speak. She felt the excitement of her body stirring. He was her husband and she was his to use as he wished.

His fingers were on his belt buckle.

'Will you not stay with me?' he whispered as he bent over her. 'Will you not cross the threshold . . .'

A scream rang through the night.

Demara watched while the features of her beloved Grimwald fused into a face unknown to her which in turn became transparent and dissolved.

The wild cry made Krispin sit bolt upright, his hand tightening on Woundflame's grip. He saw the Lady Demara sitting up and because her chemise was open and there was a look of frozen horror on her face, his first thought was that she had been assaulted.

'My lady, was it you who cried out?' he asked. In reply she shook her head from side to side.

'Lord Alwald is gone,' said Emon, climbing to his feet.

'He cannot have gone far on this islet,' Krispin said. 'Bring your axe. Margan, look to your mistress.'

'I am all right,' Demara managed to say. 'It was a nightmare.'

With his sword unsheathed Krispin forced his way through the trees to where the black boat was tied up, then with Emon close behind he started round the islet's strip of shore. A minute later they came to where Alwald lay unconscious, his breath rasping in his throat and his clothing scattered beside him. The sand about him was churned and furrowed and looking at it Emon said, 'Serene Mother! He has had a fit. Sometimes when such a seizure comes upon a man he tears his garments or casts them off.'

'There is more to it than that,' said Krispin. 'Look at those scratches on his breast.'

'Whatever happened, we must get him back to the fire, he is sleet cold. Cover his nakedness and help me carry him to the women.'

There was no sleep for the travellers for the rest of the night. Krispin restored the fire and when Alwald was placed within the range of its warmth Demara rubbed his limbs to restore his circulation.

'We must go leave at first light,' she declared. 'There is evil aboard.'

Alwald's eyes opened and seeing Demara beside him he trembled violently.

'I am punished,' he muttered and then his eyes closed again.

'Poor lad, his mind wanders,' said Emon. 'I agree, my lady, that we should quit this place. There is no luck here.'

'What could have brought this upon him?' Margan asked.

'I believe he may have met with something not fit for

219

mortal eyes,' said Demara with a shudder. 'There is a strange glamour about us tonight.'

Involuntarily they looked over their shoulders and it did seem that there were shadows on the edge of the clearing that were not cast by moonbeam and tree. Krispin heaped more branches upon the fire until its flames leapt like golden dancers; comet-tails of sparks streamed in the night breeze, and no one stirred from within its reassuring compass until it was dimmed by the approach of day.

All felt a lifting of their spirits when Alwald was laid beneath the canopy of the black boat and with a powerful thrust of the oars Krispin swung it into midstream.

'There's a full flask in my pack,' he said and Emon needed no further encouragement. A minute later all except the unconscious Alwald were revived by the spirit and chewing traveller's bread while the craft rode its reflection in a lagoon.

'We are not alone,' the soldier warned suddenly. Coming towards them was the boat they had seen as they entered the Shallows at the close of the previous day.

'Did you stay here through the night?' demanded the gangling fowler incredulously when his craft came alongside. 'Did you not heed my warning? Well, in these troubled days it does not do to question what folk do. I doubt not you had your reasons. Is he dead?' he added as he caught sight of Alwald lying on his cloak.

'He sleeps,' said Demara. 'In the night something came to him.'

'Poor soul,' said the fowler. 'Thank the Mother you are not all as he.'

'What is it about this place?' Demara asked.

'It is haunted. After sunfall no mortal man or maid is safe here. Thank you, sir,' he added as Krispin passed him the flask.

'Yet you come here yourself?'

'I come only because I have mouths to feed. Since the barbarians came to the Wald I dare not enter the marshes where I used to set my snares and nets. In the Shallows there are birds aplenty and I am safe in the daylight hours but not after nightfall.'

'And what is it that you would fear after nightfall?'

'It is an old tale, mistress, but, in a few words, long ago before the land to the south was blighted there was a chapter of necromancers, both men and women, whose magic called for human blood. They used their dark powers to murder for gain and to satisfy their lusts they bewitched the innocent. It is said that the folk of the region walked in terror of the necromancers and appealed to the Mage Ysldon who was a great sorcerer in the high days of gramarye. He took pity on the country folk and wove a great spell upon the necromancers. They tried to use their witchery in reply but the magic of Ysldon was too powerful and he forced them to the Shallows where they remain in eternal exile. As the years passed their bodies crumbled but their spirits remain to haunt the waterways and beguile travellers.'

'In what way?' Demara asked.

'They can flesh themselves into fetches of images stolen from the minds of those who enter the Shallows at night, and so allure them. Sometimes it is to relive bodily pleasures they enjoyed so long ago; sometimes, like vampires, they deceive the living into entering their world in which there is neither life nor death.

'That is the legend, mistress, as I heard it from my grandsire. And those who live by the river fear it is a realm of the weird. Once, when I stayed in the dusk to free a net, I saw shadows forming on the banks about me which I pray I may never see again.'

'Will we be able to pass through the Shallows before the light fails?' asked Krispin.

'If you row hard and do not lose your way,' the fowler

answered. 'But why? Beyond the Shallows lies the Land of Blight and only a man seeking his death would venture there.'

No one answered him.

'I must set my nets,' he said, returning the flask and grasping his oars. 'May the Mother protect you.'

They watched him disappear along a narrow channel and then, with Emon and Krispin rowing strongly and Demara at the tiller, the black boat began its voyage through the maze of islets and sandbanks.

Half way through the morning Alwald opened his eyes and looked about him in bewilderment until Margan held the flask to his lips.

'My dear, do you remember what happened?' Demara asked.

He slowly shook his head. Though he recalled every detail of the succubus, he had no wish to explain how he had come to be naked or describe the final horror which deprived him of his senses. Hours were to pass before he spoke a word.

Each time the boat rounded an islet or entered a new channel its occupants eagerly looked for open water but the monotonous vistas of stunted trees and curtains of reeds remained unaltered, and as the afternoon wore on an unspoken fear began to grow that they would have to spend another night in this shadowed region. Krispin's only consolation was that by allowing the current to lead them they were moving in the right direction.

The fear in each rose as the sun became a crimson globe above the low vegetation, its rays bloodying the ripples which spread from each laboured oar stroke. Because the day had been unduly hot a miasma was already forming and the reek of rotting vegetation and black mud rose to their nostrils. Black flies swarmed round the boat, settling thirstily on exposed skin, crawling through their hair and into their ears.

do not know about phantoms but these Mother-cursed dung-eaters will be my death,' Emon growled. He and Krispin had rowed through the day without rest and now every stroke brought agony to their aching muscles. Yet they kept on in the hope that the next islet would be the last.

'Night will be upon us soon,' said Demara sombrely.

'Yes, I can see that!' Krispin retorted with unusual irritation.

'Watch it, son,' Emon told him.

'And you watch calling me "son"! It might have gone well with your army recruits but I am an independent craftsman!'

'A toymaker!'

'Better to make toys than kill people!'

'You . . . listen, what is it?'

Softly at first came a chorus of unearthly voices raised in a wordless lament, then it grew louder as though the invisible singers were coming closer. The harmony soared and each one in the boat was filled with a bitter-sweet sense of sadness at the passing of things. Tears streamed down Margan's face, Emon clamped his lip between his teeth, and Krispin – reminded of Father Tammas and his village, of his seemingly hopeless love for his sister – felt as though something deep in his being was about to give way.

'Row!' cried Demara. But the two men rested on their oars, their eyes dreamy as the chorale changed to suggest the eternal peace which could be gained by remaining in the Shallows . . .

'It is the spirits – do not listen,' Demara implored.

But the others were too rapt in the siren song to heed her. Looking round in desperation, she saw the cooking pot. Leaning over the side she scooped it full of water and then threw the contents full in Krispin's face. He shook his head like one coming out of an intense daydream.

'Pull the oars or we are lost!' she screamed at him.

Trying to close his ears to the sweet sound sweeping over him, Krispin seized the oar grips and heaved. The boat lunged forward and veered wildly until Demara steadied the tiller, steering towards a channel between two islets. As these fell astern they found themselves sailing out on to a broad stretch of open water. Krispin continued to row with all the strength he could summon into his tired body and the twin ripples spreading from the craft lengthened steadily.

Emon and Margan looked back longingly at the low green outline of the Shallows as the singing faded, and for a long time no word was uttered.

'They wanted to hold us there until night fell,' Demara said at length.

'It was thanks to you that we escaped, lady,' Krispin said as he wearily raised his oars and allowed the increasing current to carry them. 'If you had not sluiced me we would have drifted until starshine.'

'I have a strange feeling that we have unseen protection,' Demara said thoughtfully. 'From whence it comes I do not know.'

'I trust you are right. From what Alwald told of the Land of Blight we shall need it.'

Demara looked about her. The distant banks were so low that there were no features nor landmarks; no trees spread their boughs over the smooth water, no spire pierced the purpling sky.

'Let us stay on the river tonight,' she said. 'Who knows what new danger may be on the shore.'

'It looks the most empty land I could imagine but you are right. We will let the river carry us.'

As night fell, each chewed a small piece of traveller's bread and made themselves as comfortable as possible. Now unable to see either bank, they lost their sense of direction but were content to let their craft drift like an

224

insignificant speck on the vast face of the waters. Krispin alone remained sitting upright on his oarsman's thwart to be ready in case of some unexpected emergency, but before long his head drooped and sleep overtook him.

When he next opened his eyes the moon had risen and the boat was gliding down the path of his reflection. A figure huddled in a cloak was seated on the thwart beside him.

'Margan,' said Krispin. 'Why do you not sleep?'

'I slept for a while but bad dreams would not give me peace,' she answered softly. 'They were the same as I had last night on the island.' She shivered. 'I cannot talk of them, but I feel more at ease beside you. If it had not been for you I would again be a captive of the nomads – if they had not axed off my head for trying to escape. I want you to know that my gratitude will last for the rest of my life. If there is anything I can do . . .'

Her arm encircled his waist and she rested her head on his shoulder. Her hair was soft against his unshaven cheek, its natural perfume was sweet in his nostrils. When her free hand sought his he held it.

'If only there were you and I in this boat sailing to the moon,' she said with a sigh. 'And if only we were not being carried to the Land of Blight!'

A moment later she asked, 'What is the sadness within you? Even when you smile I feel it.'

'I apologize that it shows.'

'No need. I think I am the only one that notices it.'

'And why is that?'

'Because I know what it is to have an aching heart.'

'You lost a sweetheart?'

'I lost my baby. That was after my husband left me – but he was no loss. He was a packman who had come through the High Pass after the snows cleared three years ago. In those days I lived in my parents' cottage in the Lower Wald. My father was a woodcutter who each week

225

took a load of kindling to River Garde. I was their only daughter and in fun they called me Rose Red.'

'Were you not lonely as a child by yourself in the forest?' Krispin asked.

'If you grow up in the forest you are not alone. I had my pets and made friends with wild animals – there was a deer who came to munch the apples I held out for her – and then there was the forest itself. It has a life of its own, a great spirit in which each and every tree has its own part. Where I lived the forest liked me.'

Normally Krispin would have laughed at such an idea in the same way that he had sometimes teased Jennet, but now his outlook was undergoing change. After the last few days he realized there was more possible than he had ever dreamed.

'Each day I would go out into the forest with my little dog Peta to pick certain wild flowers which I dried and made into decorations which my father sold at River Garde. Each evening I would hear my mother call, "Rose Red, Rose Red, come home for your supper." It was a simple life and I was innocent, but now I know how happy I was.

'One day I went home and there was a young packman who had come along the forest path to sell my mother needles. I had met few young men, and none like him. In my eyes he was as handsome as a prince, and I lost my heart to him within the hour.

'How I listened to the stories of his travels beyond the Wald; the crumbling old towns he visited, the villages which had fallen into ruin since The Enchantment, the slave caravans he met on the highways and the abandoned watchtowers from which knights once guarded the countryside as was the custom when Ythan had kings. Of course he told me of other things as well: the beauty of the deserts, the delight of seeing the wild geese crossing the skies at leaf-fall, the warmth of wayside inns and above all the spendour of Danaak which he said was like a jewel in a tarnished crown. He was a great talker.

'He told me that he was weary of the road and the shadows lying across Ythan which made men strangers to each other, and he wished to settle in the Wald where there was still peace and good fellowship.

'When he asked my father for my hand I was overjoyed, and my father and my uncle built us a cottage in a nearby glade and taught my husband a woodman's skills. I was more joyful than I could have believed possible, especially when I found I was with child.'

She sighed.

'In my happiness I did not think that my husband could be less happy than I, and I just laughed when he grumbled about the work being hard or the dullness of the men he drank with in the Merry Forester when he went to the village. Though I did not know it then, if he found the men dull he found wenches who were not – wenches as eager for his talk as I had been. And if he found it tiring to lift logs he found it easy to lift tankards.

'At the end of that summer, when the wild geese flew from the coming winter, the memories of Danaak and the open road became too much for him, and one morning I woke to find that he was not beside me. He left a grey goose's feather on the pillow and that told me all I needed to know.'

She became silent.

'And what happened?' Krispin asked to break her reverie.

'I had my baby but she died of fever. My father took me to River Garde where my Lady Demara had just come as a bride, and as she found that my mind was quick she chose me as her maid. But there, I was talking about you and ended telling my little tale. To turn your question – did you lose a sweetheart?'

'Yes. In a way.'

'In a way?'

'I did not lose her to another suitor but to time. When the nomads destroyed our village the shock of what she saw made her retreat into childhood. Although she is now a woman . . .'

A faint echo of Jennet's words came into his mind: *You have made me into a woman, Krispin.*

'. . . she sees the world as a child sees the world; a cat and a doll are her best friends. She does not know me.'

'And yet you leave her to go on this mad journey?'

'The journey may be mad, and I believe it is, but I play my part in the hope that some advantage for Jennet will come out of it. I have an agreement with Lady Eloira of the Peak. It is she who has given a home to Jennet.'

'Krispin, quests are not for the likes of us – me a maid and you a toymaker. Quests are for the likes of Lord Alwald and Lady Demara, fine folk who are bred to such things. From what my lady says, it is Lord Alwald who undertook the quest – for what I do not understand – and you are just the way-finder.'

Krispin smiled. 'True words.'

'Then hear me for I mean all that I am going to say. There is no hope of us going back to the Wald and ahead lies the Land of Blight. Why not you and I leave the journey now, find a place on the shore where we can build a cottage – as a forester's daughter I am handy and you are trained in woodwork – and live as man and wife. You would not regret me as your woman and I . . . I have felt a warmth for you since our escape from River Garde. You may not love me now, but in the nature of things it would grow if we were alone together. Such a life would be a hundredfold better than seeking the Dark Maid in the Land of Blight.'

For a while Krispin was silent while many thoughts went through his head. Margan withdrew her hand.

228

'If I have offended you with my words I am sorry. Mayhap you think I am wanton by speaking thus, but there is little time and it is not wanton to wish to live as a wife.'

'I would be worse than a fool to feel offence,' said Krispin. 'My silence was because . . .' He could not think of the right words.

'Because of Jennet?'

'Yes.'

'But she is locked in the past. And even if she were to remember you again, what chance do you think there is of you ever seeing her again?'

'Nevertheless, I must go on as I am for her sake.'

For a long time Margan sat without speaking, then with a sigh said, 'I would not have expected less from you but do not forget the love I have for you. I fear the future but while I breathe you will have a loving friend in me. Now, may we sit like this until the dawn. There is comfort in it.'

And so, with their arms around each other, they drifted silently on the great moon-streaked river towards the blighted land.

SEVEN
The City Without
A Name

The next day passed uneventfully. From sunrise to sundown the travellers moved through an empty landscape. No living thing stirred on the flat plain through which the river meandered, not even a bird hung in the cloudless sky. In the black craft Alwald lay without speaking, his eyes avoiding Demara, as though he had been drained both of will and strength. The two young women sat in the shade of the canopy, Demara watching Alwald anxiously and her maid occasionally giving Krispin a half smile of encouragement as he worked the oars.

In the stern Emon sat with his hand on the tiller. Though he constantly offered to take his turn at rowing, Krispin repeated that he was happy to continue for a while longer, pointing out that the river was narrowing again so consequently the current was stronger, and all that was required of him was merely to keep the boat under way enough for the rudder to be effective.

The real reason he did not change over was that the exertion of the voyage through the Shallows had had an ill effect on the soldier. A bloodstain appeared on the bandage covering his head wound and his features had taken on a greyish hue, and although he laboured at cheerfulness, he could not hide the fact that he was in pain.

Towards noon Krispin asked him to steer towards a small clump of bushes which overhung the reeds bordering the east bank. When the boat had been run through the reeds and its bows hauled up on to the bank, its occupants stepped ashore with pleasure at being able to use their limbs again. While they went off in different directions to attend to their wants, Krispin lit a small fire out of branches he had cut from the bushes with his hunting knife and started to cook a stew.

Looking over the lea he was surprised to see how the coarse grass, which had appeared lush after the Shallows, was now brownish and straggling, and even the rushes with their roots in the water were sere though it was winter.

A sickly place, Krispin thought. And a silent place.

The others had noticed this. Even when it seems silence reigns there are little background noises which, while one might not be conscious of them, negate utter silence. Here there was nothing to provide those background noises; no trees to creak, no insects to hum, no birds to call. When a green stick exploded in Krispin's fire everyone was startled not by its unexpectedness but by its sound.

It was with relief that the travellers took their places in the boat, their spirits lowered by the deadness of the surroundings, and through the rest of the day they said little as the prospect of the Land of Blight came nearer. When night fell their apprehension was increased by a mysterious radiance which hung like a pale bluish curtain ahead of them.

'Tomorrow we will be in the Land of Blight,' Alwald murmured from his resting place. 'May the Mother guard us.'

During the night they moored among the withered reeds close to the shore, and when they awoke they knew that Alwald had spoken truly. There was something so desolate in the very air that they did not need the yellowish sky or the blanched plains to tell them that they were entering the drear region. The river continued to narrow and its flow strengthened so that the boat continued at a rate that would not have been possible by rowing. Secretly each feared this speed for hastening them to their fate.

'Look,' cried Margan suddenly, and following her outstretched arm with their eyes her companions beheld the first remains of man's handiwork. It was a rank of six ancient towers bordering the river, crumbling structures of what had once been mauve-hued marble but were now eroded and discoloured by more than time and rain. Each identical shape was like no other tower any of the travellers had seen before, being in the form of an elongated cone with several balustraded platforms encircling it at different heights. Where the cone tapered almost to a point the structure became a globe above which the crowning steeple was in the shape of a spearhead.

What the five found most amazing was that several of the towers were linked by an aerial road, and judging by the debris lying between two of the towers there had been a time where all had been connected.

As the craft was swiftly borne towards the silent edifices, their great height became apparent.

'What manner of men could have built those!' Emon exclaimed.

'And why?' said Krispin.

'They must have been great sorcerers,' Demara added.

'Whoever they were their splendour has gone,' said Krispin as they passed through the great shadows of the towers, and having marvelled at them from a distance, were oppressed by their decay. The extraordinary bridge-like links between them were twisted, great cables hanging down like forest vines, and their surfaces had been so worn away that they were mere impressions of their original shapes.

Then the towers were dwindling behind the black craft, and the travellers were left with the feeling that they had finally entered the Land of Blight.

From time to time, as the force of the river carried them at an increasing pace, distant ruins were glimpsed rising from the arid plain. Although these were mere shattered monuments to a past unimaginable to the travellers, there was a despairing grandeur about the bizarre architecture which held them in awed silence.

Nearer at hand, on the banks that sloped to the swiftly moving water, vegetation changed from wizen grass straggling over the dun plain to luxuriant creeper. Again it was something outside the travellers' experience; circular leaves of deep magenta sprouted from black rope-like vines locked in savage contest for space and light.

'Look, something stirs,' Margan exclaimed.

Since they had left the Shallows one of the most unnerving things about the landscape was a complete absence of movement in it, and now they stared at the tangled banks with alarm.

Suddenly, through the leaves, a serpentine stalk reared high and swayed as though it possessed an animal power of movement. The head was melon-sized and appeared to be as black as the vine supporting it, and as it turned they saw it open and a shower of winged seeds spin away from it.

At that moment there was a threshing in the tangled vegetation below and another head appeared at the end of sinuous creeper, a head which differed from the first in that it had a gash which gave the impression of a mouth set in an otherwise empty face. It swung towards the heavy seed pod and attacked it with the saw-like teeth lining its orifice. Sap spurted from the victim which swayed away on its stalk in a desperate effort to elude the predator.

233

'Serene Mother! The plants devour each other in this place!' cried Emon.

The current bore the boat on so swiftly the travellers did not see the outcome of the encounter, but from then on they made sure that they remained a good distance from the creeper-smothered shore. As they sped further into the Land of Blight they saw that vines had swarmed over wrecked towers so that their original shapes were blurred by masses of livid foliage.

Early in the afternoon a strange grouping of ruins appeared ahead. Even from a distance it was obvious that they were much larger than those seen so far, but what was more startling was their suggestion of human shapes – a tableau of giants reared against the pallid sky. As the distance lessened it became apparent that they were not just colossal effigies but buildings. Here were the remains of a city whose long-dead architects had been obsessed by the idea of sculpting their edifices into titanic works of art.

As Krispin stared at them he experienced the same sense of recognition which had led to the discovery of the black boat. He felt that ideas were forming just beyond the edge of his consciousness, and he realized that here was the second of the landmarks that the cunning of Lady Eloira had hidden in his memory.

As the boat continued its rapid course and the outline of the dead city became clearer so the feeling of familiarity increased. He could picture wide wreckage-strewn avenues between statuesque towers as vividly as if he had walked along them, and he felt a chill of apprehension as he suddenly had the knowledge that here he must leave the craft to fulfil another step in the quest – and, glancing to where Alwald lay supine, he knew that it would have to be undertaken alone.

For an hour the travellers watched the city grow in their vision until it dwarfed their previous experience of man-built structures. Even the widely travelled Emon, whose face showed pain when he squinted at them, had to admit that they out-soared the spires of Danaak.

As mounds of creeper-swathed rubble became more and more frequent on its banks the river widened and, after the travellers sped through a sagging arch which in bygone times had been a bridge, they found themselves entering a lake reflecting the flawed façades of once stately buildings.

'To the right – head for the second quay which still has a mooring ring,' Krispin called to Emon at the tiller. Demara and Margan exchanged glances of surprise at the way he seemed to be acquainted with a locale he had never visited before.

Obediently the craft swung towards the bank which was lined with flights of broken steps running down to the water and stone wharfs where once river merchants had tied up their laden barges. As Krispin had said, the second quay they approached did have a ring of verdigrised bronze hanging from a dragon's jaws, and the painter was tied fast to this.

'Why do we tarry here?' Demara asked anxiously.

'The mission requires something to be done in this place,' Krispin replied as he buckled on his sword belt.

'You are not going to venture among the ruins?'

'It is what is required.'

'You cannot expect Alwald . . . his strength has not yet returned.'

'I shall go alone.'

'What is it that you must do?'

'That is hazy in my mind – I must find something. At this moment all I can visualize is the route I must follow. The rest will become clear at the right moment. You will remain here in the boat and I should be back within a couple of hours from what I sense of the distance I must travel. But if I do not return by the time the sun sinks between those two towers yonder you must swear to cast off.'

'But, Krispin . . .' began Margan.

'I swear,' said Demara. 'I must swear.'

'Such talk is all very well,' said Emon, 'but I am a soldier and soldiers do not remain behind.'

Krispin looked at his blanched face, the bandage once more showing signs of blood, the large hands feeling awkwardly for the nomad axe, and he realized that Emon could no longer see clearly.

'In this case a soldier is needed to guard the ladies and Alwald who since his father's death is now your master.'

With an expression of relief Emon permitted himself to be persuaded.

'You cannot be allowed to go alone,' said Margan with a vehemence not usual in ladies' maids. 'Who can tell what lurks in this dismal place.'

'Since we entered the Land of Blight the only living thing we have seen is the red vines,' Krispin said with a reassuring smile. 'It is a dead land and therefore holds no threat.'

On an impulse he opened the locker beneath the stern thwart and took out a coil of fine rope and a pouch containing a flint and steel and a candle – objects provided by the same mysterious agency which had provided the boat. Then, anxious for no more words, he climbed several steps up to the quay where he gave his companions a brief wave and strode briskly towards an avenue leading from the waterfront into the heart of the ruins.

The marble paving beneath his feet was cracked and often he had to climb over drifts of broken bricks, yet as he progressed along the avenue he had no doubt about the direction he had to take, and after a few minutes he entered a large colonnaded square in which several disfigured statues still posed on tilting plinths. It was hard to make out what they represented. Certainly they bore no human likeness and Krispin, with a shudder of distaste, concluded that they were the representations from a legendary bestiary. There was something so sinister about their grotesque shapes and watchful eyes that he was glad to hurry past them and turn into a street curving between banks of fallen masonry. As he did so something made him cast a backward glance and for a second he thought he spied a slight movement in the shadow of the colonnade on the far side of the square. It must have been a trick of the light, he decided, as all remained still.

Here and there patches of magenta creeper cascaded over broken walls and Krispin, his sword now in his hand, kept well clear of their huge circular leaves. Although nothing had happened to alarm him, he was filled with a growing uneasiness. This, he told himself, was the natural effect of his surroundings. Having lived most of his life in a village, the enormity of the ruins dwarfed his body and oppressed his spirit. Added to this was the terrible atmosphere of desolation, of ancient death and nightmare destruction, which hung like a miasma beneath the dirty sky.

Despite his misgivings he hurried on his unknown errand, recognizing a turning here, a new path through an archway there, until he came to a vast plaza much of which was covered with creeper whose stalks waved higher than his head. But it was the towering edifice in the centre which stopped him in his tracks. Bizarre even by the standards of the ruined city, it appeared to be constructed of a dull metallic material formed into a soaring conglomeration of cone-capped turrets, overhanging terraces, fantastically formed flying buttresses and steep roofs which flowed into gargoyle shapes at their corners. Surmounting it was a structure whose design put Krispin in mind of a warrior's helmet complete with visor.

At its base a broad flight of steps ascended to an entrance framed by a lancet archway which was lit by a yellow radiance from within. Even in the sickly daylight the strength of this illumination was such that it cast a long shadow behind Krispin. This, he knew, was his destination.

He stood regarding the tower until he was startled by a slight sound – the first sound, apart from the crunch of his own footfalls, since he had left the black boat. It was a soft pattering sound, the sound of naked feet on stone.

Krispin whirled round with Woundflame raised and saw that a white, vaguely man-shaped creature was slinking up behind him. It walked upright with a shambling gait, the pallid skin of its gaunt body thinly covered with long white hairs. Its hands hung low at its sides with elongated fingers tipped with claws; its bald head was wrinkled, its nostrils mere holes above which albino eyes were round and staring. Without any form of clothing, it was obvious that it was a male.

'Stay!' shouted Krispin.

It halted and made an unpleasant snuffling sound, but more unpleasant was its fetid smell which reached Krispin. He could not tell whether he was facing an unknown animal – he had heard tales of furry men-like creatures living in the branches of forests in hot climes – or some perverted being which had degenerated from human kind.

When his initial alarm faded he tried speaking kindly to it but it just snuffled and urinated with no more concern than a beast of the field. This decided Krispin that it was merely an animal which must have had its lair in the ruins, and still keeping a tight hold of his sword he turned and started across the plaza towards the light-filled archway.

Immediately the white creature broke into a shambling run, and circling Krispin it halted some distance in front of him. Waving its hand from side to side it signalled that he must not go forward. Krispin could not decide whether it was a threat or merely a friendly warning, but regardless of this he knew that something –

238

as yet he knew not what – was waiting for him within the tower.

Gesturing the creature to one side with Woundflame, he started forward again. The creature threw back its head and uttered a shrill cry which could have been a challenge or an expression of anguish, but as Krispin continued it moved out of the way. When he had gone past it picked up a large piece of broken stone and flung it with such accuracy that it struck Krispin's neck. He stumbled and gasped in pain, and when he turned he saw the creature reaching for another stone with its taloned hand.

With a shout of anger Krispin charged at the creature with Woundflame raised with the idea of frightening it off. The sight of the sword, which now shone silver, had the desired effect. It backed away waving its arms wildly until it tripped backwards into a bank of creeper. Its snuffling changed to a shriek as it vanished from sight under the huge leaves. Krispin watched in horror as the vines writhed into violent life and black pods rose on the end of swaying stalks to swoop towards the spot.

He held the grip of his sword in both hands and began to slash at the vines in the hope of freeing their victim. Reddish sap spurted after every blow, lengths of severed creeper lashed like beheaded serpents and leaves cowered from singing blade to give him a path. A pod rose up and swung at him with its mouth agape but with a quick stroke he sliced through its creeper and then, as it rolled towards his feet, he stamped it to a bloody pulp.

By the time that Krispin had cut his way to the white creature it was too late, the pods having partly devoured it. And although dead – or so he hoped – the pink eyes glared at him in reproach.

Slashing furiously, Krispin returned along his path which was already closing as more vines slithered across it. When free of the hungry foliage he once more set off

239

across the plaza and this time he reached the broad flight of steps without mishap.

When Krispin cautiously stepped through the archway into a huge pillared hall he could not see the source of the lurid light which bathed it, rather it seemed that the very air about him was glowing. Aware that he was now very close to the object that he had to obtain, he walked slowly down the centre of the hall keeping a wary eye on the columns of chalcedony which flanked it on either side.

Since his tragic encounter with the white creature his notion that nothing living could have survived in such a deserted place had been shattered, and the all-pervading light suggested that while the city might have been crumbling for centuries some remnant of its magic remained in this helmeted edifice.

Instructions buried in his memory urged him forward until he passed out of the hall, which he realized was merely an antechamber, into a gallery which ran round the walls of an enormous domed arena. Leaning over its balustrade he looked down and saw that in the centre of the floor far below was a dais of black marble supporting an ornate throne of the same material on which was seated a figure double the size of a normal man. He appeared to be wearing a suit of bulky armour crafted from silvery metal and his proudly held head was hidden by a helm similar in design to the structure surmounting the tower.

In one gauntleted hand the image held a black rod, the tip of which glowed with dazzling brightness, and it was from this that the light illuminating the tower's interior appeared to flow. For a long time Krispin gazed in wonder at the magnificent enthroned figure and then took in other details of the scene. There appeared to be a scattering of objects at the feet of the statue which were hard to make out from such a distance and, what he found disconcerting, no staircase leading down from the gallery to the lower floor nor any sign of an entrance cut in its green-stone walls.

Somewhere down there was the article he had come so far to find but it appeared that his only possible way of reaching the floor was by the rope which a subconscious command had reminded him to remove from the locker of the black boat. Now he was reassured by the foresight with which he had been prepared for his adventure by the Lady Eloira while she entranced him with her swinging pendant.

Sheathing Woundflame, whose blade had returned to its dull patina, he took the coil of rope from his shoulder and knotted one end round a baluster. After tugging the rope to test the hitch, he threw it over the coping and then carefully lowered himself to the floor below.

EIGHT
The Eidolon

When he looked round the circular space into which he had entered, Krispin realized that the area was much greater than he had imagined and the eidolon in the centre, foreshortened by the perspective from the gallery, now towered impressively on his tall throne. The light which issued from the tip of his black wand illuminated the reddish marble floor and its rune-like figures of inlaid porphyry. Krispin imagined that if only they could be deciphered that would have great significance, but centuries must have passed since there had been anyone with the ability to read them.

The young man felt a strange reluctance to seek the mysterious object which was the next step in his task. The lead should have been taken by Alwald who was of noble birth and trained in the use of weapons – he, Krispin, was merely the way-finder! He had begun to wonder if Alwald would ever recover from the mysterious languor which kept him weak and silent.

But it was no good dawdling there, he told himself. He had to be back at the black boat before the sun neared the horizon.

He set out at an angle so as to approach the front of the helmeted figure, then he stopped dead as he realized that the scattered objects he had noticed from above were human bones. They were so displaced that no skeletons remained and Krispin might not have recognized their origin had it not been for a number of skulls and weapons lying amongst them. The weapons consisted of old-fashioned swords with blades in varying stages of corrosion, a mace and a halberd whose wooden haft had long ago turned to dust.

The fact that the swords were not of the same era told Krispin that the bones were not from a party of men who had perished together but were those of victims who had died singly down the ages. It was impossible to tell how they had met their fate though such was the dislocation of the bones that they could have been torn apart.

The question uppermost in Krispin's mind was had they been killed while searching for the same object that he sought? What other reason could they have had for daring to enter this ominous region? He looked about him anxiously, hand on Woundflame's hilt.

He sought to calm himself with the thought that whatever had once guarded the eidolon must have died a very great number of years ago. Apart from the monstrous creepers and possibly a few white creatures similar to the one he had encountered on the plaza, nothing else appeared to have survived in the Land of Blight. Living beings required nourishment and the country was too barren for crops and no fish swam in the black water of the river.

'No toy ever carved itself!' he muttered aloud and felt comfort in the old village proverb. Well aware of the passing of precious time he took a deep breath and continued towards the eidolon, his feet raising small clouds of bone dust as he neared it.

Krispin halted in front of the dais which rose to the height of his shoulder with the metal-shod feet of the eidolon at eye-level. He had expected to find something on its smooth surface – what, he was not yet sure, but the directions which formed in his mind told him that he was

243

almost within touching distance of what he sought. Looking up at the massive figure in its curiously bulbous armour he saw that a large casket rested on its knees, the fingers of its left hand curled round one corner to hold it in place.

Hopeful that he was about to complete his assignment and that within a few minutes he would be on his way back to his companions, he flexed his muscles and with some difficulty hauled himself up on to the dais. Even standing upright in front of the eidolon he was able to see in the cold light which radiated from the wand the extraordinary workmanship that had gone into the making of the armour and the curious characters which had been etched into it. Looking up at the helmet above him he saw that, behind the narrow bars of the visor, there was a crystalline substance, and behind that a hint, but only a hint, of closed eyes. Could it be that the armour was not part of a statue at all but the sarcophagus of someone or something which long ago the dwellers of the nameless city had honoured as a deity?

Shrugging speculation aside, Krispin peered into the box which had been cast from the same metallic substance as the armour. It was fully illuminated by the wand light, and he saw that it contained a dazzling assortment of pebble-sized jewels and curiously shaped crystals. These crystals shone with the light of rainbows while green, blue and violet fire flashed from the gemstones, throwing multi-coloured patterns across his eager face. For an insane moment he wanted to plunge his hand into the casket, aware that if he could take even one back to Ythan he and Jennet would never have to want for anything for the rest of their lives.

Then it seemed that a voice spoke from his memory.

'*The Esav!*'

Sanity returned. The image of a heart appeared before his inward eye.

'*The Esav!*'

His eyes roved the contents of the casket and lighted on a heart-shaped crystal. As he studied it he realized it was the most beautiful of all the stones. It did not hold a rainbow like a prism or sparkle with emerald light, but was filled with a milky iridescence – a subtle sheen of mingling colours constantly changing as though some form of life was locked within its polished surface.

'*The Esav!*'

Trembling, Krispin reached down and closed his fingers round the prize. He was surprised how flat the crystal was, it could have been cut from a piece of thick glass; and how cold it was, its heart-shape could have been formed of ice. As he withdrew it he was aware of a psychic shift in the atmosphere – something terrible and *tremendous* had happened beyond the range of his senses.

Pulling open his shirt with his left hand he placed the Esav in a soft leather pouch such as was worn on a neck thong by Wald folk as a purse. Then he leapt down from the dais, missed his footing and sprawled among the bones of forgotten adventurers.

As he raised himself painfully into a sitting position he was conscious of something sliding across his throat; something damp and as fine as a thread – and invisible. The fact that whatever it was could not be seen had the effect of panicking him. He clawed his fingers down his neck in order to find it and tear it away, and as he did so another moist filament caught his wrist and tightened upon it like a hunter's snare. Other threads moved across his face causing him to jerk his head like someone in the throes of a fit, then a thicker rope-like ligament slid across his chest with the motion of an eel.

The sensation of these unseen bonds tightening on him filled Krispin with such terror that for a moment he lost the ability to think clearly. His reaction was to run but as he struggled to his feet he had the feeling of more tendrils twining about him and he knew that flight would be impossible. It was an upsurge of this terror which shocked him into action as something moist and thin and *living* probed between his lips.

With a cry of disgust his free arm wrenched Wound-flame from its sheath. The moonstone on its pommel glowed, its blade was so bright it glittered, and Krispin was reassured to feel the shock of its power flow through his hand to his wrist. Turning his body this way and that, he slashed in what he thought was the direction of the strongest of the strands holding him.

A second later the threads released their hold and he felt the heaviest uncoil from his chest. One of his strokes had found it and as it fell to the floor it became visible, a squirming pinkish tube with an orifice reminiscent of a mouth at one end. White ichor flowed from the opposite end where the sword had severed it from an invisible tentacle.

Heart pounding with fear and exertion, Krispin started across the floor with Woundflame reflecting the light like a long shard of mirror except where a smear of pale fluid stained it – a stain that was to remain as though etched by acid.

Then something brushed across Krispin's face. A heavy but still invisible tentacle fell upon his left shoulder and squirmed round his arm with the same pulsing motion of a snake. Whatever the unseen thing was, it had moved quickly to block his escape. Instead of slashing wildly, he lunged the sword at where he thought the body of his attacker would be.

A shock ran through his hand as the point made contact, there was a sound such as red hot iron makes when tempered, and for a moment the enemy became visible.

It was of man height, possessed of two lower limbs and was vaguely man shaped but there all human semblance ended. Krispin was aware of a head surrounded with threshing fibrilla, of gelatinous spheres peering through this travesty of hair, of slime glistening on skin so transparent it revealed nightmare viscera beneath, and limbs with serpentine flexibility – it was one of these that clasped his shoulder.

The ultimate horror was the mass of tentacle-like tubes which issued from the belly area, a pinkish mass of horror writhing towards Krispin with orifices gaping and suckers extended. Some were little more than threads, others had the length and strength of stockwhips.

The point of the sword was pressed against the chest and as Krispin prepared to thrust it into the pulsating organs the thing moved back with unexpected speed on spongy foot pads – and immediately became invisible.

Freed once more, Krispin backed away, sweeping the area round him with his sword and confident that Woundflame's magic would materialize his adversary if the blade touched it again. He began to work his way towards the wall in the hope of being able to clamber up the rope. Already his arm was paining with the effort of keeping his sword whistling in continuous motion, and a growing fear was that he might exhaust himself before the next attack.

When that attack came it was completely unexpected. He felt a sudden weight land on his shoulders and what seemed like a squirming net envelop him. In order to avoid the scything blade, the unseen guardian had leapt high above its arc.

Krispin was borne to the floor by the weight and bulk of his assailant and as he struggled on his knees he felt like a fly being cocooned by an industrious spider. But there was hope as long as his hand retained Woundflame. As the threads tightened about him it was impossible to wield it in the usual way so he slid his hand down the blade until there was only the length of a dagger blade to its point, and then he used it like a dagger, stabbing upwards again and again.

The tentacle net slackened.

Ichor soaked his shirt.

Filaments sliding away from his face began to take on substance.

He threw himself forward, away from the squirming behind him, and regained his feet. Turning he saw that visibility had returned to his enemy.

It was lying prone, its appendages waving with frantic helplessness, glutinous eyes wandering and fluid pulsing from its wounds. Because of the transparency of the membrane covering the body Krispin saw its inward disintegration; sacs burst, gut ruptured, nameless organs convulsed. Then the frenzy of outraged tissue slowed, colour changes took place, pumps of muscle ceased their palpitation, bladders deflated, fleshy tendrils uncoiled, bowels no longer rippled.

The guardian – no longer unseen – was dead.

As Krispin continued to regard it with horrified fascination it began to decompose, within seconds its flesh became putrescent, within a minute the whole mass was sinking into a pool of its own liquescence.

Holding his hand to his mouth, Krispin sought to escape the mephitic vapour. He reached the curving wall and leaned against it while his breath returned and he conquered his nausea. Woundflame was losing its brightness and this reassured him that he was temporarily safe.

'Now to get out of here and back to the boat,' he muttered aloud. 'Where's the rope?'

It was hard to get his bearings. The greenstone wall was featureless, the vast floor empty and in the shadowless light the rope would be impossible to see unless he was close to it. He tried to work out its position by remembering the angle at which he had originally approached the eidolon, but this proved too difficult. Placing a wooden comb, which he had carved himself in happier days, on the floor as a marker, he set off round the wall.

When he reached the comb again without having found the rope he guessed that it must have been silently pulled up out of his reach.

Krispin tried to control both a rising panic and anger at his fate. There was a cruel irony in having come so far, obtaining the Esav and surviving the attack of the unseen guardian only to find himself trapped with no visible way of returning to the outside world.

He began a second walk round the circular wall, examining it closely for a hidden exit but always he found the marble to be smooth and intact. In desperation he went round a third time, and this desperation was increased by the knowledge that outside the sun must be sinking. Soon it would be time for his companions to follow his instructions and cast off. Exhausted, he sank down with his back against the wall where he had left his comb and held Woundflame across his knees.

The touch of something on his neck, something sliding across it in a horribly familiar way, made him leap to his feet with his sword whirling about him. But it was not the tentacle of an unseen guardian – it was the end of the rope.

For a moment he gazed at its dancing end, thinking that it had been there all the time and what a fool he was not to have noticed it before.

'Krispin!'

The whispered intensity of his name made him look up.

He saw Margan leaning over the parapet, her long black tresses falling forward and her finger to her lips.

He needed no further encouragement, but, tugging the rope to make sure it was still tied fast, he began to heave himself upward. Rope climbing had been one of the sports that the elders of Toyheim, aware that their apprentices needed their muscles stretched after long hours bending over workbenches, encouraged and rewarded at village galas. Krispin's skill at this exercise now stood him in good stead though his progress was halting due to exhaustion after his contest with the invisible adversary. His arms felt as though they were about to leave their sockets, he gasped for air and several times it felt as though his fingers were about to rebel and release their grip.

'Hurry, it may be coming back,' Margan hissed from above.

Too short of breath to make the bitter retort which came into his mind, he continued the slow haul until he was able to get one arm round a baluster and rest a moment before making the final effort. Margan leaned over the coping and lent him all her strength.

'Why . . . did you come?' he asked breathlessly when he stood on trembling legs beside her. She looked at him almost pityingly for asking such a stupid question.

'The sun is low,' she said. 'Soon it will be dark and we must be away from the ruins by then.'

'Just give me a few moments.'

Margan looked apprehensively over her shoulder.

'We cannot linger. It . . .'

'It?'

'The horrid white thing.'

'A creature with hair all over it.'

She nodded. 'When I came into the great hall I saw it. It was pulling up your rope. Then it turned and came away.'

'It did not see you?'

'I kept moving round a pillar as it went past. When it had gone I came and lowered the rope again. I fear that it may come back, perhaps with others like it.'

'But how did you know I would be here?'

'I watched the way you took from the quay, and then when you did not return I set off in that direction. There

250

were your footprints in the dust to guide me, and when I saw this place looming up I guessed that this was where you had been heading.'

'And the others did not stop you?'

'They had no chance. My Lord Alwald is in another world and Emon is half blind. Please let us go now. I feel the evil of this place in my bones.'

Unsheathing Woundflame, Krispin started towards the colonnaded hall as eager as she to be under open sky again. In a few steps they reached the high archway at the end of the hall, then halted. Half way down the colonnade their way was barred by scores of white creatures.

'He did go to get others,' Margan murmured.

Krispin saw that they were holding fragments of rubble in their hands and there was no doubt in his mind that their intention was to stone them. He and Margan backed out of range and a few moments later they were back to the parapet. The creatures remained still, obviously awed by the light now flashing from Woundflame's blade.

'Forward is the only way,' said Krispin. 'Keep close behind me.' But even as he spoke he knew that they would go down under the first volley of stones – the penalty for entering this place which to the creatures was obviously hallowed. He remembered the first one he had seen gesturing him to stay away from the fantastical structure with its glowing entrance.

'They must worship that statue,' he muttered. He glanced down at the great helmeted figure on his throne, the desecrated jewel box on his lap, the light wand in his gauntleted hand.

'Margan, take Woundflame and stay here,' he said urgently. 'I shall be back in a moment.'

Without question, the girl took the sword and held it before her. The line of white creatures edged forward a shambling step, and Krispin swung himself over the parapet and down the rope.

Book Three

. . . and I have heard report of a mighty river that floweth through a dolorous waste for many days' march; and there no man dwelleth nor beast, but there stand ruins of a bygone time and diverse perils thereof. When the aforesaid river floweth through mountains it cometh unto a vale where all is peace, and everything fayre to regard, the fruits thereof good for eating; and there is no pestilence. And those fortunates who dwell in the vale venture not beyond the mountains, for they are content; and hardy travellers who mayhap gain this vale also stay for they have found the domain of their souls' content. Some would say there is no such vale and report thereof but a parable to tell of reward after travail, but though I do not know what it be clept, I believe it true.

– *The Travels of Tobias Auber*

ONE
Land Of The Scarlet Moon

Krispin raced across the floor to the dais, hauled himself up on to it as he had done before, and reached for the wand held in the metal-gloved hand of the eidolon. Unable to grasp it from this position, he clambered on to the knees of the statue and in doing so upset the box containing the gems and crystals. Like a rainbow-faceted cascade they spilled to the dais and then rolled on the floor below.

Hardly aware of what he had done, Krispin reached out and took the wand from the fingers which had held it for eons. Although enough light to illuminate the whole interior of the structure flowed from the tip there was no heat, and though the wand waved wildly as he ran back to the dangling rope the light it emitted did not cast dancing shadows.

At the wall Krispin placed the wand between his teeth and holding it thus he climbed to the parapet. As he pulled himself over the coping he saw Margan standing bravely with Woundflame held in front of her, more like a ritualistic talisman to ward off evil than a weapon. The creatures were advancing cautiously and some had their arms raised in readiness to stone her.

At the appearance of Krispin with the light wand an

inarticulate cry rose from the pallid forms – half fear, half fury – and the front rank jostled those behind.

'Now, Margan,' Krispin said. He took Woundflame from her and with the sword held high in his right hand and the wand held high in his left, he advanced into the hall of pillars with the girl following close behind. The white creatures fell back with each step he took, snuffling with dismay, colliding with each other, and fighting to get out of the path of this being who possessed the power to take the light from their god. The fact that the throned figure did not rise and strike him down only confirmed their dim conception of the stranger's power.

Before the couple were half way along the hall the creatures had turned and pelted down the wide steps leading to the plaza.

When he emerged into the leaden daylight it seemed to Krispin that hours had passed since he had entered the building in search of the Esav. He was surprised to see that although the sun was descending she still had the power to diminish the wand light to a mere glow just as the light of a candle is diminished when carried into a chamber lit by oil lamps. Below him the vast square was dotted with white figures running hither and thither in fearful confusion or leaping up and down with bewildered anger.

Then, as the two humans descended the steps, they were conscious of a menacing sound, a *growling* which seemed to come from the depths of the earth. And on reaching the broken paving of the plaza they felt it tremble as though some underworld colossus was stirring into hostile life. Its effect was to clear the plaza of the creatures.

'What can it be?' Margan asked as they hurried between banks of red-leafed creepers.

'Whatever it is, something tells me we should get back to the boat . . .'

His sentence was drowned as a ruin to their right collapsed into a swirling cloud of mortar dust. The earth was now shuddering and the growling had changed to subterranean thunder.

'Look!' shouted Margan as the masonry of other ruins avalanched into the streets leading from the plaza. Krispin turned and saw that the tower from which they had just emerged was commencing to rock and the strange cone-like structure surmounting it was moving in a way that made him think of a giant nodding his helmeted head.

'It is going to fall!'

Seizing Margan's hand he pulled her past threshing vegetation and through drifts of choking dust. Several times they were flung to the ground as extra-violent tremors surged through it. Once in the avenues which lay between the plaza and the river, their danger increased tenfold as ancient walls subsided and buildings collapsed. Just as they reached the quay a wild wind tore at their garments and the air was filled with such rending and rumbling that it seemed the whole nameless city was being destroyed.

Holding on to each other they turned and, now that a number of buildings were no longer there to block the view, they saw the last throes of the central tower. It swayed like a knight mortally wounded, its fantastical superstructure – the replica of the eidolon's helmet – tilted more and more forward just as the head of a dying warrior would droop towards his chest, and then it crashed out of sight to the plaza below. A black cloud soared like an evil spirit released from an enchanter's flask and the shock crazed the stone quay with a web of cracks.

As the sounds of titanic destruction abated, Krispin was brought back to his senses by Demara calling his name.

'Krispin! In the name of the Mother, we must get away!'

259

With Margan beside him, he ran to where the black boat was bobbing on waves now spreading across the lake. He helped the girl aboard, untied the painter from the mooring ring in the dragon's mouth and leapt into the stern. It was a work of moments to fit the oars between the thole pins and begin rowing with his last reserve of strength. Demara took the tiller and they headed out into the lake and then towards the far point where it narrowed to a river again.

No one spoke, but they kept turning their eyes to the shore where powdered brick still rose like smoke and every so often a tower would slide into rubble. The sun was low now and her beams struggling through the dust-filled air caused an inferno of a sunset to hang over the ruins.

It was with relief that they felt the tug of the current when they entered the river, and as it increased in speed, the nameless city shrank behind them. Krispin ceased rowing to wrap the light wand in his cloak and place it in the locker. The others had been looking with mounting curiosity at its bright tip. It did not emit the light that it had when it was held in the eidolon's fingers and Krispin decided that its power was waning after the downfall of the mysterious tower which housed it.

'Is that what you sought?' Demara asked.

'No, it is something that I stole.'

'Without it we would not be here,' said Margan and she launched into an account of their adventures which brought a look of interest even to Alwald's waxen face.

'But did you find that which you set out for?' he asked Krispin when the girl ran out of words.

'It was as the Lady Eloira said it would be,' he said. 'At each stage of the search an instruction came into my mind so that I knew where to go and what to do. Even when I looked into the casket of jewels I recognized the Esav because it was shaped like a heart.'

260

'The Esav?' said Demara.

'That, lady, seems to be the name of the crystal I – we were entrusted to find.'

'May I see?'

Krispin felt inside his shirt and removed the Esav, holding it up for them to see.

'It is beautiful – beyond price,' Demara cried.

'Its pale colours mingle like smoke,' Margan added. 'I think there must be a trace of every colour in the world trapped inside it.'

'What do you do with it now, son?' asked Emon, who saw the brightness of the Esav through the haze of his approaching blindness. 'In Danaak a pretty like that would fetch a stack of crowns in the Street of Gem Merchants.'

'At this moment I do not know,' Krispin replied, 'but I will know when the time comes.'

He carefully replaced it and resumed rowing.

'Have you any idea what befalls us next?' Demara asked with a note of anxiety in her voice.

'I am sorry, lady, but all I know is that we go with the river. What lies ahead is as a sealed scroll to me.'

His words, coupled with the thickening dusk about them, cast a sobering spell on the party. The river had returned to its old appearance, oil smooth and black. No fish somersaulted out of its cold depths, no birds waded among the sere reeds fringing its margin and no animal sought a resting place for the oncoming night on the arid plain stretching to the world's edge.

When it became too dark for them to see to navigate, Demara turned the tiller and ran the bow of the boat into a bank of reeds to await the moonrise.

'I shall make a light and then we can eat,' said Krispin.

'Why not use the light from the wand,' said Margan.

'That I would rather not,' said Krispin. 'There is

something I fear about it. It was the taking of the wand from the god that brought down the tower.' He shivered. 'I am of a mind to cast it into the river and be free of it.'

'That you might regret later,' murmured Alwald. 'Now it is away from its ancient master it is probably no more dangerous than the Esav.'

'Anyway, I shall light my candle,' Krispin said.

When he had done so he opened his pack and brought out the last of the traveller's bread which he broke into pieces.

'There is a fiven each,' he said as he pased them to his companions.

There was no need to tell them that the food which had been carried in the packs had only been intended for the sustenance of two, and now they had reached the end of their supply. Each ate according to his or her nature and mood. Margan swallowed hers crumb by crumb, Demara ate as she would have done at the supper board of River Garde, Emon chewed methodically, Alwald ate fast and then regretted it, and Krispin held his in his mouth until it dissolved to pap. All wondered when they would eat again, indeed *if* they would eat again, and, suddenly aware of the possible value of tallow, Krispin puffed out his candle.

'Let us rest until the moon dawn,' he said. 'I shall keep watch.'

They settled as comfortably as they could, but it was only Alwald who was visited by sleep; the others said nothing but watched mysterious lights flicker low over the horizon.

'An evil place,' muttered Emon. 'I have heard old minstrels sing of the dole of this land.'

It became colder, and soon a miasma hung over the surface of the river, and such was its property that when the moon did rise the vapour transformed the pearl of his

262

face into that of scarlet. This was reflected in arabesques of blood on the water.

Only when the great red disc climbed up among the stars did it resume its normal appearance and cast enough light for the voyage to be recommenced. As Demara sat shivering with her hand on the tiller she looked up and saw the Griffin blazing high in the sky ahead of her. It calmed her fears, a glittering reminder of old days and old joys that nothing could ever steal from her. No matter what lay ahead, she had her memories and they were hers forever. When the Dark Maid came, worldly things were lost, but memory was the one thing that her spirit could retain.

'Thank you,' she whispered to the constellation.

When the moon sank they rested again until a new day dawned over the blighted land, and then once more they were on their way. As before, Krispin only needed to row enough to give the craft steerage, and so they were carried along in an almost dreamlike state. Occasionally they lifted their heads to stare at ancient remains.

Once they passed a number of conical towers linked by aerial roads such as they had seen when they approached the nameless city; another time they passed through the shadow of a grand mansion which had been built on the riverbank. Turrets clustered each corner of its high pitched roof and tiers of balconies overhung the water.

In his imagination Krispin saw it as he thought it must have been in the days when the land was fair. The shawls of beautiful women hung over the balustrades of the balconies, graceful pleasure craft with high curved prows bobbed at its landing stages of pink and white marble, and stringed music floated on the air which captured the fragrance of the gardens. He blinked and once again it was a crumbling shell, its casements replaced by vacant gaps in its stained walls while clusters of creeper hung down in place of the ladies' shawls.

For a while Krispin wondered if he had actually had a glimpse from another time. After what he had experienced since he set foot on the shining path he had come to believe anything was possible, and what was Time anyway? It was like the river on which their boat was travelling, the past was the river behind them and the future the river ahead, yet the water was continuous – the past river just as real as the future – and it was only the boat of the present which marked the division between the two. Supposing that one could escape the confines of the boat . . .

For a moment it seemed that he was on the brink of solving a riddle which had teased him since he was a little boy, but before it became clear his thoughts rebelliously returned to food. Hunger had made him tighten his belt and now, like the others, he visualized favourite dishes and recalled memorable meals with an almost erotic attention to detail.

The Name Day feast that Jennet had prepared for them almost a year ago!

Because of the mystery surrounding their origins no one knew when they had been born or when they'd had their names bestowed upon them. Father Tammas, therefore, decided that their joint celebration should be on anniversaries of the day on which he found them in the forest. Once she had learned to cook from the village dames Jennet made sure that each anniversary was celebrated by a meal of suitable magnificence.

Krispin's mouth watered as, dish by dish and course by course, he relived the last feast . . . soup of sorrel so carefully picked; squab pie with garden onions and forest mushrooms; roast goose, with herb sauce which was the culinary achievement of Father Tammas; wildberry tart with yellow cream so thick it was spread with a knife; and the best goblets of the rare black wine of Ronimar to cleanse the palate between courses.

264

'Who is the maid who has come into your mind?' asked Margan who was seated on the thwart nearest to him.

'Wild boar meat . . . with the sauce of green apples,' Krispin murmured, and then returned to reality.

Father Tammas's best goblets were nothing but glass fragments.

Jennet had no other idea of food than holding a tiny slice of cake to her dolly's mouth!

He cursed.

'I am sorry I spoke,' said Margan.

He turned and looked at her long black hair and bright complexion – no wonder her father called her Rose Red – and apologized for his unintended churlishness.

'I was dreaming of food,' he added.

'So was I a little while ago,' she said. 'Have you ever had syllabub with mountain snow mixed with it?'

The talk spread. Demara remembered the fine white bread hot from the castle bakery which she ate with honey; Emon described how in the old Black Storm Company they used to fill a pit with coals to roast oxen that had somehow wandered into their camp . . .

'Enough!' said Alwald. 'The more we think about food the greater the pangs.'

'But I was just getting on to the gravy,' objected Emon. 'The cook used to get this huge copper pot, the lovely fat juices ran into it, and then . . .'

'The pottons take your gravy!'

'Yes, my lord.'

Emon relapsed into sulky silence.

The boat sped through the dreary landscape and lethargy fell upon the travellers. Only once during the rest of the day did anything happen to take their thoughts from their own discomforts. In the late afternoon the remains of a town built either side of the river, and once connected by a bridge, appeared ahead of them. It was the usual collection of crumbling towers, creeper-covered walls and broken quays along the banks.

'What could have happened to this land?' murmured Demara as the current took them between the ruins.

No one answered. Their eyes were fixed on one of the towers overlooking the river where a makeshift flag of green material – most probably made from a hunting cloak – fluttered in the wind.

There was no sign of whoever had raised it. There was no sound other than the moan of the wind around the decaying buildings.

With his oars Krispin turned the boat in the current and kept rowing strongly enough to hold it opposite the tower.

'What shall we do?' asked Margan. 'It could be someone in distress.'

'And it could be a trick to lure us ashore, my lady,' said Emon.

'At least let us call.'

They cupped their hands round their mouths and for the next minute a wild chorus of shouts echoed across the water.

'Apart from those white beings in the city, this is the first sign of life we have seen in the Land of Blight,' said Margan. 'It could be someone like us, perhaps someone who drifted down the river by accident – '

'We cannot risk landing,' declared Demara. 'There is too much at stake. Krispin, turn the boat round and let us leave this place as fast as we can.'

Without a word he heaved on one oar so that the current spun the boat; he straightened up and a few moments later Demara was steering them between the stone piles which had once supported a bridge. They looked back at the flag and then, as the river curved, it was lost to sight forever.

That night another scarlet moon rose and tinted the clammy mist which hung like a shroud along the river.

Hunger made them feel the cold more keenly, and although wrapped in every piece of clothing they possessed they lay in the black craft with chattering teeth and black depression in their hearts.

Although she hid her feelings most successfully – as became a young woman of aristocratic lineage – Demara suffered the most. Not only was her widowhood of a few days' duration, but the knowledge that she was carrying her dead lord's child filled her with dread rather than joy. Drifting without food or proper shelter through this dreadful landscape she pondered gloomily on what chance this spark of new life within her had of reaching its full term. And if it did, the thought of the birthing in a wilderness made her shudder. She could see no future for herself or the babe as the aptly named River of Night bore them inexorably into the unknown.

She had hinted at her condition only to Margan, for while she could understand the self-preoccupation of her male companions, it still alienated her from them. The old soldier Emon and the auburn-haired apprentice appeared incurious even about Alwald's mysterious condition. True, they had tried to fathom what had happened to him in The Shallows but when he turned his face from them like a sulky child they appeared to lose interest. Apathy is the bastard of hunger.

It was Alwald she should have been able to turn to for support, but often his mind appeared to wander. Lately his only utterances were to curse the old woman's quest which had led them into this dire situation.

With such desolate thoughts she drifted into uneasy sleep, her hands crossed protectively across her still slim belly. Margan sat close to Krispin and her need for warmth – he told himself – and her courage in coming after him into the nameless city made it impossible for him to move. Indeed, he had to admit there was something half-exciting and half-comforting in the pressure of her body against his. If he had not consigned his heart to Jennet in happier days he would have found the experience wholly pleasurable.

Her hand stole into his and he held it until it was time to begin the voyage again. It could do no harm, he thought, especially when it was doubtful if any of them would survive the next few days.

It was a little after noon when Demara suddenly pointed ahead.

'Is that low cloud or are those hills ahead of us?'

The mere suggestion that there might be an alteration in a landscape that had been unchanging for several days was enough to animate them.

'I think it is a range of hills, lady,' said Krispin. 'Perhaps we are coming to the end of this blighted plain.'

She made the Circle of the Mother and turned away her head so that the others would not see the tears of hope sparkling in her eyes.

As the afternoon wore on, details of the range became clearer. The hills were formed out of black rock and, in keeping with the dreary nature of the landscape, there was no green shading to suggest forest, yet the fact that there was something different ahead gave them new energy. Despite the pain in his head Emon insisted upon taking an oar and with him and Krispin pulling hard, coupled with the fact that the current was steadily increasing in speed, the boat appeared to fly along its dark channel.

In another hour they were approaching an enormous cleft in the towering rock into which the river disappeared; and then, almost before they realized what was happening, the current shot them into it.

The experience that Demara had gained at the tiller now came to her aid as the river swirled along a twisting gorge, and on several occasions Krispin had to fend them off with his oar to prevent the side of the craft being scraped along spray-glistening rock. But after the journey across the plain there was an exhilaration in the motion of the boat as it raced past outcrops of rock and rolled in the surge of the impatient water.

'We must come out somewhere soon,' Krispin said, but his words were lost in shouts of dismay from the others as the boat slewed round a bend.

TWO

The Vale Of Mabalon

Raising his oar for a moment Krispin turned his head and saw they had entered a broader stretch of water. Ahead mist hung like a curtain between the sides of the canyon, but it was the echoes of endless thunder which filled them with fear.

'What is it?' demanded Margan.

'Rapids,' Krispin answered grimly.

'Or falls,' said Alwald whose lethargy was replaced by panic.

'Steer for the side, lady,' Krispin called to Demara. 'We might get a hold on the rock.'

He and Emon rowed as they had never rowed before and the boat began to move across the current, but its sideways progress was painfully slow compared to the rate it was being carried towards the mist. Krispin eyed the wet rock which gave the illusion of racing past them. It would be almost impossible to get a grip on its water-worn surface or hook a hand into a fissure, and if anyone did achieve this he was likely to be torn from the boat. But he knew he had to try.

'Closer!' he shouted, and stood up ready to lean across the gunwale.

Demara wrenched the tiller over. Krispin's fingers left trails of blood as they were drawn across the rockface. Wood splintered as the current drove the boat against the side; then, caught in a whirlpool, it was flung back into the mainstream. Krispin was thrown to the bottom boards and the next thing he knew the craft was hurtling through rainbow-shot spray.

Around him his companions were screaming and clinging to the thwarts. He raised his head as the bows fell away and he saw that they were plunging down a cataract of seething water. Rocks reared out of it to meet them, to crush in the bows or tear out the bottom, but in some miraculous manner the black craft escaped them.

Several terrible moments later they spun in a pool at the bottom of the torrent until the vortex sent their keel grinding over a lip of rock and once more they were in the grip of the force. Ahead more rocks appeared like a row of black fangs, so close together that it was surely impossible for the trembling hull to shoot between them. Just as they expected to be hurled out with the impact they felt a shudder run through the framework of their craft and it twisted of its own accord, scraping between two of the rock teeth before careering down the next stretch of the rapids.

So much water cascaded over the sides that Krispin expected them to founder at any moment, yet when the black craft righted itself before the next sickening lunge he was surprised at how little water was washing over their feet.

Finally the river levelled and the boat raced through drifts of spume towards a natural gateway between black cliffs towering on either side.

For a while the boat was borne broadside on to the current and Krispin made a vain attempt to straighten it before the force of the current rolled it over and over, but again it seemed that the craft possessed the uncanny power of steering itself. As the gap loomed up it trembled and turned so that it hurtled through the race bows first.

When they emerged from the gateway the travellers

271

had an impression of bright sky and white water, then they were sweeping through yet another curtain of mist before being catapulted into space. They were no longer shooting rapids – they shot over the edge of a broad waterfall.

Down they plunged with plunging water about them. They clung to the thwarts, expecting the bows to drop so they would fall out like peas shaken from a pod. To their astonishment the boat remained level and struck the water at the base of the falls keel first. The impact drove the air from their lungs, walls of water rose on either side and swamped the boat. For a moment it seemed they were actually underwater, then, spluttering and gagging, they felt the boat lift and they were on the surface of a placid river – a river that was not black but reflected the blue, cloud-scudded sky – drifting between banks of gentle green.

The roar of the falls faded but for a while they were too stunned to move. Krispin was content to watch the banks and the vine-covered slopes slide by.

'Thanks be to the Mother, we are still alive,' murmured Margan.

'Thanks be to the Fey,' said Krispin.

'The Fey?'

'This boat must have been a Fey gift to the Lady Eloira. It came down the rapids as though it was alive and – look! – we went under the surface yet there is no water left in her.'

Nothing more was said.

If Krispin's words were true they owed gratitude to the Fey; on the other hand there was an ingrained suspicion – even fear – of these elusive forest folk.

The boat drifted on.

As the ordeal of the rapids receded they began to take more interest in their surroundings. The slopes of hills on

272

either side were covered with vineyards, squares of vivid green dissected by paths of chalky earth which told them that sooner or later they would meet people. And where there were people there was food!

Beyond the verdant hills rose the ragged tops of an encircling mountain range, the upper heights of which were covered with snow, and this gave Krispin a feeling of nostalgia for the White Virgins of the High Wald.

'Look, a house,' cried Margan, pointing to a small white building with a red door and a steep thatched roof set high among the vines. 'Shall we stop and ask the owner for food?'

'We may as well keep on,' said Demara. 'There is a village ahead of us.'

All eyes looked up the broad stretch of sky-stained water to a collection of white houses with brightly painted doors and shutters, and thatched roofs built steep to shed winter snow. In the centre rose the spire of a shrine and the whole aspect was one of tranquillity which emphasized the fact that they had escaped from the Land of Blight.

As they neared the cluster of houses they saw people hurrying to a landing stage against which several boats chafed gently. It was obvious that the black craft was the object of their excitement, the colourful crowd gesticulating for them to head for the jetty.

The oars had been lost in the rapids but as Demara moved the tiller the boat glided towards the bank as easily as though Krispin was still rowing.

It could have saved me a lot of effort if it had done this earlier on, he thought ruefully. Why had he had to bother rowing at all if the boat could move by magical means!

As they approached the jetty they saw that the people on the whole were middle-aged with figures suggesting a fondness for the good things of the table and cheerful faces browned by outdoor work. A silence fell on the villagers who looked with compassion on the travellers'

273

hungry faces and weary eyes, at Emon's bloody bandage and the limp figure of Alwald.

Leaving a wake of gentle ripples behind it, the black boat slowed and came alongside with a deftness which won the onlookers' approval. Krispin seized a pile with his bloodied hand to keep the craft in position while above him a tall woman in a flowing dress of umber-dyed wool stepped forward.

'Welcome to the Vale of Mabalon,' she said in a soft pleasing voice. 'I named Mistress Earth and I am bailiff of the valley.'

There was a muttered response from the boat, and Demara and Margan ran their fingers through their hair in a vain attempt to appear less barbarous.

'It is many seasons since we were honoured with visitors from the world beyond, and they came over the mountains,' Mistress Earth continued. 'Can it be that you have crossed the Land of Blight and survived the falls?'

When no one else answered, Krispin said, 'That indeed we have, mistress. In doing so we have been for long without food, and I have silver to pay . . .'

'It is truly marvellous that you made the journey and when you are refreshed it will be a delight for us to hear your adventures. As for food, you are welcome to all you need provided you cause no offence by offering to pay for it. We are well rewarded by the pleasure of having new faces amongst us.'

'Our thanks . . .'

'There are rooms at our inn, the Rose and Vine, and there you can borrow dry clothing, eat away your hunger and sleep as long as you need.'

Willing hands reached down to help the travellers out of the black craft, and for Alwald and Emon there were arms to lean on as they moved slowly along a broad gravelled path towards the houses which they found surrounding a central square. There was the shrine at one end and at the other a half-timbered building with a spreading tree in front of it beneath which there were stools and tables on which stood cups and pitchers of wine in varying degrees of fullness. These had been deserted at the approach of the strangers but now the villagers resumed their places, and as their talk about the new arrivals rose, inn servants were tripping over their long embroidered skirts to keep pace with the orders for more wine.

Master Corn, the landlord, and his wife took the travellers to small chambers with sloping ceilings and beds whose pillows were fragrant with aromatic herbs which had been sewn in with duck feathers. Dark woodwork shone with beeswax, patchwork quilts were vivid in the light streaming through the leaded panes of the casements, and the air was pleasantly permeated with the smell of good cooking from the kitchen below. The whole place was so restful and wholesome that after the Land of Blight the newcomers could not have imagined a more perfect haven.

Bowls of steaming water and fresh clothing were rushed to their rooms. Then, refreshed and comforted by the warmth of borrowed garments, they went down to the dining hall where bowls of broth were already steaming on a long table.

'When you hunger greatly it is best to eat gentle at first,' said Mistress Earth, who, with the landlord and a gaggle of servants at the door, watched with a smile of satisfaction as their guests, forgetting any pretence to good manners, gulped down the broth and held out their bowls to the cook's ladle for more.

The first course was followed by river fish poached in milk and served with soft vegetables. The meal ended with light wine and then Mistress Earth said that the next requirement was sleep after which they would talk.

Although the sun was only just slipping behind the

ranges which enclosed the Vale of Mabalon there was no objection to the bailiff's suggestion and the five retired to their rooms to sleep as they had never slept before.

It was mid-morning when Krispin awoke. A cup of milk had been placed beside his bed and his own clothing, now dried and cleaned, was folded over a chair. Yawning and stretching luxuriously, he crossed to the window and found himself gazing over the roofs of the village to flowered meadows where cows grazed in tail-swishing peace. The river beyond was no longer sinister but a sparkling stretch of water on which a couple of fishermen cast nets from brightly painted boats.

Figures moved among the vines on the far shore, some hoeing rhythmically while others bent with pruning knives or carried yokes from which water buckets hung on chains. Further up the slopes the vineyards gave way to rough pasture land dotted with sheep, and higher still the grass in turn gave way to stretches of mauve heather. Beyond this delightful landscape frosted mountains rose grandly against a sky so blue that it was a delight to behold after the yellowish hue above the Land of Blight.

Sighing with satisfaction, Krispin dressed and descended to the dining hall where he found Demara already in a hearth-side conversation with Mistress Earth. Seeing him, the landlord brought him a bowl of curds.

'Mistress Demara tells me that you fled down the river from the Wolf Horde,' said the bailiff.

'They have overrun our land,' Krispin said. 'My lady's castle fell through treachery, and my village was put to the torch.' With caution instilled into him by Lady Eloira he made no mention of the quest.

'It is a wonder of wonders that you reached the vale alive,' said Mistress Earth. 'A few times we have seen, floating on the river, wreckage of craft that have been dashed to pieces in the falls. Because we believed it unlikely – until your arrival – that anyone would enter the

276

Land of Blight we thought those fragments came from boats that had slipped their moorings in some region far beyond.'

'A body came once,' said Master Corn.

Mistress Earth gave a little shiver.

'It was covered with long white hairs; not of humankind and yet it had human shape. And what eyes!'

Krispin, too, shivered as memory of the white creatures returned to him.

'Tell us about this valley,' he said. 'It is a jewel of a place.'

'And like many a jewel it is well hidden,' said Master Corn. 'Here we have no truck with the outside world and so we escape its ills. No pestilence, witchfinders, spies, tax-gatherers or imperial troops find their way here. The falls and the mountains keep us free to live our lives in tranquillity as the Mother intended. So it has been since The Enchantment.'

'And nothing comes up river?'

'No. The river flows to the far end of the valley and there it vanishes into a cavern. What dangers wait there I know not, but as long as we can recall no living thing has returned after being borne into the darkness beneath the mountain, let alone travelled through from the outworld.'

'Since my father's boat was carried into it by a flood many years ago there has been a barrier of mighty stakes across the entrance so that others will not share the same fate,' said Mistress Earth quietly.

'Then the Vale of Mabalon is completely cut off?' said Krispin, hiding a pang of anxiety that having come so far and obtained the mysterious Esav he might not be able to continue the quest.

'There used to be a trail that led through the mountains,' said Master Corn. 'But who would follow that?'

'This is a goodly place,' said Mistress Earth. 'As you have lost your own homes it should not be hard for you

277

to remain here. Life is simple but rewarding, and we have only one cause for sorrow.'

'I am surprised there is even one,' said Krispin.

'Children are born few and far between,' said Master Corn. 'Slowly, slowly our numbers are lessening. Master Mist, our conjure man, believes there is some dark quality in the water flowing from the Land of Blight which makes barren the wombs of our women . . .'

'And the power of our men to make them quick,' Mistress Earth interrupted bitterly.

'Are no babies born at all?' Demara asked.

'From time to time,' said the landlord.

'Mistress Tree birthed a fine baby boy four seasons ago. But you can see why we will be happy to have you added to our number, especially . . .' Here she turned and smiled at Demara who smiled back.

'But we must go on,' said Krispin. 'Do not think me ungrateful,' he added. 'But I – and my comrade Alwald – are bound by our sacred oaths to make a journey in the service of the Lady Eloira, Reeve of the High Wald, and thus with sorrow in our hearts we will have to cross the mountains when we have rested.'

'You speak for yourself, Krispin,' said Demara. 'Lord Alwald may not ever recover his strength for such an arduous undertaking and it is imperative that Margan and I – who have sworn no oaths – remain in this valley with these good folk.'

When she saw his look of inquiry, she added, 'Oh Krispin, I am with child and it is here in this happy valley that I shall have him, and he will grow up away from the perils of the world that brought the death of his father. From feeling despair I am now filled with such joy.'

Krispin was expressing his surprise and congratulations when there was a noise behind them and turning they saw that Alwald, who had just entered the hall in time to hear Demara's words, had slipped to the rushes in a faint.

THREE
The Eagle's Way

The days passed peacefully in the Vale of Mabalon and the newcomers quickly regained their strength. The prospect of motherhood made Demara a favourite among the women of the village, and a pleasant house, empty since its elderly owner had died some years ago without heirs, was prepared for her and Margan.

At the Rose and Vine inn Emon also became a favourite. Men who had never ventured beyond the ranges which sheltered the vale hung on every word of his military stories. Under the care of Master Mist his head wound healed but no salve or potion could lighten the dusk which was settling over his world, yet he bore the approach of blindness with the same courage that he had shown in facing rebels, outcasts and wolf men. And the fact that Mistress Rain, a comely widow woman, was eager for him to share her home added to the contentment he felt at the prospect of spending the remainder of his life in this self-sufficient community.

'Son, the wine here is excellent,' he told Krispin after he had spent one evening sampling it with his cronies. 'Rain is a fine cook and she has a snug house with the softest bed of goosedown it is possible to imagine. The Wolf King robbed me of the life I knew, my dear old comrades are dead, so what regret can I have in settling here? By the time the shadow in my eyes turns to night I

279

shall know my way about the village well enough to find the path to the Rose and Vine. If you had any sense you would settle as well. That Margan is a comely wench and you should be able to read the looks she gives you.'

He laughed.

'How we tried to stop her from following you into the nameless city, but she would have none of it.'

'I have the quest . . .' Krispin murmured.

'Duty is duty, I admit,' said Emon. 'It would be different if you were a soldier, but you are a toymaker. How could an old dame expect you to be bound with a quest oath like a knight! And if you do not perish in the snows up there or get murdered by outcasts, and you do reach your journey's end – what then? Will Ythan be a better place? Will history be changed? Of course not, son.

'I have had time to think since I have been here, and I remember all the lads I helped to bury on the campaigns, and what good did their deaths do? Nothing, son, nothing. Stay here, set up a workshop and make Margan happy.'

'You probably speak wise, but I must go on,' Krispin said and in his mind he added, 'To abandon the quest would be to abandon Jennet.'

The day after his fainting spell, Alwald called Krispin to his bedside.

'My strength returns,' he said. 'The conjure man's herbals are restoring my body and the evil glamour which befell me in the Shallows is fading.'

'That I am glad to hear,' said Krispin, wondering why he sounded so sombre if he was feeling better.

'As soon as Master Mist permits I shall continue the journey – alone, if you cannot tear yourself away from the soft life here. It is impossible for *me* to remain here when honour calls.'

'Alwald, I have already learned all I can about the path which leads out of this forgotten valley,' said Krispin

280

quietly. 'We will leave the day you are strong enough to make the ascent.'

'Good. Make sure we have a goodly stock of food. And polish my blade with goose fat.'

'The Lady Demara will grieve at your going,' Krispin said.

The young man lying on the bed coloured and turned his face to the wall.

'She will be in good hands. Perhaps . . . perhaps someday . . . Now go, I would sleep.'

'As you wish,' said Krispin and left the chamber. He had already cleaned the weapons and while Alwald's sword shone as though it had just left the swordsmith's forge, he could not lighten the dullness of Woundflame's blade.

'Only battle will make you shine,' he said as he slid the sword into its scabbard. 'Best that way, or Alwald would claim you back.'

Now he wandered down to the jetty where the black boat swung with the gentle current, its sides no longer showing any signs of the battering it had received against the rocks.

A craft that heals itself! thought Krispin as he took his rolled cloak from the locker. There is more magic in the world than I dreamed when I lived in Toyheim!

He carried the cloak back to his room which was filled with the cold light of the wand as he unrolled it. He carefully bandaged it in a length of spider silk and then inserted it into a tube of thick hide which he had paid Master Snow the tanner to stitch for him. When this was done he placed it at the bottom of his pack.

There was an urgent knock at the door and when he opened it he saw an agitated maid.

'We saw a great light in your window,' she said. 'You be afire?'

'Look yourself, Mistress Grape.'

Shaking her head she returned to serving wine in the courtyard and the mystery of the 'great light in the window' remained a topic of debate for many seasons among the customers at the Rose and Vine.

There was much shaking of heads when Alwald stated that he was well enough to resume his journey, many of the vale folk believing that it would be impossible to reach the pass in the high mountains as the path must surely have been long lost to rockfall and avalanche. On the evening before he was to set out with Krispin, Master Corn held a farewell feast for them.

Alwald was seated in the chair of honour beside the Lady Demara but through the many courses and their appropriate wines – wine, its culture and drinking, being regarded as high art in the vale – he spoke few words to her and kept his eyes on his platter. Once, while the rest of the company were listening to the harping of Master Dew she took his hand in hers and said quietly, 'You have been so strange, Alfrith my dear. I miss the friendship you gave me. Tell me what it was that happened at the Shallows for I believe that it caused a shadow to come between us.'

'Shameful!' he muttered turning his head away. 'It was shameful!'

And then, to hide his emotion and prevent further talk, he added his shaky voice to a drinking song.

When the maids brought wondrous cheeses on scrubbed boards, and wine from the highest vineyard was poured reverently into fresh goblets, Mistress Earth stood up.

'It saddens our hearts that these two young men must leave us but we can only honour their devotion to the cause that calls them,' she said. 'But our sadness is lightened by the knowledge that three of you who came to us as strangers . . .'

'Strangers no more!'

'. . . are to make your homes in the Vale of Mabalon,

282

especially as it means an event that has become rare among us will bring new life to the village. A toast to the mother-to-be.'

Demara saw with dismay how Alwald bit his lip as he raised his goblet.

What has turned him against me? she wondered.

'As you five have learned since your arrival here, it is our custom to choose our own names,' Mistress Earth continued. 'A child has a baby name until he or she reaches the age of change and then at the naming ceremony he or she announces what they want to be called for the rest of their lives. These names come from nature and things for which we are daily grateful, but no two persons are allowed to have the same name. There is one name which no one bears these days, and it is our wish to bestow it upon the Lady Demara. Henceforth, lady, you will be known as Star in the Vale of Mabalon and your child shall be Star Born.'

There were handclaps and the raising of goblets and the Mother was called upon for blessings, and tears sparkled on Demara's cheeks as she acknowledged the acclaim of those who had so warmly offered her a new life.

As more pitchers of wine appeared Alwald stood up.

'Do not forget we leave at dawn,' he cried to Krispin. 'We should sleep now.'

He turned to the company, gave a formal bow and went up the creaking stairs to his chamber. For a moment the coldness of his manner – so different to the old Alfrith! Demara thought – cast a shadow over the dining hall and then Master Dew drew his fingers across his strings and voices once again rose to the rafters.

Emon sat with his arm round Mistress Rain and, when pressed, rendered the marching song of the Black Storm Company and, as all were merry with wine, the unofficial version was received with belly-shaking laughter. Soon everyone was joining in:

We march for the Regent, we march to his wars,
We hump all the rebels and slay all the whores.
We march for our captain, we beg for our pay,
If only they'd feed us we'd last another day.
And when the fighting's over, peace has come to pass,
The general gets the glory and boots us up the arse!

Krispin felt pleasantly light-headed, a reminder of the old days when he and his fellow apprentices celebrated in the Jack-in-the-Box and jokes and songs flowed as freely as the apple ale. As he looked around him with a broad smile, raising his goblet to be replenished, Demara beckoned him to sit beside her.

'Congratulations on your new name, lady,' he said.

'Lady no longer,' said Demara. 'It is fitting that from now on I have no title and instead of being a chatelaine I shall be mistress of a cottage, and I shall raise hens and take my turn in the vineyards.'

Krispin looked at her soft hands whose skin was blistered from merely holding the tiller of the black boat.

'They will harden,' she said, interpreting his glance. 'For the sake of my beloved lord and husband I shall toil to make a happy home for his unborn child. All we can do for the dead is keep faith with what we remember of them. All I can do for Grimwald is protect the child and bring him up as he would have wished.'

'I am sure you keep faith with the River Lord.'

'Which brings me to his born son Alfrith,' Demara continued. 'None of us knows what happened to him in the Shallows but his character has changed, even allowing for the hardships we have shared. He is morose when he used to laugh; he is surly when he used to be so gallant. He is like a man with a grey potton on his back. Krispin, I fear for him. Promise me that on your journey you will show him patience and protection and – should it please

284

the Mother! – guide him back here where perhaps he, too, may find peace.'

'Raising hens and pruning vines?'

She smiled at the thought.

'Perhaps. Promise me this promise.'

'By the Mother, I shall do my best, lady,' said Krispin.

'Star.'

'Lady Star.'

She laughed.

'The wine has made you merry, toymaker. Tell me, what toys did you make – hobby horses, wooden soldiers, little wagons?'

'One makes such things to begin with when the hand is still not skilled.'

'And of the toys that you have which gives you most pride?'

'A life-sized dancing doll I made for The Choosing. It was my wish then that someday the Regent would see her and want her for his collection of automata . . .'

'The Regent!'

'Then I did not know of his encouragement of the Wolf King. Now I dream that some time in the far future my doll will still go to the Citadel in Danaak but she will carry an extra gift for my lord Regent. Meantime, I have remembered something of my skill and I shall leave a toy I have made these last days in the village workshop for Star Born.'

In her pleasure Demara clapped her hands childishly.

'What is it? May I have it now?'

'In the morning. The last coat of paint is still drying. When your child can understand words it will remind you of a story to tell.'

Soon afterwards Krispin made a round of the company, shaking hands, expressing his thanks and farewells, and then with a slightly unsteady step he climbed to his chamber and laid his head on the pillow which smelled so sweetly of sleep-inducing herbs.

How easy it would be to stay in this happy valley, he thought. Much of what Emon had said made sense, and yet . . . His word had been given and there was more to life than safety and comfort . . .

. . . *like hardship and death!* mocked an inner voice, and then sleep overtook him.

It was a hand laid on his naked chest that drew Krispin back from slumber. He became conscious of warmth beside him, of gentle breathing, of soft hair against his cheek. He stretched out his hand cautiously and his blood quickened as his fingertips stroked the gentle curve of Margan's breast.

'When we left the nameless city,' she whispered, 'you told me that someday you would repay me for the help I gave you . . .'

'For saving my life,' Krispin murmured.

'. . . and tonight I claim that favour.'

'Margan, I . . .'

'Hush. At dawn you leave on your quest and it is unlikely that you and I will ever set eyes on each other again. I shall never even know if you reach the end of your journey. Therefore I want this night with you so that I shall have something to remember in the time ahead, for you know full well that since we left River Garde I have grown to love you.'

'Margan . . .'

'Hush again.'

He felt soft lips brush his.

'I remember all you told me that night we drifted along the river, but tonight will make no difference to *her* and if you truly love her it will make no difference to you. All it will mean is that I have a memory. Surely that is not too much to ask.'

286

He was conscious of her thigh against his and the stirring of his loins.

'Say that I can share the night with you.'

She smiled to herself in the darkness as her question was answered by the tensing of his body.

'Margan, I – I . . .'

'Fear not, it will be our secret.'

Her leg slid across his, her arms embraced him, her breath was warm on his skin.

'Margan, I fear . . .'

'Fear what, my love?'

'It is just that I have no skill. Laugh if you must but I . . . only once . . .'

He lost his words and she chuckled.

'Poor Krispin, you are afraid.'

'You must know so much more than I.'

'Then give me your hand and let me be your teacher.'

It seemed to Krispin, already borne along on the good wine of Mabalon, that he was caught in a vortex of pure pleasure. Margan's warmth, Margan's smooth body, Margan's erotic endearments swept away his reservation. Time after time he was overcome by the urge to take her and each time she deflected him with soft laughter until he moaned with desire that was akin to pain, and then she lay for him and allowed him to master her, and he rode his passion until he called her name and then lay heart-heaving and at peace beside her.

And later he awoke and it seemed that he was drowning in the raven hair which hung over his face, and to his astonishment his body was responding as though it had an independent will, and again he gloried in his new-found power which carried them both on a dark wave until they were cast on the dream shore of contentment.

So passed the night.

It was a blow on the door which made Krispin's eyes flicker open.

'Margan,' he whispered.

He ran his hand across the bed and found he was alone.

There was another urgent knock on the door.

'It is past sunrise and we should have started on our way,' called Alwald. 'We have far to go and you lie abed.'

'Don't scold,' answered Krispin as he groped for his garments. He stood up and an attack of giddiness made him sit on the bed again.

'I shall be with you soon. Go downstairs and have some breakfast.'

'Be quick then, we do not want to spend the night in the snows.'

When Krispin painfully made his way downstairs with his pack, the snores which echoed through the Rose and Vine testified to the success of the farewell feast. In the dining hall he found only Master Corn, Mistress Earth and his erstwhile travelling companions at the breakfast board. Margan smiled sweetly and said she hoped he had enjoyed a restful night to prepare him for the trek to the mountains.

'The paint is dry now,' he said as he handed a wooden box to Demara.

Her smile of anticipation as she opened changed to a cry of admiration. From the box she took out a replica of the black craft, complete with awning and oars, which had carried them so far along the River of Night. She placed it on the table and, while the others looked in surprise, she brought out five figures which they saw represented themselves.

'What a wonderful gift,' she said.

'Be not afraid to let your child sail it on water for I have made it strong enough, though it lacks the magic which was spelled into the original.'

Margan held up the figure which, by the long black tresses glued to the head, she recognized as a likeness of herself.

'Surely my chest is not so flat!' she exclaimed in mock indignation.

'Modesty prevented a close inspection of the subject,' Krispin answered. 'Should we . . . when we meet again I shall carve a more truthful image.'

Alwald muttered impatiently, and Krispin gulped his cup of milk, slung his pack on to his shoulder and holding his bread and cheese in one hand followed him to the door.

White mist hung over the lower meadows and curled across the river but already they could feel the warmth of the sun as she began her ascent into an azurine sky. The snow-crested mountains seemed to sparkle more brightly than before – and seemed to Krispin to be more distant than before.

'We will see you on to the path,' said Master Corn. 'And if it fails you, as well it may, you are ever welcome at the Rose and Vine.'

Without any more words they set off past the houses, across the goose meadow and up a path which meandered through the vineyards. Recognizing Krispin's condition from his pale face and wine-sheen across his brow, Emon insisted on carrying his pack for him. Margan walked sedately beside him and all she whispered when parting came at the highest row of vines was, 'Be not afraid to carry the memory as I shall.'

'Follow the path across the pasture to the woods,' said Master Corn. 'It will take you through the trees and on the other side you will follow it towards the pass. Master Leaf the goatherd tells me that the way was once marked by cairns in the mountains.'

'We shall look for them,' said Krispin.

He took his pack from the soldier and, with a wave and muttered farewell, he followed Alwald on the path which led to the distant woods. Both Demara and Margan moved forward as though to spend a little more time with them but Mistress Earth said, 'Your farewells were said last night, do not make it harder for them.' And though her words were sensible all saw that she too had tears in her eyes.

When Krispin and Alwald reached the edge of the woods they were grateful to halt and turn to look back on the valley. From this vantage point the Vale of Mabalon could not have appeared more delightful. The river winding down its centre was a ribbon of reflected blue, the water meadows on either side were emerald, while beyond the tender green cornfields orchards offered a variety of foliage shades. This lush panorama was contrasted by the mellow roofs and bright paintwork of the village and the bare whitish soil between the vine rows.

The smoke of some late-lit fires scribbled above tall chimney-pots and the bark of a dog and the slam of a door reached the ears of Krispin and Alwald with unexpected clarity.

'There lies the domain of content,' murmured Krispin.

'Come,' said Alwald and with a sigh Krispin turned and followed him into the shade of the woods.

By midday the pair had left the heather-purpled upland behind and were wearily making their way into the mountain region. The ground was stony and the only vegetation was clumps of reed-like grass forever trembling in the cold wind.

As Master Corn had said, the way was now merely marked by cairns built out of rock fragments which, over the long stretch of time since men had travelled the path, had become displaced. The result was that what had once been tall markers were spreading heaps of rubble-stone. Here and there becks of fast-flowing water had to be crossed, and as they climbed a steep valley in the early afternoon they found banks of hard snow where its walls threw permanent shadow. The cold which came off it caused them to shiver despite their packmen's cloaks.

The two young men hardly exchanged a word as they climbed wearily, with pebbles sliding from beneath their feet. Krispin in particular was suffering from the night before, and although Alwald had been declared fit by the village conjure man, he had not got all of his strength back. This meant that they stopped to catch their breath more and more frequently, and the peaks they were heading for seemed as far away as ever.

Once Krispin noticed a shadow swoop over the rocky floor towards them, and looking up he saw a huge grey eagle with white-tipped wings riding the air currents above them. Although used to the sight of eagles in the High Wald, he had never seen such a magnificent one before. From then on, whenever he looked up, he saw the great bird circling overhead, and as the afternoon passed it seemed there was something unnatural in the way it was content to keep pace with them.

They were still far from their destination when the sun set and left them in a lonely world whose only sound was the moan of wind in rocks.

Grumbling at their lack of progress Alwald threw down his pack and lit a fire of dead sticks and dry moss over which Krispin warmed a stew that Master Corn had prepared for them. Then, with a muttered goodnight, each thankfully rolled himself in cloak and blanket. Just before he went to sleep Krispin looked up and saw a dark winged silhouette against the Star Bridge.

At noon the next day they emerged from the pass between two peaks and had the sensation of looking down on the world. The mountainside sloped gently to a black lava plain which rolled away to the horizon in a series of wave-like ridges. The path which had led them from the Vale of Mabalon ended in a vast drift of black pebbles, and there was nothing to indicate which direction to take.

'Now, way-finder, point the way,' said Alwald. 'Where lies our destination?'

Krispin scanned the desolate stretch in hope of inspiration, and then saw the eagle, which had been gliding in lazy circles above them all morning, flex his wings and fly in a straight line south towards a group of rock formations which rose from the lava. The sight of them triggered a response in Krispin's memory.

'That is the way we go,' he cried, pointing to the far rocks. 'Our road leads from there.'

'And where will our road take us?'

A single word came into his conscious mind just as though it had been whispered in his ear.

'Danaak!'

FOUR
The Feast Of Fools

Danaak was a city of glitter.

The Citadel walls were lit by hundreds of huge oil-soaked flambeaux; bonfires blazed before the shrines, householders competed to illuminate their dwellings with special candle lanterns and even the meanest hovels had rush lights in their unglazed windows. Torch-lit barges glided along the Green River casting lurid reflections, and at every street corner it seemed there was a mountebank blowing flames from his mouth or jugglers spinning blazing clubs.

It was the ancient Feast of Fools, a celebration that had survived The Enchantment; a night when the citizens forgot everything except the madness of the festival. Servants acted like masters, laughing masters donned their servants' livery, and many a good dame slipped into the roaring streets to flick her skirts in the direction of masked strangers.

Only in the nether world beneath the Citadel did the carnival fever fail to penetrate. Here in the perpetual night the great capstan revolved with the failing strength of the near-naked wretches chained to its spokes. Here in the labyrinth of tunnels and cells the high-sided corpse cart rolled and gaolers, each in a halo of lanthorn light, hurried on secretive errands beneath dripping rock and filaments of nitre. Here in chambers stifling with the heat of braziers men in leather aprons manipulated their ghastly implements and scribes, with sachets of herbs beneath their nostrils, translated captives' anguished revelations into neat characters on vellum scrolls.

In a cell on the lowest level of this man-hewn hell Lord Odo crouched against the central pillar to which he was chained, unable to stand upright or sit. His feet were covered in suppurating wounds inflicted by long-haired rats, and his voice when he answered the Witchfinder General was little more than a mumble.

In smoky lantern light the black-robed witchfinder, his long ascetic features half-hidden by his cowl, regarded the list of names he had entered on the scroll which lay on his portable table.

'There must be more, my lord,' he said courteously. 'True, you have named some who conspired with you to overthrow our Lord Regent, but before I can make your lot more comfortable – accommodation without rats, mark you – I need a longer list.'

Lord Odo's chain rattled.

'If I knew of others . . .' he began.

'Tonight is the Feast of Fools,' said the witchfinder blandly. 'High up above us they are making merry in the banqueting hall. Wine is flowing. Foolery is in the air. But your friends must wonder why your seat is empty. They do not realize that one of Ythan's greatest aristocrats is the biggest of all fools . . .'

The chain rattled again.

'A rat!' screamed the prisoner.

'Quite so,' said the witchfinder. 'I was saying what a fool you are, a few more names and no more rats. In your conspiring you must have come across others who are prohibited . . . apostates, for example. Did you not ever come across those within your circle who secretly believe the Great Heresy that the All Father never fell from grace. No? A pity. Pilgrims? You must have at least heard of some who follow the Pilgrim Path. Just one name, my lord, and you can have some fresh straw and an extra crust.'

The prisoner muttered something unintelligible.

The witchfinder rose from his stool, and stooping uncomfortably beneath the low ceiling, approached the crouched man. He did not allow his distaste for the soaking straw or the stink of his victim to show, even when he bent his ear to the quivering mouth.

'You have earned your crust,' he said as he returned to his portable table. 'Perhaps when I come again you will have remembered more. We need names if you are to leave the rats behind.'

The warder raised his lantern and by its light the witchfinder carefully dipped the point of his quill into an inkhorn and, having smoothed his scroll carefully, inscribed *Lady Eloira, Reeve of the High Wald*.

High in the Citadel above, the Regent lay back on a couch with pain paling his once florid face. His arm was in a sling and its poison, spawned by the bite of the homunculus, seeped through the rest of his frame. Beside the couch the Lore Mistress Mandraga held a phial of dark liquid.

'It will give you the strength to make your appearance,' she said. 'You need not stay long, but you must be there to disprove the rumours . . .'

'I know what I must do,' said the Regent. 'How long will I have to suffer this fire in my limbs? When will the elixir you promised me be ready?'

For once the formidable old woman hesitated.

'Your taint is so rare, so outside ordinary mortal distempers because of the unnaturalness of the creature, that my cure demands equally rare elements . . . not since The Enchantment . . .'

Her words died away.

'What is needed can be found. Am I not the Regent? Cannot I command anything I need in the kingdom? Tell me what you require for your sorcery and you shall have it. Look at how I have kept Leodore supplied. He swears that if he can distil enough to arrive at the same essence from which the manikins grew he will be able to cure me, but can I wait that long?'

'There is blood aplenty in Ythan,' said Mandraga contemptuously. 'What is needed is a much rarer commodity.'

The tolling of a bell came faintly through the heavily draped casement.

'It is time,' said Mandraga, handing him the phial. He swallowed the contents in a single gulp. Immediately colour began to suffuse his face, pain ebbed and he rose to his feet. He struck a gong to summon his page.

'If only the effects of your physic would last,' he muttered. 'Tell me, what is it that is required to complete the elixir?'

'I have searched the scrolls, my son, and there is one and only one ingredient which will make the elixir effective.'

'And that?'

Mandraga sighed.

'Water from the Wells of Ythan.'

A strange look crossed the Regent's face, a mixture of fury and fear.

'That is impossible. The secret of the wells was lost an age ago . . .'

'You must find it again – quickly,' said Mandraga.

'And you must ask the Mirror . . .'

His words were interrupted by the arrival of a little page bearing a loose cape which would conceal her master's bandaged arm.

Behind her appeared the Regent's avenger in his usual armour and with crossbow cocked.

'The revellers await you, my lord,' he said. 'They are eager for the crowning of the King of Fools.'

In the city below, the excitement mounted. Groups of dancers in bizarre costumes and masks danced with linked hands along the streets, guildmen hauled wheeled stages with tableaux representing their crafts, and in every square mummers pranced on stages. In the alleys the fun was more sinister. There were throngs of roistering gentlemen disguised as bravos – and bravos dressed as gentlemen robbing them. Soldiers, about to depart on a campaign the next day, staggered in drunken determination to find the girls of their dreams – or the whores who plied their trade in doorways, shouting lewd invitations over the shoulders of their customers.

Here and there were brief flurries among the revellers as fights broke out; here by a fountain a youth dressed as a spangled troubador collapsed to the cobbles with a bodkin between his ribs, there in the shadows a girl felt the jealous hands of a jilted lover about her neck.

Hugging the shadows, the Hump moved through the gala night like a misshapen shadow himself. Sometimes, when he was forced to cross a brightly lit square, children would form a jeering circle round him and shrill cries of 'Freak show! Freak show!' mocked him until he lost himself in the darker passageways. For days now he had roamed the city in search of Gambal, the young man from the Citadel who had bought Silvermane, determined that if he found him he would learn the horsemaid's fate at the point of his cruel drong rider's spike.

Though he had loitered at the Citadel gates and visited every tavern patronized by Citadel servants, he had not caught a glimpse of the pallid youth or been able to learn of his whereabouts. Yet he continued the hunt – what else could he do? He loved Silvermane and each time he raised his eyes to the Citadel, which now appeared to float above the city in its nimbus of light, his heartbeat quickened at the thought that she must be somewhere behind its walls. Was she kept as a pet there, a beautiful oddity of nature; or was her fate more in keeping with the grotesque tales which were whispered about life – and death – in the Citadel?

The Hump's fearful thoughts made his hand close on the grip of his spike until the knuckles cracked painfully and he forced himself to continue his search.

When Grand Johan, the huge Citadel bell, boomed its summons over the city, revellers swarmed to the great square where the contest for the King of Fools would be judged beneath the cold eye of the Regent. The Hump had no wish to follow the crowds, he had no wish to see well-made men mimicking his deformity as part of their foolishness.

He found himself in a small square, one side of which overlooked the river. At the opposite end there was a tavern with tables and stools arranged in front of it. Choosing the least illuminated, he sat and waited to be served, chewing a sooma seed to lessen the pain in his broad curved back. At the next table he saw two packmen who, by the dust on their cloaks, the stubble on their faces and the shadows of weariness under their eyes, had reached the end of a hard journey.

The one with long auburn hair sat with his chin on his hands while the other sipped his wine in between muttered complaints.

'I found the way here from the Vale of Mabalon did I not?' demanded the first when his companion's complaints finally forced a response from him.

'That you did. You piloted us brilliantly across lava plain, steppe, marshland, wilderness and forest, and then along the worst roads in the kingdom but you got us here.

Only what happens now we are here? Do we visit every house in the city . . .?'

'No,' said Krispin. 'I shall know the place when I see it.'

'The old dame could at least have given you the name of the street.'

Krispin raised his shoulders and let them fall.

'We might be days before you recognize the place. Serene Mother! The way we hurried to get here, only to wander the streets like the lost children.'

'Alwald, like you I am tired,' said Krispin. 'I know you have been sore wounded and you have not been yourself since the Shallows but tonight I ask you not to rid yourself of your discontent by passing it to me through your words.'

'All right,' Alwald growled. 'You have too sensitive a nature for a toymaker.'

'And can we forget my craft!' flared Krispin. 'You sneer at an honest calling but it is time to forget your privileged birth, it avails you nothing now. When the Mother birthed the first folk there was no servant or master . . .

'When all men toiled and women span,
Who, then, was the nobleman?'

Alwald laughed.

'That couplet rings down the ages,' he said. 'And I know it to be true. I shall never call you "toymaker" again. Let me pour you another cup of this wine – not up to the standard of the Wald is it? – and forgive my ill humour.'

'We have come too far to quarrel,' said Krispin and he raised his wine cup. 'Your health.'

The conversation meant nothing to the Hump, but it struck him as unusual for two packmen. But in Danaak things were often not what they seemed.

Wine was brought to him and he washed down another

sooma seed with the first draught, and the fatigue of his hours of searching began to ebb.

At a trestle table a number of soldiers were shouting at each other with drunken hilarity.

'After we are given our weapons tomorrow we will show those green-cloaked sons-to-whores the price of heresy,' cried one.

'By the time you reach Thaan you will not have anything to show,' laughed another.

'Is it true that heretic wenches have a sideways . . .'

'Who cares. All are the same after nightfall, and heretic silver gleams as bright as any other . . .'

Several of the men began banging ale tankards on the table.

'*We march for the Regent, we march to his wars . . .*'

Sing now, you will need all your breath soon enough, thought the Hump. As a caravan guide who had made the difficult journey to the far city he knew the inhospitable terrain over which they would be marching.

The soldiers' singing was drowned by a volley of explosions and a rushing sound which filled the sky. Rockets had burst from the Citadel; the night sky was criss-crossed with trails of blue, green and red sparks as the fireworks soared to celebrate the new King of the Fools.

The beauty of the scene touched a chord in the Hump. He could not understand why the sight of those bright lights rising so free and brilliant into the heavens should bring a lump to his throat. He looked at the men and women at the other tables. The women clapped when a rocket exploded into a scatter of floating stars, the men laughed when there was an extra loud bang or smoking debris drifted down nearby, but none were touched by the longing which the spectacle inspired in him.

Azrul is right, he thought, I have a touch of madness. The mind must reflect the body.

The next moment he had knocked over his stool and leapt in the direction of a figure passing across the far end of the square.

'Gambal!' he shouted.

FIVE
Gambal

On hearing his name Gambal halted by the parapet above
the river and attempted to see who had called, but the
small square was dim except when a bursting rocket
washed it in garish light. In just such a brief glow he saw
a shape rise from a far table and move forward so urgently
that it went sprawling over the outstretched legs of a party
of drunken soldiers.

The Hump raised himself on his arms, his eyes still
fixed on Gambal.

'You clumsy son of a poxed drong!' shouted one of the
men. 'Have you not eyes in your maggot-riddled head!'

'You have spilled my ale, potton turd!' yelled another.
'And you have not the hog-humping manners to
apologize.'

Blue rocket light filled the square.

'What have we here, lads?' said a tall soldier, standing
up and looking down at the sprawled hunchback. 'Serene
Mother! Is he wearing a pack or is that part of his ill-
begotten carcase?'

He aimed a kick.

'It is flesh all right.'

'A monster!'

'A monster without manners!'

'Time he learned some!'

Fired with the same excitement as village boys tormenting a stray cur, the soldiers crowded round the Hump, prodding his bowed spine with their boots and making obscene comments on his deformity. When he tried to climb to his feet he was pushed back to the ground, and the thought that Gambal might escape angered him more than the taunts of the louts.

One picked up a pitcher of ale and poured it over his head.

'Drink for the monster!' he shouted amid the laughter which filled the square.

Fury filled the Hump. Fury that he had been created for men to mock, fury at the world which allowed such oafs to manhandle him without fear of retribution, fury at Gambal who had robbed him of his love and was now watching his humiliation. With a cry of rage he rolled over, seized the ankle of a man aiming a kick at him and, with a heave of his powerful arms, sent him crashing to the paving.

The moment of surprise which followed allowed him to gain his feet, then the anger of the soldiers broke.

One smashed a wine pitcher against the table, turning it into a deadly weapon. Holding it by the handle he swung it at the Hump. Although he drew back his head the jagged edge furrowed his cheek. The blood, which immediately covered one side of his face and gave the impression of a grotesque carnival mask, had an alarming effect on the soldiers. Before, they had been a pack amusing themselves at the expense of an individual, now the pack instinct wanted more than just amusement. Several more pitchers hit the table, a sour smell of wine filled the air and the ring of men round the Hump closed upon him with their pottery weapons outstretched.

In the glare of another rocket Gambal recognized the victim and started forward until an arm, with muscles steeled by hours of spear drill, sent him reeling. By now the other people at the tables had melted away and the tavern door was bolted and barred. Only Alwald and Krispin remained, and beneath the table they were sliding their swords from their long pedlar's packs.

Once Krispin had been as peaceable as any in Toyheim, where violence was almost unknown – never worse than a scuffle in the Jack-in-the-Box over the favours of a village maid. But now, when he felt the tingle from Wound-flame's grip, there was a curious excitement, a half-fearful half-eager urge to challenge the odds. It was something he would have never dreamed of when he wore his red apprentice's apron.

Gambal picked himself up, wiped his burst lips with the back of his hand and seizing a stool rushed into the mêlée in which the Hump appeared to be fighting for his life. At the same time Krispin and Alwald jumped to their feet with their swords in hand.

'Stop, rabble!' ordered Alwald in a voice of authority learned on the parade ground at River Garde. The reflections on the fine blade of his sword changed colour as rockets streamed overhead. On the other hand Wound-flame – perhaps because a dozen brawling soldiers could not be considered as serious enemies – remained as dull as it was when Alwald first saw it.

Alwald shouted again, but the only response he got was to have a wine cup hurled at him.

'At them!' he called to Krispin, and leapt forward to use the flat of his blade on the men who now had both the Hump and Gambal at the mercy of their boots.

One of the soldiers turned, saw Alwald coming at him and picked up a chair to parry his sword. At the same time Krispin leapt over an upturned table and brought Woundflame down in a hissing stroke that cut the chair in two, leaving the aghast man with only a small part of the backrest in his hands.

The others turned from their victims and – thanks to an ancient rule which did not allow ordinary troops to carry weapons in the city – faced Krispin and Alwald with stools, broken pitchers and knives snatched from the table.

'Begone!' Alwald ordered. 'What sort of men-at-arms be you who can find no better game than a poor hunchback! Begone, I say!'

'Fine words from a packman, eh lads,' cried the tall soldier. 'I wonder who he robbed for that fine sword. He is another who needs a lesson in manners.'

It was Woundflame that saved the hour. As the men edged closer and began to encircle the two companions, it seemed to Krispin that the sword came alive in his hand. It leapt in a series of lightning strokes from man to man, disarming them without drawing blood. Knives went spinning into the air as its metal touched them, broken pitchers – the traditional ale-house brawler's weapon in Danaak – shattered into hundreds of tiny shards, and stools were sliced into kindling.

And when their weapons were gone, the sword danced about them so they felt its draught on their faces. It happened so quickly – so *magically* – that the men stood for a moment open-mouthed, then muttering oaths they turned and disappeared into the shadows of an alley leading from the square. For some time Krispin and Alwald stood with their swords ready in case they found the courage to return while Gambal and the Hump slumped in tavern chairs wiping blood from their faces.

'I thank you, sirs,' said Gambal. 'My friend and I would have been kicked to death if it had not been for your swords.'

The tavern door was unbolted and the landlord came out clucking over the broken pitchers and stools. Some of his customers returned and a minute later wine cups were being filled again.

'A cup for these two,' said Alwald. 'Your strongest wine for they need its strength.'

'I think I could use some, too,' said Krispin as he sheathed Woundflame. 'I feel as though I have been in a battle.'

When the wine came the Hump's hands were trembling so much that Gambal held the cup to his lips.

'My friend needs rest after the blows they gave him,' he said. 'I shall see him back to his inn in the caravanserai. I am not badly hurt.'

'Do you think we might find a room there?' asked Alwald. 'Every inn we have tried in the city is full because of the feast.'

'There is always room at the caravanserai inns,' Gambal replied, 'and at half the price you would pay in the city.'

'Then we shall accompany you.'

'You do not speak like a packman,' said Gambal while Krispin handed copper coins to an inn servant for their drink, 'nor do either of you look like packmen. But do not worry, good sirs, there are many these days who are not what they seem. You may have confidence in my discretion.'

'Mayhap you are not used to pedlars such as we,' Krispin said. 'We come from a far corner of Ythan.'

'And where may that be?'

The Hump grunted as though he wanted to interject but the words were slow to come.

'A place called the Wald,' Krispin said.

'The Wolf Wald now.'

'In Danaak you know of the invasion?' asked Alwald in an attempt to sound casual.

'It is known in the Citadel.'

'And is our Lord Regent sending an army to relieve his subjects?' Alwald continued in the same tone.

'The Lord Regent must first crush the heretics of Thaan,' said Gambal and looked at the two with raised eyebrows and an innocent smile.

'Good! Heresy before invasion! How Mother-fearing our beloved master is!'

Krispin threw Alwald a warning look and said, 'Let us help to get your friend to his bed.'

The Hump climbed to his feet and, pressing an inn napkin against the wounds on his face, took a step forward and almost fell.

'Excuse me,' he muttered. 'My head rings like Grand Johan.'

Krispin took one of his arms and Gambal the other and supporting him thus they left the square. Now that the King of Fools had been crowned and received a purse of silver from the Regent's hand, the excitement of the crowds became even more feverish. Leaving the main square they surged through the streets of the city, a flood of masked and costumed revellers determined to dance until the sunrise.

Often the three young men supporting the Hump had to shoulder their way against a flow of humanity, and it was a relief when they reached a bridge leading to the caravanserai. Half way across Krispin looked over the river, now reflecting starbursts from the rockets which continued to screech above the city, and had the uneasy sensation that he had seen it before. Half-timbered houses leaned over the water, lights glittered in their casement windows and music floated from open doors leading on to small quays.

The house closest to the bridge took all his attention.

The feeling that he had experienced when he found the black boat and later in the nameless city rose within him again. Here was his destination. If it had not been for the Hump he would have gone to the door and banged its knocker shaped like a graceful dancing girl; instead he turned to Gambal and asked, 'That is a strange old house, do you know who lives in it?'

Gambal laughed.

'Trust a stranger to notice such a place. It belongs to a woman who used to be a great courtesan, and today it is one of the most expensive pleasure houses in Danaak. Gossip says that she was once the mistress of Lord Odo and she bought the house on the proceeds. Now she is probably far better off than Lord Odo who has not been seen in society of late.'

For some reason incomprehensible to Krispin the young man burst into a peal of laughter.

'Her name?'

'Merlinda. With a name ending like that you can see she has noble blood, certainly too noble for the likes of you. Only their lordships visit the Lady Merlinda's house. If you need female company there are plenty of mistresses-for-the-night at the caravanserai.'

'Not this night,' said Krispin. 'My bones are so weary that sleep is all I crave.'

Soon they were passing compounds where drongs snorted, inns filled with singing caravaneers, the gambling halls and pleasure houses which, like a red-lanterned quarter of a seaport, lived off the lust and dreams of wanderers.

'My thanks,' murmured the Hump when they reached his inn in a quieter corner of the caravanserai. 'Tomorrow may I thank you properly.'

They helped Gambal take him up the narrow stairs and when they could do no more followed an inn servant to an attic that was unoccupied.

The Hump sank on to his bed and waited for the world to steady before he spoke. Meanwhile Gambal eased off his soft leather boots and then wiped his face with a wet towel.

'You have been kind,' said the Hump.

'Why not?' said Gambal. 'You helped me once, probably more than you know.'

'In my jerkin pocket – a small auroch horn box,' the

Hump muttered. Gambal handed it to him and he took out several sooma seeds. Once they were in his mouth and his strong teeth released their potent juices the pain, particularly in his back where most of the kicks had been aimed, receded.

'It is strange that we should meet like that,' he continued in a less shaky voice. 'I have been searching the city for you.'

'Indeed?' said Gambal. 'Hold still while I get this bandage on your face. Why did you seek me?'

'To get the truth out of you, at the point of my rider's spike if necessary.'

'Rider's spike! What harm have I done you? And what truth?'

'Silvermane,' said the Hump. 'It was you who took her away – that was the harm. And the truth – I want to know her fate.'

Suddenly Gambal laughed. He laughed so much he had to sit in the Hump's only chair and there he doubled up as though he had gripe in his belly.

'You love her!' he exclaimed when he had got his breath back. 'Serene Mother! You love the horsemaid!'

The Hump said nothing. The laughter hurt him but after the way Gambal had come to his aid his feelings about the young man were confused.

'Pardon my laughter,' said Gambal. 'It was not directed at you but at myself for not realizing what should have been obvious to me when we met. Of course, you were rather drunk that night.'

'But I thought – I thought I told you about Silvermane and how I felt . . . so when I came back and you had bought her I . . .'

'Of course I remember you telling me about Silvermane, and I do remember you telling me – somewhat incoherently if you do not mind me saying so – that you

309

were in love, but you did not tell me you were in love with her.'

'Did I not?' said the Hump wonderingly. 'I thought I did, though I must admit I have no clear recollection of that night, being unused to drink.'

'You remind me of my old master, Wilk,' said Gambal as he mentally congratulated himself on having a tongue that was as quick as his mind. 'He would say things in his cups and the next day would swear he had told me something different.'

He chuckled again at a mental image of the Hump and the horsemaid making love. A short while ago the Regent would have found it equally entertaining.

'What a fool I was not to understand at the time,' he added to explain his mirth.

The Hump shifted his aching body into a less painful position. His little square of window became a little square of violet and then orange as rockets burst over the caravanserai to the drongs' high-pitched alarm.

'Then I misunderstood,' he said. 'I am sorry. But tell me, what has happened to Silvermane? All Azrul could tell me is that she went to the Citadel.'

'That is right,' said Gambal in his most open voice. 'I introduced her at the Regent's banquet. She made a sensation.'

'And?'

'Now she resides there.'

'But in what manner . . .'

'Oh, she is not behind bars like most of the freaks – if you will excuse the word – in the menagerie. Oh no, the horsemaid has her own chamber and attendant and a poet to teach her to use our tongue like a human being. The Regent has a particular interest in her. And so he should. Nothing so unusual has come to the Citadel for a long time.'

'But they say the Regent has cravings that are not of ordinary men.'

'Your Silvermane has not yet been violated if that is what you fear. I know of my master's tastes – ordinary men are burned for less – but at the moment he has no such interest.' He leaned his face closed to the Hump's ear.

'It is treason to say it, but the truth is, my friend, that there is a poison working in my master's body and he can think of little else. He is becoming a vampire because they do say – ' and his voice went even lower ' – he has an alchemist who seeks a cure by distilling blood from the hall of execution. It is further said that soon there will be more prisoners needed to keep up the quantity.'

The Hump shuddered. There was so much evil in the city, no wonder he only felt whole when he was far away leading a caravan through vast unpeopled lands.

'So have no fear for Silvermane,' Gambal continued softly. 'Horse blood would be of no value to Master Leodore.'

He went to a jug, filled a cup with water and held it to the Hump's lips.

'I owe you much.'

'Perhaps you can repay someday. Tell me, Master Guide, do you leave on a journey soon?'

'No. Azrul wanted us to go to buy toys in some distant place but it was invaded by barbarians.'

'No one has asked you to undertake a special journey, perhaps a very small party, to some far region – a hazardous journey to be made in secret.'

'Sometimes I wish it were so but that is when I despair. The truth is that I did not wish to leave Danaak without . . .'

'If someone should want you to make such a journey, I beg you to tell me.'

'Why, Gambal?'

'Because, my friend, I want to go with you. Anywhere! I need to escape from the Citadel. When the Regent became my master I was overjoyed at how clever I had been, but I had no idea of the danger, the intrigue, the ever-possible plunge from grace. Do not think I exaggerate when I say that my life is in danger.'

'How can that be?'

'By accident I discovered something – for your own sake do not ask me what – and when it becomes known to the Regent, as in time it must, I shall be taken to the dungeons as fast as the Companions of the Rose can hustle me. There is no safety for me in Danaak. I must get far from the city because the Regent's spies will hunt me for the knowledge I hold in my head.'

'I wish I could help you,' said the Hump, 'but as long as Silvermane remains in the Citadel I must remain in Danaak.'

'But if you could take her with you?'

The Hump sat upright as hope made him forget his pain.

'Would it be possible?'

'Perhaps. First I might be able to smuggle you in to see her – difficult with your shape but possible – and find out if she would *want* to leave the Citadel. After all, her own apartment and attendants are preferable to the cage of a travelling freak show.'

A curious noise came from the Hump and Gambal realized it was a laugh.

'If I could speak with her all will be well,' he said. 'My folly was that I did not speak with her before.'

'I shall return,' said Gambal. 'Remember what I have said because I have a feeling in my bones that you may soon be asked to undertake a rare journey in unmapped regions where all will depend on your sense of direction.'

'How can you think so?'

'My mother had the "sight",' he answered, and mentally added 'when she was out of her mind with Moon Bloom petals!'

A moment later he was gone and the Hump lay back, his mind filled with exciting new possibilities.

SIX

The Disk Of Livia

The angle of the sun's rays slanting through the attic window told Krispin that he had slept until the late afternoon. On the pallet on the opposite side of the small room Alwald slumbered on beneath his packman's cloak. The long and arduous journey from the Vale of Mabalon across wild terrain, and then the march along a caravan road to Danaak, had hardened their muscles and etched lines of determination on their young faces, but it had also exhausted them.

For a long, luxurious moment Krispin lay without thought just as he had lain on rest day morning in the village while Father Tammas snored peacefully in his room and below in the kitchen Jennet prepared breakfast.

Then it all came back to him – the village gone, Father Tammas dead beneath the ashes of his home, Jennet hiding in a world of childhood, and he far from his beloved Wald on a quest like a doomed character in a folk tale. A murmur of sadness escaped his lips.

He told himself not to think of the past. What mattered was now and that meant the quest – and the quest was all he had.

He rose and went to the washbowl to cleanse himself and razor the stubble from his cheeks. If he was to pay a call on the Lady Merlinda he had no wish to appear like a vagabond. Setting aside his travel-stained clothing for the inn laundress, he dressed in his doeskin breeches and jerkin of madder-dyed wool. Then he carefully placed Woundflame in his pack for he knew that while nobles and gallants might carry swords in the streets of Danaak unremarked, a youth in country clothing thus armed would attract attention.

'I think you should give me back that sword,' said Alwald who had been watching him. 'After last night's display it is clearly no ordinary blade. In return you may carry my weapon when necessary, but do try not to scratch the hilt.'

'Thank you but no,' said Krispin, knotting a light scarf which Jennet had woven for him.

'I do not understand you.'

'Then I shall explain: I am keeping Woundflame.'

Anger crossed Alwald's face.

'I took it from the reeves' vault – I lifted it from the altar . . .'

'. . . and you gave it to me. A dull blade for a dull fellow you thought.'

'It is true I thought that,' said Alwald with one of his shifts of mood, which had become extreme since the Shallows. 'Keep it, then.'

'I shall. Now hear the good news.' And he went on to tell him how, when crossing the bridge to the caravanserai, he had recognized the house which was the next step in the quest.

'And that fellow – Gambal? – said that the woman is a whore.'

'An aristocratic one. At least you will not be lowering yourself socially in talking to her.'

'Really, Krispin, there are times when your view of the social structure becomes boring. I know your arguments, some I agree with, but I did not create the manner in which we live and though you profess tolerance – an easy virtue for those who have only to gain by it – it seems to me that your words are said to get back at me. I would be obliged if you would find a more interesting way of insulting me.'

Krispin laughed.

'Well said, my lord. I shall give my mind to it. Now come down to the kitchen for I am starving and they have hams that water my mouth just to think on.'

From outside came a throb of drums and distant cheering.

'Our friends from last night must be moving off on their campaign,' said Alwald. 'I wonder where lies that city they spoke of . . .'

'Thaan.'

'. . . and why the Regent wishes to humble it.'

'I heard them say something about heretics. Now get your breeches on or I shall perish from hunger.'

Danaak was unusually quiet when the pair walked out through the caravanserai that evening. No longer illumined, the Citadel was a menacing shape against the starshine, few lights showed in the houses leaning towards each other over the narrow streets and as they passed tavern doorways no music came to their ears.

'The city has a sore head,' Alwald remarked.

'No wonder. Not even at harvest home have I seen such drinking,' said Krispin. 'I hope the Regent's spies are sleeping it off like everyone else.'

When he reached the bridge he again experienced a sense of recognition when he saw Merlinda's house.

'It looks respectable to me,' said Alwald, 'but who can tell what plays are played behind locked doors.'

Krispin crossed the cobbles and raised the knocker. In response a low voice came through a grille informing him that there was no entertainment that night.

'I have not come for entertainment,' replied Krispin. 'My companion and I would speak to the Lady Merlinda.'

There was a long pause.

'Your names?'

'They would mean nothing to her but say that we have come from the Wald and we bring a vase backwards.'

'Wait in the shadow on the other side of the street. It is not good for you to be seen loitering at this door.'

A minute later a strip of amber light appeared and widened as the door opened.

On going inside the two young men were awed by the rich furnishings and lavish decoration. Hanging lamps of finely wrought silver not only cast light but perfume; instead of rushes or woven rugs on the floor there were carpets patterned with naked nymphs and woodland creatures which made Krispin keep his eyes raised in the presence of the maid who was more finely dressed than any lady Alwald had known in the Wald.

'Follow,' she said and, with a demure walk, led them upstairs to a room whose wide casement overlooked the dark river.

'My lady will be with you in a minute,' said the maid.

The two looked about in wonder at the walls covered with soft blue leather on which were embossed silverleaf stars and crescents – Krispin recognized the constellation of the Griffin among them. Then two ladies entered. One was young with a face of unusual beauty and even more unusual hair of vivid red. The other was older and the finest of lines round her dark and lustrous eyes, almost hidden by artful cosmetics, hinted that she was older than she appeared. Her gown was of shimmering spider silk and, unlike anything either of the young men had seen before, appeared to be a single sheet of material cunningly wrapped round the body so that it gave it an outline both soft and sensuous. As she advanced towards them with a slight smile her anklets tinkled musically.

'I welcome you, young gentlemen,' she said in a voice which sounded to Krispin as soft and delightful as the cooing of woodland doves. 'May I introduce Urwen who,

317

since the mysterious absence of Lord Odo from the city, has become my dear companion as his lordship is a very old friend of mine. She was curious to see what Waldmen look like.'

'I hope that she is not disappointed,' said Alwald with a flash of his old River Garde gallantry.

'I see that you are not monsters,' Urwen said with flirtatious eyes. 'Now my curiosity is satisfied I shall leave you to your business. Merlinda, is it possible we may all dine together seeing that tonight is quiet and we are free from your young ladies.'

'Perhaps, Urwen.'

The young woman smiled and left the chamber.

Merlinda fixed her beautiful eyes on Krispin and Alwald and, after asking their names, said, 'Can you prove to me that you are the ones I have been expecting?'

'I can only state that my father was the Lord of the River March,' said Alwald. 'I do not carry my pedigree on vellum.'

'Of course not,' she said sweetly and turned to Krispin with a look of inquiry.

Without wondering how, he knew exactly what to do. From his neck he lifted the chain from which hung the medallion with its spirals of tiny runes. She took it in her hand, looked at it long and closely and said, 'This Disk of Livia is no forgery. You are welcome in my house. Tell me, is it true that you carry the Esav?'

In reply Krispin felt under his shirt and from his soft leather pouch produced the heart-shaped crystal. Merlinda took it reverently and held it beneath a perfumed lamp to study its coiling opalescence.

'I congratulate you both,' she said, handing it back. 'You have no idea how important it will be in the future. Guard it with your life.'

'I wish I knew more about it,' said Krispin. 'It is

strange, to be on a quest without understanding, without even knowing where we are going until we get there.'

She nodded them over to the casement. Through its diamond panes they saw the dark shape of a barge glide past with a lantern hanging from its prow.

'It is best for us to speak soft here,' she said. 'Spies are everywhere and I am mistrustful of my maid. You must leave Danaak as soon as possible.'

'If I but knew our next destination,' said Krispin.

'That I can tell you,' she said. 'The city of Thaan.'

'Surely that is where the army is going,' Alwald exclaimed.

'Yes, the days of the heretics are numbered. Holy people in green robes are no match for imperial troops in armour. Therefore, it is imperative that you reach Thaan before it is besieged.'

'But if the army has already left.'

'The army perforce follows the highway which, because it skirts the Wilderness of Gil, is not the direct route. If you can cross the wilderness you should arrive several days ahead of the column. There are no maps of the wilderness, it is a region shunned by men except perhaps outcasts and old miners ever hopeful of finding a lode of silver.'

'Do I have to rely on Krispin to find the way?' Alwald asked.

'Not this time. There is a remarkable man in the caravanserai,' she said in her caressing voice. 'He can find his way anywhere. They say he cannot explain how but in some mysterious manner he can pilot a caravan to its destination through the wildest uncharted country. Tomorrow I shall send my steward to fetch him and I shall hire him as your guide.'

'But will he agree?'

'If we offer enough silver – and I am not short of that, thanks to the needs of Danaak's gentry for entertainment.

319

But do not think of my house as merely a costly place for relief of the passions; here there is music and the finest food and wines. Each of my girls can play and sing and dance to harp and dulcimer. Here men enter a world of fantasy I have woven for them, a world where anything is possible or at least seems so, and dreams are made flesh.'

'You have an unusual occupation as enchantress, lady,' said Alwald.

'You mean because I was high-born? A long story, beginning with a young girl's indiscretion and . . .' she shrugged with great elegance '. . . and ending with a Pilgrim. You may wonder at that too, but I want Ythan to return to being a place where anything is possible, where dreams can come true – and where there is no need to escape into fantasy in houses such as mine.

'Return tomorrow at this hour and I hope to introduce you to your guide, and then you can leave as soon as the city gates are opened after dawn.'

The two young men walked back through the deserted streets without talk, their thoughts on the beautiful woman and her graceful way of making each feel as though he was something special to her.

At midnight they were both asleep, an empty wine pitcher between them.

At midnight the Hump chewed sooma seeds after the pain of his bruised body awoke him, and for the hundredth time he relished the hope that Gambal had given him.

At midnight Lord Odo, deep in the rock beneath the Citadel, hung in chains against his pillar and screamed when he felt the teeth of a rat.

At midnight the Regent had a cloaked visitor to his chamber who told him, 'They have arrived.'

When Krispin and Alwald returned to the house of the Lady Merlinda next evening they were surprised at the change in it. The exterior was as discreet as before, its windows shuttered; but inside it was filled with music and laughter, and as they were ushered to the lady's chamber they were aware of being watched by scornful young women in costumes whose only common factor was their richness.

Merlinda greeted them with a smile which erased the scorn.

'The guide should be here shortly to discuss my offer. Sit down and we will have a cup of wine meanwhile.'

She talked easily but tactfully did not question them about their adventures, on account of the Pilgrims' rule of knowing only what was necessary.

Suddenly she stopped midsentence as a crash vibrated through the house followed by shrill cries.

'Quick, down to the quay and disappear.'

She seized each bewildered youth by the hand and dragged them to the casement. Torches flared below and they saw armoured men on the quay with a barge moored behind them.

'Betrayed!' she murmured. 'Lord Odo has named me no doubt . . .'

The door burst open and a Companion of the Rose entered. Behind him came the Witchfinder General in his sombre robe.

'In the name of the Regent and the Empty Throne, I accuse you of treason,' he said.

'And in the name of the Regent and the Empty Throne, I arrest you on that charge,' said the companion through his visor.

Alwald and Krispin looked about them wildly but more armed men crowded into the room. They were seized, their arms wrenched behind their backs, chains locked cruelly round their wrists and they were hustled down to the quay. Here they were made to sit in the small windowless cabin of the barge while their captors rowed down river. Less than a minute had passed since the door of Merlinda's house had been burst open.

At the same time the Hump limped on to the bridge and saw Merlinda's house ahead of him. On the cobbles outside it two men in armour stood holding the bridles of a number of horses. Apart from them the street appeared unnaturally empty and he felt a vague unease. But he continued forward, telling himself that the men must be the escorts of some rich burghers or bored nobles in search of diversion.

He was half way across the bridge when a hand fell heavily on his shoulder and fingers dug into his muscles. He spun round to see Gambal.

'For the love of the Mother, come away,' he hissed. 'You will be arrested if you walk in now.'

Obediently the Hump turned and Gambal led him into a maze of alleys which he had known since childhood, and making sure that they had not been followed, entered a mean little tavern where half the customers lay drunk across trestle tables in the dim light. The remainder seemed to be in wine-inspired worlds of their own for not one cast a second glance at the Hump.

Gambal sat him at a corner table, told him that if men in armour appeared he was to pretend to be as drunk as the rest, and then bought a jug of sour wine at the metal-sheathed counter. When he returned he found a drab offering to let the Hump take her into the yard for a cup of wine. He courteously poured a drink for her and then waved her away.

'It is lucky I reached you in time,' he said. 'At the Citadel I learned that the Lady Merlinda was to be arrested with the two men who wanted to hire your services.'

'But why?' asked the puzzled Hump.

Gambal shrugged.

'Either heretics or Pilgrims – the witchfinders will decide.'

'Strange that you predicted that I would be offered a distant journey.'

'My mother had the "sight",' Gambal repeated. 'Now listen closely. It is imperative that I leave Danaak – myself and some friends.'

'Where do you wish to go?'

'As yet I cannot say, but I warn you it will be long and hazardous.'

'Silvermane . . .' began the Hump.

Gambal leaned across the table.

'Silvermane will come.'

SEVEN
Strange Company

The barge glided swiftly along the river until it reached an entrance in the rock below the walls of the Citadel. One of the companions blew a shrill note on a whistle and the portcullis which protected it creaked high enough for the craft to pass beneath.

In torchlight the craft continued along the cold tunnel until it widened into the cavern with the quay stretching along one wall. Here the prisoners were bundled out and put into the hands of a group of turnkeys who had been playing a dice game while waiting. The Witchfinder General spoke briefly to the one in charge and then reboarded the barge which turned and vanished from sight.

'Welcome to your new home,' said a warder. He removed their chains and added, 'Here you learn the rules when you break them. Come.'

There was nothing that the shocked trio could do but follow along dank passages to one of a row of oaken doors set in the rock. A warder unlocked it and they were motioned to go inside.

'Cannot I have a separate cell?' asked Merlinda. 'It is my right as a woman surely.'

'Modesty is the first thing to be lost in the underworld,' the warder answered. 'But, as you have not been convicted yet, you are allowed one tallow candle.'

He handed it to Alwald. The door crashed shut behind them, locks grated and they were left alone.

For a minute no one spoke. The ceiling was too low for them to stand fully upright, but in the dim light of the candle they saw that the room was larger than expected, having been hewn far back into the rock. The floor was ankle-deep in straw in the same way that animal cages with travelling fairs were covered with straw.

They sank down upon it with their backs against the wall, and were immediately aware of the damp which permeated it. Krispin shivered. In the worst moments of his adventure he had never felt as despondent as now. Before, no matter how grim the situation, he had faced it on his feet with Woundflame in hand. Now he was merely locked away like a criminal, and yet this was the worst predicament of all – he tried to close his mind to thoughts of what lay ahead.

'Does the quest end here, lady?' whispered Alwald.

'For us, I think,' Merlinda replied. 'When the time comes they will try to make us betray it but, thanks be to the Mother, there is little we can tell them. I have no knowledge of what you would have done in Thaan. My task was simply to arrange for you to travel there safely. What breaks my heart is the thought that time is running out. Once the city falls it will be too late . . .'

'Too late, it is always too late,' said an unknown voice.

They looked about them in alarm. In the candlelight they saw a vague movement at the end of the cell and then an extraordinary creature rose from the straw in which he had burrowed like an animal.

His head was shaved, as was his moon-like face, and he wore a motley coat and tight breeches, one leg being red and the other green. Behind his head lay a cowl, crested with a cockscomb, and bells were sewn to various parts of his clothing. In his hand he clutched a short staff bearing a small carved head that vaguely resembled his own.

'I am Ognam,' he announced in a deep, carefully modulated voice. 'As you can perceive by my attire, I have the honour to belong to the Guild of Jongleurs, that is to say that I was a member before I made an error of theatrical judgement.'

He sighed lugubriously.

As Alwald held the candle higher they saw that Ognam was in his middle years and in defiance of his captivity his greenish eyes retained a twinkle which at one moment suggested shrewdness and at another innocence. Despite prison fare his belly still threatened the buttons of his jester's coat.

'I have known better lodgings,' he continued, waving his hand about the cell. 'Some little better when one was on tour, I admit, but at least the meals were regular. Here you will have two within an hour then go for a day without a morsel. That is because in this situation the passing of time could only be measured by regular mealtimes – and here they even deprive you of time.

'I do love your candle,' he continued after another heavy sigh. 'Treasure its light, hoard the memory of its gleam. Our hosts never provide a second one.'

'Never?' murmured Merlinda with a shiver.

'Never, dear Lady. Would that I could cheer you up with a few jokes but since coming here I seem to have forgotten most of my merry quips – I seem to remember some priest-and-dancing-girl jests but they would be unsuitable in the presence of a Lady. Not that my jokes were very good if I am to be honest. It was the desire to raise greater laughter that was the cause of my present incarceration . . .'

He fell silent and Krispin felt impelled to ask why.

'Fool that I was – ha! ha! – I made mock of the Regent. My new routine was well received, dare I say that it had them rolling round my booth, but success breeds jealousy and a fellow buffoon invited one of the Regent's spies to watch the performance – and here I am. May I enquire how you come to be here?'

'Like you I was betrayed,' said Merlinda bitterly. 'Perhaps it was the act of an old friend driven by torment to give the witchfinders their favourite fare – names. Perhaps it was my maid who wanted silver. It matters not once one is brought here.'

'What is likely to happen next?' Alwald asked the jester.

'Perhaps you will be forgotten like me, perhaps in a few minutes the Witchfinder General will honour you with conversation. Try to sleep. Here dreams are the only freedom you will know.'

Ognam lay back in the straw, and grasping his staff so that its jester's head was beside his own, appeared to put his words into practice.

'That it should end thus!' cried Alwald suddenly. 'The Lord of the River March in a loathsome dungeon! The shame of it!' And in his frustration he struck his fist against the cold wall.

No one spoke and when he was sure that he was unobserved, Krispin slipped the thong holding his leather pouch over his neck and hid it and its precious contents under the straw beside him. Then, like the others, he fixed his eyes on the candle to savour every moment of its light.

The candle had guttered out when an unexpected sound made Krispin open his eyes. He had been dreaming of old days in the Wald – of a little wooden horse on wheels he had made for Jennet. Still bemused by the dream and the sudden return to frightening reality, he saw the door open and lantern rays pierce the darkness of the cell.

'Visitors,' said Ognam from where he lay half beneath the cell. His voice quavered as he added, 'Serene Mother, not me! Not this time!'

Two metal-booted warders came through the doorway.

'You,' the first said, pointing to Krispin. 'You are the one in luck. Your supper awaits . . .'

'Young sir, I beg you not to . . .' began Ognam but the warder shut him up with a blow from his truncheon.

The other warder pulled Krispin upright and pushed him towards the passage.

'Protect the Path,' Merlinda whispered after him.

The door slammed shut and after the rasping of its locks silence fell as deep as the darkness.

In the passage Krispin walked between the two warders who allowed him to move freely. They knew, and he guessed, that in the nether world there was nowhere to run to.

'What you in for, lad?' the older warder asked in a rough but kindly tone.

'I know not,' Krispin answered.

'You will find out in good time,' said the other. 'Probably all a mistake. The companions are far too zealous in arresting innocent citizens. So cheer up and make a good supper.'

'Got to keep your strength up,' said the first, and they both laughed.

They marched for several minutes, their shadows lengthening and foreshortening as they passed flaring flambeaux whose brackets were set in rock at regular intervals. They came to a cavern where several warders stood round a brazier, and Krispin was told to sit at a table in a corner. One warder remained with him and the other returned with a bowl of steaming broth.

'You are in luck, young man,' he said. 'We get no better.'

The appetizing smell made Krispin realize how hungry he was and he eagerly picked up a spoon, only to find that the saltiness of the broth made his mouth pucker.

'All right, lad?'

'Salty,' Krispin muttered.

the ungainly hand of the manikin he had thrown into the fire.

In their dungeon Alwald and Merlinda sat side by side in the dark that was darker than night, and neither had words to say. The only sounds were the rustle of a rat in the straw and the occasional snore of the jester.

Krispin clenched his teeth and wondered how many hours had passed. He had never known thirst like this, and yet with diabolical perversity his body had an urge to void. He pressed his knees together as he had as a child when he found it a strain to sit through the long ceremonial of The Choosing. He was under no illusion about the effect of the quicklime if he lost control; already his lips were blistered and his eyes half blind from the effects of the deadly powder when it had floated in the air about him.

Worst of all he knew that no matter how long he forced himself to hold out, he could not escape. He remembered a folktale about a foolish king who ordered the tide to halt, and he could no more avoid an agonizing fate than the king could hold back the waves.

The bell offered no hope. If he summoned the witch-finder he had nothing to confess . . . except the Esav! Yes! He could tell them how it had been taken from the eidolon in the nameless city, and how it now lay hidden beneath dungeon straw.

His hand moved over the rock floor towards the bell.

If he rang it now perhaps he could last until the witchfinder came and had him released.

The Esav!

He snatched his hand back.

After what he had gone through to obtain the mysterious crystal, it would negate everything he honoured to trade it for a pitcher of water and a chance to relieve himself.

Words floated into his head.

Better to die in pain than shame!

And what had the beautiful courtesan told him?

Protect the Path!

He trembled as a proud thought replaced his dread. He would end it now, and by making the choice he would triumph over the Citadel.

It would be agony, he knew, but he would be master of his fate to the end.

'Serene Mother, into thy hands . . .' he muttered aloud and then reached for the water jug.

A foot pressed down on his wrist just as his fingers reached it.

'Now is not the time to drink, Master Krispin.'

He looked up. Above him, in a robe such as the witchfinders wore, stood the young man he had met the night before.

'Get him out,' he ordered.

Two warders – speechless men from the lowest level – unsnapped the chain about his neck and hauled him from the lime-filled cavity. They attempted to brush the flour-like substance from his garments, but he shrugged them aside and seized the jug. For a moment it seemed that hell had turned to paradise as the cold liquid poured down his throat, and then he had to run into the shadows.

'There is no time to be lost,' said Gambal. 'Walk between these two and you will come to no harm.'

Holding a lanthorn high, Gambal led the way back through the large cavern where a new shift of warders stood round the brazier and then along a series of passages. Once a man in armour, a Companion of the Rose, barred their way but he saluted Gambal respectfully when he produced a square of vellum with a large wax seal affixed to it.

They halted at the door of the original cell and Gambal opened it with keys he took from his robe. Once inside with Krispin he ordered the warders to wait outside, and set his lamp down in the centre of the floor.

Alwald and Merlinda uttered Krispin's name together, but Gambal raised his hand.

'I have but little time so hear me,' he said. 'I have arranged for your escape in a few hours' time. You will go by the river at dawn when the mist hangs over it, you will leave the city by the watergate and you will meet with a guide – you know him as the Hump – who will take us on our journey. I have been planning this ever since I learned you had been arrested.'

'It is a lot for one man to arrange,' said Merlinda. 'Especially as it is said that no one has ever escaped from the Citadel.'

'At the moment I enjoy the confidence of the Regent,' said Gambal. 'But not for long. If I stay here my plight will soon be as desperate as yours; that is why I shall come with you.'

'Forgive my suspicion,' Merlinda continued, 'but would it not be easier for you to leave Danaak alone? Why should you care what happens to us?'

In reply Gambal put his hand inside his robe and produced a medallion on a silver chain. As they peered at it in the lanthorn light Krispin recognized the spiralled runes.

'You are a Pilgrim,' said Merlinda with new warmth in her voice.

'It is not only the noble-born who follow the Path.'

'How will we get past the guards?' Alwald asked.

Gambal held up his square of vellum.

'I stole the Regent's seal,' he said simply. 'It gives me great authority, but we must not take unnecessary risks. To reach the river we must pass through the guard cavern and even with this firman there could be difficulties, so I have planned for you to pass through unseen . . .'

'Excuse my interjection,' came Ognam's voice from the end of the cell, 'but I hope that I may join you.'

'I thought he slept,' Merlinda muttered.

'Mistress, when a man has had my theatrical training, a few snores come low on the repertoire. I repeat, I wish to join you.'

'Do not be a fool,' said Gambal impatiently.

'But I am a fool, sir. And if you do not take me you will have to kill me. If you leave without me I shall scream treason, and I may tell you that I am renowned for my lungs.'

Gambal ran his long fingers through his hair in a gesture of frustration.

'So be it,' he said. 'Come, but any foolishness and my dagger will be between your ribs.'

'Fool I am, but not foolish.'

Gambal turned to the others.

'I have arranged that the death cart will pass this way in an hour,' he said. 'That is when we leave. I shall return just before it arrives and unlock the door. From then on you must do exactly as I say.'

'To breathe the sweet air of Freedom I would walk hand in hand with the Dark Maid,' said Ognam, adding it was a line from a play he once performed in before he donned the motley of a jester.

'You will have your wish,' said Gambal and he laughed without humour.

The wheels of the high-sided cart creaked as the two mute warders pushed it along the passage. Shadows, thrown by their lantern, gave grotesque semblance of life to the parchment features of the dead it bore. Recognizing a symbol on one of the doors lining the passage, the warders halted the vehicle and with practised ease unloaded the corpses.

Gambal emerged from the cell door, nodded to the

334

men and called the prisoners out. 'Lie down in the cart,' he said.

Merlinda took one look and raised her hand to her mouth to stifle a scream.

'You want us to ride with corpses!' exclaimed Alwald.

'You have a choice,' Gambal hissed. 'You can ride in the death cart alive – or soon you can ride in it . . . dead!'

'Come along,' said Ognam surprisingly. 'They are no worse than some audiences it has been my misfortune to attempt to amuse.'

Clutching his staff he laid himself on the stained boards of the cart.

'Lie beside him,' Gambal snapped.

Without a word they obeyed, their bodies pressing heavily against each other in the confined space, their nostrils filled with the sweetish odour of death. Then, while they clapped their hands across their mouths and squeezed their eyes shut against the horror, the warders replaced the corpses above them.

'Fear not, these either died from hunger or the rack. I made sure none had the plague,' said Gambal.

He nodded to the warders and the creaking of the iron-shod wheels began.

Under the ghastly pile Krispin was conscious of Merlinda's body trembling next to his. Moving with difficulty beneath the cadaver of an old man who had finally escaped the Citadel by chewing through his wrist veins, he moved his hand until it touched hers and grasped it reassuringly. She responded with grateful pressure.

'You are early,' said a guard as the cart rolled slowly through the large cavern. The mute warders ceased their pushing and pointed to Gambal who, head bowed, was walking beside the wheel.

'They must be disposed of quickly,' he said, drawing out his warrant.

'What is the hurry?' asked the guard. 'Looks like you have more than usual this morning.'

'One has the Red Death.'

'Serene Mother preserve me!' cried the guard as he backed away. 'Get them to the pits!'

The cart moved forward, its axles groaning plaintively. A few minutes later it halted again.

When the mutes had lifted the corpses aside Krispin and his companions sat up and climbed out. They were in a dim passage which was filled with the dankness of underground water. Handing each mute a purse of silver, Gambal left them to replace the corpses and continue their regular task.

The fugitives passed through an arch and saw that they were back on the quay. A rowing boat was tied alongside.

'It will be a crush with an extra person,' said Gambal, taking the muffled oars. Krispin untied the painter and a moment later the boat was in midstream. Before long a half circle of pale light appeared ahead of them. Gambal extinguished his lantern and with his head twisted over his shoulder rowed towards the tunnel mouth.

As they neared the open air they were met by serpents of mist squirming over the surface and after passing beneath the dripping portcullis they moved into a bank of white vapour.

'Say not a word,' whispered Gambal. 'Silver will only buy so many.'

They were startled by a muffled rattling as the water-gate portcullis was lowered behind them.

For an hour the boat glided like a ghost through ghostly mist, the only sound was the drip of the oar blades and Gambal's laboured breathing. Then the rising sun shone through and the vapour began to disintegrate into whorls and streamers, and the fugitives saw verdant countryside about them. Pastures and cornfields slid by like a landscape in a dream and ahead coppices thickened into woodland.

At length the boat came to rest by a decayed jetty belonging to a house equally decayed. From the ruin appeard the Hump, and beside him walked a beautiful silver-haired girl in a cloak and gown that reached the ground.

'It is good to see you again,' the Hump greeted. 'The drongs are saddled and ready, but there is one more than I expected.'

'He comes part of the way,' said Gambal. 'I do not want the Companions of the Rose to tickle our whereabouts out of him.'

'I have a spare animal,' said the Hump. 'Let us be gone.'

He led them to where the drongs were tethered behind the deserted house. One of the animals was loaded with provisions and Krispin saw with gratification that their packs were among the bales. It was the work of a moment for him and Alwald to retrieve their swords from them, then all mounted – though some with difficulty – and the Hump led the snorting cavalcade along a track through the trees.

Before long the woods gave way to heathland, and the drongs, with their easy stride, bore them further and further from Danaak until even the topmost spires of the Citadel were no longer visible. Gambal often turned to look behind them but there was no sign of pursuit. The only other living creatures were birds swooping and keening over coarse grass and heather.

At midday the Hump raised his hand and the well-trained animals slowed to a stop.

'Beyond those hills yonder is an old drover's road,' he said. 'It is all but forgotten now and will be safe for us to travel.'

'And where does it lead?' asked Gambal eagerly.

'To the Wilderness of Gil.'

'And then?'

'To Thaan,' cried Merlinda with shining eyes. 'Master Guide, tell me it is possible that we may reach the city before the Regent's army.'

'If luck favours us,' the Hump replied.

'Then let us not waste time.'

The Hump goaded his drong and, with the other beasts spread out behind him, led the way towards the far hills.

Riding high on his mount Krispin felt a wild exhilaration. Woundflame moved against his thigh comfortingly and the Esav, retrieved from the dungeon straw, lay in its pouch against his skin. He regarded his companions and thought what an unusual mixture they were; there was even something strange about the silent, silver-haired girl who rode side-saddle beside the Hump, her large brown eyes so often fixed on his face. Nobleman and mountebank, courtesan and hunchback, he felt affinity with them all. But it was the thought of the quest which quickened his pulse. He realized that until now he had not understood its true significance; it had meant little more than a compact with an old sorceress in the High Wald, something to be performed for favours expected in return.

Now, after the dungeons of the Citadel, it was clear. In the Wald he had known freedom – until intrigue betrayed it to the Wolf Horde – but in Danaak a man could rot in the dark for making fun of the Lord Regent. In the Wald men died calmly; in the Citadel the death carts told their own story. In the Wald men were allowed to work as they wished; in Danaak he had seen the slave mart. The path of the Pilgrims was to restore to Ythan what the Wald had always enjoyed.

He felt the surge of the drong's powerful muscles, the wind from the hills fresh on his face, and he was filled with unexpected joy.

For Krispin the quest for Princess Livia had begun.

The FOLK OF THE AIR

PETER S BEAGLE

Bestselling author of *The Last Unicorn*

The last flourish of the pavane set the hands of the dancers free and the torchlight made their rings and their jewelled gloves flash fire, scattering tiny green and violet and silver flames like largesse to the musicians. Farrell could not find any faces in that first wonder of brightness and velvet, cloaks and gold brocade – only the beautiful clothes glittering in a great circle, moving as though they were inhabited, not by human heaviness, but by marshlights and the wind. *The folk of the air*, he thought. *These are surely the folk of the air*.

Nothing is quite as it seems in this modern-day game of medieval romance and chivalry. The revellers thought they were playing at time and magic.

No one warned them that Time can be tricky and Magic dangerous.

Peter Beagle, in his first fantasy novel since *The Last Unicorn*, again proves his mastery in a glorious tale of magic, illusion and delusion.

0 7472 3068 4   £4.95

S. P. SOMTOW

THE

SHATTERED HORSE

An era of myth is ending, an age of heroes and bronze; the time of iron and armies awaits, as yet unborn. The link is Astyanax, son of Hector, direct descendant of the Olympian Skyfather, and heir to the now ravaged lands of Troy.

Within the city walls, the great wooden horse of the Greeks lies shattered, its terrible task fulfilled, and beggars scavenge in the ruins of the once great palace. The young king returns to claim his land, though his dreams of glory and vengeance lie in dust. To save his kingdom, Astyanax must relive the acts of his uncle, Paris . . . kidnap eternal Helen – and start the Trojan War. Again.

"[He] can create a world with less apparent effort than some writers devote to creating a small room. And yet these tales are as intricately wrought as those hand-carved oriental balls within balls."
Book World

"[His] tales almost always have a taste of the epic, of myth and legend. The names roll roundly from the tongue. Acts have cosmic significance. Games are of life and death . . . he writes of worlds and beings just far enough from our lives to feel strange, yet with echoes of a familiar past. He is a mythmaker." **Analog**

FICTION/FANTASY   0 7472 3092 7   £3.50

Headline books are available at your book-shop or newsagent, or can be ordered from the following address:

Headline Book Publishing PLC
Cash Sales Department
PO Box 11
Falmouth
Cornwall
TR10 9EN
England

UK customers please send cheque or postal order (no currency), allowing 60p for postage and packing for the first book, plus 25p for the second book and 15p for each additional book ordered up to a maximum charge of £1.90 in UK.

BFPO customers please allow 60p for postage and packing for the first book, plus 25p for the second book and 15p per copy for the next seven books, thereafter 9p per book.

Overseas and Eire customers please allow £1.25 for postage and packing for the first book, plus 75p for the second book and 28p for each subsequent book.